TESS GERRITSEN

UNDER THE KNIFE

MIRA

First Published 1990
Third Australian Paperback Edition 2007
ISBN 978 1 741 16515 9

Published by
Mira Books
3 Gibbes Street
CHATSWOOD NSW 2067
AUSTRALIA

Printed and bound in Australia by
McPherson's Printing Group

To my mother and father

Tess Gerritsen is an accomplished woman with an interesting history. Once a practicing physician, she has chosen instead to write full-time. A woman of many talents, she even plays the fiddle in a band! Tess has cowritten *Adrift,* a CBS screenplay, and has several other screenplays optioned for HBO. Having lived in Hawaii, she now resides in Camden, Maine, with her physician husband and two sons.

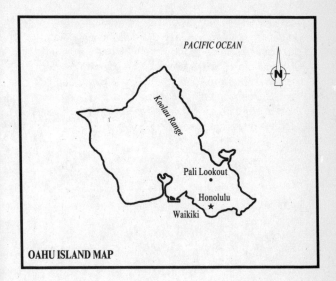

PACIFIC OCEAN

Koolau Range

Pali Lookout

Honolulu

Waikiki

OAHU ISLAND MAP

Prologue

*D*ear God, *how the past comes back to haunt us.*

From his office window, Dr. Henry Tanaka stared out at the rain battering the parking lot and wondered why, after all these years, the death of one poor soul had come back to destroy him.

Outside, a nurse, her uniform spotty with rain, dashed to her car. Another one caught without an umbrella, he thought. That morning, like most Honolulu mornings, had dawned bright and sunny. But at three o'clock the clouds had slithered over the Koolau range and now, as the last clinic employees headed for home, the rain became a torrent, flooding the streets with a river of dirty water.

Tanaka turned and stared down at the letter on his desk. It had been mailed a week ago; but like so much of his correspondence, it had been lost in the piles of obstetrical journals and supply catalogs that always littered his office. When his receptionist had finally called it to his attention this morning, he'd been alarmed by the name on the return address: Joseph Kahanu, Attorney at Law.

He had opened it immediately.

Now he sank into his chair and read the letter once again.

Dear Dr. Tanaka,
As the attorney representing Mr. Charles Decker, I hereby request any and all medical records pertaining to

the obstetrical care of Ms. Jennifer Brook, who was your patient at the time of her death....

Jennifer Brook. A name he'd hoped to forget.

A profound weariness came over him—the exhaustion of a man who has discovered he cannot outrun his own shadow. He tried to muster the energy to go home, to slog outside and climb into his car, but he could only sit and stare at the four walls of his office. His sanctuary. His gaze traveled past the framed diplomas, the medical certificates, the photographs. Everywhere there were snapshots of wrinkled newborns, of beaming mothers and fathers. How many babies had he brought into the world? He'd lost count years ago....

It was a sound in the outer office that finally drew him out of his chair: the click of a door shutting. He rose and went to peer out at the reception area. "Peggy? Are you still here?"

The waiting room was deserted. Slowly his gaze moved past the flowered couch and chairs, past the magazines neatly stacked on the coffee table, and finally settled on the outer door. It was unlocked.

Through the silence, he heard the muted clang of metal. It came from one of the exam rooms.

"Peggy?" Tanaka moved down the hall and glanced into the first room. Flicking on the light, he saw the hard gleam of the stainless-steel sink, the gynecologic table, the supply cabinet. He turned off the light and went to the next room. Again, everything was as it should be: the instruments lined up neatly on the counter, the sink wiped dry, the table stirrups folded up for the night.

Crossing the hall, he moved toward the third and last exam room. But just as he reached for the light switch, some instinct made him freeze: a sudden awareness of a presence—something malevolent—waiting for him in the darkness.

In terror, he backed out of the room. Only as he spun around to flee did he realize that the intruder was standing behind him.

A blade slashed across his neck.

Tanaka staggered backward into the exam room and toppled an instrument stand. Stumbling to the floor, he found the linoleum was already slick with his blood. Even as he felt his life drain away, a coldly rational pocket of his brain forced him to assess his own wound, to analyze his own chances. *Severed artery. Exsanguination within minutes. Have to stop the bleeding....* Numbness was already creeping up his legs.

So little time. On his hands and knees, he crawled toward the cabinet where the gauze was stored. To his half-senseless mind, the feeble light reflecting off those glass doors became his guiding beacon, his only hope of survival.

A shadow blotted out the glow from the hall. He knew the intruder was standing in the doorway, watching him. Still he kept moving.

In his last seconds of consciousness, Tanaka managed to drag himself to his feet and wrench open the cabinet door. Sterile packets rained down from the shelf. Blindly he ripped one apart, withdrew a wad of gauze and clamped it against his neck.

He didn't see the attacker's blade trace its final arc.

As it plunged deep into his back, Tanaka tried to scream but the only sound that issued from his throat was a sigh. It was the last breath he took before he slid quietly to the floor.

Charlie Decker lay naked in his small hard bed and he was afraid.

Through the window he saw the blood-red glow of a neon sign: *The Victory Hotel.* Except the *t* was missing from *Hotel.* And what was left made him think of *Hole*, which is what the place really was: *The Victory Hole*, where every triumph, every joy, sank into some dark pit of no return.

He shut his eyes but the neon seemed to burrow its way through his lids. He turned away from the window and pulled the pillow over his head. The smell of the filthy linen was suffocating. Tossing the pillow aside, he rose and paced over to the window. There he stared down at the street. On the sidewalk below, a stringy-haired blonde in a miniskirt was dickering with a man in a Chevy. Somewhere in the night people laughed and a jukebox was playing "It Don't Matter Anymore." A stench rose from the alley, a peculiar mingling of rotting trash and frangipani: the smell of the back streets of paradise. It made him nauseated. But it was too hot to close the window, too hot to sleep, too hot even to breathe.

He went over to the card table and switched on the lamp. The same newspaper headline stared up at him.

Honolulu Physician Found Slain.

He felt the sweat trickle down his chest. He threw the newspaper on the floor. Then he sat down and let his head fall into his hands.

The music from the distant jukebox faded; the next song started, a thrusting of guitars and drums. A singer growled out: "I want it bad, oh yeah, baby, so bad, so bad...."

Slowly he raised his head and his gaze settled on the photograph of Jenny. She was smiling; as always, she was smiling. He touched the picture, trying to remember how her face had felt; but the years had dimmed his memory.

At last he opened his notebook. He turned to a blank page. He began to write.

This is what they told me:
"It takes time...
Time to heal, time to forget."
This is what I told them:
That healing lies not in forgetfulness
But in remembrance
Of you.
The smell of the sea on your skin;
The small and perfect footprints you leave in the sand.
In remembrance there are no endings.
And so you lie there, now and always, by the sea.
You open your eyes. You touch me.

The sun is in your fingertips.
And I am healed.
I am healed.

1

With a steady hand, Dr. Kate Chesne injected two hundred milligrams of sodium Pentothal into her patient's intravenous line. As the column of pale yellow liquid drifted lazily through the plastic tubing, Kate murmured, "You should start to feel sleepy soon, Ellen. Close your eyes. Let go...."

"I don't feel anything yet."

"It will take a minute or so." Kate squeezed Ellen's shoulder in a silent gesture of reassurance. The small things were what made a patient feel safe. A touch. A quiet voice. "Let yourself float," Kate whispered. "Think of the sky... clouds...."

Ellen gave her a calm and drowsy smile. Beneath the harsh operating-room lights, every freckle, every flaw stood out cruelly on her face. No one, not even Ellen O'Brien, was beautiful on the operating table. "Funny," she murmured. "I'm not afraid. Not in the least...."

"You don't have to be. I'll take care of everything."

"I know. I know you will." Ellen reached out for Kate's hand. It was only a touch, a brief mingling of fingers. The warmth of Ellen's skin against hers was one more reminder that not just a body, but a woman, a friend, was lying on this table.

The door swung open and the surgeon walked in. Dr. Guy Santini was as big as a bear and he looked faintly ridiculous in his flowered paper cap. "How we doing in here, Kate?"

"Pentothal's going in now."

Guy moved to the table and squeezed the patient's hand. "Still with us, Ellen?"

She smiled. "For better or worse. But on the whole, I'd rather be in Philadelphia."

Guy laughed. "You'll get there. But minus your gallbladder."

"I don't know.... I was getting kinda...fond of the thing...." Ellen's eyelids sagged. "Remember, Guy," she whispered. "You promised. No scar...."

"Did I?"

"Yes...you did....."

Guy winked at Kate. "Didn't I tell you? Nurses make the worst patients. Demanding broads!"

"Watch it, Doc!" one of the O.R. nurses snapped. "One of these days we'll get *you* up on that table."

"Now *that's* a terrifying thought," remarked Guy.

Kate watched as her patient's jaw at last fell slack. She called softly: "Ellen?" She brushed her finger across Ellen's eyelashes. There was no response. Kate nodded at Guy. "She's under."

"Ah, Katie, my darlin'," he said, "you do such good work for a—"

"For a *girl*. Yeah, yeah. I know."

"Well, let's get this show on the road," he said, heading out to scrub. "All her labs look okay?"

"Blood work's perfect."

"EKG?"

"I ran it last night. Normal."

Guy gave her an admiring salute from the doorway. "With you around, Kate, a man doesn't even have to think. Oh, and ladies?" He called to the two O.R. nurses who were laying out the instruments. "A word of warning. Our intern's a lefty."

The scrub nurse glanced up with sudden interest. "Is he cute?"

Guy winked. "A real dreamboat, Cindy. I'll tell him you asked." Laughing, he vanished out the door.

Cindy sighed. "How does his wife stand him, anyway?"

For the next ten minutes, everything proceeded like clockwork. Kate went about her tasks with her usual efficiency. She inserted the endotracheal tube and connected the respirator. She adjusted the flow of oxygen and added the proper proportions of forane and nitrous oxide. She was Ellen's lifeline. Each step, though automatic, required double-checking, even triple-checking. When the patient was someone she knew and liked, being sure of all her moves took on even more urgency. An anesthesiologist's job is often called ninety-nine percent boredom and one percent sheer terror; it was that one percent that Kate was always anticipating, always guarding against. When complications arose, they could happen in the blink of an eye.

But today she fully expected everything to go smoothly. Ellen O'Brien was only forty-one. Except for a gallstone, she was in perfect health.

Guy returned to the O.R., his freshly scrubbed arms dripping wet. He was followed by the "dreamboat" lefty intern, who appeared to be a staggering five-feet-six in his elevator shoes. They proceeded on to the ritual donning of sterile gowns and gloves, a ceremony punctuated by the brisk snap of latex.

As the team took its place around the operating table, Kate's gaze traveled the circle of masked faces. Except for the intern, they were all comfortably familiar. There was the circulating nurse, Ann Richter, with her ash blond hair tucked neatly beneath a blue surgical cap. She was a coolheaded professional who never mixed business with pleasure. Crack a joke in the O.R. and she was likely to flash you a look of disapproval.

Next there was Guy, homely and affable, his brown eyes distorted by thick bottle-lens glasses. It was hard to believe anyone so clumsy could be a surgeon. But put a scalpel in his hand and he could work miracles.

Opposite Guy stood the intern with the woeful misfortune of having been born left-handed.

And last there was Cindy, the scrub nurse, a dark-eyed nymph with an easy laugh. Today she was sporting a brilliant new eye shadow called Oriental Malachite, which gave her a look reminiscent of a tropical fish.

"Nice eye shadow, Cindy," noted Guy as he held his hand out for a scalpel.

"Why thank you, Dr. Santini," she replied, slapping the instrument into his palm.

"I like it a lot better than that other one, Spanish Slime."

"Spanish *Moss*."

"This one's really, really striking, don't you think?" he asked the intern who, wisely, said nothing. "Yeah," Guy continued. "Reminds me of my favorite color. I think it's called Comet cleanser."

The intern giggled. Cindy flashed him a dirty look. So much for the dreamboat's chances.

Guy made the first incision. As a line of scarlet oozed to the surface of the abdominal wall, the intern automatically dabbed away the blood with a sponge. Their hands worked automatically and in concert, like pianists playing a duet.

From her position at the patient's head, Kate followed their progress, her ear tuned the whole time to Ellen's heart rhythm. Everything was going well, with no crises on the horizon. This was when she enjoyed her work most—when she knew she had everything under control. In the midst of all this stainless steel, she felt right at home. For her, the whooshes of the ventilator and the beeps of the cardiac monitor were soothing background music to the performance now unfolding on the table.

Guy made a deeper incision, exposing the glistening layer of fat. "Muscles seem a little tight, Kate," he observed. "We're going to have trouble retracting."

"I'll see what I can do." Turning to her medication cart, she reached for the tiny drawer labeled Succinylcholine. Given intravenously, the drug would relax the muscles, allowing Guy easier access to the abdominal cavity. Glancing in the drawer, she frowned. "Ann? I'm down to one vial of Succinylcholine. Hunt me down some more, will you?"

"That's funny," said Cindy. "I'm sure I stocked that cart yesterday afternoon."

"Well, there's only one vial left." Kate drew up 5 cc's of the crystal-clear solution and injected it into Ellen's IV line. It would take a minute to work. She sat back and waited.

Guy's scalpel cleared the fat layer and he began to expose the abdominal muscle sheath. "Still pretty tight, Kate," he remarked.

She glanced up at the wall clock. "It's been three minutes. You should notice some effect by now."

"Not a thing."

"Okay. I'll push a little more." Kate drew up another 3 cc's and injected it into the IV line. "I'll need another vial soon, Ann," she warned. "This one's just about—"

A buzzer went off on the cardiac monitor. Kate glanced up sharply. What she saw on the screen made her jump to her feet in horror.

Ellen O'Brien's heart had stopped.

In the next instant the room was in a frenzy. Orders were shouted out, instrument trays shoved aside. The intern clambered onto a footstool and thrust his weight again and again on Ellen's chest.

This was the proverbial one percent, the moment of terror every anesthesiologist dreads.

It was also the worst moment in Kate Chesne's life.

As panic swirled around her, she fought to stay in control. She injected vial after vial of adrenaline, first into the IV lines and then directly into Ellen's heart. *I'm losing her,* she thought. *Dear God, I'm losing her.* Then she saw one brief fluttering across the oscilloscope. It was the only hint that some trace of life lingered.

"Let's cardiovert!" she called out. She glanced at Ann, who was standing by the defibrillator. "Two hundred watt seconds!"

Ann didn't move. She remained frozen, her face as white as alabaster.

"Ann?" Kate yelled. *"Two hundred watt seconds!"*

It was Cindy who darted around to the machine and hit the charge button. The needle shot up to two hundred. Guy grabbed the defibrillator paddles, slapped them on Ellen's chest and released the electrical charge.

Ellen's body jerked like a puppet whose strings have all been tugged at once.

The fluttering slowed to a ripple. It was the pattern of a dying heart.

Kate tried another drug, then still another in a desperate attempt to flog some life back into the heart. Nothing worked. Through a film of tears, she watched the tracing fade to a line meandering aimlessly across the oscilloscope.

"That's it," Guy said softly. He gave the signal to stop cardiac massage. The intern, his face dripping with sweat, backed away from the table.

"No," Kate insisted, planting her hands on Ellen's chest. "It's not over." She began to pump—fiercely, desperately. *"It's not over."* She threw herself against Ellen, pitting her weight against the stubborn shield of rib and muscles. The heart had to be massaged, the brain nourished. She had to keep Ellen alive. Again and again she pumped, until her arms were weak and trembling. *Live, Ellen,* she commanded silently. *You have to live....*

"Kate." Guy touched her arm.

"We're not giving up. Not yet...."

"Kate." Gently, Guy tugged her away from the table. "It's over," he whispered.

Someone turned off the sound on the heart monitor. The whine of the alarm gave way to an eerie silence. Slowly, Kate turned and saw that everyone was watching her. She looked up at the oscilloscope.

The line was flat.

Kate flinched as an orderly zipped the shroud over Ellen O'Brien's body. There was a cruel finality to that sound; it struck her as obscene, this convenient packaging of what had once been a living, breathing woman. As the body was wheeled off to the morgue, Kate turned away. Long after the squeak of the gurney wheels had faded down the hall, she was still standing there, alone in the O.R.

Fighting tears, she gazed around at the bloodied gauze and empty vials littering the floor. It was the same sad debris that lingered after every hospital death. Soon it would be swept up and incinerated and there'd be no clue to the tragedy that had just been played out. Nothing except a body in the morgue.

And questions. Oh, yes, there'd be questions. From Ellen's parents. From the hospital. Questions Kate didn't know how to answer.

Wearily she tugged off her surgical cap and felt a vague sense of relief as her brown hair tumbled free to her shoulders. She needed time alone—to think, to understand. She turned to leave.

Guy was standing in the doorway. The instant she saw his face, Kate knew something was wrong.

Silently he handed her Ellen O'Brien's chart.

"The electrocardiogram," he said. "You told me it was normal."

"It was."

"You'd better take another look."

Puzzled, she opened the chart to the EKG, the electrical tracing of Ellen's heart. The first detail she noted was her own initials, written at the top, signifying that she'd seen the page. Next she scanned the tracing. For a solid minute she stared at the series of twelve black squiggles, unable to believe what she was seeing. The pattern was unmistakable. Even a third-year medical student could have made the diagnosis.

"That's why she died, Kate," Guy said.

"But— This is impossible!" she blurted. "I couldn't have made a mistake like this!"

Guy didn't answer. He simply looked away—an act more telling than anything he could have said.

"Guy, you *know* me," she protested. "You know I wouldn't miss something like—"

"It's right there in black and white. For God's sake, your *initials* are on the damn thing!"

They stared at each other, both of them shocked by the harshness of his voice.

"I'm sorry," he apologized at last. Suddenly agitated, he turned and clawed his fingers through his hair. "Dear God. She'd had a heart attack. A *heart attack*. And we took her to surgery." He gave Kate a look of utter misery. "I guess that means we killed her."

"It's an obvious case of malpractice."

Attorney David Ransom closed the file labeled O'Brien, Ellen, and looked across the broad teak desk at his clients. If he had to choose one word to describe Patrick and Mary O'Brien, it would be *gray*. Gray hair, gray faces, gray clothes. Patrick was wearing a dull tweed jacket that had long ago sagged into shapelessness. Mary wore a dress in a black-and-white print that seemed to blend together into a drab monochrome.

Patrick kept shaking his head. "She was our only girl, Mr. Ransom. Our only child. She was always so good, you know? Never complained. Even when she was a baby. She'd just lie there in her crib and smile. Like a little angel. Just like a darling little—" He suddenly stopped, his face crumpling.

"Mr. O'Brien," David said gently, "I know it's not much of a comfort to you now, but I promise you, I'll do everything I can."

Patrick shook his head. "It's not the money we're after. Sure, I can't work. My back, you know. But Ellie, she had a life insurance policy, and—"

"How much was the policy?"

"Fifty thousand," answered Mary. "That's the kind of girl she was. Always thinking of us." Her profile, caught in the window's light, had an edge of steel. Unlike her husband, Mary O'Brien was done with her crying. She sat very straight, her whole body a rigid testament to grief. David knew exactly what she was feeling. The pain. The anger. Especially the anger. It was there, burning coldly in her eyes.

Patrick was sniffling.

David took a box of tissues from his drawer and quietly placed it in front of his client. "Perhaps we should discuss the case some other time," he suggested. "When you both feel ready...."

Mary's chin lifted sharply. "We're ready, Mr. Ransom. Ask your questions."

David glanced at Patrick, who managed a feeble nod. "I'm afraid this may strike you as...cold-blooded, the things I have to ask. I'm sorry."

"Go on," prompted Mary.

"I'll proceed immediately to filing suit. But I'll need more information before we can make an estimate of damages. Part of that is lost wages—what your daughter would have earned had she lived. You say she was a nurse?"

"In obstetrics. Labor and delivery."

"Do you know her salary?"

"I'll have to check her pay stubs."

"What about dependants? Did she have any?"

"None."

"She was never married?"

Mary shook her head and sighed. "She was the perfect daughter, Mr. Ransom, in almost every way. Beautiful. And brilliant. But when it came to men, she made...mistakes."

He frowned. "Mistakes?"

Mary shrugged. "Oh, I suppose it's just the way things are these days. And when a woman gets to be a—a certain age, she feels, well, *lucky* to have any man at all...." She looked down at her tightly knotted hands and fell silent.

David sensed they'd strayed into hazardous waters. He wasn't interested in Ellen O'Brien's love life, anyway. It was irrelevant to the case.

"Let's turn to your daughter's medical history," he said smoothly, opening the medical chart. "The record states she was forty-one years old and in excellent health. To your knowledge, did she ever have any problems with her heart?''

"Never."

"She never complained of chest pain? Shortness of breath?"

"Ellie was a long-distance swimmer, Mr. Ransom. She could go all day and never get out of breath. That's why I don't believe this story about a—a heart attack."

"But the EKG was strongly diagnostic, Mrs. O'Brien. If there'd been an autopsy, we could have proved it. But I guess it's a bit late for that."

Mary glanced at her husband. "It's Patrick. He just couldn't stand the idea—"

"Haven't they cut her up enough already?" Patrick blurted out.

There was a long silence. Mary said softly, "We'll be taking her ashes out to sea. She loved the sea. Ever since she was a baby…"

It was a solemn parting. A few last words of condolence, and then the handshakes, the sealing of a pact. The O'Briens turned to leave. But in the doorway, Mary stopped.

"I want you to know it's not the money," she declared. "The truth is, I don't care if we see a dime. But they've ruined our lives, Mr. Ransom. They've taken our only baby away. And I hope to God they never forget it."

David nodded. "I'll see they never do."

After his clients had left, David turned to the window. He took a deep breath and slowly let it out, willing the emotions to drain from his body. But a hard knot seemed to linger in his stomach. All that sadness, all that rage; it clouded his thinking.

Six days ago, a doctor had made a terrible mistake. Now, at the age of forty-one, Ellen O'Brien was dead.

She was only three years older than me.

He sat down at his desk and opened the O'Brien file. Skipping past the hospital record, he turned to the curricula vitae of the two physicians.

Dr. Guy Santini's record was outstanding. Forty-eight years old, a Harvard-trained surgeon, he was at the peak of his career. His list of publications went on for five pages. Most of his research dealt with hepatic physiology. He'd been sued once, eight years ago; he'd won. Bully for him. Santini wasn't the target anyway. David had his cross hairs on the anesthesiologist.

He flipped to the three-page summary of Dr. Katharine Chesne's career.

Her background was impressive. A B.Sc in chemistry from U.C., Berkeley, an M.D. from Johns Hopkins, anesthesia residency and intensive-care fellowship at U.C., San Francisco. Now only thirty years old, she'd already compiled a respectable list of published articles. She'd joined Mid Pac Hospital as a staff anesthesiologist less than a year ago. There was no photograph, but he had no trouble conjuring up a mental picture of the stereotypical female physician: frumpy hair, no figure, and a face like a horse—albeit an extremely intelligent horse.

David sat back, frowning. This was too good a record; it didn't match the profile of an incompetent physician. How could she have made such an elementary mistake?

He closed the file. Whatever her excuses, the facts were indisputable: Dr. Katharine Chesne had condemned her patient to die under the surgeon's knife. Now she'd have to face the consequences.

He'd make damn sure she did.

George Bettencourt despised doctors. It was a personal opinion that made his job as CEO of Mid Pac Hospital all the more difficult, since he had to work so closely with the medical staff. He had both an M.B.A. and a Masters in public health. In his ten years as CEO, he'd achieved what the old doctor-led administration had been unable to do: he'd turned Mid Pac from a comatose institution into a profitable business. Yet all he ever heard from those stupid little surrogate gods in their white coats was criticism. They turned their superior noses up at the very idea that their saintly work could be dictated by profit-and-loss graphs. The cold reality was that saving lives, like selling linoleum, was a business. Bettencourt knew it. The doctors didn't. They were fools, and fools gave him headaches.

And the two sitting across from him now were giving him a migraine headache the likes of which he hadn't felt in years.

Dr. Clarence Avery, the white-haired chief of anesthesia, wasn't the problem. The old man was too timid to stand up to his own shadow, much less to a controversial issue. Ever since his wife's stroke, Avery had shuffled through his duties like a sleepwalker. Yes, he could be persuaded to cooperate. Especially when the hospital's reputation was at stake.

No, it was the other one who worried Bettencourt: the woman. She was new to the staff and he didn't know her very well. But the minute she'd walked into his office, he'd smelled trouble. She had that look in her eye, that crusader's set of the jaw. She was a pretty enough woman, though her brown hair was in a wild state of anarchy and she probably hadn't held a tube of lipstick in months. But those intense green eyes of hers were enough to make a man overlook all the flaws of that face. She was, in fact, quite attractive.

Too bad she'd blown it. Now she was a liability. He hoped she wouldn't make things worse by being a bitch, as well.

Kate flinched as Bettencourt dropped the papers on the desk in front of her. "The letter arrived in our attorney's office this morning, Dr. Chesne," he said. "Hand delivered by personal messenger. I think you'd better read it."

She took one look at the letterhead and felt her stomach drop away: *Uehara and Ransom, Attorneys at Law.*

"One of the best firms in town," explained Bettencourt. Seeing her stunned expression, he went on impatiently, "You and the hospital are being sued, Dr. Chesne. For malpractice. And David Ransom is personally taking on the case."

Her throat had gone dry. Slowly she looked up. "But how—how can they—"

"All it takes is a lawyer. And a dead patient."

"I've explained what happened!" She turned to Avery. "Remember last week—I told you—"

"Clarence has gone over it with me," cut in Bettencourt. "That isn't the issue we're discussing here."

"What *is* the issue?"

He seemed startled by her directness. He let out a sharp breath. "The issue is this: we have what looks like a million-dollar lawsuit on our hands. As your employer, we're responsible for the damages. But it's not just the money that concerns us." He paused. "There's our reputation."

The tone of his voice struck her as ominous. She knew what was coming and found herself utterly voiceless. She could only sit there, her stomach roiling, her hands clenched in her lap, and wait for the blow to fall.

"This lawsuit reflects badly on the whole hospital," he said. "If the case goes to trial, there'll be publicity. People—patients—will read those newspapers and it'll scare them." He looked down at his desk. "I realize your record up till now has been acceptable—"

Her chin shot up. "Acceptable?" she repeated incredulously. She glanced at Avery. The chief of anesthesia knew her record. And it was flawless.

Avery squirmed in his chair, his watery blue eyes avoiding hers. "Well, actually," he mumbled, "Dr. Chesne's record has been—up till now, anyway—uh, more than acceptable. That is…"

For God's sake, man! she wanted to scream. *Stand up for me!*

"There've never been any complaints," Avery finished lamely.

"Nevertheless," continued Bettencourt, "you've put us in a touchy situation, Dr. Chesne. That's why we think it'd be best if your name was no longer associated with the hospital."

There was a long silence, punctuated only by the sound of Dr. Avery's nervous cough.

"We're asking for your resignation," stated Bettencourt.

So there it was. The blow. It washed over her like a giant wave, leaving her limp and exhausted. Quietly she asked, "And if I refuse to resign?"

"Believe me, Doctor, a resignation will look a lot better on your record than a—"

"Dismissal?"

He cocked his head. "We understand each other."

"No." She raised her head. Something about his eyes, their cold self-assurance, made her stiffen. She'd never liked Bettencourt. She liked him even less now. "You don't understand me at all."

"You're a bright woman. You can see the options. In any event, we can't let you back in the O.R."

"It's not right," Avery objected.

"Excuse me?" Bettencourt frowned at the old man.

"You can't just fire her. She's a physician. There are channels you have to go through. Committees—"

"I'm well acquainted with the proper channels, Clarence! I was hoping Dr. Chesne would grasp the situation and act appropriately." He looked at her. "It really is easier, you know. There'd be no blot on your record. Just a notation that you resigned. I can have a letter typed up within the hour. All it takes is your…" His voice trailed off as he saw the look in her eyes.

Kate seldom got angry. She usually managed to keep her emotions under tight control. So the fury she now felt churning to the surface was something new and unfamiliar and almost frightening. With deadly calm she said, "Save yourself the paper, Mr. Bettencourt."

His jaw clicked shut. "If that's your decision…" He glanced at Avery. "When is the next Quality Assurance meeting?"

"It's—uh, next Tuesday, but—"

"Put the O'Brien case on the agenda. We'll let Dr. Chesne

present her record to committee." He looked at Kate. "A judgment by your peers. I'd say that's fair. Wouldn't you?"

She managed to swallow her retort. If she said anything else, if she let fly what she really thought of George Bettencourt, she'd ruin her chances of ever again working at Mid Pac. Or anywhere else, for that matter. All he had to do was slap her with the label Troublemaker; it would blacken her record for the rest of her life.

They parted civilly. For a woman who'd just had her career ripped to shreds, she managed a grand performance. She gave Bettencourt a level look, a cool handshake. She kept her composure all the way out the door and on the long walk down the carpeted hall. But as she rode the elevator down, something inside her seemed to snap. By the time the doors slid open again, she was shaking violently. As she walked blindly through the noise and bustle of the lobby, the realization hit her full force.

Dear God, I'm being sued. Less than a year in practice and I'm being sued....

She'd always thought that lawsuits, like all life's catastrophes, happened to other people. She'd never dreamed she'd be the one charged with incompetence. *Incompetence.*

Suddenly feeling sick, she swayed against the lobby telephones. As she struggled to calm her stomach, her gaze fell on the local directory, hanging by a chain from the shelf. *If only they knew the facts,* she thought. *If I could explain to them...*

It took only seconds to find the listing: *Uehara and Ransom, Attorneys at Law.* Their office was on Bishop Street.

She wrenched out the page. Then, driven by a new and desperate hope, she hurried out the door.

2

"**M**r. Ransom is unavailable."

The gray-haired receptionist had eyes of pure cast iron and a face straight out of *American Gothic*. All she needed was the pitchfork. Crossing her arms, she silently dared the intruder to try—just try—to talk her way in.

"But I have to see him!" Kate insisted. "It's about the case—"

"Of course it is," the woman said dryly.

"I only want to explain to him—"

"I've just told you, Doctor. He's in a meeting with the associates. He can't see you."

Kate's impatience was simmering close to the danger point. She leaned forward on the woman's desk and managed to say with polite fury, "Meetings don't last forever."

The receptionist smiled. "This one will."

Kate smiled back. "Then so can I."

"Doctor, you're wasting your time! Mr. Ransom *never* meets with defendants. Now, if you need an escort to find your way out, I'll be happy to—" She glanced around in annoyance as the telephone rang. Grabbing the receiver, she snapped, "Uehara and Ransom! Yes? Oh, yes, Mr. Matheson!" She pointedly turned her back on Kate. "Let's see, I have those files right here…"

In frustration, Kate glanced around at the waiting room, noting the leather couch, the Ikebana of willow and proteus, the Murashige print hanging on the wall. All exquisitely tasteful and undoubtedly expensive. Obviously, Uehara and

Ransom was doing a booming business. All off the blood and sweat of doctors, she thought in disgust.

The sound of voices suddenly drew Kate's attention. She turned and saw, just down the hall, a small army of young men and women emerging from a conference room. Which one was Ransom? She scanned the faces but none of the men looked old enough to be a senior partner in the firm. She glanced back at the desk and saw that the receptionist still had her back turned. It was now or never.

It took Kate only a split-second to make her decision. Swiftly, deliberately, she moved toward the conference room. But in the doorway she came to a halt, her eyes suddenly dazzled by the light.

A long teak table stretched out before her. Along either side, a row of leather chairs stood like soldiers at attention. Blinding sunshine poured in through the southerly windows, spilling across the head and shoulders of a lone man seated at the far end of the table. The light streaked his fair hair with gold. He didn't notice her; all his attention was focused on a sheaf of papers lying in front of him. Except for the rustle of a page being turned, the room was absolutely silent.

Kate swallowed hard and drew herself up straight. "Mr. Ransom?"

The man looked up and regarded her with a neutral expression. "Yes? Who are you?"

"I'm—"

"I'm so sorry, Mr. Ransom!" cut in the receptionist's outraged voice. Hauling Kate by the arm, the woman muttered through her teeth, "I *told* you he was unavailable. Now if you'll come with me—"

"I only want to talk to him!"

"Do you want me to call security and have you thrown out?"

Kate wrenched her arm free. "Go ahead."

"Don't tempt me, you—"

"What the hell is going on here?" The roar of Ransom's voice echoed in the vast room, shocking both women into silence. He aimed a long and withering look at Kate. "Just who *are* you?"

"Kate—" She paused and dropped her voice to what she hoped was a more dignified tone. "*Doctor* Kate Chesne."

A pause. "I see." he looked right back down at his papers and said flatly, "Show her out, Mrs. Pierce."

"I just want to tell you the facts!" Kate persisted. She tried to hold her ground but the receptionist herded her toward the door with all the skill of a sheepdog. "Or would you rather *not* hear the facts, is that it? Is that how you lawyers operate?" He studiously ignored her. "You don't give a damn about the truth, do you? You don't want to hear what really happened to Ellen O'Brien!"

That made him look up sharply. His gaze fastened long and hard on her face. "Hold on, Mrs. Pierce. I've just changed my mind. Let Dr. Chesne stay."

Mrs. Pierce was incredulous. "But—she could be violent!"

David's gaze lingered a moment longer on Kate's flushed face. "I think I can handle her. You can leave us, Mrs. Pierce."

Mrs. Pierce muttered as she walked out. The door closed behind her. There was a very long silence.

"Well, Dr. Chesne," David said. "Now that you've managed the rather miraculous feat of getting past Mrs. Pierce, are you just going to stand there?" He gestured to a chair. "Have a seat. Unless you'd rather scream at me from across the room."

His cold flippancy, rather than easing her tension, made him seem all the more unapproachable. She forced herself to move toward him, feeling his gaze every step of the way. For a man with his highly regarded reputation, he was younger than she'd expected, not yet in his forties. *Establishment* was stamped all over his clothes, from his gray pinstripe suit to his Yale tie clip. But a tan that deep and hair that sun-streaked didn't go along with an Ivy League type. *He's just a surfer boy, grown up*, she thought derisively. He certainly had a surfer's build, with those long, ropy limbs and shoulders that were just broad enough to be called impressive. A slab of a nose and a blunt chin saved him from being pretty. But it was his eyes she found herself focusing on. They were a frigid, penetrating blue; the sort of eyes that missed absolutely nothing. Right now those eyes were boring straight through her and she felt an almost irresistible urge to cross her arms protectively across her chest.

"I'm here to tell you the facts, Mr. Ransom," she said.

"The facts as you see them?"

"The facts as they *are*."

"Don't bother." Reaching into his briefcase, he pulled out Ellen O'Brien's file and slapped it down conclusively on the table. "I have all the facts right here. Everything I need." *Everything I need to hang you,* was what he meant.

"Not everything."

"And now *you're* going to supply me with the missing details. Right?" He smiled and she recognized immediately the unmistakable threat in his expression. He had such perfect, sharp white teeth. She had the distinct feeling she was staring into the jaws of a shark.

She leaned forward, planting her hands squarely on the table. "What I'm going to supply you with is the truth."

"Oh, naturally." He slouched back in his chair and regarded her with a look of terminal boredom. "Tell me something," he asked offhandedly. "Does your attorney know you're here?"

"Attorney? I—I haven't talked to any attorney—"

"Then you'd better get one on the phone. Fast. Because, Doctor, you're damn well going to need one."

"Not necessarily. This is nothing but a big misunderstanding, Mr. Ransom. If you'll just listen to the facts, I'm sure—"

"Hold on." He reached into his briefcase and pulled out a cassette recorder.

"Just what do you think you're doing?" she demanded.

He turned on the recorder and slid it in front of her. "I

wouldn't want to miss some vital detail. Go on with your story. I'm all ears.''

Furious, she reached over and flicked the Off button. "This isn't a deposition! Put the damn thing away!"

For a few tense seconds they sized each other up. She felt a distinct sense of triumph when he put the recorder back in his briefcase.

"Now, where were we?" he asked with extravagant politeness. "Oh, yes. You were about to tell me what *really* happened." He settled back, obviously expecting some grand entertainment.

She hesitated. Now that she finally had his full attention, she didn't know quite how to start.

"I'm a very…careful person, Mr. Ransom," she said at last. "I take my time with things. I may not be brilliant, but I'm thorough. And I don't make stupid mistakes."

His raised eyebrow told her exactly what he thought of that statement. She ignored his look and went on.

"The night Ellen O'Brien came into the hospital, Guy Santini admitted her. But I wrote the anesthesia orders. I checked the lab results. And I read her EKG. It was a Sunday night and the technician was busy somewhere so I even ran the strip myself. I wasn't rushed. I took all the time I needed. In fact, more than I needed, because Ellen was a member of our staff. She was one of *us*. She was also a friend. I remember sitting in her room, going over her lab tests. She wanted to know if everything was normal."

"And you told her everything was."

"Yes. Including the EKG."

"Then you obviously made a mistake."

"I just told you, Mr. Ransom. I don't make stupid mistakes. And I didn't make one that night."

"But the record shows—"

"The record's wrong."

"I have the tracing right here in black and white. And it plainly shows a heart attack."

"That's *not* the EKG I saw!"

He looked as if he hadn't heard her quite right.

"The EKG I saw that night was normal," she insisted.

"Then how did this abnormal one pop into the chart?"

"Someone put it there, of course."

"Who?"

"I don't know."

"I see." Turning away, he said under his breath: "I can't wait to see how this plays in court."

"Mr. Ransom, if I made a mistake, I'd be the first to admit it!"

"Then you'd be amazingly honest."

"Do you really think I'd make up a story as—as *stupid* as this?"

His response was an immediate burst of laughter that left her cheeks burning. "No," he answered. "I'm sure you'd come up with something much more believable." He gave her an inviting nod. In a voice thick with sarcasm, he jeered, "Please, I'm *dying* to know how this extraordinary mix-up happened. How did the wrong EKG get in the chart?"

"How should I know?"

"You must have a theory."

"I don't."

"Come on, Doctor, don't disappoint me."

"I said I don't."

"Then make a guess!"

"Maybe someone beamed it there from the *Starship Enterprise*!" she yelled in frustration.

"Nice theory," he said, deadpan. "But let's get back to reality. Which, in this case, happens to be a particular sheet of wood by-product, otherwise known as paper." He flipped the chart open to the damning EKG. "Explain *that* away."

"I told you, I can't! I've gone crazy trying to figure it out! We do dozens of EKGs every day at Mid Pac. It could have been a clerical error. A mislabeled tracing. Somehow, that page was filed in the wrong chart."

"But you've written your initials on this page."

"No, I didn't."

"Is there some other K.C., M.D.?"

"Those are my initials. But I didn't write them."

"What are you saying? That this is a forgery?"

"It—it has to be. I mean, yes, I guess it is...." Suddenly confused, she shoved back a rebellious strand of hair off her face. His utterly calm expression rattled her. Why didn't the man react, for God's sake? Why did he just sit there, regarding her with that infuriatingly bland expression?

"Well," he said at last.

"Well what?"

"How long have you had this little problem with people forging your name?"

"Don't make me sound paranoid!"

"I don't have to. You're doing fine on your own."

Now he was silently laughing at her; she could see it in his eyes. The worst part was that she couldn't blame him. Her story *did* sound like a lunatic's ravings.

"All right," he relented. "Let's assume for the moment you're telling the truth."

"Yes!" she snapped. "Please do!"

"I can think of only two explanations for why the EKG would be intentionally switched. Either someone's trying to destroy your career—"

"That's absurd. I don't have any enemies."

"Or someone's trying to cover up a murder."

At her stunned expression, he gave her a maddeningly superior smile. "Since the second explanation obviously strikes both of us as equally absurd, I have no choice but to conclude you're lying." He leaned forward and his voice was suddenly soft, almost intimate. The shark was getting chummy; that had to be dangerous. "Come on, Doctor," he prodded. "Level with me. Tell me what really happened in the O.R. Was there a slip of the knife? A mistake in anesthesia?"

"There was nothing of the kind!"

"Too much laughing gas and not enough oxygen?"

"I told you, there were *no* mistakes!"

"Then why is Ellen O'Brien dead?"

She stared at him, stunned by the violence in his voice. And the blueness of his eyes. A spark seemed to fly between them, ignited by something entirely unexpected. With a shock, she realized he was an attractive man. Too attractive. And that her response to him was dangerous. She could already feel the blush creeping into her face, could feel a flood of heat rising inside her.

"No answer?" he challenged smoothly. He settled back, obviously enjoying the advantage he held over her. "Then why don't I tell *you* what happened? On April 2, a Sunday night, Ellen O'Brien checked into Mid Pac Hospital for routine gallbladder surgery. As her anesthesiologist, you ordered routine pre-op tests, including an EKG, which you checked before leaving the hospital that night. Maybe you were rushed. Maybe you had a hot date waiting. Whatever the reason, you got careless and you made a fatal error. You missed those vital clues in the EKG: the elevated ST waves, the inverted T waves. You pronounced it normal and signed your initials. Then you left for the night—never realizing your patient had just had a heart attack."

"She never had any symptoms! No chest pain—"

"But it says right here in the nurses' notes—let me quote—" he flipped through the chart "—'Patient complaining of abdominal discomfort.'"

"That was her gallstone—"

"Or was it her heart? Anyway, the next events are indisputable. You and Dr. Santini took Ms. O'Brien to surgery. A few whiffs of anesthesia and the stress was too much for her weakened heart. So it stopped. And you couldn't restart it." He paused dramatically, his eyes as hard as diamonds. "There, Dr. Chesne. You've just lost your patient."

"That's not how it happened! I remember that EKG. It was *normal*!"

"Maybe you'd better review your textbook on EKGs."

"I don't need a textbook. I *know* what's normal!" She scarcely recognized her own voice, echoing shrilly through the vast room.

He looked unimpressed. Bored, even. "Really—" he sighed "—wouldn't it be easier just to admit you made a mistake?"

"Easier for whom?"

"For everyone involved. Consider an out-of-court settlement. It'd be fast, easy, and relatively painless."

"A settlement? But that's admitting a mistake I never made!"

What little patience he had left finally snapped. "You want to go to trial?" he shot back. "Fine. But let me tell you something about the way I work. When I try a case, I don't do it halfway. If I have to tear you apart in court, I'll do it. And when I'm finished, you'll wish you'd never turned this into some ridiculous fight for your honor. Because let's face it, Doctor. You don't have a snowball's chance in hell."

She wanted to grab him by those pinstriped lapels. She wanted to scream out that in all this talk about settlements and courtrooms, her own anguish over Ellen O'Brien's death had been ignored. But suddenly all her rage, all her strength, seemed to drain away, leaving her exhausted. Wearily she slumped back in her chair. "I wish I *could* admit I made a mistake," she said quietly. "I wish I could just say, 'I know I'm guilty and I'll pay for it.' I wish to God I could say that. I've spent the last week wondering about my memory. Wondering how this could have happened. Ellen trusted me and I let her die. It makes me wish I'd never become a doctor, that I'd been a clerk or a waitress—anything else. I love my work. You have no idea how hard it's been—how much I've given up—just to get to where I am. And now it looks as if I'll lose my job...." She swallowed and her head drooped in defeat. "And I wonder if I'll ever be able to work again...."

David regarded her bowed head in silence and fought to ignore the emotions stirring inside him. He'd always considered himself a good judge of character. He could usually look a man in the eyes and tell if he was lying. All during Kate Chesne's little speech, he'd been watching her eyes, searching for some inconsistent blip, some betraying flicker that would tell him she was lying through her teeth.

But her eyes had been absolutely steady and forthright and as beautiful as a pair of emeralds.

The last thought startled him, popping out as it did, almost against his will. As much as he might try to suppress it, he was all at once aware that she *was* a beautiful woman. She was wearing a simple green dress, gathered loosely at the waist, and it took just one glance to see that there were feminine curves beneath that silky fabric. The face that went along with those very nice curves had its flaws. She had a prizefighter's square jaw. Her shoulder-length mahogany hair was a riot of waves, obviously untamable. The curly bangs softened a forehead that was far too prominent. No, it wasn't a classically beautiful face. But then he'd never been attracted to classically beautiful women.

Suddenly he was annoyed not only at himself but at her, at her effect on him. He wasn't a dumb kid fresh out of law school. He was too old and too smart to be entertaining the peculiarly male thoughts now dancing in his head.

In a deliberately rude gesture, he looked down at his watch. Then, snapping his briefcase shut, he stood up. "I have a deposition to take and I'm already late. So if you'll excuse me…"

He was halfway across the room when her voice called out to him softly: "Mr. Ransom?"

He glanced back at her in irritation. "What?"

"I know my story sounds crazy. And I guess there's no reason on earth you should believe me. But I swear to you: it's the truth."

He sensed her desperate need for validation. She was searching for a sign that she'd gotten through to him; that she'd penetrated his hard shell of skepticism. The fact was, he didn't *know* if he believed her, and it bothered the hell out of him that his usual instinct for the truth had gone haywire, and all because of a pair of emerald-green eyes.

"Whether I believe you or not is irrelevant," he said. "So

don't waste your time on me, Doctor. Save it for the jury.''
The words came out colder than he'd intended and he saw,
from the quick flinch of her head, that she'd been stung.

"Then there's nothing I can do, nothing I can say—"

"Not a thing."

"I thought you'd listen. I thought somehow I could change
your mind—"

"Then you've got a lot to learn about lawyers. Good-day,
Dr. Chesne." Turning, he headed briskly for the door. "I'll
see you in court."

3

You don't have a snowball's chance in hell.

That was the phrase Kate kept hearing over and over as she sat alone at a table in the hospital cafeteria. And just how long did it take for a snowball to melt, anyway? Or would it simply disintegrate in the heat of the flames?

How much heat could she take before she fell apart on the witness stand?

She'd always been so adept at dealing with matters of life and death. When a medical crisis arose, she didn't wring her hands over what needed to be done; she just did it, automatically. Inside the safe and sterile walls of the operating room, she was in control.

But a courtroom was a different world entirely. That was David Ransom's territory. He'd be the one in control; she'd be as vulnerable as a patient on the operating table. How could she possibly fend off an attack by the very man who'd built his reputation on the scorched careers of doctors?

She'd never felt threatened by men before. After all, she'd trained with them, worked with them. David Ransom was the first man who'd ever intimidated her, and he'd done it effortlessly. If only he was short or fat or bald. If only she could think of him as human and therefore vulnerable. But just the thought of facing those cold blue eyes in court made her stomach do a panicky flip-flop.

"Looks like you could use some company," said a familiar voice.

Glancing up, she saw Guy Santini, rumpled as always, peering down at her through those ridiculously thick glasses.

She gave him a listless nod. "Hi."

Clucking, he pulled up a chair and sat down. "How're you doing, Kate?"

"You mean except for being unemployed?" She managed a sour laugh. "Just terrific."

"I heard the old man pulled you out of the O.R. I'm sorry."

"I can't really blame it on old Avery. He was just following orders."

"Bettencourt's?"

"Who else? He's labeled me a financial *liability*."

Guy snorted. "That's what happens when the damned M.B.A.'s take over. All they can talk about is profits and losses! I swear, if George Bettencourt could make a buck selling the gold out of patients' teeth, he'd be roaming the wards with pliers."

"And then he'd send them a bill for oral surgery," Kate added morosely.

Neither of them laughed. The joke was too close to the truth to be funny.

"If it makes you feel any better, Kate, you'll have some company in the courtroom. I've been named, too."

She looked up sharply. "Oh, Guy! I'm sorry...."

He shrugged. "It's no big deal. I've been sued before. Believe me, it's that first time that really hurts."

"What happened?"

"Trauma case. Man came in with a ruptured spleen and I couldn't save him." He shook his head. "When I saw that letter from the attorney, I was so depressed I wanted to leap out the nearest window. Susan was ready to drag me off to the psych ward. But you know what? I survived. So will you, as long as you remember they're not attacking *you*. They're attacking the job you did."

"I don't see the difference."

"And *that's* your problem, Kate. You haven't learned to separate yourself from the job. We both know the hours you put in. Hell, sometimes I think you practically live here. I'm not saying dedication's a character flaw. But you can overdo it.''

What really hurt was that she knew it was true. She did work long hours. Maybe she needed to; it kept her mind off the wasteland of her personal life.

"I'm not completely buried in my job," she said. "I've started dating again.''

"It's about time. Who's the man?''

"Last week I went out with Elliot.''

"That guy from computer programming?'' He sighed. Elliot was six-foot-two and one hundred and twenty pounds, and he bore a distinct resemblance to Pee-Wee Herman. "I bet that was a barrel of laughs.''

"Well it was sort of…fun. He asked me up to his apartment.''

"He did?''

"So I went.''

"You *did*?''

"He wanted to show me his latest electronic gear.''

Guy leaned forward eagerly. "What happened?''

"We listened to his new CDs. Played a few computer games.''

"And?''

She sighed. "After eight rounds of Zork I went home.''

Groaning, Guy sank back in his chair. "Elliot Lafferty, last of the red-hot lovers. Kate, what you need is one of these dating services. Hey, I'll even write the ad for you. 'Bright, attractive female seeks—'''

"Daddy!" The happy squeal cut straight through the cafeteria's hubbub.

Guy turned as running feet pattered toward him. "There's my Will!'' Laughing, he rose to his feet and scooped up his son. It took only a sweep of his arms to send the spindly five-year-old boy flying into the air. Little Will was so light he seemed to float for a moment like a frail bird. He fell to a very soft, very safe landing in his father's arms. "I've been waiting for you, kid,'' Guy said. "What took you so long?''

"Mommy came home late."

"Again?"

Will leaned forward and whispered confidentially. "Adele was *really* mad. Her boyfriend was s'posed to take her to the movies."

"Uh-oh. We *certainly* don't want Adele to be mad at us, do we?" Guy flashed an inquiring look at his wife Susan, who was threading her way toward them. "Hey, are we wearing out the nanny already?"

"I swear, it's that full moon!" Susan laughed and shoved back a frizzy strand of red hair. "All my patients have gone absolutely loony. I couldn't get them out of my office."

Guy muttered grumpily to Kate, "And she swore it'd be a part-time practice. Ha! Guess who gets called to the E.R. practically every night?"

"Oh, you just miss having your shirts ironed!" Susan reached up and gave her husband an affectionate pat on the cheek. It was the sort of maternal gesture one expected of Susan Santini. "My mother hen," Guy had once called his wife. He'd meant it as a term of endearment and it had fit. Susan's beauty wasn't in her face, which was plain and freckled, or in her figure, which was as stout as a farm wife's. Her beauty lay in that serenely patient smile that she was now beaming at her son.

"Daddy!" William was prancing like an elf around Guy's legs. "Make me fly again!"

"What am I, a launching pad?"

"Up! One more time!"

"Later, Will," said Susan. "We have to pick up Daddy's car before the garage closes."

"Please!"

"Did you hear that?" Guy gasped. "He said the magic word." With a lion's roar, Guy pounced on the shrieking boy and threw him into the air.

Susan gave Kate a long-suffering look. "Two children. That's what I have. And one of them weighs two hundred and forty pounds."

"I heard that." Guy reached over and slung a possessive arm around his wife. "Just for that, lady, you have to drive me home."

"Big bully. Feel like McDonald's?"

"Humph. I know someone who doesn't want to cook tonight."

Guy gave Kate a wave as he nudged his family toward the door. "So what'll it be, kid?" Kate heard him say to William. "Cheeseburger?"

"Ice cream."

"Ice cream. Now that's an alternative I hadn't thought of...."

Wistfully Kate watched the Santinis make their way across the cafeteria. She could picture how the rest of their evening would go. She imagined them sitting in McDonald's, the two parents teasing, coaxing another bite of food into Will's reluctant mouth. Then there'd be the drive home, the pajamas, the bedtime story. And finally, there'd be those skinny arms, curling around Daddy's neck for a kiss.

What do I have to go home to? she thought.

Guy turned and gave her one last wave. Then he and his family vanished out the door. Kate sighed enviously. *Lucky man.*

After he left his office that afternoon, David drove up Nuuanu Avenue and turned onto the dirt lane that wound through the old cemetery. He parked his car in the shade of a banyan tree and walked across the freshly mown lawn, past the marble headstones with their grotesque angels, past the final resting places of the Doles and the Binghams and the Cookes. He came to a section where there were only bronze plaques set flush in the ground, a sad concession to modern graveskeeping. Beneath a monkeypod tree, he stopped and gazed down at the marker by his feet.

Noah Ransom
Seven Years Old

It was a fine spot, gently sloping, with a view of the city. Here a breeze was always blowing, sometimes from the sea, sometimes from the valley. If he closed his eyes, he could tell where the wind was coming from, just by its smell.

David hadn't chosen this spot. He couldn't remember who had decided the grave should be here. Perhaps it had simply been a matter of which plot was available at the time. When your only child dies, who cares about views or breezes or monkeypod trees?

Bending down, he gently brushed the leaves that had fallen on the plaque. Then, slowly, he rose to his feet and stood in silence beside his son. He scarcely registered the rustle of the long skirt or the sound of the cane thumping across the grass.

"So here you are, David," called a voice.

Turning, he saw the tall, silver-haired woman hobbling toward him. "You shouldn't be out here, Mother. Not with that sprained foot."

She pointed her cane at the white clapboard house sitting near the edge of the cemetery. "I saw you through my kitchen window. Thought I'd better come out and say hello. Can't wait around forever for you to come visit me."

He kissed her on the cheek. "Sorry. I've been busy. But I really *was* on my way to see you."

"Oh, naturally." Her blue eyes shifted and focused on the grave. It was one of the many things Jinx Ransom shared with her son, that peculiar shade of blue of her eyes. Even at sixty-eight, her gaze was piercing. "Some anniversaries are better left forgotten," she said softly.

He didn't answer.

"You know, David, Noah always wanted a brother. Maybe it's time you gave him one."

David smiled faintly. "What are you suggesting, Mother?"

"Only what comes naturally to us all."

"Maybe I should get married first?"

"Oh, of course, of course." She paused, then asked hopefully: "Anyone in mind?"

"Not a soul."

Sighing, she laced her arm through his. "That's what I thought. Well, come along. Since there's no gorgeous female waiting for you, you might as well have a cup of coffee with your old mother."

Together they crossed the lawn toward the house. The grass was uneven and Jinx moved slowly, stubbornly refusing to lean on her son's shoulder. She wasn't supposed to be on her feet at all, but she'd never been one to follow doctors' orders. A woman who'd sprained her ankle in a savage game of tennis certainly wouldn't sit around twiddling her thumbs.

They passed through a gap in the mock-orange hedge and climbed the steps to the kitchen porch. Gracie, Jinx's middle-aged companion, met them at the screen door.

"There you are!" Gracie sighed. She turned her mouse-brown eyes to David. "I have absolutely *no* control over this woman. None at all."

He shrugged. "Who does?"

Jinx and David settled down at the breakfast table. The kitchen was a dense jungle of hanging plants: asparagus fern and baby's tears and wandering Jew. Valley breezes swept in from the porch, and through the large window, there was a view of the cemetery.

"What a shame they've trimmed back the monkeypod," Jinx remarked, gazing out.

"They had to," said Gracie as she poured coffee. "Grass can't grow right in the shade."

"But the view's just not the same."

David batted away a stray fern. "I never cared for that view anyway. I don't see how you can look at a cemetery all day."

"I like my view," Jinx declared. "When I look out, I see my old friends. Mrs. Goto, buried there by the hedge. Mr.

Carvalho, by the shower tree. And on the slope, there's our Noah. I think of them all as sleeping.''

"Good Lord, Mother."

"Your problem, David, is that you haven't resolved your fear of death. Until you do, you'll never come to terms with life."

"What do you suggest?"

"Take another stab at immortality. Have another child."

"I'm not getting married again, Mother. So let's just drop the subject."

Jinx responded as she always did when her son made a ridiculous request. She ignored it. "There was that young woman you met in Maui last year. Whatever happened to her?"

"She got married. To someone else."

"What a shame."

"Yeah, the poor guy."

"Oh, David!" cried Jinx, exasperated. "When are you going to grow up?"

David smiled and took a sip of Gracie's tar-black coffee, on which he promptly gagged. Another reason he avoided these visits to his mother. Not only did Jinx stir up a lot of bad memories, she also forced him to drink Gracie's god-awful coffee.

"So how was *your* day, Mother?" he asked politely.

"Getting worse by the minute."

"More coffee, David?" urged Gracie, tipping the pot threateningly toward his cup.

"No!" David gasped, clapping his hand protectively over the cup. The women stared at him in surprise. "I mean, er, no, thank you, Gracie."

"So touchy," observed Jinx. "Is something wrong? I mean, besides your sex life."

"I'm just a little busier than usual. Hiro's still laid up with that bad back."

"Humph. Well, you don't seem to like your work much

anymore. I think you were much happier in the prosecutor's office. Now you take the job so damned seriously.''

"It's a serious business."

"Suing doctors? Ha! It's just another way to make a fast buck."

"My doctor was sued once," Gracie remarked. "I thought it was terrible, all those things they said about him. Such a saint…"

"Nobody's a saint, Gracie," David said darkly. "Least of all, doctors." His gaze wandered out the window and he suddenly thought of the O'Brien case. It had been on his mind all afternoon. Or rather, *she'd* been on his mind, that green-eyed, perjuring Kate Chesne. He'd finally decided she was lying. This case was going to be even easier than he'd thought. She'd be a sitting duck on that witness stand and he knew just how he'd handle her in court. First the easy questions: name, education, postgraduate training. He had a habit of pacing in the courtroom, stalking circles around the defendant. The tougher the questions, the tighter the circles. By the time he came in for the kill, they'd be face-to-face. He felt an unexpected thump of dread in his chest, knowing what he'd have to do to finish it. Expose her. Destroy her. That was his job, and he'd always prided himself on a job well done.

He forced down a last sip of coffee and rose to his feet. "I have to be going," he announced, ducking past a lethally placed hanging fern. "I'll call you later, Mother."

Jinx snorted. "When? Next year?"

He gave Gracie a sympathetic pat on the shoulder and muttered in her ear, "Good luck. Don't let her drive you nuts."

"*I*? Drive *her* nuts?" Jinx snorted. "Ha!"

Gracie followed him to the porch door where she stood and waved. "Goodbye, David!" she called sweetly.

For a moment, Gracie paused in the doorway and watched David walk through the cemetery to his car. Then she turned sadly to Jinx.

"He's *so* unhappy!" she said. "If only he could forget."

"He won't forget." Jinx sighed. "David's just like his father that way. He'll carry it around inside him till the day he dies."

4

Ten-knot winds were blowing in from the northeast as the launch bearing Ellen O'Brien's last remains headed out to sea. It was such a clean, such a natural resolution to life: the strewing of ashes into the sunset waters, the rejoining of flesh and blood with their elements. The minister tossed a lei of yellow flowers off the old pier. The blossoms drifted away on the current, a slow and symbolic parting that brought Patrick O'Brien to tears.

The sound of his crying floated on the wind, over the crowded dock, to the distant spot where Kate was standing. Alone and ignored, she lingered by the row of tethered fishing boats and wondered why she was here. Was it some cruel and self-imposed form of penance? A feeble attempt to tell the world she was sorry? She only knew that some inner voice, begging for forgiveness, had compelled her to come.

There were others here from the hospital: a group of nurses, huddled in a quiet sisterhood of mourning; a pair of obstetricians, looking stiffly uneasy in their street clothes; Clarence Avery, his white hair blowing like dandelion fuzz in the wind. Even George Bettencourt had made an appearance. He stood apart, his face arranged in an impenetrable mask. For these people, a hospital was more than just a place of work; it was another home, another family. Doctors and nurses delivered each other's babies, presided over each other's deaths. Ellen O'Brien had helped bring many of their children into the world; now they were here to usher her out of it.

The far-off glint of sunlight on fair hair made Kate focus

on the end of the pier where David Ransom stood, towering above the others. Carelessly he pushed a lock of windblown hair into place. He was dressed in appropriately mournful attire—a charcoal suit, a somber tie—but in the midst of all this grief, he displayed the emotions of a stone wall. She wondered if there was anything human about him. *Do you ever laugh or cry? Do you ever hurt? Do you ever make love?*

That last thought had careened into her mind without warning. Love? Yes, she could imagine how it would be to make love with David Ransom: not a sharing but a claiming. He'd demand total surrender, the way he demanded surrender in the courtroom. The fading sunlight seemed to knight him with a mantle of unconquerability. What chance did she stand against such a man?

Wind gusted in from the sea, whipping sailboat halyards against masts, drowning out the minister's final words. When at last it was over, Kate found she didn't have the strength to move. She watched the other mourners pass by. Clarence Avery stopped, started to say something, then awkwardly moved on. Mary and Patrick O'Brien didn't even look at her. As David approached, his eyes registered a flicker of recognition, which was just as quickly suppressed. Without breaking stride, he continued past her. She might have been invisible.

By the time she finally found the energy to move, the pier was empty. Sailboat masts stood out like a row of dead trees against the sunset. Her foosteps sounded hollow against the wooden planks. When she finally reached her car, she felt utterly weary, as though her legs had carried her for miles. She fumbled for her keys and felt a strange sense of inevitability as her purse slipped out of her grasp, scattering its contents across the pavement. She could only stand there, paralyzed by defeat, as the wind blew her tissues across the ground. She had the absurd image of herself standing here all night, all week, frozen to this spot. She wondered if anyone would notice.

David noticed. Even as he waved goodbye and watched his clients drive away, he was intensely aware that Kate Chesne was somewhere on the pier behind him. He'd been startled to see her here. He'd thought it a rather clever move on her part, this public display of penitence, obviously designed to impress the O'Briens. But as he turned and watched her solitary walk along the pier, he noticed the droop of her shoulders, the downcast face, and he realized how much courage it had taken for her to show up today.

Then he reminded himself that some doctors would do anything to head off a lawsuit.

Suddenly disinterested, he started toward his car. Halfway across the parking lot, he heard something clatter against the pavement and he saw that Kate had dropped her purse. For what seemed like forever, she just stood there, the car keys dangling from her hand, looking for all the world like a bewildered child. Then, slowly, wearily, she bent down and began to gather her belongings.

Almost against his will, he was drawn toward her. She didn't notice his approach. He crouched beside her, scooped a few errant pennies from the ground, and held them out to her. Suddenly she focused on his face and then froze.

"Looks like you need some help," he said.

"Oh."

"I think you've got everything now."

They both rose to their feet. He was still holding out the loose change, of which she seemed oblivious. Only after he'd deposited the money in her hand did she finally manage a weak "Thank you."

For a moment they stared at each other.

"I didn't expect to see you here," he remarked. "Why did you come?"

"It was—" she shrugged "—a mistake, I think."

"Did your lawyer suggest it?"

She looked puzzled. "Why would he?"

"To show the O'Briens you care."

Her cheeks suddenly flushed with anger. "Is that what you think? That this is some sort of—of *strategy*?"

"It's not unheard of."

"Why are *you* here, Mr. Ransom? Is this part of *your* strategy? To prove to your clients you care?"

"I do care."

"And you think I don't."

"I didn't say that."

"You implied it."

"Don't take everything I say personally."

"I take everything you say personally."

"You shouldn't. It's just a job to me."

Angrily, she shoved back a tangled lock of hair. "And what *is* your job? Hatchet man?"

"I don't attack people. I attack their mistakes. And even the best doctors make mistakes."

"You don't need to tell me that!" Turning, she looked off to sea, where Ellen O'Brien's ashes were newly drifting. "I live with it, Mr. Ransom. Every day in that O.R. I know that if I reach for the wrong vial or flip the wrong lever, it's someone's life. Oh, we find ways to deal with it. We have our black jokes, our gallows humor. It's terrible, the things we laugh about, and all in the name of survival. Emotional survival. You have no idea, you lawyers. You and your whole damned profession. You don't know what it's like when everything goes wrong. When we lose someone."

"I know what it's like for the family. Every time you make a mistake, someone suffers."

"I suppose *you* never make mistakes."

"Everyone does. The difference is, you bury yours."

"You'll never let me forget it, will you?"

She turned to him. Sunset had painted the sky orange, and the glow seemed to burn in her hair and in her cheeks. Suddenly he wondered how it would feel to run his fingers through those wind-tumbled strands, wondered what that face would feel like against his lips. The thought had popped out of nowhere and now that it was out, he couldn't get rid of it. Certainly it was the last thing he ought to be thinking. But she was standing so dangerously close that he'd either have to back away or kiss her.

He managed to hold his ground. Barely. "As I said, Dr. Chesne, I'm only doing my job."

She shook her head and her hair, that sun-streaked, mahogany hair, flew violently in the wind. "No, it's more than that. I think you have some sort of vendetta. You're out to hang the whole medical profession. Aren't you?"

David was taken aback by her accusation. Even as he started to deny it, he knew she'd hit too close to home. Somehow she'd found his old wound, had reopened it with the verbal equivalent of a surgeon's scalpel. "Out to hang the whole profession, am I?" he managed to say. "Well, let me tell you something, Doctor. It's incompetents like you that make my job so easy."

Rage flared in her eyes, as sudden and brilliant as two coals igniting. For an instant he thought she was going to slap him. Instead she whirled around, slid into her car and slammed the door. The Audi screeched out of the stall so sharply he had to flinch aside.

As he watched her car roar away, he couldn't help regretting those unnecessarily brutal words. But he'd said them in self-defense. That perverse attraction he'd felt to her had grown too compelling; he knew it had to be severed, right there and then.

As he turned to leave, something caught his eye, a thin shaft of reflected light. Glittering on the pavement was a silver pen; it had rolled under her car when she'd dropped her purse. He picked it up and studied the engraved name: Katharine Chesne, M.D.

For a moment he stood there, weighing the pen, thinking about its owner. Wondering if she, too, had no one to go home to. And it suddenly struck him, as he stood alone on the windy pier, just how empty he felt.

Once, he'd been grateful for the emptiness. It had meant the blessed absence of pain. Now he longed to feel something—anything—if only to reassure himself that he was alive. He knew the emotions were still there, locked up somewhere inside him. He'd felt them stirring faintly when he'd looked into Kate Chesne's burning eyes. Not a full-blown emotion, perhaps, but a flicker. A blip on the tracing of a terminally ill heart.

The patient wasn't dead. Not yet.

He felt himself smiling. He tossed the pen up in the air and caught it smartly. Then he slipped it into his breast pocket and walked to his car.

The dog was deeply anesthetized, its legs spread-eagled, its belly shaved and prepped with iodine. It was a German shepherd, obviously well-bred and just as obviously unloved.

Guy Santini hated to see such a handsome creature end up on his research table, but lab animals were scarce these days and he had to use whatever the supplier sent him. He consoled himself with the knowledge that the animals suffered no pain. They slept blissfully through the entire surgical procedure and when it was over, the ventilator was turned off and they were injected with a lethal dose of Pentothal. Death came peacefully; it was a far better end than the animals would have faced on the streets. And each sacrifice yielded data for his research, a few more dots on a graph, a few more clues to the mysteries of hepatic physiology.

He glanced at the instruments neatly laid out on the tray: the scalpel, the clamps, the catheters. Above the table, a pressure monitor awaited final hookup. Everything was ready. He reached for the scalpel.

The whine of the door swinging closed made him pause. Footsteps clipped toward him across the polished lab floor. Glancing across the table, he saw Ann Richter standing there. They looked at each other in silence.

"I see you didn't go to Ellen's services, either," he said.

"I wanted to. But I was afraid."

"Afraid?" He frowned. "Of what?"

"I'm sorry, Guy. I no longer have a choice." Silently, she

held out a letter. "It's from Charlie Decker's lawyer. They're asking questions about Jenny Brook."

"What?" Guy stripped off his gloves and snatched the paper from her hand. What he read there made him look up at her in alarm. "You're not going to tell them, are you? Ann, you can't—"

"It's a subpoena, Guy."

"Lie to them, for God's sake!"

"Decker's out, Guy. You didn't know that, did you? He was released from the state hospital a month ago. He's been calling me. Leaving little notes at my apartment. Sometimes I even think he's following me...."

"He can't hurt you."

"Can't he?" She nodded at the paper he was holding. "Henry got one, just like it. So did Ellen. Just before she..." Ann stopped, as if voicing her worst fears somehow would turn them to reality. Only now did Guy notice how haggard she was. Dark circles shadowed her eyes, and the ash-blond hair, of which she'd always been so proud, looked as if it hadn't been combed in days. "It has to end, Guy," she said softly. "I can't spend the rest of my life looking over my shoulder for Charlie Decker."

He crumpled the paper in his fist. He began to pace back and forth, his agitation escalating to panic. "You could leave the islands—you could go away for a while—"

"How long, Guy? A month? A year?"

"As long as it takes for this to settle down. Look, I'll give you the money—" He fumbled for his wallet and took out fifty dollars, all the cash he had. "Here. I promise I'll send you more—"

"I'm not asking for your money."

"Go on, take it."

"I told you, I—"

"For God's sake, *take it*!" His voice, harsh with desperation, echoed off the stark white walls. "Please, Ann," he urged quietly. "I'm asking you, as a friend. Please."

She looked down at the money he was holding. Slowly,

she reached out and took it. As her fingers closed around the bills she announced, "I'm leaving tonight. For San Francisco. I have a brother—"

"Call me when you get there. I'll send you all the money you need." She didn't seem to hear him. "Ann? You'll do this for me. Won't you?"

She looked off blankly at the far wall. He longed to reassure her, to tell her that nothing could possibly go wrong; but they'd both know it was a lie. He watched as she walked slowly to the door. Just before she left, he said, "Thank you, Ann."

She didn't turn around. She simply paused in the doorway. Then she gave a little shrug, just before she vanished out the door.

As Ann headed for the bus stop, she was still clutching the money Guy had given her. Fifty dollars! As if that was enough! A thousand, a million dollars wouldn't be enough.

She boarded the bus for Waikiki. From her window seat she stared out at a numbing succession of city blocks. At Kalakaua, she got off and began to walk quickly toward her apartment building. Buses roared past, choking her with fumes. Her hands turned clammy in the heat. Concrete buildings seemed to press in on all sides and tourists clotted the sidewalks. As she wove her way through them, she felt a growing sense of uneasiness.

She began to walk faster.

Two blocks north of Kalakaua, the crowd thinned out and she found herself at a corner, waiting for a stoplight to change. In that instant, as she stood alone and exposed in the fading sunlight, the feeling suddenly seized her: *someone is following me.*

She swung around and scanned the street behind her. An old man was shuffling down the sidewalk. A couple was pushing a baby in a stroller. Gaudy shirts fluttered on an outdoor clothing rack. Nothing out of the ordinary. Or so it seemed....

The light changed to green. She dashed across the street and didn't stop running until she'd reached her apartment.

She began to pack. As she threw her belongings into a suitcase, she was still debating her next move. The plane to San Francisco would take off at midnight; her brother would put her up for a while, no questions asked. He was good that way. He understood that everyone had a secret, everyone was running away from something.

It doesn't have to be this way, a stray voice whispered in her head. *You could go to the police....*

And tell them what? The truth about Jenny Brook? Do I tear apart an innocent life?

She began to pace the apartment, thinking, fretting. As she walked past the living-room mirror, she caught sight of her own reflection, her blond hair in disarray, her eyes smudged with mascara. She hardly recognized herself; fear had transformed her face into a stranger's.

It only takes a single phone call, a confession. A secret, once revealed, is no longer dangerous....

She reached for the telephone. With unsteady hands she dialed Kate Chesne's home phone number. Her heart sank when, after four rings, a recording answered, followed by the message beep.

She cleared the fear from her throat. "This is Ann Richter," she said. "Please, I have to talk to you. It's about Ellen. I know why she died."

Then she hung up and waited for the phone to ring.

It was hours before Kate heard the message.

After she left the pier that afternoon, she drove aimlessly for a while, avoiding the inevitable return to her empty house. It was Friday night. T.G.I.F. She decided to treat herself to an evening out. So she had supper alone at a trendy little seaside grill where everyone but her seemed to be having a grand old time. The steak she ordered was utterly tasteless and the chocolate mousse so cloying she could barely force it down her throat. She left an extravagant tip, almost as an apology for her lack of appetite.

Next she tried a movie. She found herself wedged between a fidgety eight-year-old boy on one side and a young couple passionately making out on the other.

She walked out halfway through the film. She never did remember the title—only that it was a comedy, and she hadn't laughed once.

By the time she got home, it was ten o'clock. She was half undressed and sitting listlessly on her bed when she noticed that the telephone message light was blinking. She let the messages play back as she wandered over to the closet.

"Hello, Dr. Chesne, this is Four East calling to tell you Mr. Berg's blood sugar is ninety-eight.... Hello, this is June from Dr. Avery's office. Don't forget the Quality Assurance meeting on Tuesday at four.... Hi, this is Windward Realty. Give us a call back. We have a listing we think you'd like to see...."

She was hanging up her skirt when the last message played back.

"This is Ann Richter. Please, I have to talk to you. It's about Ellen. I know why she died...."

There was the click of the phone hanging up, and then a soft whir as the tape automatically rewound. Kate scrambled back to the recorder and pressed the replay button. Her heart was racing as she listened again to the agonizingly slow sequence of messages.

"It's about Ellen. I know why she died...."

Kate grabbed the phone book from her nightstand. Ann's address and phone number were listed; her line was busy. Again and again Kate dialed but she heard only the drone of the busy signal.

She slammed down the receiver and knew immediately what she had to do next.

She hurried back to the closet and yanked the skirt from its hanger. Quickly, feverishly, she began to dress.

*   *   *

The traffic heading into Waikiki was bumper-to-bumper.

As usual, the streets were crowded with a bizarre mix of tourists and off-duty soldiers and street people, all of them moving in the surreal glow of city lights. Palm trees cast their spindly shadows against the buildings. An otherwise distinguished-looking gentleman was flaunting his white legs and Bermuda shorts. Waikiki was where one came to see the ridiculous, the outrageous. But tonight, Kate found the view through her car window frightening—all those faces, drained of color under the glow of streetlamps, and the soldiers, lounging drunkenly in nightclub doorways. A wild-eyed evangelist stood on the corner, waving a Bible as he shouted "The end of the world is near!"

As she pulled up at a red light, he turned and stared at her and for an instant she thought she saw, in his burning eyes, a message meant only for her. The light turned green. She sent the car lurching through the intersection. His shout faded away.

She was still jittery ten minutes later when she climbed the steps to Ann's apartment building. As she reached the door, a young couple exited, allowing Kate to slip into the lobby.

It took a moment for the elevator to arrive. Leaning back against the wall, she forced herself to breathe deeply and let the silence of the building calm her nerves. By the time she finally stepped into the elevator, her heart had stopped its wild hammering. The doors slid closed. The elevator whined upward. She felt a strange sense of unreality as she watched the lights flash in succession: three, four, five. Except for a faint hydraulic hum, the ride was silent.

On the seventh floor, the doors slid open.

The corridor was deserted. A dull green carpet stretched out before her. As she walked toward number 710, she had the strange sensation that she was moving in a dream, that none of this was real—not the flocked wallpaper or the door looming at the end of the corridor. Only as she reached it did she see it was slightly ajar. "Ann?" she called out.

There was no answer.

She gave the door a little shove. Slowly it swung open and she froze, taking in, but not immediately comprehending, the scene before her: the toppled chair, the scattered magazines, the bright red splatters on the wall. Then her gaze followed the trail of crimson as it zigzagged across the beige carpet, leading inexorably toward its source: Ann's body, lying face-down in a lake of blood.

Beeps issued faintly from a telephone receiver dangling off an end table. The cold, electronic tone was like an alarm, screaming at her to move, to take action. But she remained paralyzed; her whole body seemed stricken by some merciful numbness.

The first wave of dizziness swept over her. She crouched down, clutching the doorframe for support. All her medical training, all those years of working around blood, couldn't prevent this totally visceral response. Through the drumbeat of her own heart she became aware of another sound, harsh and irregular. Breathing. But it wasn't hers.

Someone else was in the room.

A flicker of movement drew her gaze across to the living room mirror. Only then did she see the man's reflection. He was cowering behind a cabinet, not ten feet away.

They spotted each other in the mirror at the same instant. In that split second, as the reflection of his eyes met hers, she imagined she saw, in those hollows, the darkness beckoning to her. An abyss from which there was no escape.

He opened his mouth as if to speak but no words came out, only an unearthly hiss, like a viper's warning just before it strikes.

She lurched wildly to her feet. The room spun past her eyes with excruciating slowness as she turned to flee. The corridor stretched out endlessly before her. She heard her own scream echo off the walls; the sound was as unreal as the image of the hallway flying past.

The stairwell door lay at the other end. It was her only feasible escape route. There was no time to wait for elevators.

She hit the opening bar at a run and shoved the door into the concrete stairwell. One flight into her descent, she heard the door above spring open again and slam against the wall. Again she heard the hiss, as terrifying as a demon's whisper in her ear.

She stumbled to the sixth-floor landing and grappled at the door. It was locked tight. She screamed and pounded. Surely someone would hear her! Someone would answer her cry for help!

Footsteps thudded relentlessly down the stairs. She couldn't wait; she had to keep running.

She dashed down the next flight and hit the fifth floor landing too hard. Pain shot through her ankle. In tears, she wrenched and pounded at the door. It was locked.

He was right behind her.

She flew down the next flight and the next. Her purse flew off her shoulder but she couldn't stop to retrieve it. Her ankle was screaming with pain as she hurtled toward the third-floor landing. Was it locked, as well? Were they all locked? Her mind flew ahead to the ground floor, to what lay outside. A parking lot? An alley? Is that where they'd find her body in the morning?

Sheer panic made her wrench with superhuman strength at the next door. To her disbelief, it was unlocked. Stumbling through, she found herself in the parking garage. There was no time to think about her next move; she tore off blindly into the shadows. Just as the stairwell door flew open again, she ducked behind a van.

Crouching by the front wheel, she listened for footsteps but heard nothing except the torrent of her own blood racing in her ears. Seconds passed, then minutes. Where was he? Had he abandoned the chase? Her body was pressed so tightly against the van, the steel bit into her thigh. She felt no pain; every ounce of concentration was focused on survival.

A pebble clattered across the ground, echoing like a pistol shot in the concrete garage.

She tried in vain to locate the source but the explosions seemed to come from a dozen different directions at once. *Go away!* she wanted to scream. *Dear God, make him go away....*

The echoes faded, leaving total silence. But she sensed his presence, closing in. She could almost hear his voice whispering to her *I'm coming for you. I'm coming....*

She had to know where he was, if he was drawing close.

Clinging to the tire, she slowly inched her head around and peered beneath the van. What she saw made her reel back in horror.

He was on the other side of the van and moving toward the rear. Toward her.

She sprang to her feet and took off like a rabbit. Parked cars melted into one continuous blur. She plunged toward the exit ramp. Her legs, stiff from crouching, refused to move fast enough. She could hear the man right behind her. The ramp seemed endless, spiraling around and around, every curve threatening to send her sprawling to the pavement. His footsteps were gaining. Air rushed in and out of her lungs, burning her throat.

In a last, desperate burst of speed, she tore around the final curve. Too late, she saw the headlights of a car coming up the ramp toward her.

She caught a glimpse of two faces behind the windshield, a man and a woman, their mouths open wide. As she slammed into the hood, there was a brilliant flash of light, like stars exploding in her eyes. Then the light vanished and she saw nothing at all. Not even darkness.

5

"**M**ango season," Sergeant Brophy said as he sneezed into a soggy handkerchief. "Worst time of year for my allergies." He blew his nose, then sniffed experimentally, as if checking for some new, as yet undetected obstruction to his nasal passages. He seemed completely unaware of his gruesome surroundings, as though dead bodies and blood-spattered walls and an army of crime-lab techs were always hanging about. When Brophy got into one of his sneezing jags, he was oblivious of everything but the sad state of his sinuses.

Lieutenant Francis "Pokie" Ah Ching had grown used to hearing the sniffles of his junior partner. At times, the habit was useful. He could always tell which room Brophy was in; all he had to do was follow the man's nose.

That nose, still bundled in a handkerchief, vanished into the dead woman's bedroom. Pokie refocused his attention on his spiral notebook, in which he was recording the data. He wrote quickly, in the peculiar shorthand he'd evolved over his twenty-six years as a cop, seventeen of them with homicide. Eight pages were filled with sketches of the various rooms in the apartment, four pages of the living room alone. His art was crude but to the point. Body there. Toppled furniture here. Blood all over.

The medical examiner, a boyish, freckle-faced woman known to everyone simply as M.J., was making her walk-around before she examined the body. She was wearing her usual blue jeans and tennis shoes—sloppy dress for a doctor, but in her specialty, the patients never complained. As she circled the room, she dictated into a cassette recorder.

"Arterial spray on three walls, pattern height about four to five feet.... Heavy pooling at east end of living room where body is located.... Victim is female, blond, age thirty to forty, found in prone position, right arm flexed under head, left arm extended.... No hand or arm lacerations noted." M.J. crouched down. "Marked dependent mottling. Hmm." Frowning, she touched the victim's bare arm. "Significant body cooling. Time is now 12:15 a.m." She flicked off the cassette and was silent for a moment.

"Somethin' wrong, M.J.?" Pokie asked.

"What?" She looked up. "Oh, just thinking."

"What's your prelim?"

"Let's see. Looks like a single deep slash to the left carotid, very sharp blade. And very fast work. The victim never got a chance to raise her arms in defense. I'll get a better look when we wash her down at the morgue." She stood up and Pokie saw her tennis shoes were smeared with blood. How many crime scenes had those shoes tramped through?

Not as many as mine, he thought.

"Slashed carotid," he said thoughtfully. "Does that remind you of somethin'?"

"First thing I thought of. What was that guy's name a few weeks back?"

"Tanaka. He had a slash to the left carotid."

"That's him. Just as bloody a mess as this one, too."

Pokie thought a moment. "Tanaka was a doctor," he remarked. "And this one..." He glanced down at the body. "This one's a nurse."

"Was a nurse."

"Makes you wonder."

M.J. snapped her lab kit closed. "There's lots of doctors and nurses in this town. Just because these two end up on my slab doesn't mean they knew each other."

A loud sneeze announced Brophy's emergence from the

bedroom. "Found a plane ticket to San Francisco on her dresser. Midnight flight." He glanced at his watch. "Which she just missed."

A plane ticket. A packed suitcase. So Ann Richter was about to skip town. Why?

Mulling over that question, Pokie made another circuit of the apartment, going through the rooms one by one. In the bathroom, he found a lab tech microscopically peering down at the sink.

"Traces of blood in here, sir. Looks like your killer washed his hands."

"Yeah? Cool cat. Any prints?"

"A few here and there. Most of 'em old, probably the victim's. Plus one fresh set off the front doorknob. Could belong to your witness."

Pokie nodded and went back to the living room. That was their ace in the hole. The witness. Though dazed and in pain, she'd managed to alert the ambulance crew to the horrifying scene in apartment 710.

Thereby ruining a good night's sleep for Pokie.

He glanced at Brophy. "Have you found Dr. Chesne's purse yet?"

"It's not in the stairwell where she dropped it. Someone must've picked it up."

Pokie was silent a moment. He thought of all the things women carried in their purses: wallets, driver's licenses, house keys.

He slapped his notebook closed. "Sergeant?"

"Sir?"

"I want a twenty-four-hour guard placed on Dr. Chesne's hospital room. Effective immediately. I want a man in the lobby. And I want you to trace every call that comes in asking about her."

Brophy looked dubious. "All that? For how long?"

"Just as long as she's in the hospital. Right now she's a sitting duck."

"You really think this guy'd go after her in the hospital?"

"I don't know." Pokie sighed. "I don't know what we're dealing with. But I've got two identical murders." Grimly he slid the notebook into his pocket. "And she's our only witness."

Phil Glickman was making a pest of himself as usual.

It was Saturday morning, the one day of the week David could work undisturbed, the one day he could catch up on all the paperwork that perpetually threatened to bury his desk. But today, instead of solitude, he'd found Glickman. While his young associate was smart, aggressive and witty, he was also utterly incapable of silence. David suspected the man talked in his sleep.

"So I said, 'Doctor, do you mean to tell me the posterior auricular artery comes off *before* the superficial temporal?' And the guy gets all flustered and says, 'Oh, did I say that? No, of course it's the other way around.' Which blew it right there for him." Glickman slammed his fist triumphantly into his palm. "Wham! He's dead meat and he knows it. We just got the offer to settle. Not bad, huh?" At David's lackluster nod, Glickman looked profoundly disappointed. Then he brightened and asked, "How's it going with the O'Brien case? They ready to yell uncle?"

David shook his head. "Not if I know Kate Chesne."

"What, is she dumb?"

"Stubborn. Self-righteous."

"So it goes with the white coat."

David tiredly dragged his fingers through his hair. "I hope this doesn't go to trial."

"It'll be like shooting rabbits in a cage. Easy."

"Too easy."

Glickman laughed as he turned to leave. "Never seemed to bother you before."

Why the hell does it bother me now? David wondered.

The O'Brien case was like an apple falling into his lap. All he had to do was file a few papers, issue a few threatening statements, and hold his hand out for the check. He should be breaking out the champagne. Instead, he was moping around on a gorgeous Saturday morning, feeling sleazy about the whole affair.

Yawning, he leaned back and rubbed his eyes. It'd been a lousy night, spent tossing and turning in bed. He'd been plagued by dreams—disturbing dreams; the kind he hadn't had in years.

There had been a woman. She'd stood very still, very quiet in the shadows, her face silhouetted against a window of hazy light. At first he'd thought she was his ex-wife, Linda. But there were things about her that weren't right, things that confused him. She'd stood motionless, like a deer pausing in the forest. Eagerly he'd reached out to undress her, but his hands had been impossibly clumsy and in his haste, he'd torn off one of her buttons. She had laughed, a deliciously throaty sound that reminded him of brandy.

That's when he knew she wasn't Linda. Looking up, he'd stared into the green eyes of Kate Chesne.

There were no words between them, only a look. And a touch: her fingers, sliding gently down his face.

He'd awakened, sweating with desire. He'd tried to fall back to sleep. Again and again the dream had returned. Even now, as he sank back in his chair and closed his eyes, he saw her face again and he felt that familiar ache.

Brutally wrenching his thoughts back to reality, he dragged himself over to the window. He was too old for this nonsense. Too old and too smart to even fantasize about an affair with the opposition.

Hell, attractive women walked into his office all the time. And every so often, one of them would give off the sort of signals any red-blooded man could recognize. It took only a certain tilt of the head, a provocative flash of thigh. He'd always been amused but never tempted; bedding down clients wasn't included in his list of services.

Kate Chesne had sent out no such signals. In fact she plainly despised lawyers as much as he despised doctors. So why, of all the women who'd walked through his door, was she the one he couldn't stop thinking about?

He reached into his breast pocket and pulled out the silver pen. It suddenly occurred to him that this wasn't the sort of item a woman would buy for herself. Was it a gift from a boyfriend? he wondered, and was startled by his instant twinge of jealousy.

He should return it.

The thought set his mind off and racing. Mid Pac Hospital was only a few blocks away. He could drop off the pen on his way home. Most doctors made Saturday-morning rounds, so there was a good chance she'd be there. At the prospect of seeing her again, he felt a strange mixture of anticipation and dread, the same churning in his stomach he used to feel as a teenager scrounging up the courage to ask a girl for a date. It was a very bad sign.

But he couldn't get the idea out of his mind.

The pen felt like a live wire. He shoved it back in his pocket and quickly began to stuff his papers into the brief-case.

Fifteen minutes later he walked into the hospital lobby and went to a house telephone. The operator answered.

"I'm trying to reach Dr. Kate Chesne," David said. "Is she in the building?"

"Dr. Chesne?" There was a pause. "Yes, I believe she's in the hospital. Who's calling?"

He started to give his name, then thought better of it. If Kate knew it was his page, she'd never answer it. "I'm a friend," he replied lamely.

"Please hold."

A recording of some insipid melody came on, the sort of music they probably played on elevators in hell. He caught himself drumming the booth impatiently. That's when it struck him just how eager he was to see her again.

I must be nuts, he thought, abruptly hanging up the phone. Or desperate for female companionship. Maybe both.

Disgusted with himself, he turned to leave, only to find

that his exit was blocked by two very impressive-looking cops.

"Mind coming with us?" one of them asked.

"Actually," responded David, "I would."

"Then lemme put it a different way," said the cop, his meaning absolutely clear.

David couldn't help an incredulous laugh. "What did I do, guys? Double-park? Insult your mothers?"

He was grasped firmly by both arms and directed across the lobby, into the administrative wing.

"Is this an arrest or what?" he demanded. They didn't answer. "Hey, I think you're supposed to inform me of my rights." They didn't. "Okay," he amended. "Then maybe it's time *I* informed *you* of my rights." Still no answer. He shot out his weapon of last resort. "I'm an attorney!"

"Goody for you" was the dry response as he was led toward a conference room.

"You know damn well you can't arrest me without charges!"

They threw open the door. "We're just following orders."

"*Whose* orders?"

The answer was boomed out in a familiar voice. "*My* orders."

David turned and confronted a face he hadn't seen since his days with the prosecutor's office. Homicide Detective Pokie Ah Ching's features reflected a typical island mix of bloods: a hint of Chinese around the eyes, some Portuguese in the heavy jowls, a strong dose of dusky Polynesian coloring. Except for a hefty increase in girth, he had changed little in the eight years since they'd last worked together. He was even wearing the same old off-the-rack polyester suit, though it was obvious those front buttons hadn't closed in quite some time.

"If it isn't Davy Ransom," Pokie grunted. "I lay out my nets, and look what comes swimming in."

"Yeah," David muttered, jerking his arm free. "The wrong fish."

Pokie nodded at the two policemen. "This one's okay."

The officers retreated. The instant the door closed, David barked out: "What the hell's going on?"

In answer, Pokie moved forward and gave David a long, appraising look. "Private practice must be bringin' in the bucks. Got yourself a nice new suit. Expensive shoes. Humph. Italian. Doing well, huh, Davy?"

"I can't complain."

Pokie settled down on the edge of the table and crossed his arms. "So how's it, workin' out of a nice new office? Miss the ol' cockroaches?"

"Oh, sure."

"I made lieutenant a month after you left."

"Congratulations."

"But I'm still wearin' the same old suit. Driving the same old car. And the shoes?" He stuck out a foot. "Taiwan."

David's patience was just about shredded. "Are you going to tell me what's going on? Or am I supposed to guess?"

Pokie reached in his jacket for a cigarette, the same cheap brand he'd always smoked, and lit up. "You a friend of Kate Chesne's?"

David was startled by the abrupt shift of subject. "I know her."

"How well?"

"We've spoken a few times. I came to return her pen."

"So you didn't know she was brought to the E.R. last night? Trauma service."

"What?"

"Nothing serious," Pokie said quickly. "Mild concussion. Few bruises. She'll be discharged today."

David's throat had suddenly tightened beyond all hope of speech. He watched, stunned, as Pokie took a long, blissful drag on his cigarette.

"It's a funny thing," Pokie remarked, "how a case'll just sit around forever, picking up dust. No clues. No way of closing the file. Then, pow! We get lucky."

"What happened to her?" David asked in a hoarse voice.

"She was in the wrong place at the wrong time." He blew out a lungful of smoke. "Last night she walked in on a very bad scene."

"You mean...she's a witness? To what?"

Pokie's face was impassive through the haze drifting between them. "Murder."

Through the closed door of her hospital room, Kate could hear the sounds of a busy hospital: the paging system, crackling with static, the ringing telephones. All night long she'd strained to hear those sounds; they had reminded her she wasn't alone. Only now, as the sun spilled in across her bed and a profound exhaustion settled over her, did she finally drift toward sleep. She didn't hear the first knock, or the voice calling to her through the door. It was the gust of air sweeping into the room that warned her the door had swung open. She was vaguely aware that someone was approaching her bed. It took all her strength just to open her eyes. Through a blur of sleep, she saw David's face.

She felt a feeble sense of outrage struggle to the surface. He had no right to invade her privacy when she was so weak, so exposed. She knew what she *ought* to say to him, but exhaustion had sapped her last reserves of emotion and she couldn't dredge up a single word.

Neither could he. It seemed they'd both lost their voices.

"No fair, Mr. Ransom," she whispered. "Kicking a girl when she's down..." Turning away, she gazed down dully at the sheets. "You seem to have forgotten your handy tape recorder. Can't take a deposition without a tape recorder. Or are you hiding it in one of your—"

"Stop it, Kate. Please."

She fell instantly still. He'd called her by her first name. Some unspoken barrier between them had just fallen, and she didn't know why. What she did know was that he was here, that he was standing so close she could smell the scent of his after-shave, could almost feel the heat of his gaze.

"I'm not here to...kick you while you're down." Sighing,

he added, "I guess I shouldn't be here at all. But when I heard what happened, all I could think of was…"

She looked up and found him staring at her mutely. For the first time, he didn't seem so forbidding. She had to remind herself that he *was* the enemy; that this visit, whatever its purpose, had changed nothing between them. But at that moment, what she felt wasn't threatened but protected. It was more than just his commanding physical presence, though she was very aware of that, too; he had a quiet aura of strength. Competence. If only he'd been *her* attorney; if only he'd been hired to defend, not prosecute her. She couldn't imagine losing any battle with David Ransom at her side.

"All you could think of was what?" she asked softly.

Shifting, he turned awkwardly toward the door. "I'm sorry. I should let you sleep."

"Why did you come?"

He halted and gave a sheepish laugh. "I almost forgot. I came to return this. You dropped it at the pier."

He placed the pen in her hand. She stared down in wonder, not at the pen, but at his hands. Large, strong hands. How would it feel, to have those fingers tangled in her hair?

"Thank you," she whispered.

"Sentimental value?"

"It was a gift. From a man I used to—" Clearing her throat, she looked away and repeated, "Thank you."

David knew this was his cue to walk out. He'd done his good deed for the day; now he should cut whatever threads of conversation were being spun between them. But some hidden force seemed to guide his hand toward a chair and he pulled it over to the bed and sat down.

Her hair lay tangled on the pillow and a bruise had turned one cheek an ugly shade of blue. He felt an instinctive flood of rage against the man who'd tried to hurt her. The emotion was entirely unexpected; it surprised him by its ferocity.

"How are you feeling?" he asked, for want of anything else to say.

She gave a feeble shrug. "Tired. Sore." She paused and added with a weak laugh, "Lucky to be alive."

His gaze shifted to the bruise on her cheek and she automatically reached up to hide what stood out so plainly on her face. Slowly she let her hand fall back to the bed. He found it a very sad gesture, as if she was ashamed of being the victim, of bearing that brutal mark of violence.

"I'm not exactly at my most stunning today," she said.

"You look fine, Kate. You really do." It was a stupid thing to say but he meant it. She looked beautiful; she was alive. "The bruise will fade. What matters is that you're safe."

"Am I?" She looked at the door. "There's been a guard sitting out there all night. I heard him, laughing with the nurses. I keep wondering why they put him there...."

"I'm sure it's just a precaution. So no one bothers you."

She frowned at him, suddenly puzzled. "How did *you* get past him?"

"I know Lt. Ah Ching. We worked together, years ago. When I was with the prosecutor's office."

"You?"

He smiled. "Yeah. I've done my civic duty. Got my education in sleaze. At slave wages."

"Then you've talked to Ah Ching? About what happened?"

"He said you're a witness. That your testimony's vital to his case."

"Did he tell you Ann Richter tried to call me? Just before she was killed. She left a message on my recorder."

"About what?"

"Ellen O'Brien."

He paused. "I didn't hear about this."

"She *knew* something, Mr. Ransom. Something about Ellen's death. Only she never got a chance to tell me."

"What was the message?"

"'I know why she died.' Those were her exact words."

David stared at her. Slowly, reluctantly, he found himself

drawn deeper and deeper into the spell of those green eyes. "It may not mean anything. Maybe she just figured out what went wrong in surgery—"

"The word she used was *why*. 'I know *why* she died.' That implies there was a reason, a—a *purpose* for Ellen's death."

"Murder on the operating table?" He shook his head. "Come on."

She turned away. "I should have known you'd be skeptical. It would ruin your precious lawsuit, wouldn't it? To find out the patient was murdered."

"What do the police think?"

"How would I know?" she shot back in frustration. Then, in a tired voice, she said, "Your friend Ah Ching never says much of anything. All he does is scribble in that notebook of his. Maybe he thinks it's irrelevant. Maybe he doesn't want to hear any confusing facts." Her gaze shifted to the door. "But then I think about that guard. And I wonder if there's something else going on. Something he won't tell me…"

There was a knock on the door. A nurse came in with the discharge papers. David watched as Kate sat up and obediently signed each one. The pen trembled in her hand. He could hardly believe this was the same woman who'd stormed into his office. That day he'd been impressed by her iron will, her determination.

Now he was just as impressed by her vulnerability.

The nurse left and Kate sank back against the pillows.

"Do you have somewhere to go?" he asked. "After you leave here?"

"My friends…they have this cottage they hardly ever use. I hear it's on the beach." She sighed and looked wistfully out the window. "I could use a beach right now."

"You'll be staying there alone? Is that safe?"

She didn't answer. She just kept looking out the window. It made him uneasy, thinking of her in that cottage, alone, unprotected. He had to remind himself that she wasn't his concern. That he'd be crazy to get involved with this woman.

Let the police take care of her; after all, she was their responsibility.

He stood up to leave. She just sat there, huddled in the bed, her arms crossed over her chest in a pitiful gesture of self-protection. As he walked out of the room, he heard her say, softly, "I don't think I'll ever feel safe again."

6

"It's just a little place," explained Susan Santini as she and Kate drove along the winding North Shore highway. "Nothing fancy. Just a couple of bedrooms. An absolutely ancient kitchen. Prehistoric, really. But it's cozy. And it's so nice to hear the waves...." She turned off the highway onto a dirt road carved through the dense shrubbery of halekoa. Their tires threw up a cloud of rich red dust as they bounced toward the sea. "Seems like we hardly use the place these days, what with one of us always being on call. Sometimes Guy talks about selling. But I'd never dream of it. You just don't find bits of paradise like this anymore."

The tires crunched onto the gravel driveway. Beneath a towering stand of ironwood trees, the small plantation-era cottage looked like nothing more than a neglected dollhouse. Years of sun and wind had faded the planks to a weathered green. The roof seemed to sag beneath its burden of brown ironwood needles.

Kate got out and stood for a moment beneath the trees, listening to the waves hiss onto the sand. Under the midday sun, the sea shone a bright and startling blue.

"There they are," said Susan, pointing down the beach at her son William, who was dancing a joyous little jig in the sand. He moved like an elf, his long arms weaving delicately, his head bobbing back and forth as he laughed. The baggy swim trunks barely clung to his scrawny hips. Framed against the brilliance of the sky, he seemed like nothing more than a collection of twigs among the trees, a mythical creature who might vanish in the blink of an eye. Nearby, a young woman with a sparrowlike face was sitting on a towel and flipping listlessly through a magazine.

"That's Adele," Susan whispered. "It took us half a dozen ads and twenty-one interviews to find her. But I just don't think she's going to work out. What worries me is William's already getting attached to her."

William suddenly spotted them. He stopped in his tracks and waved. "Hi, Mommy!"

"Hello, darling!" Susan called. Then she touched Kate's arm. "We've aired out the cottage for you. And there should be a pot of coffee waiting."

They climbed the wooden steps to the kitchen porch. The screen door squealed open. Inside hung the musty smell of age. Sunlight slanted in through the window and gleamed dully on the yellowed linoleum floor. A small pot of African violets sat on the blue-tiled countertop. Taped haphazardly to the walls was a whimsical collection of drawings: blue and green dinosaurs, red stick men, animals of various colors and unidentifiable species, each labeled with the artist's name: William.

"We keep the line hooked up for emergencies," Susan informed her, pointing to the wall telephone. "I've already stocked the refrigerator. Just the basics, really. Guy said we can pick up your car tomorrow. That'll give you a chance to do some decent grocery shopping." She made a quick circuit of the kitchen, pointing out various cabinets, the pots and pans, the dishes. Then, beckoning to Kate, she led the way to the bedroom. There she went to the window and spread apart the white lace curtains. Her red hair glittered in the stream of sunlight. "Look, Kate. Here's that view I promised you." She gazed out lovingly at the sea. "You know, people wouldn't need psychiatrists if they just had this to look at every day. If they could lie in the sun, hear the waves, the birds." She turned and smiled at Kate. "What do you think?"

"I think…" Kate gazed around at the polished wood floor, the filmy curtains, the dusty gold light shimmering through the window. "I think I never want to leave," she replied with a smile.

Footsteps pattered on the porch. Susan looked around as the screen door slammed. "So endeth the peace and quiet." She sighed.

They returned to the kitchen and found little William singing tunelessly as he laid out a collection of twigs on the kitchen table. Adele, her bare shoulders glistening with suntan oil, was pouring him a cup of apple juice. On the counter lay a copy of *Vogue*, dusty with sand.

"Look, Mommy!" exclaimed William, pointing proudly to his newly gathered treasure.

"My goodness, what a collection," said Susan, appropriately awed. "What are you going to do with all those sticks?"

"They're not sticks. They're swords. To kill monsters."

"Monsters? But, darling, I've told you. There aren't any monsters."

"Yes, there are."

"Daddy put them all in jail, remember?"

"Not all of them." Meticulously, he lay another twig down on the table. "They're hiding in the bushes. I heard one last night."

"William," Susan said quietly. "What monsters?"

"In the bushes. I told you, last night."

"Oh." Susan flashed Kate a knowing smile. "That's why he crawled into our bed at two in the morning."

Adele placed the cup of juice beside the boy. "Here, William. Your…" She frowned. "What's that in your pocket?"

"Nothing."

"I saw it move."

William ignored her and took a slurp of juice. His pocket twitched.

"William Santini, give it to me." Adele held out her hand.

William turned his pleading eyes to the court of last appeals: his mother. She shook her head sadly. Sighing, he reached into his pocket, scooped out the source of the twitch-ing, and dropped it in Adele's hand.

Her shriek was startling, most of all to the lizard, which promptly flung itself to freedom, but only after dropping its writhing tail in Adele's hand.

"He's getting away!" wailed William.

There followed a mad scrambling on hands and knees by everyone in the room. By the time the hapless lizard had been recaptured and jailed in a teacup, they were all breathless and weak from laughter. Susan, her red hair in wild disarray, collapsed onto the kitchen floor, her legs sprawled out in front of her.

"I can't *believe* it," she gasped, falling back against the refigerator. "Three grown women against one itty-bitty liz-ard. Are we helpless or what?"

William wandered over to his mother and stared at the sunlight sparkling in her red hair. In silent fascination, he reached for a loose strand and watched it glide sensuously across his fingers. "My mommy," he whispered.

She smiled. Taking his face in her hands, she kissed him tenderly on the mouth. "My baby."

"You haven't told me the whole story," said David. "Now I want to know what you've left out."

Pokie Ah Ching took a mammoth bite of his Big Mac and chewed with the fierce concentration of a man too long de-nied his lunch. Swiping a glob of sauce from his chin, he grunted, "What makes you think I left something out?"

"You've thrown some heavy-duty manpower into this case. That guard outside her room. The lobby stakeout. You're fishing for something big."

"Yeah. A murderer." Pokie took a pickle slice out of his sandwich and tossed it disgustedly on a mound of napkins. "What's with all the questions, anyway? I thought you left the prosecutor's office."

"I didn't leave behind my curiosity."

"Curiosity? Is that all it is?"

"Kate happens to be a friend of mine—"

"Hogwash!" Pokie shot him an accusing look. "You think I don't ask questions? I'm a detective, Davy. And I happen to know she's no friend of yours. She's the defendant in one of your lawsuits." He snorted. "Since when're you getting chummy with the opposition?"

"Since I started believing her story about Ellen O'Brien. Two days ago, she came to me with a story so ridiculous I laughed her out of my office. She had no facts at all, nothing but a disjointed tale that sounded flat-out paranoid. Then this nurse, Ann Richter, gets her throat slashed. Now *I'm* beginning to wonder. Was Ellen O'Brien's death malpractice? Or murder?"

"Murder, huh?" Pokie shrugged and took another bite. "That'd make it my business, not yours."

"Look, I've filed a lawsuit that claims it was malpractice. It's going to be pretty damned embarrassing—not to mention a waste of my time—if this turns out to be murder. So before I get up in front of a jury and make a fool of myself, I want to hear the facts. Level with me, Pokie. For old times' sake."

"Don't pile on the sentimental garbage, Davy. You're the one who walked away from the job. Guess that fat paycheck was too hard to resist. Me? I'm still here." He shoved a drawer closed. "Along with this crap they call furniture."

"Let's get one thing straight. My leaving the job had nothing to do with money."

"So why did you leave?"

"It was personal."

"Yeah. With you it's always *personal*. Still tight as a clam, aren't you?"

"We were talking about the case."

Pokie sat back and studied him for a moment. Through the open door of his office came the sound of bedlam—loud voices and ringing telephones and clattering typewriters. A normal afternoon in the downtown police station. In disgust, Pokie got up and shoved his office door closed. "Okay." He sighed, returning to his chair. "What do you want to know?"

"Details."

"Gotta be specific."

"What's so important about Ann Richter's murder?"

Pokie answered by grabbing a folder from the chaotic pile of papers on his desk. He tossed it to David. "M.J.'s preliminary autopsy report. Take a look."

The report was three pages long and cold-bloodedly graphic. Even though David had served five years as deputy prosecutor, had read dozens of such reports, he couldn't help shuddering at the clinical details of the woman's death.

Left carotid artery severed cleanly…razor-sharp instrument…. Laceration on right temple probably due to incidental impact against coffee table…. Pattern of blood spatter on wall consistent with arterial spray….

"I see M.J. hasn't lost her touch for turning stomachs," David said, flipping to the second page. What he read there made him frown. "Now, this finding doesn't make sense. Is M.J. sure about the time of death?"

"You know M.J. She's always sure. She's backed up by mottling and core body temp."

"Why the hell would the killer cut the woman's throat and then hang around for three hours? To enjoy the scenery?"

"To clean up. To case the apartment."

"Was anything missing?"

Pokie sighed. "No. That's the problem. Money and jewelry were lying right out in the open. Killer didn't touch any of it."

"Sexual assault?"

"No sign of it. Victim's clothes were intact. And the killing was too efficient. If he was out for thrills, you'd think he would've taken his time. Gotten a few more screams out of her."

"So you've got a brutal murder and no motive. What else is new?"

"Take another look at that autopsy report. Read me what M.J. wrote about the wound."

"'Severed left carotid artery. Razor-sharp instrument.'" He looked up. "So?"

"So those are the same words she used in another autopsy report two weeks ago. Except that victim was a man. An obstetrician named Henry Tanaka."

"Ann Richter was a nurse."

"Right. And here's the interesting part. Before she joined the O.R. staff, she used to moonlight in obstetrics. Chances are, she knew Henry Tanaka."

David suddenly went very, very still. He thought of another nurse who'd worked in obstetrics. A nurse who, like Ann Richter, was now dead. "Tell me more about that obstetrician," he said.

Pokie fished out a pack of cigarettes and an ashtray. "Mind?"

"Not if you keep talking."

"Been dying for one all morning," Pokie grunted. "Can't light up when Brophy's around, whining about his damned sinuses." He flicked off the lighter. "Okay." He sighed, gratefully expelling a cloud of smoke. "Here's the story. Henry Tanaka's office was over on Liliha. You know, that god-awful concrete building. Two weeks ago, after the rest of his staff had left, he stayed behind in the office. Said he had to catch up on some paperwork. His wife says he always got home late. But she implied it wasn't paperwork that was keeping him out at night."

"Girlfriend?"

"What else?"

"Wife know any names?"

"No. She figured it was one of the nurses over at the hospital. Anyway, about seven o'clock that night, couple of janitors found the body in one of the exam rooms. At the time we thought it was just a case of some junkie after a fix. There were drugs missing from the cabinet."

"Narcotics?"

"Naw, the good stuff was locked up in a back room. The killer went after worthless stuff, drugs that wouldn't bring you a dime on the streets. We figured he was either stoned or dumb. But he was smart enough not to leave prints. Anyway, with no other evidence, the case sort of hit a wall. The only lead we had was something one of the janitors saw. As he was coming into the building, he spotted a woman running across the parking lot. It was drizzling and almost dark, so he didn't get a good look. But he says she was definitely a blonde."

"Was he positive it was a woman?"

"What, as opposed to a man in a wig?" Pokie laughed. "That's one I didn't think of. I guess it's possible."

"So what came of your lead?"

"Nothing much. We asked around, didn't come up with any names. We were starting to think that mysterious blonde was a red herring. Then Ann Richter got killed." He paused. "She was blond." He snuffed out his cigarette. "Kate Chesne's our first big break. Now at least we know what our man looks like. The artist's sketch'll hit the papers Monday. Maybe we'll start pulling in some names."

"What kind of protection are you giving Kate?"

"She's tucked away on the North Shore. I got a patrol car passing by every few hours."

"That's all?"

"No one'll find her up there."

"A professional could."

"What am I supposed to do? Slap on a permanent guard?" He nodded at the stack of papers on his desk. "Look at those files, Davy! I'm up to my neck in stiffs. I call myself lucky if a night goes by without a corpse rolling in the door."

"Professionals don't leave witnesses."

"I'm not convinced he *is* a pro. Besides, you know how tight things are around here. Look at this junk." He kicked the desk. "Twenty years old and full of termites. Don't even mention that screwy computer. I still gotta send fingerprints

to California to get a fast ID!'' Frustrated, he flopped back
in his twenty-year-old chair. ''Look, Davy. I'm reasonably
sure she'll be okay. I'd like to guarantee it. But you know
how it is.''

Yeah, David thought. *I know how it is.* Some things about
police work never changed. Too many demands and not
enough money in the budget. He tried to tell himself that his
only interest in this case was as the plaintiff's attorney; it
was his job to ask all these questions. He had to be certain
his case wouldn't crumble in the light of new facts. But his
thoughts kept returning to Kate, sitting so alone, so vulnerable, in that hospital bed.

David wanted to trust the man's judgment. He'd worked
with Pokie Ah Ching long enough to know the man was, for
the most part, a competent cop. But he also knew that even
the best cops made mistakes. Unfortunately cops and doctors
had something in common: they both buried their mistakes.

The sun slanted down on Kate's back, its warmth lulling
her into an uneasy sleep. She lay with her face nestled in her
arms as the waves lapped at her feet and the wind riffled the
pages of her paperback book. On this lonely stretch of beach,
where the only disturbance was the birds bickering and
thrashing in the trees, she had found the perfect place to hide
away from the world. To be healed.

She sighed and the scent of coconut oil stirred in her nostrils. Little by little, she was tugged awake by the wind in
her hair, by a vague hunger for food. She hadn't eaten since
breakfast and already the afternoon had slipped toward evening.

Then another sensation wrenched her fully awake. It was
the feeling that she was no longer alone. That she was being
watched. It was so definite that when she rolled over and
looked up she was not at all surprised to see David standing
there.

He was wearing jeans and an old cotton shirt, the sleeves
rolled up in the heat. His hair danced in the wind, sparkling

like bits of fire in the late-afternoon sunlight. He didn't say a thing; he simply stood there, his hands thrust in his pockets, his gaze slowly taking her in. Though her swimsuit wasn't particularly revealing, something about his eyes—their boldness, their directness—seemed to strip her against the sand. Sudden warmth flooded her skin, a flush deeper and hotter than any the sun could ever produce.

"You're a hard lady to track down," he said.

"That's the whole idea of going into hiding. People aren't supposed to find you."

He glanced around, his gaze quickly surveying the lonely surroundings. "Doesn't seem like such a bright idea, lying out in the open."

"You're right." Grabbing her towel and book, she rose to her feet. "You never know who might be hanging around out here. Thieves. Murderers." Tossing the towel smartly over her shoulder, she turned and walked away. "Maybe even a lawyer or two."

"I have to talk to you, Kate."

"I have a lawyer. Why don't you talk to him?"

"It's about the O'Brien case—"

"Save it for the courtroom," she snapped over her shoulder. She stalked away, leaving him standing alone on the beach.

"I may not be seeing you in the courtroom," he yelled.

"What a pity."

He caught up to her as she reached the cottage, and was right on her heels as she skipped up the steps. She let the screen door swing shut in his face.

"Did you hear what I said?" he shouted from the porch.

In the middle of the kitchen she halted, suddenly struck by the implication of his words. Slowly she turned and stared at him through the screen. He'd planted his hands on either side of the doorframe and was watching her intently. "I may not be in court," he said.

"What does that mean?"

"I'm thinking of dropping out."

"Why?"

"Let me in and I'll tell you."

Still staring at him, she pushed the screen door open. "Come inside, Mr. Ransom. I think it's time we talked."

Silently he followed her into the kitchen and stood by the breakfast table, watching her. The fact that she was barefoot only emphasized the difference in their heights. She'd forgotten how tall he was, and how lanky, with legs that seemed to stretch out forever. She'd never seen him out of a suit before. She decided she definitely liked him better in blue jeans. All at once she was acutely aware of her own state of undress. It was unsettling, the way his gaze followed her around the kitchen. Unsettling, and at the same time, undeniably exciting. The way lighting a match next to a powder keg was exciting. Was David Ransom just as explosive?

She swallowed nervously. "I—I have to dress. Excuse me."

She fled into the bedroom and grabbed the first clean dress within reach, a flimsy white import from India. She almost ripped it in her haste to pull it on. Pausing by the door, she forced herself to count to ten but found her hands were still unsteady.

When she finally ventured back into the kitchen, she found him still standing by the table, idly thumbing through her book.

"A war novel," she explained. "It's not very good. But it kills the time. Which I seem to have a lot of these days." She waved vaguely toward a chair. "Sit down, Mr. Ransom. I—I'll make some coffee." It took all her concentration just to fill the kettle and set it on the stove. She found she was having trouble with even the simplest task. First she knocked the box of paper filters into the sink. Then she managed to dump coffee grounds all over the counter.

"Let me take care of that," he said, gently nudging her aside.

She watched, voiceless, as he wiped up the spilled coffee. Her awareness of his body, of its closeness, its strength, was suddenly overwhelming. Just as overwhelming was the unexpected wave of sexual longing. On unsteady legs, she moved to the table and sank into a chair.

"By the way," he asked over his shoulder, "can we cut out the 'Mr. Ransom' bit? My name's David."

"Oh. Yes. I know." She winced, hating the breathless sound of her own voice.

He settled into a chair across from her and their eyes met levelly over the kitchen table.

"Yesterday you wanted to hang me," she stated. "What made you change your mind?"

In answer, he pulled a piece of paper out of his shirt pocket. It was a photocopy of a local news article. "That story appeared about two weeks ago in the *Star-Bulletin*."

She frowned at the headline: Honolulu Physician Found Slashed To Death. "What does this have to do with anything?"

"Did you know the victim, Henry Tanaka?"

"He was on our O.B. staff. But I never worked with him."

"Look at the newspaper's description of his wounds."

Kate focused again on the article. "It says he died of wounds to the neck and back."

"Right. Wounds made by a very sharp instrument. The neck was slashed only once, severing the left carotid artery. Very efficient. Very fatal."

Kate tried to swallow and found her throat was parched. "That's how Ann—"

He nodded. "Same method. Identical results."

"How do you know all this?"

"Lt. Ah Ching saw the parallels almost immediately. That's why he slapped a guard on your hospital room. If these murders are connected, there's something systematic about all this, something rational—"

"*Rational?* The killing of a doctor? A nurse? If anything, it sounds more like the work of a psychotic!"

"It's a strange thing, murder. Sometimes it has no rhyme or reason to it. Sometimes the act makes perfect sense."

"There's no such thing as a *sensible* reason to kill someone!"

"It's done every day, by supposedly sane people. And all for the most mundane of reasons. Money. Power." He paused. "Then again," he said softly, "there's the crime of passion. It seems Henry Tanaka was having an affair with one of the nurses."

"Lots of doctors have affairs."

"So do lots of nurses."

"Which nurse are we talking about?"

"I was hoping you could tell me."

"I'm sorry, but I'm not up on the latest hospital gossip."

"Even if it involves your patients?"

"You mean Ellen? I—I wouldn't know. I don't usually delve into my patients' personal lives. Not unless it's relevant to their health."

"Ellen's personal life may have been very relevant to her health."

"Well, she was a beautiful woman. I'm sure there were…men in her life." Kate's gaze fell once again to the article. "What does this have to do with Ann Richter?"

"Maybe nothing. Maybe everything. In the last two weeks, three people on Mid Pac's staff have died. Two were murdered. One had an unexpected cardiac arrest on the operating table. Coincidence?"

"It's a big hospital. A big staff."

"But those three particular people knew each other. They even worked together."

"But Ann was a surgical nurse—"

"Who used to work in obstetrics."

"What?"

"Eight years ago, Ann Richter went through a very messy divorce. She ended up with a mile-high stack of credit-card bills. She needed extra cash, fast. So she did some moonlighting as an O.B. nurse. The night shift. That's the same shift Ellen O'Brien worked. They knew each other, all right. Tanaka, Richter, O'Brien. And now they're all dead."

The scream of the boiling kettle tore through the silence but she was too numb to move. David rose and took the kettle off the stove. She heard him set out the cups and pour the water. The smell of coffee wafted into her awareness.

"It's strange," she remarked. "I saw Ann almost every day in that O.R. We'd talk about books we'd read or movies we'd seen. But we never really talked about *ourselves*. And she was always so private. Almost unapproachable."

"How did she react to Ellen's death?"

Kate was silent for a moment, remembering how, when everything had gone wrong, when Ellen's life had hung in the balance, Ann had stood white-faced and frozen. "She seemed…paralyzed. But we were all upset. Afterward she went home sick. She didn't come back to work. That was the last time I saw her. Alive, I mean…." She looked down, dazed, as he slid a cup of coffee in front of her.

"You said it before. She must have known something. Something dangerous. Maybe they all did."

"But, David, they were just ordinary people who worked in a hospital—"

"All kinds of things can go on in hospitals. Narcotics theft. Insurance fraud. Illicit love affairs. Maybe even murder."

"If Ann knew something dangerous, why didn't she go to the police?"

"Maybe she couldn't. Maybe she was afraid of self-incrimination. Or she was protecting someone else."

A deadly secret, Kate thought. Had all three victims shared it? Softly she ventured, "Then you think Ellen was murdered."

"That's why I'm here. I want you to tell *me*."

She shook her head in bewilderment. "How can I?"

"You have the medical expertise. You were there in the O.R. when it happened. How could it be done?"

"I've already gone over it a thousand times—"

"Then do it again. Come on, Kate, *think*. Convince me it was murder. Convince me I *should* drop out of this case."

His blunt command seemed to leave her no alternative. She

felt his eyes goading her to recall every detail, every event leading up to those frantic moments in the O.R. She remembered how everything had gone so smoothly, the induction of anesthesia, the placement of the endotracheal tube. She'd double-checked the tanks and the lines; she knew the oxygen had been properly hooked up.

"Well?" he prodded.

"I can't think of anything."

"Yes, you can."

"It was a completely routine case!"

"What about the surgery itself?"

"Faultless. Guy's the best surgeon on the staff. Anyway, he'd just started the operation. He was barely through the muscle layer when—" She stopped.

"When what?"

"He—he complained about the abdominal muscles being too tight. He was having trouble retracting them."

"So?"

"So I injected a dose of succinylcholine."

"That's pretty routine, isn't it?"

She nodded. "I give it all the time. But in Ellen, it didn't seem to work. I had to draw up a second dose. I remember asking Ann to fetch me another vial."

"You had only one vial?"

"I usually keep a few in my cart. But that morning there was only one in the drawer."

"What happened after you gave the second dose of succinylcholine?"

"A few seconds went by. Maybe it was ten. Fifteen. And then—" Slowly she looked up at him. "Her heart stopped."

They stared at each other. Through the window, the last light of day slanted in, knifelike, across the kitchen. He leaned forward, his eyes hard on hers. "If you could prove it—"

"But I can't! That empty vial went straight to the incinerator, with all the rest of the trash. And there's not even a body left to autopsy." She looked away, miserable. "Oh, he

was smart, David. Whoever the killer was, he knew exactly
what he was doing."

"Maybe he's too smart for his own good."

"What do you mean?"

"He's obviously sophisticated. He knew exactly which
drugs you'd be likely to give in the O.R. And he managed
to slip something deadly into one of those vials. Who has
access to the anesthesia carts?"

"They're left in the operating rooms. I suppose anyone on
the hospital staff could get to them. Doctors. Nurses. Maybe
even the janitors. But there were always people around."

"What about nights? Weekends?"

"If there's no surgery scheduled, I guess they just close
the suite down. But there's always a surgical nurse on duty
for emergencies."

"Does she stay in the O.R. area?"

She shrugged helplessly. "I'm only there if we have a
case. I have no idea what happens on a quiet night."

"If the suite's left unguarded, then anyone on the staff
could've slipped in."

"It's not someone on the staff. I *saw* the killer, David!
That man in Ann's apartment was a stranger."

"Who could have an associate. Someone in the hospital.
Maybe even someone you know."

"A conspiracy?"

"Look at the systematic way these murders are being carried out. As if our killer—or killers—has some sort of list.
My question is: Who's next?"

The clatter of her cup dropping against the saucer made
Kate jump. Glancing down, she saw that her hands were
shaking. *I saw his face,* she thought. *If he has a list, then my
name's on it.*

The afternoon had slid into dusk. Agitated, she rose and
paced to the open doorway. There she stood, staring out at
the sea. The wind, so steady just moments before, had died.
There was a stillness in the air, as if evening were holding
its breath.

"He's out there," she whispered. "Looking for me. And I don't even know his name." The touch of David's hand on her shoulder made her tremble. He was standing behind her, so close she could feel his breath in her hair. "I keep seeing his eyes, staring at me in the mirror. Black and sunken. Like one of those posters of starving children…"

"He can't hurt you, Kate. Not here." David's breath seared her neck. A shudder ran through her body—not one of fear but of arousal. Even without looking at him, she could sense his need, simmering to the surface.

Suddenly it was more than his breath scorching her flesh; it was his lips. His face burrowed through the thick strands of her hair to press hungrily against her neck. His fingers gripped her shoulders, as if he was afraid she'd pull away. But she didn't. She couldn't. Her whole body was aching for him.

His lips left a warm, moist trail as they glided to her shoulder, and then she felt the rasp of his jaw.

He swung her around to face him. The instant she turned, his mouth was on hers.

She felt herself falling under the force of his kiss, falling into some deep and bottomless well, until her back suddenly collided with the kitchen wall. With the whole hard length of his body he pinned her there, belly against belly, thigh against thigh. Her lips parted and his tongue raged in, claiming her mouth as his. There was no doubt in her mind he intended to claim the rest of her, as well.

The match had been struck; the powder keg was about to explode, and her with it. She willingly flung herself into the conflagration.

No words were spoken; there were only the low, aching moans of need. They were both breathing so hard, so fast, that her ears were filled with the sound. She scarcely heard the telephone ringing. Only when it had rung again and again did her feverish brain finally register what it was.

It took all her willpower to swim against the flood of desire. She struggled to pull away. "The—the telephone—"

"Let it ring." His mouth slid down to her throat.

But the sound continued, grating and relentless, nagging her with its sense of urgency.

"David. Please…"

Groaning, he wrenched away and she saw the astonishment in his eyes. For a moment they stared at each other, neither of them able to believe what had just happened between them. The phone rang again. Jarred to her senses at last, she forced herself across the kitchen and picked up the reciever. Clearing her throat, she managed a hoarse "Hello?"

She was so dazed it took her a few seconds to register the silence on the line. "Hello?" she repeated.

"Dr. Chesne?" a voice whispered, barely audible.

"Yes?"

"Are you alone?"

"No, I— Who is this?" Her voice suddenly froze as the first fingers of terror gripped her throat.

There was a pause, so long and empty she could hear her own heart pounding in her ears. *"Hello?"* she screamed. *"Who is this?"*

"Be careful, Kate Chesne. For death is all around us."

7

The receiver slipped from her grasp and clattered on the linoleum floor. She reeled back in terror against the counter. "It's him," she whispered. Then, in a voice tinged with hysteria she cried out: *"It's him!"*

David instantly scrabbled on the floor for the receiver. "Who is this? Hello? *Hello?*" Cursing, he slammed the receiver back in the cradle and turned to her. "What did he say? Kate!" He took her by the shoulders and gave her a shake. "What did he say?"

"He—he said to be careful—that death was all around...."

"Where's your suitcase?" he snapped.

"What?"

"Your suitcase!"

"In—in the bedroom closet."

He stalked into the bedroom. Automatically she followed him and watched as he dragged her Samsonite down from the shelf. "Get your things together. You can't stay here."

She didn't ask where they were going. She only knew that she had to escape; that every minute she remained in this place just added to the danger.

Suddenly driven by the need to get away, she began to pack. By the time they were ready to leave, her compulsion to escape was so strong she practically flew down the porch steps to his car.

As he thrust the key in the ignition, she was seized by a wild terror that the car wouldn't start; that like some unfortunate victim in a horror movie, she would be stranded here, doomed to meet her death.

But at the first turn of the key, the engine started. The ironwood trees lunged at them as David sent the BMW wheeling around. Branches slashed the windshield. She felt another stab of panic as their tires spun uselessly in the sand. Then the car leaped free. The headlights trembled as they bounced up the dirt lane.

"How did he find me?" she sobbed.

"That's what I'm wondering." David hit the gas pedal as the car swung onto paved road. The BMW responded instantly with a burst of power that sent them hurtling down the highway.

"No one knew I was here. Only the police."

"Then there's been a leak of information. Or—" he shot a quick look at the rearview mirror "—you were followed."

"Followed?" She whipped her head around but saw only a deserted highway, shimmering under the dim glow of street lamps.

"Who took you to the cottage?" he asked.

She turned and focused on his profile, gleaming faintly in the darkness. "My—my friend Susan drove me."

"Did you stop at your house?"

"No. We went straight to the cottage."

"What about your clothes? How'd you get them?"

"My landlady packed a suitcase and brought it to the hospital."

"He might have been watching the lobby entrance. Waiting for you to be discharged."

"But we didn't see anyone follow us."

"Of course you didn't. People almost never do. We normally focus our attention on what's ahead, on where we're going. As for your phone number, he could've looked it up in the book. The Santinis have their name on the mailbox."

"But it doesn't make sense," she cried. "If he wants to kill me, why not just do it and get it over with? Why threaten me with phone calls?"

"Who knows how he thinks? Maybe he gets a thrill out

of scaring his victims. Maybe he just wants to keep you from cooperating with the police.''

''I was alone. He could have done it right there…on the beach….'' She tried desperately not to think of what could have happened, but she couldn't shut out the image of her own blood seeping into the sand.

High on the hillside, the lights of houses flashed by, each one an unreachable haven of safety. In all that darkness, was there a haven for her? She huddled against the car seat, wishing she never had to leave this small cocoon of safety.

Closing her eyes, she forced herself to concentrate on the hum of the engine, on the rhythm of the highway passing beneath their wheels—anything to banish the bloodstained image. BMW. The ultimate driving machine, she thought inanely. Wasn't that what the ads said? High-tech German engineering. Cool, crisp performance. Just the kind of car she'd expect David to own.

''…and there's plenty of room. So you can stay as long as you need to.''

''What?'' Bewildered, she turned and looked at him. His profile was a hard, clean shadow against the passing streetlights.

''I said you can stay as long as you need to. It's not the Ritz, but it'll be safer than a hotel.''

She shook her head. ''I don't understand. Where are we going?''

He glanced at her and the tone of his voice was strangely unemotional. ''My house.''

''Home,'' said David, pushing open the front door. It was dark inside. Through the huge living-room windows, moonlight spilled in, faintly illuminating a polished wood floor, the dark and hulking silhouettes of furniture. David guided her to a couch and gently sat her down. Then, sensing her desperate need for light, for warmth, he quickly walked around the room, turning on all the lamps. She was vaguely aware of the muted clink of a bottle, the sound of something being poured. Then he returned and put a glass in her hand.

"Drink it," he said.

"What—what is it?"

"Whiskey. Go on. I think you could use a stiff one."

She took a deep and automatic gulp; the fiery sting instantly brought tears to her eyes. "Wonderful stuff." She coughed.

"Yeah. Isn't it?" He turned to leave the room and she felt a sudden, irrational burst of panic that he was abandoning her.

"David?" she called.

He immediately sensed the terror in her voice. Turning back, he spoke quietly: "It's all right, Kate. I won't leave you. I'll be right next door, in the kitchen." He smiled and touched her face. "Finish that drink."

Fearfully she watched him vanish through the doorway. Then she heard his voice, talking to someone on the phone. The police. As if there was anything they could do now. Clutching the glass in both hands, she forced down another sip of whiskey. The room seemed to swim as her eyes flooded with tears. She blinked them away and slowly focused on her surroundings.

It was, somehow, every inch a man's house. The furniture was plain and practical, the oak floor unadorned by even a single throw rug. Huge windows were framed by stark white curtains and she could hear, just outside, waves crashing against the seawall. Nature's violence, so close, so frightening.

But not nearly as frightening as the violence of man.

After David hung up, he paused in the kitchen, trying to scrape together some semblance of composure. The woman was already frightened enough; seeing his agitation would only make things worse. He quickly ran his fingers through his ruffled hair. Then, taking a deep breath, he pushed open the kitchen door and walked back into the living room.

She was still huddled pitifully on the couch, her hands clenched around the half-empty glass of whiskey. At least a trace of color had returned to her face, but it was barely enough to remind him of a frost-covered rose petal. A little more whiskey was what she needed. He took the glass, filled it to the brim and placed it back in her hands. Her skin was icy. She looked so stunned, so vulnerable. If he could just take her hands in his, if he could warm her in his arms, maybe he could coax some life back into those frozen limbs. But he was afraid to give in to the impulse; he knew it could lead to far more compelling urges.

He turned and poured himself a tall one. What she needed from him right now was protection. Reassurance. She needed to know that she would be taken care of and that things were still right with the world, though the truth of the matter was, her world had just gone to hell in a hand basket.

He took a deep gulp of whiskey, then set it down. What she really needed was a sober host.

"I've called the police," he said over his shoulder.

Her response was almost toneless. "What did they say?"

He shrugged. "What could they say? Stay where you are. Don't go out alone." Frowning at his glass, he thought, What the hell, and recklessly downed the rest of the whiskey. Bottle in hand, he returned to the couch and set the whiskey down on the coffee table. They were sitting only a few feet apart but it felt like miles of emptiness between them.

She stirred and looked toward the kitchen. "My—my friends—they won't know where I am. I should call them."

"Don't worry about it. Pokie'll let them know you're safe." He watched her sink back listlessly on the couch. "You should eat something," he said.

"I'm not hungry."

"My housekeeper makes great spaghetti sauce."

She lifted one shoulder—only one, as if she hadn't the energy for a full-blown shrug.

"Yep," he continued with sudden enthusiasm. "Once a week Mrs. Feldman takes pity on a poor starving bachelor

and she leaves me a pot of sauce. It's loaded with garlic.
Fresh basil. Plus a healthy slug of wine.''

There was no response.

"Every woman I've ever served it to swears it's a powerful
aphrodisiac.''

At last there was a smile, albeit a very small one. "How
helpful of Mrs. Feldman," she remarked.

"She thinks I'm not eating right. Though I don't know
why. Maybe it's all those frozen-dinner trays she finds in my
trash can.''

There was another smile. If he kept this up, he just might
coax a laugh out of her by next week. Too bad he was such
a lousy comedian. Anyway, the situation was too damned
grim for jokes.

The clock on the bookshelf ticked loudly—a nagging reminder of how much silence had passed between them. Kate
suddenly stiffened as a gust rattled the windows.

"It's just the wind," he said. "You'll get used to it. Sometimes, in a storm, the whole house shudders and it feels like
the roof will blow off." He gazed up affectionately at the
beams. "It's thirty years old. Probably should have been torn
down years ago. But when we bought it, all we could see
were the possibilities.''

"We?" she asked dully.

"I was married then.''

"Oh." She stirred a little, as though trying to show some
semblance of interest. "You're divorced.''

He nodded. "We lasted a little over seven years—not bad,
in this day and age." He gave a short, joyless laugh. "Con-
trary to the old cliché, it wasn't an itch that finished us. It
was more like a...fading out. But—" he sighed "—Linda
and I are still friendly. Which is more than most divorced
couples can say. I even like her new husband. Great guy.
Very devoted, caring. Something I guess I wasn't...." He
looked away, uncomfortable. He hated talking about himself.
It made him feel exposed. But at least all this small talk was
doing the trick. It was bringing her back to life, nudging the

fear from her mind. "Linda's in Portland now," he went on quickly. "I hear they've got a baby on the way."

"You didn't have any children?" It was a perfectly natural question. He wished she hadn't asked it.

He nodded shortly. "A son."

"Oh. How old is he?"

"He's dead." How flat his voice sounded. As if Noah's death were as casual a topic as the weather. He could already see the questions forming on her lips. And the words of sympathy. That was the last thing he wanted from her. He'd heard enough well-meaning words of sympathy to last him the rest of his life.

"So anyway," he said, shifting the subject, "I'm what you'd call a born-again bachelor. But I like it this way. Some men just aren't meant to be married, I guess. And it's great for my career. Nothing to distract me from the practice, which seems to be going big guns these days."

Damn. She was still looking at him with those questions in her eyes. He headed them off with another change of topic.

"What about you?" he asked quickly. "Were you ever married?"

"No." She looked down, as if contemplating the benefits of another slug of whiskey. "I lived with a man for a while. In fact, he's the reason I came to Honolulu. To be near him." She gave a bitter laugh. "Guess that'll teach me."

"What?"

"Not to go chasing after some stupid man."

"Sounds like a nasty breakup."

She hiccuped. "It was very…civil, actually. I'm not saying it didn't hurt. Because it did." Shrugging, she surrendered to another gulp of whiskey. "It's hard, you know. Trying to be everything at once. I guess I couldn't give him what he needed: dinner waiting on the table, my undivided attention."

"Is that what he expected?"

"Isn't that what every man expects?" she snorted angrily. "Well, I didn't need all that—that male crap. I had a job that required me to jump at every phone call. Rush in for every emergency. He didn't understand.''

"Was it worth it?''

"Was what worth it?''

"Sacrificing your love life for your career?''

She didn't answer for a while. Then her head drooped. "I used to think so,'' she said quietly. "Now I think of all those hours I put in. All those ruined weekends. I thought I was indispensable to the hospital. And then I find out I'm just as dispensable as anyone else. All it took was a lawsuit. Hell of an eye-opener.'' She tipped her glass at him bitterly. "Thanks for the revelation, counselor.''

"Why blame me? I was just hired to do a job.''

"For a nice fat fee, I imagine.''

"I took the case on contingency. I won't be seeing a cent.''

"You gave up all that money? Just because you think I'm telling the truth?'' She shook her head in amazement. "I'm surprised the truth means so much to you.''

"You have a nice way of making me sound like scum. But yes, the truth does matter to me. A great deal, in fact.''

"A lawyer with principles? I didn't know there was such a thing.''

"We're a recognized subspecies.'' His gaze inadvertently slid to the neckline of her gauze dress. The memory of how that silky skin had felt under his exploring fingers suddenly hit him with such force that he quickly turned and reached for the whiskey. There was no glass handy so he took a swig straight from the bottle. *Right,* he thought. *Get yourself drunk. See how many stupid things you can say before morning.*

Actually, they were both getting thoroughly soused. But he figured she needed it. Twenty minutes ago she'd been in a state of shock. Now, at least, she was talking. In fact she'd just managed to insult him. That had to be a good sign.

She gazed fervently into her glass. "God, I hate whiskey!'' she said with sudden passion and gulped down the rest of the drink.

"I can tell. Have some more."

She eyed him suspiciously. "I think you're trying to get me drunk."

"Whatever gave you that idea?" He laughed, shoving the bottle toward her.

She regarded it for a moment. Then, with a look of utter disgust, she refilled her glass. "Good old Jack Daniel's," she sighed. Her hand was unsteady as she recapped the bottle. "What a laugh."

"What's so funny?"

"It was Dad's favorite brand. He used to swear this stuff was medicinal. Absolutely *hated* all my hair-of-the-dog lectures. Boy, would he get a kick out of seeing me now." She took a swallow and winced. "Maybe he's right. Anything that tastes this awful *has* to be medicinal."

"I take it your father wasn't a doctor."

"He wanted to be." She stared down moodily at her drink. "Yeah, that was his dream. He planned on being a country doctor. You know, the kind of guy who'd deliver a baby in exchange for a few dozen eggs. But I guess things didn't work out. I came along and then they needed money and…" She sighed. "He had a repair shop in Sacramento. Oh, he was handy! I used to watch him putter around in that basement. Dad could fix anything you put in his hands. TVs. Washing machines. He even held seventeen patents, none of them worth a damn cent. Except maybe the Handy Dandy apple slicer." She glanced at him hopefully. "Ever heard of it?"

"Sorry. No."

She shrugged. "Neither has anyone else."

"What does it do, exactly?"

"One flick of the wrist and whack! Six perfect slices." At his silence she gave him a rueful smile. "I can see you're terribly impressed."

"But I am. I'm impressed that your father managed to invent you. He must've been happy you became a doctor."

"He was. When I graduated from med school, he told me

it was the very best day of his life.'' She stopped, her smile suddenly fading. ''I think that's sad, don't you? That out of all the years of his life, that was the one single day he was happiest….'' She cleared her throat. ''After he died, Mom sold the shop. She got married to some high-powered banker in San Francisco. What a snooty guy. We can't stand each other.'' She looked down at her glass and her voice dropped. ''I still think about that shop sometimes. I miss the old basement. I miss all those dumb, useless gadgets of his. I miss—''

He saw her lower lip tremble and he thought with sudden panic: *Oh, no. Now she's going to cry.* He could deal with sobbing clients. He knew exactly how to respond to their tears. Pull out the box of Kleenex. Pat them on the back. Tell them he'd do everything he could.

But this was different. This wasn't his office but his living room. And the woman on the verge of tears wasn't a client but someone he happened to like very much.

Just as he thought the dam would burst, she managed to drag herself together. He saw only the briefest glitter of tears in her eyes, then she blinked and they were gone. Thank God. If she started bawling now, he'd be utterly useless.

He took her glass and deliberately set it down on the table. ''I think you've had enough for tonight. Come on, doctor lady. It's time for bed. I'll show you the way.'' He reached for her hand but she reflexively pulled back. ''Something wrong?''

''No. It's just…''

''Don't tell me you're worried about how it looks? Your staying here, I mean.''

''A little. Not much, actually. I mean, not under the circumstances.'' She gave an awkward laugh. ''Fear does strange things to one's sense of propriety.''

''Not to mention one's sense of legal ethics.'' At her puzzled look, he said, ''I've never done this before.''

''What? Brought a woman home for the night?''

''Well, I haven't done *that* in a while, either. What I meant was, I make it a point never to get involved with any of my clients. And certainly never with the opposition.''

''Then I'm the exception?''

''Yes. You are definitely the exception. Believe it or not, I don't normally paw every female who walks into my office.''

''Which ones do you paw?'' she asked, a faint smile suddenly tracing her lips.

He moved toward her, drawn by invisible threads of desire. ''Only the green-eyed ones,'' he murmured. Gently he touched her cheek. ''Who happen to have a bruise here and there.''

''That last part sounds suspiciously kinky,'' she whispered.

''No, it's not.'' The intimate tone of his voice made Kate suddenly fall very still. His finger left a scorching trail as it stroked down her face.

She knew the danger of this moment. This was the man who'd once vowed to ruin her. He could still ruin her. *Consorting with the enemy,* she thought in sudden panic as his face drew closer. But she couldn't seem to move. A sense of unreality swept over her; a feeling that none of this could be happening, that it was only some hot, drunken fantasy. Here she was, sharing a couch with the very man she'd once despised, and all she could think of was how much she wanted him to haul her into his arms and kiss her.

His lips were gentle. It was no more than a brushing of mouths, a cautious savoring of what they both knew might follow, but it was enough to touch off a thousand flames inside her. Jack Daniel's had never tasted so good!

''And what will the bar association say to that?'' she murmured.

''They'll call it outrageous....''

''Unethical.''

''And absolutely insane. Which it is.'' Drawing away, he studied her for a moment; and his struggle for control showed plainly in his face. To her disappointment, common sense won out. He rose from the couch and tugged her to her feet.

"When you file your complaint with the state bar, don't forget to mention how apologetic I was."

"Will it make a difference?"

"Not to them. But I hope it does to you."

They stood before the window, staring at each other. The wind lashed the panes, a sound as relentless as the pounding of her own heartbeat in her ears.

"I think it's time to go to bed," he said hoarsely.

"What?"

He cleared his throat. "I mean it's time you went to your bed. And I went to mine."

"Oh."

"Unless..."

"Unless?"

"You don't want to."

"Want to what?"

"Go to bed."

They looked at each other uneasily. She swallowed. "I think maybe I'd better."

"Yeah." He turned away and agitatedly plowed his fingers through his hair. "I think so, too."

"David?"

He glanced over his shoulder. "Yes?"

"Is it really a violation of legal ethics? Letting me stay here?"

"Under the circumstances?" He shrugged. "I think I'm still on safe ground. Barely. As long as nothing happens between us." He scooped up the whiskey bottle. Matter-of-factly he slid it into the liquor cabinet and shut the door. "And nothing will."

"Of course not," she responded quickly. "I mean, I don't need that kind of complication in my life. Certainly not now."

"Neither do I. But for the moment, we seem to need each other. So I'll provide you with a safe place to stay. And you can help me figure out what really happened in that O.R. A convenient arrangement. I ask only one thing."

"What's that?"

"We keep this discreet. Not just now but also after you leave. This sort of thing can only hurt both our reputations."

"I understand. Perfectly."

They both took a simultaneous breath.

"So...I think I'll say good-night," she said. Turning, she started across the living room. Her whole body felt like rubber. She only prayed she wouldn't fall flat on her face.

"Kate?"

Her heart did a quick somersault as she spun around to face him. "Yes?"

"Your room's the second door on the right."

"Oh. Thanks." Her flip-flopping heart seemed to sink like a stone as she left him standing there in the living room. Her only consolation was that he looked every bit as miserable as she felt.

Long after Kate had gone to her room, David sat in the living room, thinking. Remembering how she had tasted, how she had trembled in his arms. And wondering how he'd gotten himself into this mess. It was bad enough, letting the woman sleep under his roof, but to practically seduce her on his couch—that was sheer stupidity. Though he'd wanted to. God, how he'd wanted to.

He could tell by the way she'd melted against him that she hadn't been kissed in a very long time. Terrific. Here they were, two normal, healthy, *deprived* adults, sleeping within ten feet of each other. You couldn't ask for a more explosive situation.

He didn't want to think about what his old ethics professor would say to this. Strictly speaking, he couldn't consider himself off the O'Brien case yet. Until he actually handed the file over to another firm, he still had to behave as their attorney and was bound by legal ethics to protect their interests. To think how scrupulous he'd always been about separating his personal from his professional life!

If he'd had his head screwed on straight, he would have

avoided the whole mess by taking Kate to a hotel or a friend's house. Anywhere but here. The problem was, he'd been having trouble thinking straight since the day he met her. Tonight, after that phone call, he'd had only one thought in mind: to keep her safe and warm and protected. It was a fiercely primitive instinct over which he had no control; and he resented it. He also resented her for stirring up all these inconvenient male responses.

Annoyed at himself, he rose from the couch and circled the living room, turning off lights. He decided he wasn't interested in being any woman's white knight. Besides, Kate Chesne wasn't the kind of woman who needed a hero. Or any man, for that matter. Not that he didn't like independent women. He did like them.

He also liked *her.* A lot.

Maybe too much.

Kate lay curled up in bed, listening to David's restless pacing in the living room. She held her breath as his footsteps creaked up the hall past her door. Was it her imagination or did he pause there for a moment before continuing on to the next room? She could hear him moving around, opening and closing drawers, rattling hangers in the closet. *My God,* she thought. *He's sleeping right next door.*

Now the shower was running. She wondered if it was a cold shower. She tried not to think about what he'd look like, standing under the stream of water, but the image had already formed in her head, the soapsuds sliding down his shoulders, the gold hairs matted and damp on his chest.

Now stop it. Right now.

She bit her lip—bit it so hard the image wavered a little. Damn. So this was lust, pure and unadulterated. Well, maybe slightly adulterated—by whiskey. Here she was, thirty years old, and she'd never wanted any man so badly. She wanted him on a level that was raw and wild and elemental.

She'd certainly never felt this way about Eric. Her relationship with Eric had been excruciatingly civilized; nothing

as primitive as this—this animal heat. Even their parting had
been civilized. They'd discussed their differences, decided
they were irreconcilable, and had gone their separate ways.
At the time she'd thought it devastating, but now she realized
what had been hurt most by the breakup was her pride. All
these months, she'd nursed the faint hope that Eric would
come back to her. Now she could barely conjure up a picture
of his face. It kept blurring into the image of a man in a
shower.

She buried her head in the pillow, an act that made her
feel about as brilliant as an ostrich. And she was supposed
to be so bright, so levelheaded. Why, it was even official,
having been stated in her performance evaluation as a resi-
dent: *Dr. Chesne is a superbly competent, levelheaded physician.* Ha! Levelheaded? Try dim-witted. Besotted. Or just
plain dumb—for lusting after the man who'd once threatened
to ruin her in court.

She had so many important things to worry about; matters,
literally, of life and death. She was losing her job. Her career
was on the skids. A killer was searching for her.

And she was wondering how much hair David Ransom
had on his chest.

She was running down hundreds of steps, plunging deeper
and deeper into a pit of darkness. She didn't know what lay
at the end; all she knew was that something was right behind
her, something terrible; she didn't dare look back to see its
face. There were no doors, no windows, no other avenue of
escape. Her flight was noiseless, like the flickering reel of a
movie with no sound. In this silence lay the worst terror of
all: no one would hear her scream.

With a sob, Kate wrenched herself awake and found herself staring up wildly at an unfamiliar ceiling. Somewhere a
telephone was ringing. Daylight glowed in the window and
she heard waves lapping the seawall. The ringing telephone
suddenly stopped; David's voice murmured in another room.

I'm safe, she told herself. *No one can hurt me. Not here. Not in this house.*

The knock on the door made her sit up sharply.

"Kate?" David called through the closed door.

"Yes?"

"You'd better get dressed. Pokie wants us down at the station."

"Right now?"

"Right now."

It was his low tone of urgency that alarmed her. She scrambled out of bed and opened the door. "Why? What is it?"

His gaze slid briefly to her nightgown, then focused, utterly neutral, on her face. "The killer. They know his name."

8

Pokie slid the book of mug shots toward Kate. "See anyone you know, Dr. Chesne?"

Kate scanned the photographs and immediately focused on one face. It was a cruel portrait; every wrinkle, every hollow had been brought into harsh clarity by the camera lights. Yet the man didn't squint. He gazed straight ahead with wide eyes. It was the look of a lost soul. Softly she said, "That's him."

"You positive?"

"I—I remember his eyes." Swallowing hard, she turned away. Both men were watching her intently. They were probably worried she'd faint or get hysterical or do something equally ridiculous. But she wasn't feeling much of anything. It was as if she were detached from her body and were floating somewhere near the ceiling, watching a stock scene from a police procedural: the witness unerringly pointing out the face of the killer.

"That's our man," Pokie said with grim satisfaction.

A wan sergeant in plainclothes brought her a cup of hot coffee. He seemed to have a cold; he was sniffling. Through the glass partition, she saw him return to his desk and take out a bottle of nose spray.

Her gaze returned to the photo. "Who is he?" she asked.

"A nut case," replied Pokie. "The name's Charles Decker. That photo was taken five years ago, right after his arrest."

"On what charge?"

"Assault and battery. He kicked down the door of a medical office. Tried to strangle the doctor right there in front of the whole staff.''

''A doctor?'' David's head came up. ''Which one?''

Pokie sat back, his weight eliciting a squeal of protest from the old chair. ''Guess.''

''Henry Tanaka.''

Pokie's answer was a satisfied display of nicotine-stained teeth. ''One and the same. It took us a while, but the name finally popped up on a computer search.''

''Arrest records?''

''Yeah. We should've picked it up earlier, but it kind of slipped by during the initial investigation. See, we asked Mrs. Tanaka if her husband had any enemies. You know, routine question. She gave us some names. We followed up on 'em but they all came up clean. Then she mentioned that five years back, some nut had attacked her husband. She didn't remember his name and as far as she knew, the man was still in the state hospital. We went to the files and finally pulled out an arrest report. It was Charlie Decker's. And this morning I got word from the lab. Remember that set of fingerprints on the Richter woman's doorknob?''

''Charlie Decker's?''

Pokie nodded. ''And now—'' he glanced at Kate ''—our witness gives us a positive ID. I'd say we got our man.''

''What was his motive?''

''I told you. He's crazy.''

''So are thousands of other people. Why did this one turn killer?''

''Hey, I'm not the guy's shrink.''

''But you have an answer, don't you?''

Pokie shrugged. ''All I got is a theory.''

''That man threatened my life, Lieutenant,'' said Kate. ''I think I have the right to know more than just his name.''

''She does, Pokie,'' agreed David quietly. ''You won't find it in any of your police manuals. But I think she has the right to know who this Charles Decker is.''

Sighing, Pokie fished a spiral notebook out of his desk.

"Okay," he grunted, flipping through the pages. "Here's what I got so far. Understand, it's still gotta be confirmed. Decker, Charles Louis, white male born Cleveland thirty-nine years ago. Parents divorced. Brother killed in a gang fight at age fifteen. Great start. One married sister, living in Florida."

"You talked to her?"

"She's the one who gave us most of this info. Let's see. Joined the navy at twenty-two. Based in various ports. San Diego. Bremerton. Got shipped here to Pearl six years ago. Served as corpsman aboard the USS *Cimarron*—"

"Corpsman?" Kate questioned.

"Assistant to the ship's surgeon. According to his superior officers, Decker was kind of a loner. Pretty much kept to himself. No history of emotional problems." Here he let out a snort. "So much for the accuracy of military files." He flipped to the next page. "Had a decent service record, couple of commendations. Seemed to be moving up the ranks okay. And then, five years ago, it seems something snapped."

"Nervous breakdown?" asked David.

"Lot more than that. He went berserk. And it all had to do with a woman."

"You mean a girlfriend?"

"Yeah. Some gal he'd met here in the Islands. He put in for permission to get married. It was granted. But then he and his ship sailed for six months of classified maneuvers off Subic Bay. Sailor in the next bunk remembers Decker spent every spare minute writing poems for that girlfriend. Must've been nuts about her. Just nuts." Pokie shook his head and sighed. "Anyway, when the *Cimarron* returned to Pearl, the girlfriend wasn't waiting on the pier with all the other honeys. Here's the part where things get a little confused. All we know is Decker jumped ship without permission. Guess it didn't take long for him to find out what'd happened."

"She found another guy?" David guessed.

"No. She was dead."

There was a long silence. In the next office, a telephone was ringing and typewriters clattered incessantly.

Kate asked softly, "What happened to her?"

"Complications of childbirth," explained Pokie. "She had some kind of stroke in the delivery room. The baby girl died, too. Decker never even knew she was pregnant."

Slowly, Kate's gaze fell to the photograph of Charlie Decker. She thought of what he must have gone through, that day in Pearl Harbor. The ship pulling into the crowded dock. The smiling families. *How long did he search for her face?* she wondered. *How long before he realized she wasn't there? That she'd never be there?*

"That's when the man lost it," continued Pokie. "Somehow he found out Tanaka was his girlfriend's doctor. The arrest record says he showed up at the clinic and just about strangled the doctor on the spot. After a scuffle, the police were called. A day later, Decker got out on bail. He went and bought himself a Saturday-night special. But he didn't use it on the doctor. He put the barrel in his own mouth. Pulled the trigger." Pokie closed the notebook.

The ultimate act, thought Kate. *Buy a gun and blow your own head off.* He must have loved that woman. And what better way to prove it than to sacrifice himself on her altar?

But he wasn't dead. He was alive. And he was killing people.

Pokie saw her questioning look. "It was a very cheap gun. It misfired. Turned his mouth into bloody pulp. But he survived. After a few months in a rehab facility, he was transferred to the state hospital. The nuthouse. Their records show he regained function of just about everything but his speech."

"He's mute?" asked David.

"Not exactly. Vocal cords were ripped to shreds during the resuscitation. He can mouth words, but his voice is more like a—a hiss."

A hiss, thought Kate. The memory of that unearthly sound,

echoing in Ann's stairwell, seemed to reach out from her worst nightmares. *The sound of a viper about to strike.*

Pokie continued. "About a month ago, Decker was discharged from the state hospital. He was supposed to be seeing some shrink by the name of Nemechek. But Decker never showed up for the first appointment."

"Have you talked to Nemechek?" asked Kate.

"Only on the phone. He's at a conference in L.A. Should be back on Tuesday. Swears up and down that his patient was harmless. But he's covering his butt. Looks pretty bad when the patient you just let out starts slashing throats."

"So that's the motive," said David. "Revenge. For a dead woman."

"That's the theory."

"Why was Ann Richter killed?"

"Remember that blond woman the janitors saw running through the parking lot?"

"You think that was her?"

"It seems she and Tanaka were—how do I put it?—very well acquainted."

"Does that mean what I think it means?"

"Let's just say Ann Richter's neighbors had no trouble recognizing Tanaka's photo. He was seen at her apartment more than once. The night he was killed, I think she went to pay her favorite doctor a little social call. Instead she found something that scared the hell out of her. Maybe she saw Decker. And he saw her."

"Then why didn't she go to the police?" asked Kate.

"Maybe she didn't want the world to know she was having an affair with a married man. Or maybe she was afraid she'd be accused of killing her lover. Who knows?"

"So she was just a witness," said Kate. "Like me."

Pokie looked at her. "There's one big difference between you and her. Decker can't get to *you.* Right now no one outside this office knows where you're staying. Let's keep it that way." He glanced at David. "There's no problem, keeping her at your house?"

David's face was unreadable. "She can stay."

"Good. And it's better if she doesn't use her own car."

"My car?" Kate frowned. "Why not?"

"Decker has your purse. And a set of your car keys. So he knows you drive an Audi. He'll be watching for one."

Watching for me, she thought with a shudder. "For how long?" she whispered.

"What?"

"How long before it's all over? Before I have my life back?"

Pokie sighed. "It might take a while to find him. But hang in there, Doc. The man can't hide forever."

Can't he? wondered Kate. She thought of all the places a man could hide on Oahu: the nooks and crannies of Chinatown where no one ever asks questions. The tin-roofed fishing shacks of Sand Island. The concrete alleys of Waikiki. Somewhere, in some secret place, Charlie Decker was quietly mourning for a dead woman.

They rose to leave and a question suddenly came to her mind. "Lieutenant," she asked. "What about Ellen O'Brien?"

Pokie, who was gathering a pile of papers into a folder, glanced up. "What about her?"

"Does she have some connection to all this?"

Pokie looked down one last time at Charlie Decker's photo. Then he shut the folder. "No," he answered. "No connection at all."

"But there *has* to be a connection!" Kate blurted as they walked out of the station into the midmorning heat. "Some piece of evidence he hasn't found—"

"Or won't tell us about," finished David.

She frowned at him. "Why wouldn't he? I thought you two were friends."

"I deserted the trenches, remember?"

"You make police work sound like jungle warfare."

"For some cops, the job *is* a war. A holy war. Pokie's got

a wife and four kids. But you'd never know it, looking at all the hours he puts in.''

''So you do think he's a good cop?''

David shrugged. ''He's a plough horse. Solid but not brilliant. I've seen him screw up on occasion. He could be wrong this time, too. But right now I have to agree with him. I don't see how Ellen O'Brien fits into this case.''

''But you heard what he said! Decker was a corpsman. Assistant to the ship's surgeon—''

''Decker's profile doesn't fit the pattern, Kate. A psycho who works like Jack the Ripper doesn't bother with drug vials and EKGs. That takes a totally different kind of mind.''

She stared down the street in frustration. ''The trouble is, I can't see any way to prove Ellen *was* murdered. I can't even be sure it's possible.''

David paused on the sidewalk. ''Okay.'' He sighed. ''So we can't prove anything. But let's think about the logistics.''

''You mean of murder?''

He nodded. ''Let's take a man like Decker. An outsider. Someone who knows a little about medicine. And surgery. Tell me, step by step. How would he go about getting into the hospital and killing a patient?''

''I suppose he'd have to…to…'' Her gaze wandered up the street. She frowned as her eyes focused on a paperboy, waving the morning edition to passing cars. ''Today's Sunday,'' she said suddenly.

''So?''

''Ellen was admitted on a Sunday. I remember being in her room, talking to her. It was eight o'clock on a Sunday night.'' She glanced feverishly at her watch. ''That's in ten hours. We could go through the steps.…''

''Wait a minute. You've lost me. What, exactly, are we doing in ten hours?''

She turned to him. Softly she said, ''Murder.''

The visitor parking lot was nearly empty when David swung his BMW into the hospital driveway at ten o'clock that night. He parked in a stall near the lobby entrance, turned off the engine and looked at Kate. "This won't prove a thing. You know that, don't you?"

"I want to see if it's possible."

"Possibilities don't hold up in court."

"I don't care how it plays in court, David. As long as *I* know it's possible."

She glanced out at the distant red Emergency sign, glowing like a beacon in the darkness. An ambulance was parked at the loading dock. On a nearby bench, the driver sat idly smoking a cigarette and listening to the crackle of his dispatch radio.

A Sunday night, quiet as usual. Visiting hours were over. And in their rooms, patients would already be settling into the blissful sleep of the drugged.

David's face gleamed faintly in the shadows. "Okay." He sighed, shoving open his door. "Let's do it."

The lobby doors were locked. They walked in the E.R. entrance, through a waiting room where a baby screamed in the lap of its glassy-eyed mother, where an old man coughed noisily into a handkerchief and a teenage boy clutched an ice bag to his swollen face. The triage nurse was talking on the telephone; they walked right past her and headed for the elevators.

"We're in, just like that?" David asked.

"The E.R. nurse knows me."

"But she hardly looked at you."

"That's because she was too busy ogling *you*," Kate said dryly.

"Boy, have you got a wild imagination." He paused, glancing around the empty lobby. "Where's Security? Isn't there a guard around?"

"He's probably making rounds."

"You mean there's only one?"

"Hospitals are really pretty boring places, you know," she replied and punched the elevator button. "Besides, it's Sunday."

They rose up to the fourth floor and stepped off into the antiseptic-white corridor. Freshly waxed linoleum gleamed under bright lights. A row of gurneys sat lined up against the wall, as though awaiting a deluge of the wounded. Kate pointed to the double doors marked No Admittance.

"The O.R.'s through there."

"Can we get in?"

She took a few experimental steps forward. The doors automatically slid open. "No problem."

Inside, only a single dim light shone over the reception area. A cup, half filled with lukewarm coffee, sat abandoned on the front desk awaiting its owner's return. Kate pointed to a huge wallboard where the next day's surgery schedule was posted.

"All tomorrow's cases are listed right there," she explained. "One glance will tell you which O.R. the patient will be in, the procedure, the names of the surgeon and anesthesiologist."

"Where was Ellen?"

"The room's right around the corner."

She led him down an unlit hall and opened the door to O.R. 5. Through the shadows they saw the faint gleam of stainless steel. She flicked on the wall switch; the sudden flood of light was almost painful.

"The anesthesia cart's over there."

He went over to the cart and pulled open one of the steel drawers. Tiny glass vials tinkled in their compartments. "Are these drugs always left unlocked?"

"They're worthless on the street. No one would bother to steal any of those. As for the narcotics—" she pointed to a wall cabinet "—we keep them locked in there."

His gaze slowly moved around the room. "So this is where you work. Very impressive. Looks like a set for a sci-fi movie."

She grinned. "Funny. I've always felt right at home in here." She circled the room, affectionately patting the equipment as she moved. "I think it's because I'm the daughter of a tinkerer. Gadgets don't scare me. I actually like playing with all these buttons and dials. But I suppose some people do find it all pretty intimidating.''

''And you've never been intimidated?''

She turned and found he was staring at her. Something about his gaze, about the intensity of those blue eyes, made her fall very still. ''Not by the O.R.,'' she said softly.

It was so quiet she could almost hear her own heartbeat thudding in that stark chamber. For a long time they stared at each other, as though separated by some wide, unbreachable chasm. Then, abruptly, he shifted his attention to the anesthesia cart.

''How long would it take to tamper with one of these drug vials?'' he asked. She had to admire his control. At least he could still speak; she was having trouble finding her own voice.

''He'd—he'd have to empty out the succinylcholine vials. It would probably take less than a minute.''

''As easy as that?''

''As easy as that.'' Her gaze shifted reluctantly to the operating table. ''They're so helpless, our patients. We have absolute control over their lives. I never saw it that way before. It's really rather frightening.''

''So murder in the O.R. isn't that difficult.''

''No,'' she conceded. ''I guess it isn't.''

''What about switching the EKG? How would our killer do that?''

''He'd have to get hold of the patient's chart. And they're all kept on the wards.''

''That sounds tricky. The wards are crawling with nurses.''

''True. But even in this day and age, nurses are still a little intimidated by a white coat. I bet if we put you in uniform, you'd be able to breeze your way right into the nurses' station, no questions asked.''

He cocked his head. ''Want to try it?''

''You mean right now?''

"Sure. Find me a white coat. I've always wanted to play doctor."

It took only a minute to locate a stray coat hanging in the surgeons' locker room. She knew it was Guy Santini's, just by the coffee stains on the front. The size 46 label only confirmed it.

"I didn't know King Kong was on your staff," David grunted, thrusting his arms into the huge sleeves. He buttoned up and stood straight. "What do you think? Are they going to fall down laughing?"

Stepping back, she gave him a critical look. The coat sagged on his shoulders. One side of the collar was turned up. But the truth was, he looked absolutely irresistible. And perversely untouchable. She smoothed down his collar. Just that brief contact, that brushing of her fingers against his neck, seemed to flood her whole arm with warmth.

"You'll do," she said.

"I look that bad?" He glanced down at the coffee stains. "I feel like a slob."

She laughed. "The owner of that particular coat *is* a slob. So don't worry about it. You'll fit right in." As they walked to the elevators, she added, "Just remember to think *doctor*. Get into the right mind-set. You know—brilliant, dedicated, compassionate."

"Don't forget *modest*."

She gave him a slap on the back. "Go get'em, Dr. Kildare."

He stepped into the elevator. "Look, don't vanish on me, okay? If they get suspicious, I'll need you to back me up."

"I'll be waiting in the O.R. Oh, David…one last bit of advice."

"What's that?"

"Don't commit malpractice, Doctor. You might have to sue yourself."

He let out a groan as the doors snapped shut between them. The elevator whined faintly as it descended to the third floor. Then there was silence.

It was a simple test. Even if David was stopped by Security, it would take only a word from Kate to set him free. Nothing could possibly go wrong. But as she headed up the hallway, her uneasiness grew.

Back in O.R. 5, she settled into her usual seat near the head of the table and thought of all the hours she'd spent anchored to this one spot. A very small world. A very safe world.

The sound of a door slapping shut made her glance up. Why was David back so soon? Had there been trouble? She hopped off the stool and pushed into the corridor. There she halted.

Just down the hall, a faint crack of light shone through the door to O.R. 7. She listened for a moment and heard the rattle of cabinets, the squeal of a drawer sliding open.

Someone was rummaging through the supplies. A nurse? Or someone else—someone who didn't belong?

She glanced toward the far end of the corridor—her only route of escape. The reception desk lay around that corner. If she could just get safely past O.R. 7, she could slip out and call Security. She had to decide now; whoever was going through O.R. 7 might proceed to the other rooms. If she didn't move now, she'd be trapped.

Noiselessly she headed down the hall. The slam of a cabinet told her she wouldn't make it. O.R. 7's door suddenly swung open. Panicked, she reeled backward to see Dr. Clarence Avery freeze in the doorway. Something slid out of his hand and the sound of shattering glass seemed to reverberate endlessly in the hall. She took one look at his bloodlessly white face, and her fear instantly turned to concern. For a terrifying moment she thought he'd keel over right then and there of a heart attack.

"Dr.—Dr. Chesne," he stammered weakly. "I—I didn't expect— I mean, I..." Slowly he stared down at his feet; that's when she noticed, through the shadows, the sparkle of glass lying on the floor. He shook his head helplessly. "What...what a mess I've made...."

"It's not that bad," she responded quickly. "Here, I'll help you clean it up."

She flicked on the corridor lights. He didn't move. He just stood there, blinking in the sudden glare. She had never seen him look so old, so frail; the white hair seemed to tremble on his head. She grabbed a handful of paper towels from the scrub sink dispenser and offered him a few sheets, but he still didn't move. So she crouched at his feet and began gathering up the broken glass. He was wearing one blue sock and one white sock. As she reached for one of the shards, she noticed a label was still affixed.

"It's for my dog," he said weakly.

"Excuse me?"

"The potassium chloride. It's for my dog. She's very sick."

Kate looked up at him blankly. "I'm sorry" was all she could think of saying.

He lowered his head. "She needs to be put to sleep. All morning, she's been whimpering. I can't stand listening to it anymore. And she's old, you know. Over ninety in dog years. But it—it seems cruel, taking her to the vet for that. A total stranger. It would terrify her."

Kate rose to her feet. Avery just stood there, clutching the paper towels as if not quite sure what to do with them.

"I'm sure the vet would be gentle," she replied. "You don't have to do it yourself."

"But it's so much better if I do, don't you think? If I'm the one to tell her goodbye?"

She nodded. Then she turned to the anesthesia cart and took out a vial of potassium chloride. "Here—" She offered quietly, placing it in his hand. "This should be enough, don't you think?"

He nodded. "She's not a very…big dog." He let out a shaky breath and turned to leave. Then he stopped and looked back at her. "I've always liked you, Kate. You're the only one who never seemed to be laughing behind my back. Or dropping hints that I'm too old, that I ought to retire." He sighed and shook his head. "But maybe they're right, after all." As he turned to leave, she heard him say, "I'll do what I can at your hearing."

His footsteps creaked off into the corridor. As the sound faded away, her gaze settled on the bits of broken glass in the trash can. The label KCL stared up at her. Potassium chloride, she thought with a frown. When pushed intravenously, it was a deadly poison, resulting in sudden cardiac arrest. And it occurred to her that the same poison that would kill a dog could just as easily be used to kill a human being.

The clerk on ward 3B was hunched at her desk, clutching a paperback book. On the cover, a half-naked couple grappled beneath the blazing scarlet title: *His Wanton Bride*. She flipped a page. Her eyes widened. She didn't even notice David walk by. Only when he was standing right beside her in the nurses' station did she bother to glance up. Instantly flushing, she slapped down the book.

"Oh! Can I help you, Doctor…uh…"

"Smith," finished David and flashed her such a dazzling smile that she sank like melted jelly into her chair. *Wow,* he thought as he gazed into a pair of rapturous violet eyes. *This white coat really does the trick.* "I need to see one of your charts," he said.

"Which one?" she asked breathlessly.

"Room…er…" He glanced over at the chart rack. "Eight."

"A or B?"

"B."

"Mrs. Loomis?"

"Yes, that's the name. Loomis."

She seemed to float out of her chair. Swaying over to the chart rack, she struck a pose of slinky indifference. It took her an inordinately long time to locate Room 8B's chart, despite the fact it was staring her right in the face. David glanced down at the book cover and suddenly felt like laughing.

"Here it is," she chirped, holding it out to him in both hands, like some sort of sacred offering.

"Why, thank you, Ms...."

"Mann. Janet. Miss."

"Yes." He cleared his throat. Then, turning, he fled to a chair as far away as possible from Miss Janet Mann. He could almost hear her sigh of disappointment as she turned to answer a ringing telephone.

"Oh, all right." She sighed. "I'll bring them down right now." She grabbed a handful of red-stoppered blood tubes from the pickup tray and hurried out, leaving David alone in the station.

So that's all there is to it, he thought, flipping open the metal chart cover. The unfortunate Mrs. Loomis in room 8B was obviously a complicated case, judging by the thickness of her record and the interminable list of doctors on her case. Not only did she have a surgeon and anesthesiologist, there were numerous consultation notes by an internist, psychiatrist, dermatologist and gynecologist. He was reminded of the old saying about too many cooks. Like the proverbial broth, this poor lady didn't have a chance.

A nurse walked past, wheeling a medication cart. Another nurse slipped in for a moment to answer the ringing telephone then hurried out again. Neither woman paid him the slightest attention.

He flipped to the EKG, which was filed at the back of the chart. It would take maybe ten seconds to remove that one page and replace it with another. And with so many doctors passing through the ward—six for Mrs. Loomis alone—no one would notice a thing.

Murder, he decided, couldn't be easier. All it took was a white coat.

9

_____

"I guess you proved your point tonight," said David as he set two glasses of hot milk on the kitchen table. "About murder in the O.R."

"No, we didn't." Kate looked down bleakly at the steaming glass. "We didn't prove a thing, David. Except that the chief of anesthesia's got a sick dog." She sighed. "Poor old Avery. I must have scared the wits out of him."

"Sounds like you scared the wits out of each other. By the way, does he have a dog?"

"He wouldn't lie to me."

"I'm just asking. I don't know the man." He took a sip of milk and it left a faint white mustache on his stubbled lip. He seemed dark and out of place in his gleaming kitchen. A faint beard shadowed his jaw, and his shirt, which had started out so crisp this morning, was now mapped with wrinkles. He'd undone his top button and she felt a peculiar sense of weightlessness as she caught a glimpse of dark gold hair matting his chest.

She looked down fiercely at her milk. "I'm pretty sure he does have a dog," she continued. "In fact, I remember seeing a picture on his desk."

"He keeps a picture of a dog on his desk?"

"It's of his wife, really. She's holding this sort of brownish terrier. She was really very beautiful."

"I take it you mean his wife."

"Yes. She had a stroke a few months ago. It devastated that poor man, to put her in a nursing home. He's been shuffling through his duties ever since.'' Mournfully she took a sip. ''I bet he couldn't do it.''

''Do what?''

''Kill his dog. Some people are incapable of hurting a fly.''

''While others are perfectly capable of murder.''

She looked at him. ''You still think it *was* murder?''

He didn't answer for a moment, and his silence frightened her. Was her only ally slipping away? ''I don't know what I think.'' He sighed. ''So far I've been going on instinct, not facts. And that won't hold up in a courtroom.''

''Or a committee hearing,'' she added morosely.

''Your hearing's on Tuesday?''

''And I still haven't the faintest idea what to tell them.''

''Can't you get a delay? I'll cancel my appointments tomorrow. Maybe we can pull together some evidence.''

''I've already asked for a delay. It was turned down. Anyway, there doesn't seem to *be* any evidence. All we have is a pair of murders, with no obvious connection to Ellen's death.''

He sat back, frowning at the table. ''What if the police are barking up the wrong tree? What if Charlie Decker's just a wild card?''

''They found his fingerprints, David. And I saw him there.''

''But you didn't actually see him kill anyone.''

''No. But who else had a motive?''

''Let's think about this for a minute.'' Idly, David reached for the saltshaker and set it in the center of the table. ''We know Henry Tanaka was a very busy man. And I'm not talking about his practice. He was having an affair—'' David moved the pepper shaker next to the salt ''—probably with Ann Richter.''

''Okay. But where does Ellen fit in?''

''That's the million-dollar question.'' He reached over and tapped the sugar jar. ''Where does Ellen O'Brien fit in?''

Kate frowned. ''A love triangle?''

''Possible. But a man doesn't have to stop at one mistress.

He could've had a dozen. And they each in turn could have had jealous lovers.''

"Triangles within triangles? This sounds wilder by the minute. All this romping around in bedrooms! Doctors having affairs left and right! I just can't picture it.''

"It happens. And not just in hospitals.''

"Law offices too, hmm?''

"I'm not saying *I've* done it. But we're all human.''

She couldn't help smiling. "It's funny. When we first met, I didn't think of you as being particularly human.''

"No?''

"You were a threat. The enemy. Just another damn lawyer.''

"Oh. Scum of the earth, you mean.''

"You did play the part well.''

He winced. "Thanks a lot.''

"But it's not that way anymore,'' she said quickly. "I can't think of you as just another lawyer. Not since…''

Her voice faded as their eyes suddenly locked.

"Not since I kissed you,'' he finished softly.

Warmth flooded her cheeks. Abruptly she rose to her feet and carried the glass to the sink, all the time aware of his gaze on her back. "It's all gotten so complicated,'' she commented with a sigh.

"What? The fact I'm human?''

"The fact we're *both* human,'' she blurted out. Even without looking at him, she could sense the attraction, the electricity, crackling between them.

She washed the glass. Twice. Then, calmly, deliberately, she sat back down at the table. He was watching her, a wry look of amusement on his face.

"I'll be the first to admit it,'' he said, his eyes twinkling. "It *is* a hell of an inconvenience, being human. A slave to all those pesky biological urges.''

Biological urges. What a hopelessly pale description of the hormonal storm now raging inside her. Avoiding his gaze, she focused on the saltshaker, sitting at the center of the table.

She thought suddenly of Henry Tanaka. Of triangles within triangles. Had all those deaths been a consequence of nothing more than lust and jealousy gone berserk?

"You're right," she agreed, thoughtfully touching the salt-shaker. "Being human leads to all sorts of complications. Even murder."

She sensed his tension before he even spoke a word. His gaze fell on the table and all at once he went completely still. "I can't believe we didn't think of it."

"Of what?" she asked.

He shoved his empty glass toward the sugar jar. It gave the diagram a fourth corner. "We're not dealing with a triangle. It's a *square*."

There was a pause. "Your grasp of geometry is really quite amazing," she said politely.

"What if Tanaka *did* have a second girlfriend—Ellen O'Brien?"

"That's our old triangle."

"But we've left someone out. Someone very important." He tapped the empty milk glass.

Kate frowned at the four objects on the table. "My God," she whispered. "Mrs. Tanaka."

"Exactly."

"I never even thought of his wife."

He looked up. "Maybe it's time we did."

The japanese woman who opened the clinic door was wearing fire-engine-red lipstick and face powder that was several shades too pale for her complexion. She looked like a fugitive from a geisha house. "Then you're not with the police?" she asked.

"Not exactly," replied David. "But we do have a few questions—"

"I'm not talking to any more reporters." She started to shut the door.

"We're not reporters, Mrs. Tanaka. I'm an attorney. And this is Dr. Kate Chesne."

"Well, what do you want, then?"

"We're trying to get information about another murder. It's related to your husband's death."

Sudden interest flickered in the woman's eyes. "You're talking about that nurse, aren't you? That Richter woman."

"Yes."

"What do you know about her?"

"We'll be glad to tell you everything we know. If you'll just let us come in."

She hesitated, curiosity and caution waging a battle in her eyes. Curiosity won. She opened the door and gestured for them to come into the waiting room. She was tall for a Japanese; taller, even, than Kate. She was wearing a simple blue dress and high heels and gold seashell earrings. Her hair was so black it might have looked artificial had there not been the single white strand tracing her right temple. Mari Tanaka was a remarkably beautiful woman.

"You'll have to excuse the mess," she apologized, pausing in the impeccably neat waiting room. "But there's been so much confusion. So many things to take care of." She gazed around at the deserted couches, as though wondering where all the patients had gone. Magazines were still arrayed on the coffee table and a box of children's toys sat in the corner, waiting to be played with. The only hint that tragedy had struck this office was the sympathy card and a vase of white lilies, sent by a grieving patient. Through a glass partition in front of the reception desk, two women could be seen in the adjoining office, surrounded by stacks of files.

"There are so many patients to be referred," said Mrs. Tanaka with a sigh. "And all those outstanding bills. I had no idea things would be so chaotic. I always let Henry take care of everything. And now that he's gone…" She sank tiredly onto the couch. "I take it you know about my husband and that—that woman."

David nodded. "Did you?"

"Yes. I mean, I didn't know her name. But I knew there had to be someone. Funny, isn't it? How they say the wife is always the last to know." She gazed at the two women behind the glass partition. "I'm sure *they* knew about her. And people at the hospital, they must have known, as well. I was the only one who didn't. The *stupid* wife." She looked up. "You said you'd tell me about this woman. Ann Richter. What do you know about her?"

"I worked with her," Kate began.

"Did you?" Mrs. Tanaka shifted her gaze to Kate. "I never even met her. What was she like? Was she pretty?"

Kate hesitated, knowing instinctively that the other woman was only searching for more information with which to torture herself. Mari Tanaka seemed consumed by some bizarre need for self-punishment. "Ann was…attractive, I suppose," she said.

"Intelligent?"

Kate nodded. "She was a good nurse."

"So was I." Mrs. Tanaka bit her lip and looked away. "She was a blonde, I hear. Henry liked blondes. Isn't that ironic? He liked the one thing I couldn't be." She glanced at David with sudden feminine hostility. "And I suppose *you* like Oriental women."

"A beautiful woman is a beautiful woman," he replied, unruffled. "I don't discriminate."

She blinked back a veil of tears. "Henry did."

"Have there been other women?" Kate asked gently.

"I suppose." She shrugged. "He was a man, wasn't he?"

"Did you ever hear the name Ellen O'Brien?"

"Did she have some…connection with my husband?"

"We were hoping you could tell us."

Mrs. Tanaka shook her head. "He never mentioned any names. But then, I never asked any questions."

Kate frowned. "Why not?"

"I didn't want him to lie to me." Somehow, by the way she said it, it made perfect sense.

"Have the police told you there's a suspect?" David asked.

"You mean Charles Decker?" Mrs. Tanaka's gaze shifted

back to David. "Sergeant Brophy came to see me yesterday afternoon. He showed me the man's photograph."

"Did you recognize the face?"

"I never saw the man, Mr. Ransom. I didn't even know his name. All I knew was that my husband was attacked by some psychotic five years ago. And that the stupid police let the man go the very next day."

"But your husband refused to press charges," said David.

"He what?"

"That's why Decker was released so quickly. It seems your husband wanted the matter dropped."

"He never told me that."

"What did he tell you?"

"Almost nothing. But there were lots of things we never talked about. That's how we managed to stay together all these years. By not talking about certain things. It was almost an agreement. He didn't ask how I spent the money. I didn't ask about his women."

"Then you don't know anything more about Decker?"

"No. But maybe Peggy can help you."

"Peggy?"

She nodded toward the office. "Our receptionist. She was here when it happened."

Peggy was a blond, fortyish Amazon wearing white stretch pants. Though invited to sit, she preferred to stand. Or maybe she simply preferred not to occupy the same couch as Mari Tanaka.

"Remember the man?" Peggy repeated. "I'll never forget him. I was cleaning up one of the exam rooms when I heard all this yelling. I came right out and that psychotic was here, in the waiting room. He had his hands around Henry's—the doctor's—neck and he kept screaming at him."

"You mean cursing him?"

"No, not cursing. He said something like 'What did you do with her?'"

"Those were his words? You're sure?"

"Pretty sure."

"And who was this 'her' he was referring to? One of the patients?"

"Yes. And the doctor felt just awful about that case. She was such a nice woman, and to have both her and the baby die. Well…"

"What was her name?"

"Jenny… Let me think. Jenny something. Brook. I think that was it. Jennifer Brook."

"What did you do after you saw the doctor being attacked?"

"Well, I pulled the man away, of course. What do you think I did? He was holding on tight, but I got him off. Women aren't completely helpless, you know."

"Yes, I'm quite aware of that."

"Anyway, he sort of collapsed then."

"The doctor?"

"No, the man. He crumpled in this little heap over there, by the coffee table and he just sat there, crying. He was still there when the police arrived. A few days later, we heard he'd shot himself. In the mouth." She paused and stared at the floor, as though seeing some ghostlike remnant of the man, still sitting there. "It's weird, but I couldn't help feeling sorry for him. He was crying like a baby. I think even Henry felt sorry.…"

"Mrs. Tanaka?" The other clerk poked her head into the waiting room. "You have a phone call. It's your accountant. I'll transfer it to the back office."

Mrs. Tanaka rose. "There's really nothing more we can tell you," she said. "And we do have to get back to work." She shot Peggy a meaningful glance. Then, with only the barest nod of goodbye, she walked sleekly out of the waiting room.

"Two weeks' notice," Peggy muttered sullenly. "That's what she gave us. And then she expects us to get the whole damn office in order. No wonder Henry didn't want that witch hanging around." She turned to go back to her desk.

"Peggy?" asked Kate. "Just one more question, if you

don't mind. When your patients die, how long do you keep the medical records?''

"Five years. Longer if it's an obstetrical death. You know, in case some malpractice suit gets filed.''

"Then you still have Jenny Brook's chart?''

"I'm sure we do.'' She went into the office and pulled open the filing cabinet. She went through the B drawer twice. Then she checked the J's. In frustration, she slammed the drawer closed. "I can't understand it. It should be here.''

David and Kate glanced at each other. "It's missing?'' said Kate.

"Well, it's not here. And I'm very careful about these things. Let me tell you, I do not run a sloppy office.'' She turned and glared at the other clerk as though expecting a dissenting opinion. There was none.

"What are you saying?'' said David. "That someone's removed it?''

"He must have,'' replied Peggy. "But I can't see why he would. It's barely been five years.''

"Why *who* would?''

Peggy looked at him as if he was dim-witted. "Dr. Tanaka, of course.''

"Jennifer Brook,'' said the hospital records clerk in a flat voice as she typed the name into the computer. "Is that with or without an *e* at the end?''

"I don't know,'' answered Kate.

"Middle initial?''

"I don't know.''

"Date of birth?''

Kate and David looked at each other. "We don't know,'' replied Kate.

The clerk turned and peered at them over her horn-rimmed glasses. "I don't suppose you'd know the medical-record number?'' she asked in a weary monotone.

They shook their heads.

"That's what I was afraid of.'' The clerk swiveled back

to her terminal and punched in another command. After a few seconds, two names appeared on the screen, a Brooke and a Brook, both with the first name Jennifer. "Is it one of these?" she questioned.

A glance at the dates of birth told them one was fifty-seven years old, the other fifteen.

"No," said Kate.

"It figures." The clerk sighed and cleared the screen. "Dr. Chesne," she continued with excruciating patience, "why, exactly, do you need this particular record?"

"It's a research project," Kate said. "Dr. Jones and I—"

"Dr. Jones?" The clerk looked at David. "I don't remember a Dr. Jones on our staff."

Kate said quickly, "He's with the University—"

"Of Arizona," David finished with a smile.

"It's all been cleared through Avery's office. It's a paper on maternal death and—"

"Death?" The clerk blinked. "You mean this patient is deceased?"

"Yes."

"Well, no wonder. We keep those files in a totally different place." From her tone, their other file room might have been on Mars. She rose reluctantly from her chair. "This will take a while. You'll have to wait." Turning, she headed at a snail's pace toward a back door and vanished into what was no doubt the room for deceased persons' files.

"Why do I get the feeling we'll never see her again?" muttered David.

Kate sagged weakly against the counter. "Just be glad she didn't ask for your credentials. I could get in big trouble for this, you know. Showing hospital records to the enemy."

"Who, me?"

"You're a lawyer, aren't you?"

"I'm just poor old Dr. Jones from Arizona." He turned and glanced around the room. At a corner table, a doctor was yawning as he turned a page. An obviously bored clerk wheeled a cart up the aisle, collecting charts and slapping them onto an already precarious stack. "Lively place," he remarked. "When does the dancing start?"

They both turned at the sound of footsteps. The clerk with the horn-rimmed glasses reappeared, empty-handed.

"The chart's not there," she announced.

Kate and David stared at her in stunned silence.

"What do you mean, it's not there?" asked Kate.

"It should be. But it's not."

"Was it released from the hospital?" David snapped.

The clerk looked aridly over her glasses. "We don't release originals, Dr. Jones. People always lose them."

"Oh. Well, of course."

The clerk sank down in front of the computer and typed in a command. "See? There's the listing. It's supposed to be in the file room. All I can say is it must've been misplaced." She added, under her breath, "Which means we'll probably never see it again." She was about to clear the screen when David stopped her.

"Wait. What's that notation there?" he asked, pointing to a cryptic code.

"That's a chart copy request."

"You mean someone requested a copy?"

"Yes," the clerk sighed wearily. "That is what it means, Doctor."

"Who asked for it?"

She shifted the cursor and punched another button. A name and address appeared magically on the screen. "Joseph Kahanu, Attorney at Law, Alakea Street. Date of request: March 2."

David frowned. "That's only a month ago."

"Yes, Doctor, I do believe it is."

"An attorney. Why the hell would he be interested in a death that happened five years ago?"

The clerk turned and looked at him dryly over her horn-rimmed glasses. "You tell me."

The paint in the hall was chipping and thousands of footsteps had worn a path down the center of the threadbare carpet. Outside the office hung a sign:

Joseph Kahanu, Attorney at Law
Specialist in Divorce, Child Custody, Wills, Accidents,
Insurance, Drunk Driving, and Personal Injury

"Great address," whispered David. "Rats must outnumber the clients." He knocked on the door.

It was answered by a huge Hawaiian man dressed in an ill-fitting suit. "You're David Ransom?" he asked gruffly.

David nodded. "And this is Dr. Chesne."

The man's silent gaze shifted for a moment to Kate's face. Then he stepped aside and gestured sullenly toward a pair of rickety chairs. "Yeah, come in."

The office was suffocating. A table fan creaked back and forth, churning the heat. A half-open window, opaque with dirt, looked out over an alley. In one glance, Kate recognized all the signs of a struggling law practice: the ancient typewriter, the cardboard boxes stuffed with client files, the secondhand furniture. There was scarcely enough room for the lone desk. Kahanu looked unbearably hot in his suit jacket; he'd probably pulled it on at the last minute, just for the benefit of his visitors.

"I haven't called the police yet," said Kahanu, settling into an unreliable-looking swivel chair.

"Why not?" asked David.

"I don't know how you run *your* practice, but I make it a point not to squeal on my clients."

"You're aware Decker's wanted for murder."

Kahanu shook his head. "It's a mistake."

"Did Decker tell you that?"

"I haven't been able to reach him."

"Maybe it's time the police found him for you."

"Look," Kahanu shot back. "We both know I'm not in your league, Ransom. I hear you got some big-shot office over on Bishop Street. Couple of dozen lapdog associates. Probably spend your weekends on the golf course, cozying up to some judge or other. Me?'' He waved around at his office and laughed. ''I got just a few clients. Most times they don't even remember to pay me. But they're my clients. And I don't like to go against 'em.''

''You know two people have been murdered.''

''They got no proof he did it.''

''The police say they do. They say Charlie Decker's a dangerous man. A sick man. He needs help.''

''That what they call a jail cell these days? Help?'' Disgusted, he fished out a handkerchief and mopped his brow, as though buying time to think. ''Guess I got no choice now,'' he muttered. ''One way or the other, police'll be banging on my door.'' Slowly he folded the handkerchief and tucked it back in his pocket. Then, reaching into his drawer, he pulled out a folder and tossed it on the battered desk. ''There's the copy you asked for. Seems you're not the only who one wants it.''

David frowned as he reached for the folder. ''Has someone else asked for it?''

''No. But someone broke into my office.''

David looked up sharply. ''When?''

''Last week. Tore apart all my files. Didn't steal anything, and I even had fifty bucks in the cash box. I couldn't figure it out at the time. But this morning, after you told me about those missing records, I got to thinking. Wondering if that file's what he was after.''

''But he didn't get it.''

''The night he broke in, I had the papers at home.''

''Is this your only copy?''

''No. I ran off a few just now. Just to be safe.''

''May I take a look?'' Kate asked.

David hesitated, then handed her the chart. ''You're the doctor. Go ahead.''

She stared for a moment at the name on the cover: Jennifer Brook. Then, flipping it open, she began to read.

Recorded on the first few pages was a routine obstetrical admission. The patient, a healthy twenty-eight-year-old woman at thirty-six weeks of pregnancy, had entered Mid Pac Hospital in the early stages of labor. The initial history and physical exam, performed by Dr. Tanaka, were unremarkable. The fetal heart tones were normal, as were all the blood tests. Kate turned to the delivery-room record.

Here things began to go wrong. Terribly wrong. The nurse's painstakingly neat handwriting broadened into a frantic scrawl. The entries became terse, erratic. A young woman's death was distilled down to a few coldly clinical phrases.

Generalized seizures... No response to Valium and Dilantin... Stat page to E.R. for assistance... Respirations now irregular... Respirations ceased... No pulse... Cardiac massage started... Fetal heart tones audible but slowing... Still no pulse... Dr. Vaughn from E.R. to assist with stat C-section...
Live infant...

The record became a short series of blotted-out sentences, totally unreadable.

On the next page was the last entry, written in a calm hand.

Resuscitation stopped. Patient pronounced dead at 01: 30.

"She died of a cerebral hemorrhage," Kahanu said. "She was only twenty-eight."

"And the baby?" Kate asked.

"A girl. She died an hour after the mother."

"Kate," David murmured, nudging her arm. "Look at the bottom of the page. The names of the personnel in attendance."

Kate's gaze dropped to the three names. As she took them in one by one, her hands went icy.

Henry Tanaka, M.D.
Ann Richter, RN
Ellen O'Brien, RN

"They left out a name," Kate pointed out. She looked up. "There was a Dr. Vaughn, from the E.R. He might be able to tell us—"

"He can't," said Kahanu. "You see, Dr. Vaughn had an accident a short time after Jennifer Brook died. His car was hit head-on."

"You mean he's dead?"

Kahanu nodded. "They're all dead."

The chart slid from her frozen fingers onto the desk. There was something dangerous about this document, something evil. She stared down, unwilling to touch it, for fear the contagion would rub off.

Kahanu turned his troubled gaze to the window. "Four weeks ago Charlie Decker came to my office. Who knows why he chose me? Maybe I was convenient. Maybe he couldn't afford anyone else. He wanted a legal opinion about a possible malpractice suit."

"On this case?" said David. "But Jenny Brook died five years ago. And Decker wasn't even a relative. You know as well as I do the lawsuit would've been tossed right out."

"He paid for my services, Mr. Ransom. In cash."

In cash. Those were magic words for a lawyer who was barely surviving.

"I did what he asked. I subpoenaed the chart for him. I contacted the doctor and the two nurses who'd cared for Jenny Brook. But they never answered my letters."

"They didn't live long enough," explained David. "Decker got to them first."

"Why should he?"

"Vengeance. They killed the woman he loved. So he killed them."

"My client didn't kill anyone."

"Your client had the motive, Kahanu. And you provided him with their names and addresses."

"You've never met Decker. I have. And he's not a violent man."

"You'd be surprised how ordinary a killer can seem. I used to face them in court—"

"And I *defend* them! I take on the scum no one else'll touch. I *know* a killer when I see one. There's something different about them, about their eyes. Something's missing. I don't know what it is. A soul, maybe. I tell you, Charlie Decker wasn't like that."

Kate leaned forward. "What was he like, Mr. Kahanu?" she asked quietly.

The Hawaiian paused, his gaze wandering out the dirty window to the alley below. "He was—he was real... ordinary. Not tall, but not too short, either. Mostly skin and bones, like he wasn't eating right. I felt sorry for him. He looked like a man who's had his insides kicked out. He didn't say much. But he wrote things down for me. I think it hurt him to use his voice. He's got something wrong with his throat and he couldn't talk much louder than a whisper. He was sitting right there in that chair where you are now, Dr. Chesne. Said he didn't have much money. Then he took out his wallet and counted out these twenty-dollar bills, one at a time. I could see, just by the way he handled them, real slow and careful, that it was everything he had." Kahanu shook his head. "I still don't see why he even bothered, you know? The woman's dead. The baby's dead. All this digging around in the past, it won't bring 'em back."

"Do you know where to find him?" asked David.

"He has a P.O. box," said Kahanu. "I already checked. He hasn't picked up his mail in three days."

"Do you have his address? Phone number?"

"Never gave me one. Look, I don't know where he is. I'll

leave it to the police to find him. That's their job, isn't it?''
He pushed away from the desk. ''That's all I know. If you
want anything else, you'll have to get it from Decker.''

''Who happens to be missing,'' said David.

To which Kahanu added darkly: ''Or dead.''

10

In his forty-eight years as cemetery groundskeeper, Ben Hoomalu had seen his share of peculiar happenings. His friends liked to say it was because he was tramping around dead people all day, but in fact it wasn't the dead who caused all the mischief but the living: the randy teenagers groping in the darkness among the gravestones; the widow scrawling obscenities on her husband's nice new marble tombstone; the old man caught trying to bury his beloved poodle next to his beloved wife. Strange goings-on—that's what a fellow saw around cemeteries.

And now here was that car, back again.

Every day for the past week Ben had seen the same gray Ford with the darkly tinted windows drive through the gates. Sometimes it'd show up early in the morning, other times late in the afternoon. It would park over by the Arch of Eternal Comfort and just sit there for an hour or two. The driver never got out; that was odd, too. If a person came all this way to visit a loved one, wouldn't you think he'd at least get out and take a look at the grave?

There was no figuring out some folks.

Ben picked up the hedge clippers and started trimming the hibiscus bush. He liked hearing the clack, clack of the blades in the afternoon stillness. He looked up as a beat-up old Chevy drove through the gate and parked. A spindly man emerged from the car and waved at Ben. Smiling, Ben waved back. The man was carrying a bunch of daisies as he headed toward the woman's grave. Ben paused and watched the man go about his ritual. First, he gathered up the wilted flowers left behind on his previous visit and meticulously collected all the dead leaves and twigs. Then, after laying his new offering beside the stone, he settled reverentially on the grass. Ben knew the man would sit there a long time; he always did. Every visit was exactly the same. That was part of the comfort.

By the time the man got up to leave, Ben had finished with the hibiscus and was working on the bougainvillea. He watched the man walk slowly back to the car and felt a twinge of sadness as the old Chevy wound along the road toward the cemetery gates. He didn't even know the man's name; he only knew that whoever lay buried in that grave was still very much loved. He dropped his hedge clippers and wandered over to where the fresh daisies lay bundled together in a pink ribbon. There was still a dent in the grass where the man had knelt.

The purr of another car starting up caught his attention and he saw the gray Ford pull away from the curb and slowly follow the Chevy out the cemetery gates.

And what did *that* mean? Funny goings-on, all right.

He looked down at the name on the stone: Jennifer Brook, 28 years old. Already a dead leaf had blown onto the grave and now lay trembling in the wind. He shook his head.

Such a young woman. Such a shame.

"You got a ham on rye, hold the mayo, and a call on line four," said Sergeant Brophy, dropping a brown bag on the desk.

Pokie, faced with the choice between a sandwich and a blinking telephone, reached for the sandwich. After all, a man had to set his priorities, and he figured a growling stomach ranked somewhere near the top of anyone's priority list. He nodded at the phone. "Who's calling?"

"Ransom."

"Not again."

"He's demanding we open a file on the O'Brien case."

"Why the hell's he keep bugging us about that case, anyway?"

"I think he's got a thing for that—that—" Brophy's face suddenly screwed up as he teetered on the brink of a sneeze and he whipped out a handkerchief just in time to muffle the explosion "—doctor lady. You know. Hearts 'n' flowers."

"Davy?" Pokie laughed out a clump of ham sandwich. "Men like Davy don't go for hearts 'n' flowers. Think they're too damn smart for all that romantic crap."

"No man's that smart," Brophy said glumly.

There was a knock on the door and a uniformed officer poked his head into the office. "Lieutenant? You got a summons from on high."

"Chief?"

"He's stuck with an office full of reporters. They're askin' about that missing Sasaki girl. Wants ya up there like ten minutes ago."

Pokie looked down regretfully at his sandwich. Unfortunately, on that cosmic list of priorities, a summons from the chief ranked somewhere on a par with breathing. Sighing, he left the sandwich on his desk and pulled on his jacket.

"What about Ransom?" reminded Brophy, nodding at the blinking telephone.

"Tell him I'll call him back."

"When?"

"Next year," Pokie grunted as he headed for the door. He added under his breath, "If he's lucky."

David muttered an oath as he slid into the driver's seat and slammed the car door. "We just got the brush-off."

Kate stared at him. "But they've seen Jenny Brook's file. They've talked to Kahanu—"

"They say there's not enough evidence to open a murder investigation. As far as they're concerned, Ellen O'Brien died of malpractice. End of subject."

"Then we're on our own."

"Wrong. We're pulling out." Suddenly agitated, he started

the engine and drove away from the curb. "Things are getting too dangerous."

"They've been dangerous from the start. Why are you getting cold feet now?"

"Okay, I admit it. Up till now I wasn't sure I believed you—"

"You thought I was *lying*?"

"There was always this—this nagging doubt in the back of my mind. But now we're hearing about stolen hospital charts. People breaking into lawyer's offices. There's something weird going on here, Kate. This isn't the work of a raging psychopath. It's too reasoned. Too methodical." He frowned at the road ahead. "And it all has to do with Jenny Brook. There's something dangerous about her hospital chart, something our killer wants to keep hidden."

"But we've gone over that thing a dozen times, David! It's just a medical record."

"Then we're overlooking something. And I'm counting on Charlie Decker to tell us what it is. I say we sit tight and wait for the police to find him."

Charlie Decker, she thought. Her doom or her salvation? She stared out at the late-afternoon traffic and tried to remember his face. Up till now, the image had been jelled in fear; every time she'd thought of his face in the mirror, she'd felt an automatic surge of terror. Now she tried to ignore the sweat forming on her palms, the racing of her pulse. She forced herself to think of that face with its tired, hollow eyes. Killer's eyes? She didn't know anymore. She looked down at Jenny Brook's chart, lying on her lap. Did it contain some vital clue to Decker's madness?

"I'll corner Pokie tomorrow," said David, weaving impatiently through traffic. "See if I can't change his mind about the O'Brien case."

"And if you can't convince him?"

"I'm very convincing."

"He'll want more evidence."

"Then let *him* find it. I think we've gone as far as we can on this. It's time for us to back off."

"I can't, David. I have a career at stake—"

"What about your life?"

"My career is my life."

"There's one helluva big difference."

She turned away. "I can't really expect you to understand. It's not your fight."

But he did understand. And it worried him, that note of stubbornness in her voice. She reminded him of one of those ancient warriors who'd rather fall on their swords than accept defeat.

"You're wrong," he told her. "About it not being my fight."

"You don't have anything at stake."

"Don't forget I pulled out of the case—a potentially lucrative case, I might add."

"Oh. Well, I'm sorry I cost you such a nice fee."

"You think I care about the money? I don't give a damn about the money. It's my reputation I put on the line. And all because I happened to believe that crazy story of yours. Murder on the operating table! I'm going to look like a fool if it can't be proved. So don't tell me I have nothing to lose!" By now he was yelling. He couldn't help it. She could accuse him of any number of things and he wouldn't bat an eye. But accusing him of not giving a damn was something he couldn't stand.

Gripping the steering wheel, he forced his gaze back to the road. "The worst part is," he muttered, "I'm a lousy liar. And I think the O'Briens can tell."

"You mean you didn't tell them the truth?"

"That I think their daughter was murdered? Hell, no. I took the easy way out. I told them I had a conflict of interest. A nice, noncommittal excuse. I figured they couldn't get too upset since I'm referring the case to a good firm."

"You're doing *what*?" She stared at him.

"I was their attorney, Kate. I have to protect their interests."

"Naturally."

"This hasn't been easy, you know," he went on. "I don't like to shortchange my clients. Any of them. They're dealing with enough tragedy in their lives. The least I can do is see they get a decent shot at justice. It bothers the hell out of me when I can't deliver what I promise. You understand that, don't you?"

"Yes. I understand perfectly well."

He knew by the hurt tone of her voice that she really didn't. And that annoyed him because he thought she should understand.

She sat motionless as he pulled into the driveway. He parked the car and turned off the engine but she made no move to get out. They lingered there in the shadowy heat of the garage as the silence between them stretched into minutes. When she finally spoke again, it was in the flat tones of a stranger.

"I've put you in a compromising position, haven't I?"

His answer was a curt nod.

"I'm sorry."

"Look, forget about it, okay?" He got out and opened her door. She was still sitting there, rigid as a statue. "Well?" he asked. "Are you coming inside?"

"Only to pack."

He felt an odd little thump of dismay in his chest, which he tried to ignore. "You're leaving?"

"I appreciate what you've done for me," she answered tightly. "You went out on a limb and you didn't have to. Maybe, at the start, we needed each other. But it's obvious this…arrangement is no longer in your best interests. Or mine, for that matter."

"I see," he said, though he didn't. In fact he thought she was acting childishly. "And just where do you plan to go?"

"I'll stay with friends."

"Oh, great. Spread the danger to them."

"Then I'll check into a hotel."

"Your purse was stolen, remember? You don't have any money, credit cards." He paused for dramatic effect. "No nothing."

"Not at the moment, but—"

"Or are you planning to ask me for a loan?"

"I don't need your help," she snapped. "I've never needed any man's help!"

He briefly considered the old-fashioned method of brute force, but knowing her sense of pride, he didn't think it would work. So he simply retorted, "Suit yourself," and stalked off to the house.

While she was packing, he paced back and forth in the kitchen, trying to ignore his growing sense of uneasiness. He grabbed a carton of milk out of the refrigerator and took a gulp straight from the container. *I should order her to stay,* he thought. *Yes, that's exactly what I should do.* He shoved the milk back in the refrigerator, slammed the door and stormed toward her bedroom.

But just as he got there, he pulled himself up short. Bad idea. He knew exactly how she'd react if he started shouting out orders. You just didn't push a woman like Kate Chesne around. Not if you were smart.

He hulked in the doorway and watched as she folded a dress and tucked it neatly into a suitcase. The fading daylight was glimmering behind her in the window. She swept back a stray lock of hair and a lead weight seemed to lodge in his throat as he glimpsed the bruised cheek. It reminded him how vulnerable she really was. Despite her pride and her so-called independence, she was really just a woman. And like any woman, she could be hurt.

She noticed him in the doorway and she paused, night-gown in hand. "I'm almost finished," she said, matter-of-factly tossing the nightgown on top of the other clothes. He couldn't help glancing twice at the mound of peach-colored silk. He felt that lead weight drop into his belly. "Have you called a cab yet?" she asked, turning back to the dresser.

"No, I haven't."

"Well, I shouldn't be a minute. Could you call one now?"

"I'm not going to."

She turned and frowned at him. "What?"

"I said I'm not going to call a cab."

His announcement seemed to leave her momentarily stunned. "Fine," she said calmly. "Then I'll call one myself." She started for the door. But as she walked past him, he caught her by the arm.

"Kate, don't." He pulled her around to face him. "I think you should stay."

"Why?"

"Because it's not safe out there."

"The world's never been safe. I've managed."

"Oh, yeah. What a tough broad you are. And what happens when Decker catches up?"

She yanked her arm away. "Don't you have better things to worry about?"

"Like what?"

"Your sense of ethics? After all, I wouldn't want to ruin your precious reputation."

"I can take care of my own reputation, thank you."

She threw her head back and glared straight up at him. "Then maybe it's time I took better care of mine!"

They were standing so close he could almost feel the heat mounting in waves between them. What happened next was as unexpected as a case of spontaneous combustion. Their gazes locked. Her eyes suddenly went wide with surprise. And need. Despite all her false bravado, he could see it brimming there in those deep, green pools.

"What the hell," he growled, his voice rough with desire. "I think both our reputations are already shot."

And then he gave in to the impulse that had been battering at his willpower all day. He hauled her close into his arms and kissed her. It was a long and savagely hungry kiss. She gave a weak murmur of protest, just before she sagged backward against the doorway. Almost immediately he felt her respond, her body molding itself against his. It was a perfect fit. Absolutely perfect. Her arms twined around his neck and as he urged her lips apart with his, the kiss became desperately urgent. Her moan sent a sweet agony of desire knifing through to his belly.

The same sweet fire was now engulfing Kate. She felt him fumbling for the buttons of her dress but his fingers seemed as clumsy as a teenager's exploring the unfamiliar territory of a woman's body. With a groan of frustration, he tugged the dress off her shoulders; it seemed to fall in slow motion, hissing down her hips to the floor. The lace bra magically melted away and his hand closed around her breast, branding her flesh with his fingers. Under his pleasuring stroke, her nipple hardened instantly and they both knew that this time there would be no retreat; only surrender.

Already she was groping at his shirt, her breath coming in hot, frantic little whimpers as she tried to work the buttons free. Damn. Damn. Now they were both yanking at the shirt. Together they stripped it off his shoulders and she immediately sought his chest, burying her fingers in the bristling gold hairs.

By the time they'd stumbled down the hall and into the evening glow of his bedroom, his shoes and socks were tossed to the four corners of the room, his pants were unzipped and his arousal was plainly evident.

The bed creaked in protest as he fell on top of her, his hands trapping her face beneath his. There were no preludes, no formalities. They couldn't wait. With his mouth covering hers and his hands buried in her hair, he thrust into her, so deeply that she cried out against his lips.

He froze, his whole body suddenly tense. "Did I hurt you?" he whispered.

"No...oh, no...."

It took only one look at her face to tell him it wasn't pain that had made her cry out, but pleasure—in him, in what he was doing to her. She tried to move; he held her still, his face taut as he struggled for control. Somehow, she'd always known he would claim her. Even when the voice of common sense had told her it was impossible, she'd known he would be the one.

She couldn't wait. She was moving in spite of him, matching agony for agony.

He let her take him to the very brink and then, when he knew it was inevitable, he surrendered himself to the fall. In a frenzy he took control and plunged them both over the cliff.

The drop was dizzying.

The landing left them weak and exhausted. An eternity passed, filled with the sounds of their breathing. Sweat trickled over his back and onto her naked belly. Outside, the waves roared against the seawall.

"Now I know what it's like to be devoured," she whispered as the glow of sunset faded in the window.

"Is that what I did?"

She sighed. "Completely."

He chuckled and his mouth glided warmly to her earlobe. "No, I think there's still something here to eat."

She closed her eyes, surrendering to the lovely ripples of pleasure his mouth inspired. "I never dreamed you'd be like this."

"Like what?"

"So...consuming."

"Just what did you expect?"

"Ice." She laughed. "Was I ever wrong!"

He took a strand of her hair and watched it drift like a cloud of silk through his fingers. "I guess I can seem pretty icy. It runs in my family. My father's side, anyway. Stern old New England stock. It must've been terrifying to face him in court."

"He was a lawyer, too?"

"Circuit-court judge. He died four years ago. Keeled over on the bench, right in the middle of sentencing. Just the way he would've wanted to go." He smiled. "Run-'em-in Ransom, they used to call him."

"Oh. The law-and-order type?"

"Absolutely. Unlike my mother, who thrives on anarchy."

She giggled. "It must have been an explosive combination."

"Oh, it was." He stroked his finger across her lips. "Almost as explosive as we are. I never did figure out their relationship. It didn't make sense to me. But you could almost see the chemistry working between them. The sparks. That's what I remember about my parents, all those sparks, flying around the house."

"So they were happy?"

"Oh, yeah. Exhausted, maybe. Frustrated, a lot. But they were definitely happy."

Twilight glowed dimly through the window. In silent awe, he ran his hand along the peaks and valleys of her body, a slow and leisurely exploration that left her skin tingling. "You're beautiful," he whispered. "I never thought..."

"What?"

"That I'd end up in bed with a lawyer-hating doctor. Talk about strange bedfellows."

She laughed softly. "And I feel like a mouse cozying up to the cat."

"Does that mean you're still afraid of me?"

"A little. A lot."

"Why?"

"I can't quite get over the feeling you're the enemy."

"If I'm the enemy," he said, his lips grazing her ear, "then I think one of us has just surrendered."

"Is this all you ever think about, counselor?"

"Since I met you, it is."

"And before you met me?"

"Life was very, very dull."

"I find that hard to believe."

"I'm not saying I've been celibate. But I'm a careful man. Maybe too careful. I find it hard to...get close to people."

"You seem to be doing a pretty good job tonight."

"I mean, emotionally close. It's just the way I am. Too

many things can go wrong and I'm not very good at dealing with them.''

By the evening glow, she studied his face hovering just above hers. "What did go wrong with your marriage, David?"

"Oh. My marriage." He rolled over on his back and sighed. "Nothing, really. Nothing I can put my finger on. I guess that just goes to show you what an insensitive clod I am. Linda used to complain I was lousy at expressing my feelings. That I was cold, just like my father. I told her that was a lot of bull. Now I think she was right."

"And I think it's just an act of yours. An icy mask you like to hide behind." She rolled onto her side, to look at him. "People show affection in different ways."

"Since when did you go into psychiatry?"

"Since I got involved with a very complex man."

Gently he tucked a strand of hair behind her ear. His gaze lingered on her cheek. "That bruise of yours is already fading. Every time I see it I get angry."

"You told me once it turned you on."

"What it really does is make me feel protective. Must be some ancient male instinct. From the days when we had to keep the other cavemen from roughing up our personal property."

"Oh, my. We're talking *that* ancient, are we?"

"As ancient as—" his hand slid possessively down the curve of her hip "—this."

"I'm not so sure 'protective' is what you're feeling right now," she murmured.

"You're right. It's not." He laughed and gave her an affectionate pat on the rump. "What I'm feeling is starved—for food. Why don't we heat up some of Mrs. Feldman's spaghetti sauce. Open a bottle of wine. And then…" He drew her toward him and his skin seemed to sear right into hers.

"And then?" she whispered.

"And then…" His lips lingered maddeningly close. "I'll

do to you what lawyers have been doing to doctors for decades.''

"David!" she squealed.

"Hey, just kidding!" He threw his arms up in self-defense as she swung at him. "But I think you get the general idea." He pulled her out of bed and into his arms. "Come on. And stop looking so luscious, or we'll never get out of the room. They'll find us sprawled on the bed, starved to death."

She gave him a slow, naughty look. "Oh," she murmured, "but what a way to go."

It was the sound of the waves slapping the seawall that finally tugged Kate awake. Drowsily she reached out for David but her hand met only an empty pillow, warmed by the morning sun. She opened her eyes and felt a sharp sense of abandonment when she discovered that she was alone in the wide, rumpled bed.

"David?" she called out. There was no answer. The house was achingly silent.

She swung her legs around and sat up on the side of the bed. Naked and dazed, she peered slowly around the sunlit room and felt the color rise in her cheeks as the night's events came back to her. The bottle of wine. The wicked whispers. The hopelessly twisted sheets. She noticed that the clothes they'd both tossed aside so recklessly had all been picked up from the floor. His pants were hanging on the closet door; her bra and underwear were now draped neatly across a chair. It made her flush even hotter to think of him gathering up all her intimate apparel. Giggling, she hugged the sheets and found they still bore his scent. But where was he?

"David?"

She rose and went into the bathroom; it was empty. A damp towel hung on the rack. Next she wandered out into the living room and marveled at the morning sun, slanting in gloriously through the windows. The empty wine bottle was still sitting on the coffee table, mute evidence of the night's intoxication. She still felt intoxicated. She poked her head into the kitchen; he wasn't there, either. Back in the living room, she paused in that brilliant flood of sunlight and called out his name. The whole house seemed to echo with loneliness.

Her sense of desolation grew as she headed back up the hall, searching, opening doors, peeking into rooms. She had the strange feeling that she was exploring an abandoned house, that this wasn't the home of a living, breathing human being, but a shell, a cave. An inexplicable impulse sent her to his closet where she stood and touched each one of those forbidding suits hanging inside. It brought him no closer to her. Back in the hallway, she opened the door to a book-lined office. The furniture was oak, the lamps brass, and everything was as neat as a pin. A room without a soul.

Kate moved down the hall, to the very last room. She was prying, she knew it. But she missed him and she longed for some palpable clue to his personality. As she opened the door, stale air puffed out, carrying the smell of a space shut away too long from the rest of the world. She saw it was a bedroom. A child's room.

A mobile of prisms trembled near the window, scattering tiny rainbows around the room. She stood there, transfixed, watching the lights dance across the wallpaper with its blue Swedish horses, across the sadly gaping toy shelves, across the tiny bed with the flowered coverlet. Almost against her will, she felt herself moving forward, as though some small, invisible hand were tugging her inside. Then, just as suddenly, the hand was gone and she was alone, so alone, in a room that ached with emptiness.

For a long time she stood there among the dancing rainbows, ashamed that she had disturbed the sanctity of this room. At last she wandered over to the dresser where a stack of books lay awaiting their owner's return. She opened one of the covers and stared at the name on the inside flap. Noah Ransom.

"I'm sorry," she whispered, tears stinging her eyes. "I'm sorry...."

She turned and fled the room, closing the door behind her.

Back in the kitchen, she huddled over a cup of coffee and read and reread the terse note she'd finally discovered, along with a set of keys, on the white-tiled counter.

Catching a ride with Glickman. The car's yours today.
See you tonight.

Hardly a lover's note, she thought. No little words of endearment, not even a signature. It was cold and matter-of-fact, just like this kitchen, just like everything else about this house. So that was David. Man of ice, master of a soulless house. They had just shared a night of passionate lovemaking. She'd been swept off her feet. He left impersonal little notes on the kitchen counter.

She had to marvel at how he'd compartmentalized his life. He had walled off his emotions into nice, neat spaces, the way he'd walled off his son's room. But she couldn't do that. Already she missed him. Maybe she even loved him. It was crazy and illogical; and she wasn't used to doing crazy, illogical things.

Suddenly annoyed at herself, she stood up and furiously rinsed her coffee cup in the sink. Dammit, she had more important things to worry about. Her committee hearing was this afternoon; her career hung in the balance. It was a stupid time to be fretting over a man.

She turned and picked up Jenny Brook's hospital chart, which had been lying on the breakfast table. This sad, mysterious document. Slowly she flipped through it, wondering what could possibly be so dangerous about a few pages of medical notes. But something terrible had happened the night Jenny Brook gave birth—something that had reached like a claw through time to destroy every name mentioned on these pages. Mother and child. Doctors and nurses. They were all dead. Only Charlie Decker knew why. And he was a puzzle in himself, a puzzle with pieces that didn't fit.

A maniac, the police had called him. A monster who slashed throats.

A harmless man, Kahanu had said. A lost soul with his insides kicked out.

A man with two faces.

She closed the chart and found herself staring at the back cover. A chart with two sides.

A man with two faces.

She sat up straight, suddenly comprehending. Of course. Jekyll and Hyde.

"The multiple personality is a rare phenomenon. But it's well described in psychiatric literature." Susan Santini swiveled around and reached for a book from the shelf behind her. Turning back to her desk, she perused the index for the relevant pages. Her red hair, usually so unruly, was tied back in a neat little knot. On the wall behind her hung an impressive collection of medical and psychiatric degrees, testimony to the fact Susan Santini was more than just Guy's wife; she was also a professional in her own right, and a well-respected one.

"Here it is," she said, leaning forward. "'From Eve to Sybil. A collection of case histories.' It's really a fascinating topic."

"Have you had any cases in your practice?" asked Kate.

"Wish I had. Oh, I thought I had one, when I was working with the courts. But that creep turned out to be just a great actor trying to beat a murder rap. I tell you, he could go from Caspar Milquetoast to Hulk Hogan in the blink of an eye. What a performance!"

"It is possible, though? For a man to have two completely different personalities?"

"The human psyche is made up of so many clashing parts. Call it id versus ego, impulse versus control. Look at violence, for example. Most of us manage to bury our savage tendencies. But some people can't. Who knows why? Childhood abuse? Some abnormality in brain chemistry? Whatever the reason, these people are walking time bombs. Push them too far and they lose all control. The scary part is, they're all around us. But we don't recognize them until something inside them, some inner dam, bursts. And then the violent side shows itself.''

"Do you think Charlie Decker could be one of these walking time bombs?"

Susan leaned back in her leather chair and considered the possibility. "That's a hard question, Kate. You say he came from a broken home. And he was arrested for assault and battery five years ago. But there's no lifelong pattern of violence. And the one time he used a gun, he turned it on himself." She looked doubtful. "I suppose, if he had some precipitating stress, some crisis…"

"He did."

"You mean this?" Susan gestured to the copy of Jenny Brook's medical chart.

"The death of his fiancée. The police think it triggered some sort of homicidal rage. That he's been killing the people he thought were responsible."

"It sounds weird, but the most compelling reason for violence does seem to be love. Think of all those crimes of passion. All those jealous spouses. Spurned lovers."

"Love and violence," said Kate. "Two sides of the same coin."

"Exactly." Susan handed the medical record back to Kate. "But I'm just speculating. I'd have to talk to this man Decker before I can pass judgment. Are the police getting close?"

"I don't know. They won't tell me a thing. A lot of this information I had to dig up myself."

"You're kidding. Isn't it their job?"

Kate sighed. "That's the problem. For them it's nothing but a job, another file to be closed."

The intercom buzzed. "Dr. Santini?" said the receptionist. "Your three-o'clock appointment's waiting."

Kate glanced at her watch. "Oh, I'm sorry. I've been keeping you from your patients."

"You know I'm always glad to help out." Susan rose and walked with her to the door. There she touched Kate's arm. "This place you're staying—you're absolutely sure it's safe?"

Kate turned and saw the worry in Susan's eyes. "I think so. Why?"

Susan hesitated. "I hate to frighten you, but I think you ought to know. If you're correct, if Decker is a multiple personality, then you're dealing with a very unstable mind. Someone totally unpredictable. In the blink of an eye, he could change from a man to a monster. So, please, be very, very careful."

Kate's throat went dry. "You—you really think he's that dangerous?"

Susan nodded. "Extremely dangerous."

11

It looked like a firing squad and she was the one who'd been handed the blindfold.

She was sitting before a long conference table. Arranged in a grim row in front of her were six men and a woman, all physicians, none of them smiling. Though he'd promised to attend, Dr. Clarence Avery, the chief of anesthesia, was not present. The one friendly face in the entire room was Guy Santini's, but he'd been called only as a witness. He was sitting off to the side and he looked every bit as nervous as she felt.

The committee members asked their questions politely but doggedly. They responded to her answers with impassive stares. Though the room was air-conditioned, her cheeks were on fire.

"And you personally examined the EKG, Dr. Chesne?"

"Yes, Dr. Newhouse."

"And then you filed it in the chart."

"That's correct."

"Did you show the tracing to any other physician?"

"No, sir."

"Not even to Dr. Santini?"

She glanced at Guy, who was hunched down in his chair, staring off unhappily. "Screening the EKG was my responsibility, not Dr. Santini's," she said evenly. "He trusted my judgment."

How many times do I have to repeat this story? she asked herself wearily. *How many times do I have to answer the same damn questions?*

"Dr. Santini? Any comment?"

Guy looked up reluctantly. "What Dr. Chesne says is true. I trusted her judgment." He paused, then added emphatically, "I still trust her judgment."

Thank you, Guy, she thought. Their eyes met and he gave her a faint smile.

"Let's return to the events during surgery, Dr. Chesne," continued Dr. Newhouse. "You say you performed routine induction with IV Pentothal...."

The nightmare was relived. Ellen O'Brien's death was dissected as thoroughly as a cadaver on the autopsy table.

When the questions were over, she was allowed a final statement. She delivered it in a quiet voice. "I know my story sounds bizarre. I also know I can't prove any of it—at least, not yet. But I know this much: I gave Ellen O'Brien the very best care I could. The record shows I made a mistake, a terrible one. And my patient died. But did I kill her? I don't think so. I really don't think so...." Her voice trailed off. There was nothing else to say. So she simply murmured, "Thank you." And then she left the room.

It took them twenty minutes to reach a decision. She was called back to her chair. As her gaze moved along the table, she noticed with distinct uneasiness that two new faces had joined the group. George Bettencourt and the hospital attorney were sitting at one end of the table. Bettencourt looked coldly satisfied. She knew, before a word was even spoken, what the decision would be.

Dr. Newhouse, the committee chairman, delivered the verdict. "We know your recall of the case is at odds with the record, Dr. Chesne. But I'm afraid the record is what we must go on. And the record shows, unquestionably, that your care of patient Ellen O'Brien was substandard." Kate winced at the last word, as though the worst insult imaginable had just been hurled at her. Dr. Newhouse sighed and removed his glasses—a tired gesture that seemed to carry all the weight of the world. "You're new to the staff, Dr. Chesne. You've been with us for less than a year. This sort of...mishap, after so short a time on the staff, concerns us very much. We regret this. We really do. But based on what we've heard, we're forced to refer the case to the Disciplinary Committee. They'll decide what action to take in regards to your position here at Mid Pac. Until then—'' he glanced at Bettencourt ''—we have no objection to the measures already taken by the hospital administration regarding your suspension.''

So it's over, she thought. *I was stupid to hope for anything else.*

They allowed her a chance to respond but she'd lost her voice; it was all she could manage to remain calm and dry-eyed in front of these seven people who'd just torn her life apart.

As the committee filed out, she remained in her chair, unable to move or even to raise her head. ''I'm sorry, Kate,'' Guy said softly. He lingered beside her for a moment, as though hunting for something else to say. Then he, too, drifted out of the room.

Her name was called twice before she finally looked up to see Bettencourt and the attorney standing in front of her.

''We think it's time to talk, Dr. Chesne,'' announced the attorney.

She frowned at them in bewilderment. ''Talk? About what?''

''A settlement.''

Her back stiffened. ''Isn't this a little premature?''

''If anything, it's too late.''

''I don't understand.''

''A reporter was in my office a few hours ago. It appears the whole case is out in the open. Obviously the O'Briens took their story to the newspapers. I'm afraid you'll be tried—and convicted—in print.''

''But the case was filed only last week.''

''We have to get this out of the public eye. Now. And the best way to do it is a very fast, very quiet settlement. All we need is your agreement. I plan to start negotiations at around half a million, though we fully expect they'll push for more.''

Half a million dollars, she thought. It struck her as obscene, placing a monetary value on a human life. "No," she said.

The attorney blinked. "Excuse me?"

"The evidence is still coming in. By the time this goes to trial, I'm sure I'll be able to prove—"

"It won't go to trial. This case *will* be settled, Doctor. With or without your permission."

Her mouth tightened. "Then I'll pay for my own attorney. One who'll represent me and not the hospital."

The two men glanced at each other. When the attorney spoke again, his tone was distinctly unpleasant. "I don't think you fully understand what it means to go to trial. Dr. Santini will, in all probability, be dropped from the case. Which means *you* will be the principal defendant. *You'll* be the one sweating on that stand. And it'll be *your* name in the newspapers. I know their attorney, David Ransom. I've seen him rip a defendant to shreds in the courtroom. Believe me, you don't want to go through that."

"Mr. Ransom is no longer on the case," she said.

"What?"

"He's withdrawn."

He snorted. "Where on earth did you hear that rumor?"

"He told me."

"Are you saying you talked to him?"

Not to mention went to bed with him, she reflected, flushing. "It happened last week. I went to his office. I told him about the EKGs—"

"Dear God." The attorney turned and threw his pencil in his briefcase. "Well, that's it, folks. We're in big trouble."

"Why?"

"He'll use that crazy story of yours to push for a higher settlement."

"But he believed me! That's why he's withdrawing—"

"He couldn't possibly believe you. I know the man."

I know him too! she wanted to yell.

But there was no point; she'd never be able to convince them. So she simply shook her head. "I won't settle."

The attorney snapped his briefcase shut and turned in frustration to Bettencourt. "George?"

Kate shifted her attention to the chief administrator. Bettencourt was watching her with an utterly smooth expression. No hostility. No anger. Just that quintessential poker player's gaze.

"I'm concerned about your future, Dr. Chesne," he said.

So am I, she felt like snapping back.

"There's a good chance, unfortunately, that the Disciplinary Committee will view your case harshly. If so, they'll probably recommend you be terminated. And that would be a shame, having that on your record. It would make it almost impossible for you to find another job. Anywhere." He paused, to let his words sink in. "That's why I'm offering you this alternative, Doctor. I think it's far preferable to an out-and-out firing."

She stared down at the sheet of paper he was holding out to her. It was a typed resignation, already dated, with a blank space awaiting her signature.

"That's all that'd appear in your file. A resignation. There'd be no damning conclusions from the Disciplinary Committee. No record of termination. Even with this lawsuit, you could probably find another job, though not in this town." He took out a pen and held it out to her. "Why don't you sign it? It really is for the best."

She kept staring at the paper. The whole process was so neat, so efficient. Here was this ready-made document. All it needed was her signature. Her capitulation.

"We're waiting, Dr. Chesne," challenged Bettencourt. "Sign it."

She rose to her feet. She took the resignation sheet. Looking him straight in the eye, she ripped the paper in half. "There's my resignation," she declared. Then she turned and walked out the door.

Only as she stalked away past the administrative suite did

it occur to her what she'd just done. She'd burned her bridges. There was no going back now; her only course was to slog it out to the very end.

Halfway down the hall, her footsteps slowed and finally stopped. She wanted to cry but couldn't. She stood there, staring down the corridor, watching the last secretary straggle away toward the elevators. It was five-fifteen and only a janitor remained at the far end of the hall, listlessly shoving a vacuum cleaner across the carpet. He rounded the corner and the sound of the machine faded away, leaving only a heavy stillness. Farther down the hall, a light was shining through the open door of Clarence Avery's office. It didn't surprise her that he was still at work; he often stayed late. But she wondered why he hadn't attended the hearing as he'd promised. Now, more than ever, she needed his support.

She went to the office. Glancing inside, she was disappointed to find only his secretary, tidying up papers on the desk.

The woman glanced up. "Oh. Dr. Chesne."

"Is Dr. Avery still in the hospital?" Kate asked.

"Haven't you heard?"

"Heard what?"

The secretary looked down sadly at the photograph on the desk. "His wife died last night, at the nursing home. He hasn't been in the hospital all day."

Kate felt herself sag against the doorway. "His…wife?"

"Yes. It was all rather unexpected. A heart attack, they think, but— Are you all right?"

"What?"

"Are you all right? You don't look well."

"No, I'm—I'm fine." Kate backed into the hall. "I'm fine," she repeated, walking in a daze toward the elevators. As she rode down to the lobby, a memory came back to her, an image of shattered glass sparkling at the feet of Clarence Avery.

She needs to be put to sleep…. It's so much better if I do it, if I'm there to say goodbye. Don't you think?

The elevator doors hissed open. The instant she stepped out into the bright lights of the lobby, a sudden impulse seized her, the need to flee, to find safety. To find David. She walked outside into the parking lot and the urge became compelling. She couldn't wait; she had to see him now. If she hurried, she might catch him at his office.

Just the thought of seeing his face filled her with such irrational longing that she began to run. She ran all the way to the car.

Her route took her into the very heart of downtown. Late-afternoon sunlight slanted in through the picket shadows of steel-and-glass high rises. Rush-hour traffic clogged the streets; she felt like a fish struggling upstream. With every minute that passed, her hunger to see him grew. And with it grew a panic that she would be too late, that she'd find his office empty, his door locked. At that moment, as she fought through the traffic, it seemed that nothing in her life had ever been as important as reaching the safety of his arms.

Please be there, she prayed. *Please be there....*

"An explanation, Mr. Ransom. That's all I'm asking for. A week ago you said our chances of winning were excellent. Now you've withdrawn from the case. I want to know why."

David gazed uneasily into Mary O'Brien's silver-gray eyes and wondered how to answer her. He wasn't about to tell her the truth—that he was having an affair with the opposition. But he did owe her some sort of explanation and he knew, from the look in her eye, that it had better be a good one.

He heard the agitated creaking of wood and leather and he glanced in irritation at Phil Glickman, who was squirming nervously in his chair. David shot him a warning look to cool it. If that was possible. Glickman already knew the truth. And damned if he didn't look ready to blurt it all out.

Mary O'Brien was still waiting.

David's answer was evasive but not entirely dishonest. "As I said earlier, Mrs. O'Brien, I've discovered a conflict of interest."

"I don't understand what that means," Mary O'Brien said impatiently. "This conflict of interest. Are you telling me you work for the hospital?"

"Not exactly."

"Then what does it mean?"

"It's…confidential. I really can't discuss it." Smoothly changing the subject, he continued, "I'm referring your case to Sullivan and March. It's an excellent firm. They'll be happy to take it from here, assuming you have no objections."

"You haven't answered my question." She leaned forward, her eyes glinting, her bony hands bunched tightly on his desk. Claws of vengeance, he thought.

"I'm sorry, Mrs. O'Brien. I just can't serve your needs objectively. I have no choice but to withdraw."

It was a very different parting from the last visit. A cold and businesslike handshake, a nod of the head. Then he and Glickman escorted her out of his office.

"I expect there'll be no delays because of this," she said.

"There shouldn't be. All the groundwork's been laid." He frowned as he saw the frantic expression of his secretary at the far end of the hall.

"You still think they'll try to settle?"

"It's impossible to second-guess.…" He paused, distracted. His secretary now looked absolutely panicked.

"You told us before they'd want to settle."

"Hmm? Oh." Suddenly anxious to get rid of her, he guided her purposefully toward the reception room. "Look, don't worry about it, Mrs. O'Brien," he practically snapped out. "I can almost guarantee the other side's discussing a settlement right—" His feet froze in their tracks. He felt as though he were mired in concrete and would never move again.

Kate was standing in front of him. Slowly, her disbelieving gaze shifted to Mary O'Brien.

"Oh, my God," Glickman groaned.

It was a tableau taken straight out of some soap opera: the shocked parties, all staring at one another.

"I can explain everything," David blurted out.

"I doubt it," retorted Mary O'Brien.

Wordlessly Kate spun around and walked out of the suite. The slam of the door shook David out of his paralysis. Just before he rushed out into the hall he heard Mary O'Brien's outraged voice say: "Conflict of interest? Now I know what he meant by *interest*!"

Kate was stepping into an elevator.

He scrambled after her but before he could yank her out, the door snapped shut between them. "Dammit!" he yelled, slamming his fist against the wall.

The next elevator took forever to arrive. All the way down, twenty floors, he paced back and forth like a caged animal, muttering oaths he hadn't used in years. By the time he emerged on the ground floor, Kate was nowhere to be seen.

He ran out of the building and down the steps to the sidewalk. Scanning the street, he spotted, half a block away, a bus idling near the curb. Kate was walking toward it.

Shoving frantically through a knot of pedestrians, he managed to grab her arm and haul her back as she was about to step aboard the bus.

"Let me go!" she snapped.

"Where the hell do you think you're going?"

"Oh, sorry. I almost forgot!" Thrusting her hand in her skirt pocket, she pulled out his car keys and practically threw them at him. "I wouldn't want to be accused of stealing your precious BMW!"

She looked around in frustration as the bus roared off without her. Yanking her arm free, she stormed away. He was right behind her.

"Just give me a chance to explain."

"What did you tell your client, David? That she'll get her settlement now that you've got the dumb doctor eating out of your hand?"

"What happened between you and me has nothing to do with the case."

"It has everything to do with the case! You were hoping all along I'd settle."

"I only asked you to think about it."

"Ha!" She whirled on him. "Is this something they teach you in law school? When all else fails, get the opposition into bed?"

That was the last straw. He grabbed her arm and practically dragged her off the sidewalk and into a nearby pub. Inside, he plunged straight through the boisterous crowd that had gathered around the bar and hauled her through the swirling cigarette smoke to an empty booth at the back. There he plopped her down unceremoniously onto the wooden bench. Sliding into the seat across from her, he shot her a look that said she was damn well going to hear him out.

"First of all—" he started.

"Good evening," said a cheery voice.

"Now what?" he barked at the startled waitress who'd arrived to take their order.

The woman seemed to shrink back into her forest-green costume. "Did you…uh, want anything—"

"Just bring us a couple of beers," he snapped.

"Of course, sir." With a pitying look at Kate, the waitress turned ruffled skirts and fled.

For a solid minute, David and Kate stared at each other with unveiled hostility. Then David let out a sigh and clawed his fingers through his already unruly hair. "Okay," he said. "Let's try it again."

"Where do we start? Before or after your client popped out of your office?"

"Did anyone ever tell you you've got a lousy sense of timing?"

"Oh, you're wrong there, mister. My sense of timing happens to be just dandy. What did I hear you say to her? 'Don't worry, there's a settlement in the works'?"

"I was trying to get her out of my office!"

"So how did she react to your straddling both sides of the lawsuit?"

"I wasn't—" he looked pained "—straddling."

"Working for her and going to bed with me? I'd call that straddling."

"For an intelligent woman, you seem to have a little trouble comprehending one little fact: I'm off the case. Permanently. And voluntarily. Mary O'Brien came to my office demanding to know why I withdrew."

"Did you—did you tell her about us?"

"You think I'm nuts? You think I'd come out and announce I had a roll in the hay with the opposition?"

His words hit her like a slap across her face. Was that all it had meant to him? She'd imagined their lovemaking meant far more than just the simple clash of hormones. A joining of souls, perhaps. But for David, the affair had only meant complications. An angry client, a forced withdrawal from a case. And now the humiliation of having to confess an illicit romance. That he'd tried so hard to conceal their affair gave it all a lurid glow. People only hid what they were ashamed of.

"A weekend fling," she said. "Is that what I was?"

"I didn't mean it that way!"

"Well, don't worry about it, David," she assured him with regal composure as she rose to her feet. "I won't embarrass you any more. This is one skeleton who'll gladly step back into the closet."

"*Sit down.*" It was nothing more than a low growl but it held enough threat to make her pause. "Please," he added. Then, in a whisper, he said it again. "Please."

Slowly, she sat back down.

They fell silent as the waitress returned and set down their beers. Only when they were alone again did David say, quietly, "You're not just a fling, Kate. And as for the O'Briens, it's none of their business what I do on my weekends. Or weekdays." He shook his head in amazement. "You know, I've withdrawn from other cases, but it was always for perfectly logical reasons. Reasons I could defend without getting red in the face. This time, though…'' He let out a brittle laugh. "At my age, getting red in the face isn't supposed to happen anymore.''

Kate stared down at her glass. She hated beer. She hated arguing. Most of all, she hated this chasm between them. "If I jumped to conclusions,'' she admitted grudgingly, "I'm sorry. I guess I never did trust lawyers.''

He grunted. "Then we're even. I never did trust doctors.''

"So we're an unlikely pair. What else is new?''

They suffered through another one of those terrible loaded silences.

"We really don't know each other very well, do we?'' she finally said.

"Except in bed. Which isn't the best place to get acquainted.'' He paused. "Though we certainly tried.''

She looked up and saw an odd little tilt to his mouth, the beginnings of a smile. A lock of hair had slipped down over his brow. His shirt collar gaped open and his tie had been yanked into a limp version of a hangman's noose. She'd never seen him look so wrenchingly attractive.

"Are you going to get in trouble, David? What if the O'Briens complain to the state bar?'' she asked softly.

He shrugged. "I'm not worried. Hell, the worst they can do is disbar me. Throw me in jail. Maybe send me to the electric chair.''

"David.''

"Oh, you're right, I forgot. Hawaii doesn't have an electric chair.'' He noticed she wasn't laughing. "Okay, so it's a lousy joke.'' He lifted his mug and was about to take a gulp of beer when he focused on her morose expression. "Oh, I completely forgot. What happened at your hearing?''

"There were no surprises.''

"It went against you?''

"To say the least.'' Miserable, she stared down at the table. "They said my work was substandard. I guess that's a polite way of calling me a lousy doctor.''

His silence, more than anything he could have said, told her how much the news disturbed him. With a sense of wonder she watched his hand close gently around hers.

"It's funny," she remarked with an ironic laugh. "I never planned on being anything but a doctor. Now that I'm losing my job, I see how poorly qualified I am for anything else. I can't type. I can't take dictation. For God's sake, I can't even *cook*."

"Uh-oh. Now that's a serious deficiency. You may have to beg on street corners."

It was another lousy joke, but this time she managed a smile. A meager one. "Promise to drop a few quarters in my hat?"

"I'll do better than that. I'll buy you dinner."

She shook her head. "Thanks. But I'm not hungry."

"Better take me up on the offer," he urged, squeezing her hand. "You never know where you next meal's coming from."

She lifted her head and their gazes met across the table. The eyes she'd once thought so icy now held all the warmth of a summer's day. "All I want is to go home with you, David. I want you to hold me. And not necessarily in that order."

Slowly he moved around the table and slid next to her. Then he pulled her into his arms and held her long and close. It was what she needed, this silent embrace, not of a lover but a friend.

They both stiffened at the sound of the waitress clearing her throat. "I don't believe this woman's timing," David muttered as he pulled away.

"Anything else?" asked the waitress.

"Yes," David replied, smiling politely through clenched teeth. "*If* you don't mind."

"What's that, sir?"

"A little privacy."

Kate let him talk her into dinner. A full stomach and a few glasses of wine left her flushed and giddy as they walked the dark streets to the parking garage. The lamps spilled a hazy glow across their faces. She clung to his arm and felt like singing, like laughing.

She was going home with David.

She slid onto the leather seat of the BMW and the familiar feeling of security wrapped around her like a blanket. She was in a capsule where no one, nothing, could hurt her. The feeling lasted all the way down the Pali Highway, clung to her as they slipped into the tunnel through the Koolau Mountains, kept her warm on the steep and winding road down the other side of the ridge.

It shattered when David glanced in the rearview mirror and swore softly.

She glanced sideways and saw the faint glow of a car's headlights reflected on his face. "David?"

He didn't answer. She felt the rising hum of the engine as they accelerated.

"David, is something wrong?"

"That car. Behind us."

"What?"

He frowned at the mirror. "I think we're being followed."

12

Kate whipped her head around and stared at the pair of headlights twinkling in the distance. "Are you sure?"

"I only noticed because it has a dead left parking light. I know it pulled out behind us when we left the garage. It's been on our tail ever since. All the way down the mountain."

"That doesn't mean he's following us!"

"Let's try a little experiment." He took his foot off the gas pedal.

She went rigid in alarm. "Why are you slowing down?"

"To see what he does."

As her heart accelerated wildly, Kate felt the BMW drift down to forty-five, then forty. Below the speed limit. She waited for the headlights to overtake them but they seemed to hang in the distance, as though some invisible force kept the cars apart.

"Smart guy," said David. "He's staying just far enough behind so I can't read his license."

"There's a turnoff! Oh, please, let's take it!"

He veered off the highway and shot onto a two-lane road cut through dense jungle. Vine-smothered trees whipped past, their overhanging branches splattering the windshield with water. She twisted around and saw, through the backdrop of jungle, the same pair of headlights, twinkling in the darkness. Phantom lights that refused to vanish.

"It's him," she whispered. She couldn't bring herself to say the name, as if, just by uttering it, she would unleash some terrible force.

"I should have known," he muttered. "Dammit, I should've known!"

"What?"

"He was watching the hospital. That's the only way he could've followed you—"

He must have been right behind me, she thought, suddenly sick with the realization of what could have happened. *And I never even knew he was there.*

"I'm going to lose him. Hold on."

She was thrown sideways by the violent lurch of the car. It was all she could do to hang on for dear life. The situation was out of her hands; this show was entirely David's.

Houses leaped past, a succession of brightly lit windows punctuated by the silhouettes of trees and shrubbery. The BMW weaved like a slalom skier through the darkness, rounding corners at a speed that made her claw the dashboard in terror.

Without warning, he swerved into a driveway. The seat belt sliced into her chest as they jerked to a sudden standstill in a pitch-dark garage. Instantly, David cut off the engine. The next thing she knew, he was pulling her down into his arms. There she lay, wedged between the gearshift and David's chest, listening, waiting. She could feel his heart hammering against her, could hear his harsh, uneven breaths. At least he was still able to breathe; she scarcely dared to.

With mounting terror, she watched a flicker of light slowly grow brighter and brighter in the rearview mirror. From the road came the faint growl of an engine. David's arms tensed around her. Already he had shifted his weight and now lay on top of her, shielding her body with his. For an eternity she lay crushed in his embrace, listening, waiting, as the sound of the engine faded away. Only when there was total silence did they finally creep up and peer through the rear window.

The road was dark. The car had vanished.

"What now?" she whispered.

"We get the hell out of here. While we still can." He

turned the key; the engine's purr seemed deafening. With his headlights killed, he let the car creep slowly out of the garage.

As they wound their way out of the neighborhood, she kept glancing back, searching for the twin lights dancing beyond the trees. Only when they'd reached the highway did she allow herself a breath of relief. But to her alarm, David turned the car back toward Honolulu.

"Where are we going?"

"We can't go home. Not now."

"But we've lost him!"

"If he followed you from the hospital, then he trailed you straight to my office. To me. Unfortunately, I'm in the phone book. Address and all."

She sank back in shock and struggled to absorb this latest blow. They entered the Pali Tunnel. The succession of lights passing overhead was wildly disorienting, flash after flash that shocked her eyes.

Where do I go now? she wondered. *How long before he finds me? Will I have time to run? Time to scream?* She shuddered as they emerged from the tunnel and were plunged into sudden darkness.

"It's my last resort," David said. "But it's the only place I can think of. You won't be alone. And you'll be perfectly safe." He paused and added with an odd note of humor, "Just don't drink the coffee."

She turned and stared at him in bewilderment. "Where are we going?"

His answer had a distinctly apologetic ring. "My mother's."

The tiny gray-haired woman who opened the door was wearing a ratty bathrobe and pink bunny slippers. For a moment she stood there, blinking like a surprised mouse at the unexpected visitors. Then she clapped her hands and squeaked: "My goodness, David! How nice you've come for a visit! Oh, but this is naughty of you, not to call. You've caught us in our pajamas, like two ol—''

"You're gorgeous, Gracie," cut in David as he tugged Kate into the house. Quickly he locked and bolted the door. Then, glancing out the curtained window, he demanded, "Is Mother awake?"

"Why, yes, she's…uh…" Gracie gestured vaguely at the foyer.

From another room, a querulous voice called out: "For heaven's sake, get rid of whoever it is and get in here! It's your turn! And you'd better come up with something good. I just got a triple word score!"

"She's beating me again." Gracie sighed mournfully.

"Then she's in a good mood?"

"I wouldn't know. I've never seen her in one."

"Get ready," David muttered to Kate as he guided her across the foyer. "Mother?" he called out pleasantly. *Too* pleasantly.

In a mauve and mahogany living room, a regal woman with blue-gray hair was sitting with her back turned to them. Her wrapped foot was propped up on a crushed velvet ottoman. On the tea table beside her lay a Scrabble board, criss-crossed with tiles. "I don't believe it," she announced to the wall. "It must be an auditory hallucination." She turned and squinted at him. "Why, my son has actually come for a visit! Is the world at an end?"

"Nice to see you, too, Mother," he responded dryly. He took a deep breath, like a man gathering up the nerve to yank out his own teeth. "We need your help."

The woman's eyes, as glitteringly sharp as crystals, suddenly focused on Kate. Then she noticed David's arm, which was wrapped protectively around Kate's shoulder. Slowly, knowingly, she smiled. With a grateful glance at the heavens she murmured fervently: "Glory hallelujah!"

"You never tell me anything, David," Jinx Ransom complained as she sat with her son in the fern-infested kitchen an hour later.

They were huddled over cups of cocoa, a ritual they hadn't shared since he was a boy. *How little it takes to be transported back to childhood,* he reflected. One sip of chocolate, one disapproving look from his mother, and the pangs of filial guilt returned. Good old Jinx; she really knew how to make a guy feel young again. In fact, she made him feel about six years old.

"Here you have a woman in your life," said Jinx, "and you hide her from me. As if you're ashamed of her. Or ashamed of me. Or maybe you're ashamed of us both."

"There's nothing to talk about. I haven't known her that long."

"You're just ashamed to admit you're human, aren't you?"

"Don't psychoanalyze me, Mother."

"I'm the one who diapered you. I'm the one who watched you skin your knees. I even saw you break your arm on that blasted skateboard. You almost never cried, David. You still don't cry. I don't think you can. It's some gene you inherited from your father. The Plymouth Rock curse. Oh, the emotions are in there somewhere, but you're not about to let them show. Even when Noah died—"

"I don't want to talk about Noah."

"You see? The boy's been gone eight years now and you still can't hear his name without getting all tight in the face."

"Get to the point, Mother."

"Kate."

"What about her?"

"You were holding her hand."

He shrugged. "She has a very nice hand."

"Have you gone to bed with her yet?"

David sputtered hot chocolate all over the table. "Mother!"

"Well it's nothing to be ashamed of. People do it all the time. It's what nature intended, though I sometimes think you imagine yourself immune to the whole blasted process. But tonight, I saw that look in your eye.''

Swatting away a stray fern, he went to the sink for a paper towel and began dabbing the cocoa from his shirt.

''Am I right?'' asked Jinx.

''Looks like I'll need a clean shirt for tomorrow,'' he muttered. ''This one's shot.''

''Use one of your father's shirts. So am I right?''

He looked up. ''About what, Mother?'' he asked blankly.

She raised her arm and made a throttling motion at the heavens. ''I knew it was a mistake to have only one child!''

Upstairs there was a loud thud. David glanced up at the ceiling. ''What the hell is Gracie doing up there, anyway?''

''Digging up some clothes for Kate.''

David shuddered. Knowing Gracie's incomparable taste in clothes, Kate would come down swathed from head to toe in some nauseating shade of pink. With bunny slippers to match. The truth was, he didn't give a damn what she was wearing, if only she'd hurry downstairs. They'd been apart only fifteen minutes and already he missed her. It annoyed him, all these inconvenient emotions churning around inside him. It made him feel weak and helpless and all too…human.

He turned eagerly at hearing a creak on the stairs and saw it was only Gracie.

''Is that hot chocolate, Jinx?'' Gracie demanded. ''You know the milk upsets your stomach. You really should have tea instead.''

''I don't want tea.''

''Yes, you do.''

''No, I don't.''

''Where's Kate?'' David called out bleakly.

''Oh, she's coming,'' said Gracie. ''She's up in your room, looking at your old model airplanes.'' Giggling, she confided to Jinx, ''I told her they were proof that David was once a child.''

''He was never a child,'' grumbled Jinx. ''He sprang from the womb a fully mature adult. Though smaller, of course.

Perhaps he'll do it backward. Perhaps he'll get younger as the years go by. We'll see him loosen up and become a real child.''

"Like you, Mother?''

Gracie put on the teakettle and sighed happily. ''It's so nice to have company, isn't it?'' She glanced around, startled, as the phone rang. ''My goodness, it's after ten. Who on earth—''

David shot to his feet. ''I'll get it.'' He grabbed the receiver and barked out: ''Hello?''

Pokie's voice boomed triumphantly across the wires. ''Have I got news for you.''

"You've tracked down that car?''

"Forget the car. We got the man.''

"Decker?''

"I'll need Dr. Chesne down here to identify him. Half an hour, okay?''

David glanced up to see Kate standing in the kitchen doorway. Her eyes were filled with questions. Grinning, he snapped her a victorious thumbs-up sign. ''We'll be right over,'' he told Pokie. ''Where you holding him? Downtown station?''

There was a pause. ''No, not the station.''

"Where, then?''

"The morgue.''

"Hope you have strong stomachs.'' The medical examiner, a grotesquely chirpy woman named M.J., pulled open the stainless-steel drawer. It glided out noiselessly. Kate cringed against David as M.J. casually reached in and unzipped the plastic shroud.

Under the harsh morgue lights, the corpse's face looked artificial. This wasn't a man; it was some sort of waxen image, a mockery of life.

"Some yachtie found him this evening, floating facedown in the harbor,'' explained Pokie.

Kate felt David's arm tighten around her waist as she

forced herself to study the dead man's bloated features. Distorted as he was, the open eyes were recognizable. Even in death they seemed haunted.

Nodding, Kate whispered, "That's him."

Pokie grinned, a response that struck her as surreal in that nightmarish room. "Bingo," he grunted.

M.J. ran her gloved hand over the dead man's scalp. "Feels like we got a depressed skull fracture here...." She whisked off the shroud, revealing the naked torso. "Looks like he's been in the water quite a while."

Suddenly nauseated, Kate turned and buried her face against David's shoulder. The scent of his after-shave muted the stench of formalin.

"For God's sake, M.J.," David muttered. "Cover him up, will you?"

M.J. zipped up the shroud and slid the drawer closed. "You've lost the old ironclad stomach, hey, Davy boy? If I remember right, you used to shrug off a lot worse."

"I don't hang around stiffs the way I used to." He guided Kate away from the body drawers. "Come on. Let's get the hell out of here."

The medical examiner's office was a purposefully cheerful room, complete with hanging plants and old movie posters, a bizarre setting for the gruesome business at hand. Pokie poured coffee from the automatic brewer and handed two cups to David and Kate. Then, sighing with satisfaction, he settled into a chair across from them. "So that's how it wraps up," he said. "No trial. No hassles. Just a convenient corpse. Too bad justice ain't always this easy."

Kate stared down at her coffee. "How did he die, Lieutenant?" she whispered.

Pokie shrugged. "Happens now and then. Get some guy who's had a little too much to drink. Falls off a pier, bashes his head on the rocks. Hell, we find floaters all the time. Boat bums, mostly." He glanced at M.J. "What do you think?"

"Can't rule out anything yet," mumbled M.J. She was hunched at her desk and wolfing down a late supper. A meatloaf sandwich dripping with ketchup, Kate noted, her stomach threatening to turn inside out. "When a body's been in the water that long, anatomy gets distorted. I'll tell you after the autopsy."

"Just how long was he in the water?" asked David.

"A day. More or less."

"A *day*?" He looked at Pokie. "Then who the hell was following us tonight?"

Pokie grinned. "You just got yourself an active imagination."

"I'm telling you, there was a car!"

"Lot of cars out on the road. Lot of headlights look the same."

"Well, it sure wasn't my guy in the drawer," said M.J., crumpling up her sandwich wrappings. She chomped enthusiastically into a bright red apple. "Far as I know, dead men don't drive."

"When are you going to know the cause of death?" David snapped.

"Still need skull X rays. I'll open him up tonight, check the lungs for water. That'll tell us if he drowned." She took another bite of apple. "But that's *after* I finish my dinner. In the meantime—" swiveling around, she grabbed a cardboard box from a shelf and tossed it down on the desk "—his personal effects."

Methodically she took out the items, each one sealed in its own plastic bag. "Plastic comb, black, pocket-size...cigarettes, Winston, half empty...matchbook, unlabeled...man's wallet, brown vinyl, containing fourteen dollars...various ID cards..." She reached in for the last item. "And these." The set of keys clattered on the desk. Attached was a plastic tag with gaudy red lettering: The Victory Hotel.

Kate picked up the key ring. "The Victory Hotel," she murmured. "Is that where he was living?"

Pokie nodded. "We checked it out. What a dive. Rats crawling all over the place. We know he was there Saturday night. But that's the last time he was seen. Alive, anyway."

Slowly Kate lay the keys down and stared at the mockingly bright lettering. She thought about the face in the mirror, about the torment in those eyes. And as she gazed at the sad and meager pile of belongings, an unexpected wave of sorrow welled up in her, sorrow for a man's shattered dreams. *Who were you, Charlie Decker?* she wondered. *Madman? Murderer?* Here were the bits and pieces of his life, and they were all so ordinary.

Pokie gave her a grin. "Well, it's over, Doc. Our man's dead. Looks like you can go home."

She glanced at David, but he was staring off in another direction. "Yes," she said in a weary voice. "Now I can go home."

Who were you, Charlie Decker?

That refrain played over and over in her head as she sat in the darkness of David's car and watched the streetlights flash by. *Who were you?* She thought of all the ways he'd suffered, all the pain he'd felt, that man without a voice. Like everyone else, he'd been a victim.

And now he was a convenient corpse.

"It's too easy, David," she said softly.

He glanced at her through the gloom of the car. "What is?"

"The way it's all turned out. Too simple, too neat..." She stared off into the darkness, remembering the reflection of Charlie Decker's face in the mirror. "My God. I saw it in his eyes," she whispered. "It was right there, staring at me, only I was too panicked to recognize it."

"What?"

"The fear. He was terrified. He must have known something, something awful. And it killed him. Just like it killed the others...."

"You're saying he was a victim? Then why did he threaten you? Why did he make that call to the cottage?"

"Maybe it wasn't a threat...." She looked up with sudden

comprehension. "Maybe he was warning me. About some-one else."

"But the evidence—"

"What evidence? A few fingerprints on a doorknob? A corpse with a psychiatric record?"

"And a witness. You saw him in Ann's apartment."

"What if he was the real witness? A man in the wrong place at the wrong time." She watched their headlights slash the darkness. "Four people, David. And the only thing that linked them together was a dead woman. If I only knew why Jenny Brook was so important."

"Unfortunately, dead men don't talk."

Maybe they do. "The Victory Hotel," she said suddenly. "Where is it?"

"Kate, the man's dead. The answers died with him. Let's just forget it."

"But there's still a chance—"

"You heard Pokie. The case is closed."

"Not for me, it isn't."

"Oh, for God's sake, Kate! Don't turn this into an obsession!" Gripping the steering wheel, he forced out an agitated breath. When he spoke again, his voice was quiet. "Look, I know how much it means to you, clearing your name. But in the long run, it may not be worth the fight. If vindication's what you're after, I'm afraid you won't get it. Not in the courtroom, anyway."

"You can't be sure what a jury will think."

"Second-guessing juries is part of my job. I've made a good living, cashing in on doctors' mistakes. And I've done it in a town where a lot of lawyers can barely pay their rent. I'm not any smarter than the other guy, I just pick my cases well. And when I do, I'm not afraid to get down and get dirty. By the time I'm finished, the defendant's scarred for life."

"Lovely profession you're in."

"I'm telling you this because I don't want it to happen to you. That's why I think you should settle out of court. Let the matter die quietly. Discreetly. Before your name gets dragged through the mud.''

"Is that how they do it in the prosecutor's office? 'Plead guilty and we'll make you a *deal*'?''

"There's nothing wrong with a settlement."

"Would you settle? If you were me?"

There was a long pause. "Yes. I would."

"Then we must be very different." Stubbornly she gazed ahead at the highway. "Because I can't let this die. Not without a fight."

"Then you're going to lose." It was more than an opinion; it was a pronouncement, as final as the thud of a judge's gavel in the courtroom.

"And I suppose lawyers don't take on losing battles, do they?"

"Not this lawyer."

"Funny. Doctors take them on all the time. Try arguing with a stroke. Or cancer. We don't make bargains with the enemy."

"And that's exactly how I make my living," he retorted. "On the arrogance of doctors!"

It was a vicious blow; he regretted it the instant he said it. But she was headed for trouble, and he had to stop her before she got hurt. Still, he hadn't expected such brutal words to pop out. It was one more reminder of how high the barriers were between them.

They drove the rest of the way in silence. A cloud of gloom filled the space of the car. They both seemed to sense that things were coming to an end; he guessed it had been inevitable from the start. Already he could feel her pulling away.

Back at his house, they drifted toward the bedroom like a pair of strangers. When she pulled down her suitcase and started to pack, he said simply, "Leave it for the morning," and shoved it back in the closet. That was all. He couldn't bring himself to say he wanted her to stay, needed her to stay. He just shut the closet door.

Then he turned to her. Slowly he removed his jacket and tossed it on the chair. He went to her, took her face in his hands and kissed her. Her lips felt chilled. He took her in his arms and held her, warmed her.

They made love, of course. One last time. He was there and she was there and the bed was there. Love among the ruins. No, not love. Desire. Need. Something entirely different, all-consuming yet wholly unsatisfying.

And afterward he lay beside her in the darkness, listening to her breathing. She slept deeply, the unarousable slumber of exhaustion. He should be sleeping, too. But he couldn't. He was too busy thinking about all the reasons he shouldn't fall in love.

He didn't like being in love. It left him far too vulnerable. Since Noah's death, he'd avoided feeling much of anything. At times he'd felt like a robot. He'd functioned on automatic pilot, breathing and eating out of necessity, smiling only when it was expected. When Linda finally left him, he'd hardly noticed; their divorce was a mere drop in an ocean of pain. He guessed he'd loved her, but it wasn't the same total, unconditional love he'd felt for his son. For David, love was quantified by how much he suffered by its loss.

And now here was this woman, lying beside him. He studied the dark pool of her hair against the pillow, the glow of her face. He tried to think of the last time there'd been a woman in his bed. It had been a long time ago, a blonde. But he couldn't even dredge up her name. That's how little she'd meant to him.

But Kate? He'd remember her name, all right. He'd remember this moment, the way she slept, curled up like a tired kitten, the way her very presence seemed to warm the darkness. He'd remember.

He rose from the bed and wandered into the hall. Some strange yearning pulled him toward Noah's room. He went inside and stood for a moment, bathed in the window's moonlight. For so long he'd avoided this room. He'd hated the sight of that unoccupied bed. He'd always remembered

how it used to be, tiptoeing in to watch his son sleep. Noah,
by some strange instinct, always seemed to choose that moment to awaken. And in the darkness, they'd murmur their
ritual conversation.

Is that you, Daddy?

Yes, Noah, it's me. Go back to sleep.

Hug first. Please.

Good night. Don't let the bedbugs bite.

David sat down on the bed, listening to the echoes of the
past, remembering how much it had hurt to love.

At last he went back to Kate's bed, crawled in beside her
and fell asleep.

He woke up before dawn. In the shower he purposefully
washed off all traces of their lovemaking. He felt renewed.
He dressed for work, donning each item of clothing as if it
was a piece of armor to shield him from the world. Alone in
the kitchen, he had a cup of coffee.

Now that Decker was dead, there was no reason for Kate
to stay. David had done his moral duty; he'd played the white
knight and kept her safe. It had been clear from the start that
none of this was for keeps. He'd never led her on. His conscience was clear. Now it was time for her to go home; and
they both knew it. Perhaps her leaving was all for the better.
A few days, a few weeks apart, might give him a saner per-
spective. Maybe he'd decide this was all a case of temporary,
hormonal madness.

Or maybe he was only kidding himself.

He worried about all the things that could happen to her
if she kept on digging into Charlie Decker's past. He also
knew she would keep on digging. Last night he hadn't told
her the truth: that he thought she was right, that there was
more to this case than a madman's vengeance. Four people
were dead; he didn't want her to be the fifth.

He got up and rinsed his cup. Then he went back to the
bedroom. There he sat at the foot of the bed—a safe distance—and watched her sleep. Such a beautiful, stubborn,
maddeningly independent woman. He used to think he liked

independent women. Now he wasn't so sure. He almost wished Decker was still alive, just so Kate would go on needing him. How incredibly selfish.

Then he decided she did still need him. They'd shared two nights of passion. For that he owed her one last favor.

He nudged her gently. "Kate?"

Slowly she opened her eyes and looked at him. Those sleepy green eyes. He wanted so badly to kiss her but decided it was better if he didn't.

"The Victory Hotel," he said. "Do you still want to go?"

13

Mrs. Tubbs, the manager of the Victory Hotel, was a toad-like woman with two pale slits for eyes. Despite the heat, she was wearing a ratty gray sweater over her flowered dress. Through a hole in her sock poked an enormously swollen big toe. "Charlie?" she asked, cautiously peering at David and Kate through her half-open door. "Yeah, he lived here."

In the room behind her, a TV game show blared and a man yelled, "You retard! I coulda guessed that one!"

The woman turned and yelled: "Ebbie! Turn that thing down! Can't you see I'm talkin' to someone?" She looked back at David and Kate. "Charlie don't live here no more. Got hisself killed. Po-lice already come by."

"If it's all right, we'd like to see his room," said Kate.

"What for?"

"We're looking for information."

"You from the po-lice?"

"No, but—"

"Can't let you up there without a warrant. Po-lice give me too much trouble already. Gettin' everyone in the building all nervous. 'Sides, I got orders. No one goes up." Her tone implied that someone very high, perhaps even God Himself, had issued those orders. To emphasize the point, she started to close the door. She looked outraged when David stopped it with a well-placed hand.

"Seems to me you could use a new sweater, Mrs. Tubbs," David remarked quietly.

The door swung open a fraction of an inch. Mrs. Tubbs's pale eyes peered at him through the crack. "I could use a lot of new things," she grunted. From the apartment came a man's loud and enthusiastic burp. "New husband, mostly."

"Afraid I can't help you there."

"No one can, 'cept maybe the good Lord."

"Who works His magic in unexpected ways." David's smile was dazzling; Mrs. Tubbs stared, waiting for the proffered miracle to occur.

David produced it in the form of two twenty-dollar bills, which he slipped discreetly into her fat hands.

She looked down at the money. "Hotel owner'll kill me if he finds out."

"He won't."

"Don't pay me nearly enough to manage this here trash heap. Plus I'm s'posed to pay off the city inspector." David slipped her another twenty. "But you ain't no inspector, right?" She wadded up the bills and stuffed them into the dark and bottomless recess of her bosom. "No inspector I seen ever come dressed like you." Shuffling out into the hall, she closed the door on Ebbie and the TV. In her stockinged feet, she led David and Kate toward the staircase. It was a climb of only one flight, but for her each step seemed to be agony. By the time she reached the top, she was wheezing like an accordion. A brown carpet—or had it once been mustard yellow?—stretched out into the dim hallway. She stopped before room 203 and fumbled for the keys.

"Charlie was here 'bout a month," she gasped out, a few words at a time. "Real quiet. Caused no...no trouble, not like some...some of them others...."

At the other end of the hall, a door suddenly opened and two small faces peered out.

"Charlie come back?" the little girl called.

"I already told you," Mrs. Tubbs said. "Charlie gone and left for good."

"But when's he comin' back?"

"You kids deaf or somethin'? How come you ain't in school?"

"Gabe's sick," explained the girl. As if to confirm the fact, little Gabe swiped his hand across his snotty nose.

"Where's your ma?"

The girl shrugged. "Out workin'."

"Yeah. Leaves you two brats here to burn down the place."

The children shook their heads solemnly. "She took away our matches," replied Gabe.

Mrs. Tubbs got the door unlocked. "There y'are," she said and pushed it open.

As the room swung into view, something small and brown rustled across the floor and into the shadows. The mingled odors of cigarette smoke and grease hung in the gloom. Pinpoints of light glittered through a tattered curtain. Mrs. Tubbs went over and shoved the curtain aside. Sunshine splashed in through the grimy window.

"Go 'head, have a look 'round," she said, planting herself in a corner. "But don't take nothin'."

It was easy to see why a visit by the city inspector might cause her alarm. A baited rattrap, temporarily unoccupied, lay poised near a trash can. A single light bulb hung from the ceiling, its wires nakedly exposed. On a one-burner hot plate sat a frying pan coated with a thick layer of congealed fat. Except for the one window, there was no ventilation and any cooking would have made the air swirl with grease.

Kate's gaze took in the miserable surroundings: the rumpled bed, the ashtray overflowing with cigarette butts, the card table littered with loose scraps of paper. She frowned at one of the pages, covered with scribblings.

Eight was great
Nine was fine,
And now you're ten years old.
Happy Birthday, Jocelyn,
The best will yet unfold!

"Who's Jocelyn?" she asked.

"That brat in 210. Mother's never around to watch 'em.

Always out workin'. Or so she calls it. Kids just 'bout burned the place down last month. Woulda throwed 'em all out, 'cept they always pay me in cash.''

"Just how much is the rent?" David asked.

"Four hundred bucks."

"You've got to be kidding."

"Hey, we got us a good location. Close to the bus lines. Free water 'n 'lectricity." At that instant, a cockroach chose to scuttle across the floor. "And we take pets."

Kate looked up from the pile of papers. "What was he like, Mrs. Tubbs?"

"Charlie?" She shrugged. "What's to say? Kept to hisself. Never made no noise. Never blasted the radio like some of these no-accounts. Never complained 'bout nothin' far as I remember. Hell, we hardly knew he was here. Yeah, a real good tenant."

By those standards, the ideal tenant would have been a corpse.

Mrs. Tubbs settled into a chair and watched as they searched the room. Their inspection revealed a few wrinkled shirts hanging in the closet, a dozen cans of Campbell's soup neatly stacked in the cabinet under the sink, some laundered socks and men's underwear in the dresser drawer. It was a meager collection of belongings; they held few clues to the personality of their owner.

At last Kate wandered to the window and looked down at a glass-littered street. Beyond a chain-link fence there was a condemned building with walls that sagged outward, as though a giant had stepped on it. A grim view of the world, this panorama of broken bottles and abandoned cars and drunks lolling on the sidewalk. This was a dead end, the sort of place you landed when you could fall no farther.

No, that wasn't quite right. There was one place lower you could fall: the grave.

"Kate?" said David. He'd been rummaging in the nightstand. "Prescription pills," he said, holding up a bottle. "Haldol, prescribed by Dr. Nemechek. State hospital."

"That's his psychiatrist."

"And look. I also found this." He held out a small, framed photograph.

The instant Kate saw the face, she knew who the woman was. She took the picture and studied it by the window's light. It was only a snapshot in time, a single image captured on a sheet of photographic paper, but the young woman who'd smiled into the camera's lens had the glow of eternity in her eyes. They were rich brown eyes, full of laughter, narrowed slightly in the sunlight. Behind her, a brassy sky met the turquoise blue of the sea. A strand of dark hair had blown across her face and clung almost wistfully to the curve of her cheek. She was wearing a simple white bathing suit; and though she'd struck a purposely sexy pose, kneeling there in the sand, there was a sweet gawkiness about her, like a child playing grown-up in her mother's clothes.

Kate slipped the photo out of its frame. The edges were tattered, lovingly worn by years of handling. On the other side was a handwritten message: "Till you come back to me. Jenny."

"Jenny," Kate said softly.

For a long time she stood there, staring at those words, written by a woman long since dead. She thought about the emptiness of this room, about the soup cans, so carefully stacked, about the pile of socks and underwear in the drawer. Charlie Decker had owned so very little. The one possession he'd guarded through the years, the one thing he'd treasured, had been this fading photograph of a woman with eternity in her eyes. It was hard to believe that such a glow could ever be extinguished, even in the depths of a grave.

She turned to Mrs. Tubbs. "What will happen to his things? Now that he's dead?"

"Guess I'll have to sell it all off," replied Mrs. Tubbs. "Owed me a week's rent. Gotta get it somehow. Though there ain't much of value in here. 'Cept maybe what you're holding.''

Kate looked down at the smiling face of Jenny Brook. ''Yes. She's beautiful, isn't she?''

''Naw, I don't mean the picture.''

Kate frowned. ''What?''

''The frame.'' Mrs. Tubbs went to the window and snapped the curtain closed. ''It's silver.''

Jocelyn and her brother were hanging like monkeys on the chain-link fence. As David and Kate came out of the Victory Hotel, the children dropped to the ground and watched expectantly as though something extraordinary was about to happen. The girl—if she was indeed ten—was small for her age. Toothpick legs stuck out from under her baggy dress. Her bare feet were filthy. The little boy, about six and equally filthy, held a clump of his sister's skirt in his fist.

''He's dead, isn't he?'' Jocelyn blurted out. Seeing Kate's sad nod, the girl slouched back against the fence and addressed one of the smudges on her bodice. ''You see, I knew it. Stupid grown-ups. Don't ever tell us the truth, any of 'em.''

''What did they tell you about Charlie?'' asked Kate.

''They just said he went away. But he never even gave me my present.''

''For your birthday?''

Jocelyn stared down at her nonexistent breasts. ''I'm ten.''

''And I'm seven,'' her brother said automatically, as if it was called for in the script.

''You and Charlie must have been good friends,'' David remarked.

The girl looked up, and seeing his smile—a smile that could melt the heart of any woman, much less that of a ten-year-old—immediately blushed. Looking back down, she coyly traced one brown toe along a crack in the sidewalk. ''Charlie didn't have any friends. I don't, either. 'Cept Gabe here, but he's just my brother.''

Little Gabe smiled and rubbed his slimy nose on his sister's dress.

"Did anyone else know Charlie very well?" David asked. "I mean, besides you."

Jocelyn chewed her lip thoughtfully. "Well…you could try over at Maloney's. Up the street."

"Who's Maloney?"

"Oh, he's nobody."

"If he's nobody, then how does he know Charlie?"

"He's not a him. He's a place. I mean, *it's* a place."

"Oh, of course," said David, looking down into Jocelyn's dazzled eyes. "How stupid of me."

"What're you kids doing in here again? Go on. Get out before I lose my license!"

Jocelyn and Gabe skipped through the air-conditioned gloom, past the cocktail tables and up to the bar. They clambered onto two counter stools. "Some people here to see you, Sam," announced Jocelyn.

"There's a sign out there says you gotta be twenty-one to come in here. You kids twenty-one yet?"

"I'm seven," answered Gabe. "Can I have an olive?"

Grumbling, the bartender dipped his soapy hand in a glass jar and plopped half a dozen green olives on the counter. "Okay, now get going before someone sees you in—" His head jerked up as he noticed David and Kate approaching through the shadows. From his wary look, it was obvious Maloney's was seldom frequented by such well-heeled clientele. He blurted out: "It's not my doing! These brats come runnin' in off the street. I was just gonna throw 'em out."

"They're not liquor inspectors," said Jocelyn with obvious disdain as she popped an olive in her mouth.

Apparently everyone in this part of town lived in fear of some dreaded inspector or another.

"We need information," said David. "About one of your customers. Charlie Decker."

Sam took a long and careful look at David's clothes, and

his train of thought was clearly mirrored in his eyes. *Nice suit. Silk tie. Yessir, all very expensive.* "He's dead," the bartender grunted.

"We know that."

"I don't speak ill of the dead." There was a long, significant pause. "You gonna order something?"

David sighed and finally settled onto a bar stool. "Okay. Two beers."

"That's all?"

"And two pineapple juices," added Jocelyn.

"That'll be twelve bucks."

"Cheap drinks," said David, sliding a twenty-dollar bill across the counter.

"Plus tax."

The children dumped the remaining olives in their drinks and began slurping down the juice.

"Tell us about Charlie," Kate prodded.

"Well, he used to sit right over there." Sam nodded at a dark corner table.

David and Kate leaned forward, waiting for the next pearl of information. Silence. "And?" prompted David.

"So that's where he sat."

"Doing what?"

"Drinking. Whiskey, mostly. He liked it neat. Then sometimes, I'd make him up a Sour Sam. That's if the mood hit him for somethin' different. That's my invention, the Sour Sam. Yeah, he'd drink one of those 'bout once a week. But mostly it was whiskey. Neat."

There was another silence. The talking machine had run out of money and needed a refill.

"I'll try a Sour Sam," said Kate.

"Don't you want your beer?"

"You can have it."

"Thanks. But I never touch the stuff." He turned his attention to mixing up a bizarre concoction of gin, club soda, and the juice of half a lemon, which undoubtedly accounted for the drink's name.

"Five bucks," he announced, passing it to Kate. "So how do you like it?"

She took a sip and gasped. "Interesting."

"Yeah, that's what everyone tells me."

"We were talking about Charlie," David reminded him.

"Oh, yeah, Charlie." The talking machine was back in order. "Let's see, he came around just 'bout every night. Think he liked the company, though he couldn't talk much, what with that bad throat of his. He'd sit there and drink, oh, one or two."

"Whiskeys. Neat," David supplied.

"Yeah, that's right. Real moderate, you know. Never got out-and-out drunk. He was a regular for 'bout a month. Then, few days ago, he stopped comin'. Too bad, you know? Hate to lose a steady one like that."

"You have any idea why he stopped?"

"They say police were looking for him. Word was out he killed some people."

"What do you think?"

"Charlie?" Sam laughed. "Not a chance."

Jocelyn handed Sam her empty glass. "Can I have another pineapple juice?"

Sam poured out two more pineapple juices and slid them over to the kids. "Eight bucks." He looked at David, who resignedly reached for his wallet.

"You forgot the olives," said Gabe.

"Those are free." The man wasn't entirely heartless.

"Did Charlie ever mention the name Jenny Brook?" Kate asked.

"Like I said, he never talked much. Yeah, ol' Charlie, he'd just sit over at that table and write those ol' poems. He'd scribble and scribble for hours just to get one right. Then he'd get mad and toss it. There'd be all these wadded-up papers on the floor whenever he left."

Kate shook her head in wonder. "I never imagined he'd be a poet."

"Everyone's a poet these days. That Charlie, though, he

was real serious about it. That last day he was here, didn't have no money to pay for his drink. So he tears out one of his poems and gives it to me. Says it'll be worth somethin' some day. Ha! I'm such a sucker.'' He picked up a dirty rag and began to give the counter an almost sensuous rubdown.

"Do you still have the poem?'' asked Kate.

"That's it, tacked over on the wall there.''

The cheap, lined paper hung by a few strips of Scotch tape. By the dim light of the bar, the words were barely readable.

This is what I told them:
That healing lies not in forgetfulness
But in remembrance
Of you.
The smell of the sea on your skin.
The small and perfect footprints you leave in the sand.
In remembrance there are no endings.
And so you lie there, now and always, by the sea.
You open your eyes. You touch me.
The sun is in your fingertips.
And I am healed.
I am healed.

"So,'' said Sam, "think it's any good?''

"Gotta be,'' said Jocelyn. "If Charlie wrote it.''

Sam shrugged. "Don't mean nothin'.''

"Seems like we've hit a dead end,'' David commented as they walked out into the blinding sunshine.

He might as well have said it of their relationship. He was standing with his hands thrust deep in his pockets as he gazed down the street at a drunk slouched in a doorway. Shattered glass sparkled in the gutter. Across the street, lurid red letters spelled out the title *Victorian Secrets* on an X-rated movie marquee.

If only he'd give her a smile, a look, anything to indicate

that things weren't drawing to a close between them. But he didn't. He just kept his hands in his pockets. And she knew, without him saying a word, that more than Charlie Decker had died.

They passed an alley, scattering shards of broken beer bottles as they walked.

"So many loose ends," she remarked. "I don't see how the police can close the case."

"When it comes to police work, there are always loose ends, nagging doubts."

"It's sad, isn't it?" She gazed back at the Victory Hotel. "When a man dies and he leaves nothing behind. No trace of who or what he was."

"You could say the same about all of us. Unless we write great books or put up buildings, what's left of us after we're gone? Nothing."

"Only children."

For a moment he was silent. Then he said, "That's if we're lucky."

"We do know one thing about him," she concluded softly. "He loved her. Jenny." Staring down at the cracked sidewalk, she thought of the face in the photograph. An unforgettable woman. Even five years after her death, Jenny Brook's magic had somehow affected the lives of four people: the one who had loved her and the three who'd watched her die. She was the one tragic thread weaving through the tapestry of their deaths.

What would it be like, she wondered, to be loved as fiercely as Jenny had been? What enchantment had she possessed? *Whatever it was, I certainly don't have it.*

She said, without conviction, "It'll be good to get home again."

"Will it?"

"I'm used to being on my own."

He shrugged. "So am I."

They'd both retreated to their separate emotional corners. So little time left, she thought with a sense of desolation.

And here they were, mouthing words like a pair of strangers. This morning, she'd awakened to find him showered and shaved and dressed in his most forbidding suit. Over breakfast they'd discussed everything but the subject that was uppermost in her mind. He could have made the first move. The whole time she was packing, he'd had the chance to ask her to stay. And she would have.

But he didn't say a thing.

Thank God she'd always been so good at holding on to her dignity. Never any tears, any hysterics. Even Eric had said as much. You've always been so sensible about things, he'd told her as he'd walked out the door.

Well, she'd be sensible this time, too.

The drive was far too short. Glancing at his profile she remembered the day they'd met. An eternity ago. He looked just as forbidding, just as untouchable.

They pulled up at her house. He carried her suitcase briskly up the walkway; he had the stride of a man in a hurry.

"Would you like to come in for a cup of coffee?" she asked, already knowing what his answer would be.

"I can't. Not right now. But I'll call you."

Famous last words. She understood perfectly, of course. It was all part of the ritual.

He cast a furtive glance at his watch. *Time to move on,* she reflected. *For both of us.*

Automatically she thrust the key in the lock and gave the door a shove. It swung open. As the room came into view, she halted on the threshold, unable to believe what she was seeing.

Dear God, she thought. *Why is this happening? Why now?*

She felt David's steadying hand close around her arm as she swayed backward in horror. The room swam, just for an instant, and then her eyes refocused on the opposite wall.

On the flowered wallpaper the letters "MYOB" had been spray painted in bloodred. And below them was the hollow-eyed figure of a skull and crossbones.

14

"No dice, Davy. The case is closed."

Pokie Ah Ching splashed coffee from his foam cup as he weaved through the crammed police station, past the desk sergeant arguing into the phone, past clerks hurrying back and forth with files, past a foul-smelling drunk shouting epithets at two weary-looking officers. Through it all, he moved as serenely as a battleship gliding through stormy waters.

"Don't you see, it was a warning!"

"Probably left by Charlie Decker."

"Kate's neighbor checked the house Tuesday morning. That message was left sometime later, when Decker was already dead."

"So it's a kid's prank."

"Yeah? Why would some kid write MYOB? Mind your own business?"

"You understand kids? I don't. Hell, I can't even figure out my own kids." Pokie headed into his office and scooted around to his chair. "Like I said, Davy, I'm busy."

David leaned across the desk. "Last night I told you we were followed. You said it was all in my head."

"I still say so."

"Then Decker turns up in the morgue. A nice, convenient little accident."

"I'm starting to smell a conspiracy theory."

"Your sense of smell is amazing."

Pokie set his cup down, slopping coffee on his papers. "Okay." He sighed. "You got one minute to tell me your theory. Then I'm throwing you out."

David grabbed a chair and sat down. "Four deaths. Tanaka. Richter. Decker. And Ellen O'Brien—"

"Death on the operating table isn't in my jurisdiction."

"But murder is. There's a hidden player in this game, Pokie. Someone who's managed to get rid of four people in a matter of two weeks. Someone smart and quiet and medically sophisticated. And very, very scared."

"Of what?"

"Kate Chesne. Maybe Kate's been asking too many questions. Maybe she knows something and just doesn't realize it. She's made our killer nervous. Nervous enough to scrawl warnings all over that wall."

"Unseen player, huh? I suppose you already got me a list of suspects."

"Starting with the chief of anesthesia. You check out that story on his wife yet?"

"She died Tuesday night in the nursing home. Natural causes."

"Oh, sure. The night after he walks off with a bunch of lethal drugs, she kicks the bucket."

"Coincidence."

"The man lives alone. There's no one to track his comings and goings—"

"I can just see the old geezer now." Pokie laughed. "Geriatric Jack the Ripper."

"It doesn't take much strength to slit someone's throat."

"But what's the old guy's motive, huh? Why would he go after members of his own staff?"

David let out a frustrated sigh. "I don't know," he admitted. "But it's got something to do with Jenny Brook."

Ever since he'd laid eyes on her photograph, he'd been unable to get the woman out of his mind. Something about her death, about the cold details recorded in her medical chart kept coming back to him, like a piece of music being played over and over in his head.

Uncontrollable seizures.

An infant girl, born alive.

Mother and child, two soft sparks of humanity, extinguished in the glare of the operating room.

Why, after five years, did their deaths threaten Kate Chesne?

There was a knock on the door. Sergeant Brophy, red-eyed and sniffling, dropped some papers on Pokie's desk. "Here's that report you been waiting for. Oh, and we got us another sighting of that Sasaki girl."

Pokie snorted. "Again? What does that make it? Forty-three?"

"Forty-four. This one's at Burger King."

"Geez. Why do they always spot 'em at fast-food chains?"

"Maybe she's sittin' there with Jimmy Hoffa and—and—" Brophy sneezed. "Elvis." He blew his nose three times. They were great loud honks that, in the wild, could have attracted geese. "Allergies," he said, as if that was a far more acceptable excuse than the common cold. He aimed a spiteful glance out the window at his nemesis: a mango tree, seething with blossoms. "Too many damn trees around here," he muttered, retreating from the office.

Pokie laughed. "Brophy's idea of paradise is an air-conditioned concrete box." Reaching for the report, he sighed. "That's it, Davy. I got work to do."

"You going to reopen the case?"

"I'll think about it."

"What about Avery? If I were you, I'd—"

"I said I'll think about it." He flipped open the report, a rude gesture that said the meeting was definitely over.

David saw he might as well bang his head against a brick wall. He rose to leave. He was almost to the door when Pokie suddenly snapped out: "Hold it, Davy."

David halted, startled by the sharpness of Pokie's voice. "What?"

"Where's Kate right now?"

"I took her to my mother's. I didn't want to leave her alone."

"Then she is in a safe place."

"If you can call being around my mother safe. Why?"

Pokie waved the report he was holding. "This just came in from M.J.'s office. It's the autopsy on Decker. He didn't drown."

"What?" David moved over to the desk and snatched up the report. His gaze shot straight to the conclusions.

Skull X rays show compression fracture, probably caused by lethal blow to the head. Cause of death: epidural hematoma.

Pokie sank back wearily and spat out an epithet. "The man was dead hours before he hit the water."

"Vengeance?" said Jinx Ransom, biting neatly into a freshly baked gingersnap. "It's a perfectly reasonable motive for murder. If, that is, one accepts there is such a thing as a reasonable motive for murder."

She and Kate were sitting on the back porch, overlooking the cemetery. It was a windless afternoon. Nothing moved—not the leaves on the trees, not the low-lying clouds, not even the air, which hung listless over the valley. The only creature stirring was Gracie, who shuffled out of the kitchen with a tray of rattling coffee cups and teaspoons. Pausing outside, Gracie cocked her head up at the sky.

"It's going to rain," she announced with absolute confidence.

"Charlie Decker was a poet," said Kate. "He loved children. Even more important, children loved him. Don't you think they'd know? They'd sense it if he was dangerous?"

"Nonsense. Children are as stupid as all the rest of us. And as for his being a mild-mannered poet, that doesn't mean a thing. He had five years to brood about his loss. That's certainly long enough to turn an obsession into violence.''

"But the people who knew him all agree he wasn't a violent man."

"We're all violent. Especially when it concerns the ones we love. They're intimately connected, love and hate."

"That's a pretty grim view of human nature."

"But a realistic one. My husband was a circuit-court judge. My son was once a prosecutor. Oh, I've heard all their stories and believe me, reality's much grimmer than we could ever imagine."

Kate gazed out at the gently sloping lawn, at the flat bronze plaques marching out like footsteps across the grass. "Why did David leave the prosecutor's office?"

"Hasn't he told you?"

"He said something about slave wages. But I get the feeling money doesn't really mean much to him."

"Money doesn't mean diddly squat to David," Gracie interjected. She was looking down at a broken gingersnap, as if she wasn't quite sure whether to eat it or toss it to the birds.

"Then why did he leave?"

Jinx gave her one of those crystal-blue looks. "You were a surprise to me, Kate. It's rare enough for David to bring any woman to meet me. And then, when I heard you were a doctor…Well." She shook her head in amazement.

"David doesn't like doctors much," Gracie explained helpfully.

"It's a bit more than just dislike, dear."

"You're right," agreed Gracie after a few seconds' thought. "I suppose *loathe* is a better word."

Jinx reached for her cane and stood up. "Come, Kate," she beckoned. "There's something I think you should see."

It was a slow and solemn walk, through the feathery gap in the mock orange hedge, to a shady spot beneath the monkeypod tree. Insects drifted like motes in the windless air. At their feet, a small bunch of flowers lay wilting on a grave.

Noah Ransom
Seven years old.

"My grandson," said Jinx.

A leaf fluttered down from the tree and lay trembling on the grass.

"It must have been terrible for David," Kate murmured. "To lose his only child."

"Terrible for anyone. But especially for David." Jinx nudged the leaf aside with her cane. "Let me tell you about my son. He's very much like his father in one way: he doesn't love easily. He's like a miser, holding on to some priceless hoard of gold. But then, when he does release it, he gives it all and that's it. There's no turning back. That's why it was so hard on him, losing Noah. That boy was the most precious thing in his life and he still can't accept the fact he's gone. Maybe that's why he has so much trouble with you." She turned to Kate. "Do you know how the boy died?"

"He said it was a case of meningitis."

"Bacterial meningitis. Curable illness, right?"

"If it's caught early enough."

"*If.* That's the word that haunts David." She looked down sadly at the wilted flowers. "He was out of town—some convention in Chicago—when Noah got sick. At first, Linda didn't think much of it. You know how kids are, always coming down with colds. But the boy's fever wouldn't go away. And then Noah said he had a headache. His usual pediatrician was on vacation so Linda took the boy to another doctor, in the same building. For two hours they sat in the waiting room. After all that, the doctor spent only five minutes with Noah. And then he sent him home."

Kate stared down at the grave, knowing, fearing, what would come next.

"Linda called the doctor three times that night. She must have known something was wrong. But all she got from him was a scolding. He told her she was just an anxious mother. That she ought to know better than to turn a cold into a crisis.

When she finally brought Noah into Emergency, he was delirious. He just kept mumbling, asking for his Daddy. The hospital doctors did what they could, but…'' Jinx gave a little shrug. ''It wasn't easy for either of them. Linda blamed herself. And David…he just withdrew. He shrank into his tight little shell and refused to come out, even for her. I'm not surprised she left him.'' Jinx looked off, toward the house. ''It came out later, about the doctor. That he was an alcoholic. That he'd lost his license in California. That's when David turned it into his personal crusade. Oh, he ruined the man, all right. He did a very thorough job of it. But it took over his life, wrecked his marriage. That's when he left the prosecutor's office. He's made a lot of money since then, destroying doctors. But the money's not why he does it. Somewhere, in the back of his mind, he'll always be crucifying that one doctor. The one who killed Noah.''

That's why we never had a chance, Kate thought. *I was always the enemy. The one he wanted to destroy.*

Jinx wandered slowly back to the house. For a long time, Kate stood alone in the shadow of the old tree, thinking about Noah Ransom, seven years old. About how powerful a force it was, this love for a child; as cruelly obsessive as anything between a man and a woman. Could she ever compete with the memory of a son? Or ever escape the blame for his death?

All these years, David had held on to that pain. He'd used it as some mystical source of power to fight the same battle over and over again. The way Charlie Decker had used his pain to sustain him through five long years in a mental hospital.

Five years in a hospital.

She frowned, suddenly remembering the bottle of pills in Decker's nightstand. Haldol. Pills for psychotics. Was he, in fact, crazy?

Turning, she looked back at the porch and saw it was empty. Jinx and Gracie had gone into the house. The air was so heavy she could feel it weighing oppressively on her shoulders. A storm on the way, she thought.

If she left now, she might make it to the state hospital before the rain started.

Dr. Nemechek was a thin, slouching man with tired eyes and a puckered mouth. His shirt was rumpled and his white coat hung in folds on his frail shoulders. He looked like a man who'd slept all night in his clothes.

They walked together on the hospital grounds. All around them, white-gowned patients wandered aimlessly like dandelion fluffs drifting about the lawn. Every so often, Dr. Nemechek would stop to pat a shoulder or murmur a few words of greeting. *How are you, Mrs. Solti? Just fine, Doctor. Why didn't you come to group therapy? Oh, it's my old trouble, you know. All those mealyworms in my feet. I see. I see. Well, good afternoon, Mrs. Solti. Good afternoon, Doctor.*

Dr. Nemechek paused on the grass and gazed around sadly at his kingdom of shattered minds. "Charlie Decker never belonged here," he remarked. "I told them from the beginning that he wasn't criminally insane. But the court had their so-called expert from the mainland. So he was committed." He shook his head. "That's the trouble with courts. All they look at is their evidence, whatever that means. I look at the man."

"And what did you see when you looked at Charlie?"

"He was withdrawn. Very depressed. At times, maybe, delusional."

"Then he was insane."

"But not criminally so." Nemechek turned to her as if he wanted to be absolutely certain she understood his point. "Insanity can be dangerous. Or it can be nothing more than a gentle affliction. A merciful shield against pain. That's what it was for Charlie: a shield. His delusion kept him alive. That's why I never tried to tamper with it. I felt that if I ever took away that shield, it would kill him."

"The police say he was a murderer."

"Ridiculous."

"Why?"

"He was a perfectly benign creature. He'd go out of his way to avoid stepping on a cricket."

"Maybe killing people was easier."

Nemechek gave a dismissive wave. "He had no reason to kill anyone."

"What about Jenny Brook? Wasn't she his reason?"

"Charlie's delusion wasn't about Jenny. He'd accepted her death as inevitable."

Kate frowned. "Then what was his delusion?"

"It was about their child. It was something one of the doctors told him, about the baby being born alive. Only Charlie got it twisted around in his head. That was his obsession, this missing daughter of his. Every August, he'd hold a little birthday celebration. He'd tell us, 'My girl's five years old today.' He wanted to find her. Wanted to raise her like a little princess, give her dresses and dolls and all the things girls are supposed to like. But I knew he'd never really try to find her. He was terrified of learning the truth: that the baby really was dead."

A sprinkling of rain made them both glance up at the sky. Wind was gusting the clouds and on the lawn, nurses hurried about, coaxing patients out of the coming storm.

"Is there any possibility he was right?" she asked. "That the girl's still alive?"

"Not a chance." A curtain of drizzle had drifted between them, blotting out his gray face. "The baby's dead, Dr. Chesne. For the last five years, the only place that child existed was in Charlie Decker's mind."

The baby's dead.

As Kate drove the mist-shrouded highway back to Jinx's house, Dr. Nemechek's words kept repeating in her head.

The baby's dead. The only place that child existed was in Charlie Decker's mind.

If the girl had lived, what would she be like now? Kate wondered. Would she have her father's dark hair? Would she have her mother's glow of eternity in her five-year-old eyes?

The face of Jenny Brook took shape in her mind, an impish smile framed by the blue sky of a summer day. At that instant, fog puffed across the road and Kate strained to see through the mist. As she did, the image of Jenny Brook wavered, dissolved; in its place was another face, a small one, framed by ironwood trees. There was a break in the clouds; suddenly, the mist vanished from the road. And as the sunlight broke through, so did the revelation. She almost slammed on the brakes.

Why the hell didn't I see it before?

Jenny Brook's child was still alive.

And he was five years old.

"Where the hell is she?" muttered David, slamming the telephone down. "Nemechek says she left the state hospital at five. She should be home by now." He glanced irritably across his desk at Phil Glickman, who was poking a pair of chopsticks into a carton of chow mein.

"You know," Glickman mumbled as he expertly shuttled noodles into his mouth, "this case gets more confusing every time I hear about it. You start off with a simple act of malpractice and you end up with murder. In plural. Where's it gonna lead next?"

"I wish I knew." David sighed. Swiveling around toward the window, he tried to ignore the tempting smells of Glickman's take-out supper. Outside, the clouds were darkening to a gunmetal gray. It reminded him of just how late it was. Ordinarily, he'd be packing up his briefcase for home. But he'd needed a chance to think, and this was where his mind seemed to work best—right here at this window.

"What a way to commit murder, slashing someone's throat," Glickman said. "I mean, think of all that blood! Takes a lot of nerve."

"Or desperation."

"And it can't be that easy. You'd have to get up pretty close to slice that neck artery." He slashed a chopstick through the air. "There are so many easier ways to do the job."

"Sounds like you've put some thought into the matter."

"Don't we all? Everyone has some dark fantasy. Cornering your wife's lover in the alley. Getting back at the punk who mugged you. We can all think of someone we'd really like to put away. And it can't be that hard, you know? Murder. If a guy's smart, he does it with subtlety." He slurped up a mouthful of noodles. "Poison, for instance. Something that kills fast and can't be traced. Now there's the perfect murder."

"Except for one thing."

"What's that?"

"Where's the satisfaction if your victim doesn't suffer?"

"A problem," Glickman conceded. "So you make 'em suffer through terror. Warnings. Threats."

David shifted uneasily, remembering the bloodred skull on Kate's wall. Through narrowed eyes, he watched the clouds hanging low on the horizon. With every passing minute, his sense of impending disaster grew stronger.

He rose to his feet and began throwing papers into his briefcase. It was useless, hanging around here; he could worry just as effectively at his mother's house.

"You know, there's one thing about this case that still bothers me," remarked Glickman, gulping the last of his supper.

"What's that?"

"That EKG. Tanaka and Richter were killed in just about the bloodiest way possible. Why should the murderer go out of his way to make Ellen O'Brien's death look like a heart attack?"

"The one thing I learned in the prosecutor's office," said David, snapping his briefcase shut, "is that murder doesn't have to make sense."

"Well, it seems to me our killer went to a lot of trouble just to shift the blame to Kate Chesne."

David was already at the door when he suddenly halted. "What did you say?"

"That he went to a lot of trouble to pin the blame—"

"No, the word you used was *shift*. He *shifted* the blame!"

"Maybe I did. So?"

"So who gets sued when a patient dies unexpectedly on the operating table?"

"The blame's usually shared by..." Glickman stopped. "Oh, my God. Why the hell didn't I think of that before?"

David was already reaching for the telephone. As he dialed the police, he cursed himself for being so blind. The killer had been there all along. Watching. Waiting. He must have known that Kate was hunting for answers, and that she was getting close. Now he was scared. Scared enough to scrawl a warning on Kate's wall. Scared enough to tail a car down a dark highway.

Maybe even scared enough to kill one more time.

It was five-thirty and most of the clerks in Medical Records had gone for the day. The lone clerk who remained grudgingly took Kate's request slip and went to the computer terminal to call up the chart location. As the data appeared, she frowned.

"This patient's deceased," she noted, pointing to the screen.

"I know," said Kate, wearily remembering the last time she'd tried to retrieve a chart from the Deceased Persons' room.

"So it's in the inactive files."

"I understand that. Could you please get me the chart?"

"It may take a while to track it down. Why don't you come back tomorrow?"

Kate resisted the urge to reach over and grab the clerk by her frilly dress. "I need the chart *now*." She felt like adding: *It's a matter of life and death.*

The clerk looked at her watch and tapped her pencil on

the desk. With agonizing slowness, she rose to her feet and vanished into the file room.

Fifteen minutes passed before she returned with the record. Kate retreated to a corner table and stared down at the name on the cover: Brook, Baby Girl.

The child had never even had a name.

The chart contained pitifully few pages, only the hospital face sheet, death certificate, and a scrawled summary of the infant's short existence. Death had been pronounced August 17 at 2:00 a.m., an hour after birth. The cause of death was cerebral anoxia: the tiny brain had been starved of oxygen. The death certificate was signed by Dr. Henry Tanaka.

Kate next turned her attention to the copy of Jenny Brook's chart, which she'd brought with her. She'd read these pages so many times before; now she studied it line by line, pondering the significance of each sentence.

"...28-year-old female, G1P0, 36 weeks' gestation, admitted via E.R. in early labor..."

A routine report, she thought. There were no surprises, no warnings of the disaster to come. But at the bottom of the first page she stopped, her gaze focusing on a single statement: "Because of maternal family history of spina bifida, amniocentesis was performed at eighteen weeks of pregnancy and revealed no abnormalities."

Amniocentesis. Early in her pregnancy, fluid had been withdrawn from Jenny Brook's womb for analysis. This would have identified any fetal malformations. It also would have identified the baby's sex.

The amniocentesis report was not included in the hospital chart. That didn't surprise her; the report had probably been filed away in Jenny Brook's outpatient record.

Which had conveniently vanished from Dr. Tanaka's office, she realized with a start.

Kate closed the chart. Suddenly feverish, she rose and returned to the file clerk. "I need another record," she said.

"Not another deceased patient, I hope."

"No, this one's still alive."

"Name?"

"William Santini."

It took only a minute for the clerk to find it. When Kate finally held it in her hands, she was almost afraid to open it, afraid to see what she already knew lay inside. She stood there beside the clerk's desk, wondering if she really wanted to know.

She opened the cover.

A copy of the birth certificate stared up at her.

Name: William Santini.
Date of Birth: August 17
Time: 03:00.

August 17, the same day. But not quite the same time. Exactly one hour after Baby Girl Brook had left the world, William Santini had entered it.

Two infants; one living, one dead. Had there ever been a better motive for murder?

"Don't tell me you still have charts to finish," remarked a shockingly familiar voice.

Kate's head whipped around. Guy Santini had just walked in the door. She slapped the chart closed but instantly realized the name was scrawled in bold black ink across the cover. In a panic, she hugged the chart to her chest as an automatic smile congealed on her face.

"I'm just…cleaning up some last paperwork." She swallowed and managed to add, conversationally, "You're here late."

"Stranded again. Car's back in the shop so Susan's picking me up." He glanced across the counter, searching for the clerk, who'd temporarily vanished. "Where's the help around here, anyway?"

"She was, uh, here just a minute ago," said Kate, inching toward the exit.

"I guess you heard the news. About Avery's wife. A blessing, really, considering her—'' He looked at her and she froze, just two feet from the door.

He frowned. ''Is something wrong?''

''No. I've just— Look, I've really got to go.'' She turned and was about to flee out the door when the file clerk yelled: ''Dr. Chesne!''

''What?'' Kate spun around to see the woman peering at her reproachfully from behind a shelf.

''The chart. You can't take it out of the department.''

Kate looked down at the folder she was still holding to her chest and frantically debated her next move. She didn't dare return the chart while Guy was standing right beside the counter; he'd see the name. But she couldn't stand here like a half-wit, either.

They were both frowning at her, waiting for her to say something.

''Look, if you're not finished with it, I can hold it right here,'' the clerk offered, moving to the counter.

''No. I mean…''

Guy laughed. ''What's in that thing, anyway? State secrets?''

Kate realized she was clutching the chart as though terrified it would be forcibly pried from her grasp. With her heart hammering, she willed her feet to move forward. Her hand was barely steady as she placed the chart facedown on the counter. ''I'm not finished with it.''

''Then I'll hold it for you.'' The clerk reached over and for one terrifying second seemed poised to expose the patient's name. Instead she merely scooped up the request list that Guy had just laid on the counter. ''Why don't you sit down, Dr. Santini?'' she suggested. ''I'll bring your records over to you.'' Then she turned and vanished into the file room.

Time to get the hell out of here, thought Kate.

It took all her self-control not to bolt out the door. She felt Guy's eyes on her back as she moved slowly and deliberately toward the exit. Only when she'd actually made it into the hall, only when she heard the door thud shut behind her, did the impact of what she'd discovered hit her full force. Guy Santini was her colleague. Her friend.

He was also a murderer. And she was the only one who knew.

Guy stared at the door through which Kate had just retreated. He'd known Kate Chesne for almost a year now and he'd never seen her so jittery. Puzzled, he turned and headed to the corner table to wait. It was his favorite spot, this little nook; it gave him a sense of privacy in this vast, impersonal room. Someone else obviously favored it, as well. There were two charts still lying there, waiting to be refiled. He grabbed a chair and was about to nudge the folders aside when his gaze suddenly froze on the top cover. He felt his legs give away. Slowly he sank into the chair and stared at the name.

Brook, Baby Girl. Deceased.

Dear God, he thought. *It can't be the same Brook.*

He flipped it open and hunted for the mother's name on the death certificate. What he saw sent panic knifing through him.

Mother: Brook, Jennifer.

The same woman. The same baby. He had to think; he had to stay calm. Yes, he would stay calm. There was nothing to worry about. No one could connect him to Jenny Brook or the child. The four people involved with that tragedy of five years ago were now dead. There was no reason for anyone to be curious.

Or was there?

He shot to his feet and hurried back to the counter. The chart that Kate had so reluctantly parted with was still lying there, face down. He flipped it over. His own son's name stared up at him.

Kate Chesne knew. She *had* to know. And she had to be stopped.

"Here you are," said the file clerk, emerging from the shelves with an armload of charts. "I think I've got all—" She halted in amazement. "Where are you going? Dr. Santini!"

Guy didn't answer; he was too busy running out the door.

The hospital lobby was reassuringly bright when Kate stepped off the elevator. A few visitors still lingered by the lobby doors, staring out at the storm. A security guard lounged at the information desk, chatting with a pretty volunteer. Kate hurried over to the public telephones. An out-of-order sign was taped to the first phone; a man was feeding a quarter into the other. She planted herself right behind him and waited. Wind rattled the lobby windows; outside, the parking lot was obscured by a heavy curtain of rain. She prayed that Lieutenant Ah Ching would be at his desk.

But at that moment it wasn't Ah Ching's voice she longed to hear most of all; it was David's.

The man was still talking on the phone. Glancing around, she was alarmed to see the security guard had vanished. The volunteer was already closing down the information desk. The place was emptying out too fast. She didn't want to be left alone—not here, not with what she knew.

She fled the hospital and headed out into the downpour.

She'd parked Jinx's car at the far end of the lot. The storm had become a fierce, tropical battering of wind and rain. By the time she'd dashed across to the car, her clothes were soaked. It took a few seconds to fumble through the unfamiliar set of keys, another few seconds to unlock the door. She was so intent on escaping the storm that she scarcely noticed the shadow moving toward her through the gloom.

Just as she slid onto the driver's seat, the shadow closed in. A hand seized her arm.

She stared up to see Guy Santini towering over her.

15

"**M**ove over," he said.

"Guy, my arm—"

"I said move over."

Desperate, she glanced around for some passerby who might hear her screams. But the lot was deserted and the only sound was the thudding of rain on the car's roof.

Escape was impossible. Guy was blocking the driver's exit and she'd never be able to scramble out the passenger door in time.

Before she could even plan her next move, Guy shoved her aside and slid onto the driver's seat. The door slammed shut. Through the window, the gray light of evening cast a watery glow on his face.

"Your keys, Kate," he demanded.

The keys had dropped beside her on the seat; she made no move to retrieve them.

"Give me the damn keys!" He suddenly spotted them in the dim light. Snatching them up, he shoved the key into the ignition. The second he did, she lashed out. Like a trapped animal, she clawed at his face but at the last instant, some inner revulsion at the viciousness of her attack made her hesitate. It was only a split second, but it was enough time for him to react.

Flinching aside, he seized her wrist and wrenched her sideways so hard she was thrown back against the seat.

"If I have to," he said in a deadly quiet voice, "I swear I'll break your arm." He threw the gear in reverse and the car jerked backward. Then, hitting the gas, he spun the car out of the parking lot and into the street.

"Where are you taking me?" she asked.

"Somewhere. Anywhere. I'm going to talk and you're going to listen."

"About—about what?"

"You know what the hell about!"

Her chin snapped up expectantly as they approached an intersection. If she could throw herself out—

But he'd already anticipated her move. Seizing her arm, he yanked her toward him and sped through the intersection just as the signal turned red.

That was the last stoplight before the freeway. The car accelerated. She watched in despair as the speedometer climbed to sixty. She'd missed her chance. If she tried to leap out now, she'd almost certainly break her neck.

He knew as well as she did that she'd never be so reckless. He released her arm. "It was none of your business, Kate," he said, his eyes shifting back to the road. "You had no right to pry. No right at all."

"Ellen was my patient—*our* patient—"

"That doesn't mean you can tear my life apart!"

"What about her life? And Ann's? They're dead, Guy!"

"And the past died with them! I say let it stay dead."

"My God, I thought I knew you. I thought we were friends—"

"I have to protect my son. And Susan. You think I'd stand back and let them be destroyed?"

"They'd never take the boy away from you! Not after five years! The courts are bound to give you custody—"

"You think all I'm worried about is custody? Oh, we'd keep William all right. There's no judge on earth who'd be able to take him away from me! Who'd hand him over to some lunatic like Decker! No. It's Susan I'm thinking of."

The highway was slick with rain, the road treacherous. Both his hands were fully occupied on the steering wheel. If she lunged at him now, the car would surely spin out of control, killing them both. She had to wait for another time, another chance to escape.

"I don't understand," she persisted, scanning the road ahead for a stalled car, a traffic jam, anything to slow them down. "What do you mean, it's Susan you're worried about?"

"She doesn't know." At Kate's incredulous look, he nodded. "She thinks William is hers."

"How can she not know?"

"I've kept it from her. For five years, it's been my little secret. She was under anesthesia when our baby was born. It was a nightmare, all that rush, all that panic to do an emergency C-section. That was our third baby, Kate. Our last chance. And she was born dead...." He paused and cleared his throat; when he spoke again, his voice was still thick with pain. "I didn't know what to do. What to tell Susan. There she was, sleeping. So peaceful, so happy. And there I was, holding our dead baby girl."

"You took Jenny Brook's baby as your own."

He hastily scraped the back of his hand across his face. "It was—it was an act of God. Can't you see that? *An act of God.* That's how it seemed to me at the time. The woman had just died. And there was her baby boy, this absolutely *perfect* baby boy, crying in the next room. No one to hold him. Or love him. No one knew a thing about the child's father. There didn't seem to be any relatives, anyone who cared. And there was Susan, already starting to wake up. Can't you understand? It would have killed her to find out. God *gave* us that boy! It was as if—as if He had planned it that way. We all felt it. Ann. Ellen. Only Tanaka—"

"He didn't agree?"

"Not at first. I argued with him. I practically begged him. It was only when Susan opened her eyes and asked for her baby that he finally gave in. So Ellen brought the boy to the room. She put him in Susan's arms. And my Susan—she just looked at him and then she—she started to cry...." Guy wiped his sleeve across his face. "That's when we knew we'd done the right thing."

Yes, Kate could see the perfection of that moment. A decision as wise as Solomon's. What better proof of its rightness than the sight of a newborn baby curled up in his mother's arms?

But that same decision had led to the murder of four people.

Soon it would be five.

The car suddenly slowed; with a new burst of hope, she looked up. Traffic was growing heavier. Far ahead lay the Pali tunnel, curtained off by rain. She knew there was an emergency telephone somewhere near the entrance. If he would just slow down a little more, if she could shove the car door open, she might be able to fling herself out before he could stop her.

The chance never came. Instead of heading into the tunnel, Guy veered off onto a thickly wooded side road and roared past a sign labeled: Pali Lookout. The last stop, she thought. Set on a cliff high above the valley, this was the overhang where suicidal lovers sealed their pacts, where ancient warriors once were flung to their deaths. It was the perfect spot for murder.

A last flood of desperation made her claw for the door. Before she could get it open, he yanked her back. She turned and flew at him with both fists. Guy struggled to fight her off and lost control of the wheel. The car swerved off the road. By the erratic beams of their headlights, she caught glimpses of trees looming ahead. Branches thudded against the windshield but she was beyond caring whether they crashed; her only goal was escape.

It was Guy's overwhelming strength that decided the battle. He threw all his weight into shoving her back. Then, cursing, he grabbed the wheel and spun it wildly to the left. The right fender scraped trees as the car veered back onto the road. Kate, sprawled against the seat, could only watch in defeat as they weaved up the last hundred yards to the lookout.

Guy stopped the car and killed the engine. For a long time he sat in silence, as though summoning up the courage to get the job done. Outside, the rain had slowed to a drizzle and beyond the cliff's edge, mist swirled past, shrouding the fatal plunge from view.

"That was a damned crazy stunt you pulled," he said quietly. "Why the hell did you do it?"

Slowly she bowed her head; she felt a profound sense of weariness. Of inevitability. "Because you're going to kill me," she whispered. "The way you killed the others."

"I'm going to *what*?"

She looked up, searching his eyes for some trace of remorse. If only she could reach inside him and drag out some last scrap of humanity! "Was it easy?" she asked softly. "Cutting Ann's throat? Watching her bleed to death?"

"You mean— You really think I— Dear God!" He dropped his head in his hands. Suddenly he began to laugh. It was soft at first, then it grew louder and wilder until his whole body was racked by what sounded more like sobs than laughter. He didn't notice the new set of headlights, flickering like a beacon through the mist. She glanced around and saw that another car had wandered up the road. This was her chance to throw open the door, to run for help. But she didn't. In that instant she knew that Guy had never really meant to hurt her. That he was incapable of murder.

Without warning, he shoved his door open and stumbled out into the fog. At the edge of the lookout, he halted, his head and shoulders bowed as if in prayer.

Kate got out of the car and followed him. She didn't say a thing. She simply reached out and touched his arm. She could almost feel the pain, the confusion, coursing through his body.

"Then you didn't kill them," she said.

He looked up and slowly took in a deep breath of air. "I'd do almost anything to keep my son. But murder?" He shook his head. "No. God, no. Oh, I thought about killing Decker. Who would have missed him? He was nothing, just a—a scrap of human garbage. And it seemed like such an easy way out. Maybe the only way out. He wouldn't give up. He kept hounding people for answers. Demanding to know where the baby was."

"How did he know the baby was alive?"

"There was another doctor in the delivery room that night—"

"You mean Dr. Vaughn?"

"Decker talked to him. Learned just enough."

"And then Vaughn died in a car accident."

Guy nodded. "I thought it'd all be okay, then. I thought it was over. But then Decker got out of the state hospital. Sooner or later, someone would've talked. Tanaka was ready to. And Ann was scared out of her mind. I gave her some money, to leave the islands. But she never made it. Decker got to her first."

"That doesn't make sense, Guy. Why would he kill the only people who could give him the answers?"

"He was psychotic."

"Even psychotics have some sort of logic."

"He must have done it. There was no one else who—"

From somewhere in the mist came the hard click of metal. Kate and Guy froze as footsteps rapped slowly across the pavement. Out of the gathering darkness, a figure emerged, like vapor taking on substance until it stood before them. Even in the somber light of dusk, Susan Santini's red hair seemed to sparkle with fire. But it was the dull gray of the gun that held Kate's gaze.

"Move out of the way, Guy," Susan ordered softly.

Guy was too stunned to move or speak; he could only stare mutely at his wife.

"It was you," Kate murmured in astonishment. "All the time *you* were the one. Not Decker."

Slowly, Susan turned her unfocused gaze on Kate. Through the veil of mist drifting between them, her face was as vague and formless as a ghost's. "You don't understand, do you? But you've never had a baby, Kate. You've never been afraid of someone hurting it or taking it away. That's all a mother ever thinks about. Worries about. It's all *I* ever worried about."

A low groan escaped Guy's throat. "My God, Susan. Do you understand what you've done?"

"You wouldn't do it. So I had to. All those years, I never knew about William. You should have told me, Guy. You should have told me. I had to hear it from Tanaka."

"You killed four people, Susan!"

"Not four. Only three. I didn't kill Ellen." Susan looked at Kate. "She did."

Kate stared at her. "What do you mean?"

"That wasn't succinylcholine in the vial. It was potassium chloride. You gave Ellen a lethal dose." Her gaze shifted back to her husband. "I didn't want you to be blamed, darling. I couldn't stand to see you hurt, the way you were hurt by the last lawsuit. So I changed the EKG. I put *her* initials on it."

"And I got the blame," finished Kate.

Nodding, Susan raised the gun. "Yes, Kate. You got the blame. I'm sorry. Now please, Guy. Move away. It has to be done, for William's sake."

"No, Susan."

She frowned at him in disbelief. "They'll take him away from me. Don't you see? They'll take my baby away."

"I won't let them. I promise."

Susan shook her head. "It's too late, Guy. I've killed the others. She's the only one who knows."

"But *I* know!" Guy blurted out. "Are you going to kill me, too?"

"You won't tell. You're my husband."

"Susan, give me the gun." Guy moved slowly forward, his hand held out to her. His voice dropped, became gentle, intimate. "Please, darling. Nothing will happen. I'll take care of everything. Just give it to me."

She retreated a step and almost lost her balance on the uneven terrain. Guy froze as the barrel of the gun swayed for an instant in his direction.

"You're not going to hurt me, Susan."

"Please, Guy…"

He took a step forward. "Are you?"

"I love you," she moaned.

"Then give me the gun. Yes, darling. Give it to me…."

The distance between them slowly evaporated. Guy's hand stretched out to her, coaxing her with the promise of warmth and safety. She stared at it with longing, as though knowing in some deep part of her mind that it was forever beyond her reach. The gun was only inches from Guy's fingers and still she didn't move; she was paralyzed by the inevitability of defeat.

Guy, at last sensing he had won, quickly closed the gap between them. Seizing the gun by the barrel, he tried to tug it from her hands.

But she didn't surrender it. At that instant, something inside her, some last spark of resistance, seemed to flare up and she tried to wrench it back.

"Let go!" she screamed.

"Give it to me," Guy demanded, wrestling for control of the weapon. "Susan, give it to me!"

The gun's blast seemed to trap them in freeze-frame. They stared at each other in astonishment, neither of them willing to believe what had just happened. Then Guy stumbled backward, clutching his leg.

"No!" Susan's wail rose up and drifted, ghostlike, through the mist. Slowly she turned toward Kate. The glow of desperation was in her eyes. And she was still clutching the gun.

That's when Kate ran. Blindly, desperately, into the mist. She heard a pistol shot. A bullet whistled past and thudded into the dirt near her feet. There was no time to get her bearings, to circle back toward the road. She just kept running and prayed that the fog would shroud her from Susan.

The ground suddenly rose upward. Through fingers of

mist, she saw the sheer face of the ridge, sparsely stubbled with brush. She spun around and realized instantly that the way back to the main road was blocked by Susan's approach. Her only escape route lay to the left, down the crumbling remains of the old Pali road. It was the original cliff pass. The road had long ago been abandoned to the elements. She had no idea how far it would take her; parts of it, she knew, had collapsed down the sheer slope.

The sound of footsteps closing in left her no choice. She scrambled over a low concrete wall and at once found herself sliding helplessly down a muddy bank. Clawing at branches and vines, she managed to break her fall until she landed, scratched and breathless, on a slab of pavement. The old Pali road.

Somewhere above, hidden among the clouds, bushes rustled. "There's nowhere to run, Kate!" Susan's disembodied voice seemed to come from everywhere at once. "The old road doesn't go very far. One wrong step and you'll be over the cliff. So you'd better be careful...."

Careful...careful... The shouted warning echoed off the ridge and shattered into terrifying fragments of sound. The rustling of bushes moved closer. Susan was closing in. She was taking her time, advancing slowly, steadily. Her victim was trapped. And she knew it.

But trapped wasn't the same as helpless.

Kate leaped to her feet and began to run. The old road was full of cracks and potholes. In places it had crumbled away entirely and young trees poked through, their roots rippling the asphalt. She strained to see through the fog but could make out no more than a few feet ahead. Darkness was falling fast; it would cut off the last of her visibility. But it would also be a cloak in which to hide.

But where could she hide? On her right, the ridge loomed steeply upward; on her left, the pavement broke off sharply at the cliff's edge. She had no choice; she had to keep running.

She stumbled over a loose boulder and sprawled onto the

brutal asphalt. At once she was back on her feet, mindless of the pain searing her knees. Even as she ran, she forced herself to think ahead. Would there be a barrier at the road's end? Or would there simply be a straight drop to oblivion? In either case, there'd be no escape. There would only be a bullet, and then a plunge over the cliff. How long would it be before they found her body?

A gust of wind swept the road. For an instant, the mist cleared. She saw looming to her right the face of the ridge, covered by dense brush. Halfway up, almost hidden by the overgrowth, was the mouth of a cave. If she could reach it, if she could scramble up those bushes before Susan passed this way, she could hide until help arrived. If it arrived.

She threaded her way into the shrubbery and began clambering up the mountainside. Rain had muddied the slope; she had to claw for roots and branches to pull herself up. All the time, there was the danger of dislodging a boulder, of sending it thundering to the road. The crash would certainly alert Susan. And here she'd be, poised like a fly on the wall. One well-placed bullet would end it all.

The sound of footsteps made her freeze. Susan was approaching. Desperately, Kate hugged the mountain, willing herself to blend into the bushes.

The footsteps slowed, stopped. At that instant, the wind nudged the clouds against the ridge, draping Kate in silvery mist. The footsteps moved on, slowly clipping across the pavement. Only when the sound had faded did Kate dare continue her climb.

By the time she reached the cave's mouth, her hands had cramped into claws. In took her last ounce of strength to drag herself up into the muddy hollow. There she collapsed, fighting to catch her breath. Dampness trickled from the tree roots above and dripped onto her face. She heard, deep in the shadows, the rustle of movement and something scuttled across her arm. A beetle. She didn't have the energy to brush it off. Exhausted and shivering, she curled up like a tired puppy in the mud. The wind rose, sweeping the clouds from the pass.

Already the mist was fading. If she could just hold out until nightfall. That was the most she could hope for: darkness.

Closing her eyes, she focused on a mental image of David. If only he could hear her silent plea for help. But he couldn't help her. No one could. She wondered how he'd react to her death. Would he feel any grief? Or would he simply shrug it off as a tragic end to a fading love affair? That was what hurt most—the thought of his indifference.

She cradled her face in her arms, and warm tears mingled with the icy water on her cheeks. She'd never felt so alone, so abandoned. Suddenly it didn't matter whether she lived or died; only that someone cared.

But I'm the only one who really cares.

A desperate new strength stirred inside her. Slowly she unfolded her limbs and looked out at the thin wisps of fog drifting past the cave. And she felt a new sense of fury that her life might be stolen from her and that the man she loved wasn't even here to help.

If I want to be saved, I have to do it myself.

It was the footsteps, moving slowly back along the road, that told her darkness would come too late to save her. Through the tangle of branches fringing the cave mouth, she saw against the sky's fading light the velvety green of a distant ridge. The mist had vanished; so had her invisibility.

"You're up there, aren't you?" Susan's voice floated up from the road, a sound so chilling Kate trembled. "I almost missed it. But there's one unfortunate thing about caves. Something I'm sure you've realized by now. They're dead ends."

Rocks rattled down the slope and slammed onto the road, their impact echoing like gunshot. *She's climbing the ridge,* Kate thought frantically. *She's coming for me....*

Her only escape route was back out through the cave mouth. Right into Susan's line of fire.

A twig snapped and more rocks slithered down the mountain. Susan was closing in. Kate had no choice left; either she bolted now or she'd be trapped like a rat.

Swiftly she groped around in the mud and came up with a fist-size rock. It wasn't much against a gun, but it was all she had. Cautiously, she eased her head out. To her horror, she saw that Susan was already halfway up the slope.

Their eyes met. In that instant, each recognized the other's desperation. One was fighting for her life, the other for her child. There could be no compromise, no surrender, except in death.

Susan took aim; the barrel swung up toward her prey's head.

Kate hurled the rock.

It skimmed the bushes and thudded against Susan's shoulder. Crying out, Susan slid a few feet down the mountainside before she managed to grab hold of a branch. There she clung for a moment, stunned.

Kate scrambled out of the cave and began clawing her way up the ridge. Even as she pulled herself up, branch by branch, some rational part of her brain was screaming that the ascent was impossible, that the cliff face was too steep, the bushes too straggly to support her weight. But her arms and legs seemed to move on their own, guided not by logic but by the instinct to survive. Her sleeves were shredded by thorns and her hands and arms were already scraped raw but she was too numbed by terror to feel pain.

A bullet ricocheted off a boulder. Kate cringed as shattered rock and earth spat out and stung her face. Susan's aim was wide; she couldn't cling to the mountain and shoot accurately at the same time.

Kate looked up to find herself staring at an overhanging rock, laced with vines. Was she strong enough to drag herself over the top? Would the vines hold her weight? The surface was impossibly steep and she was so tired, so very tired....

Another shot rang out; the bullet came so close she could feel it whistle past her cheek. Kate frantically grabbed a vine and began to drag herself up the rock face. Her shoes slid uselessly downward, then found a toe hold. She shimmied up a few precious inches, then a few more, her knees scraping the harsh volcanic boulder. High above, clouds raced across the sky, taunting her with the promise of freedom. How many bullets were left?

It only takes one....

Every inch became an agony. Her muscles screamed for rest. Even if a bullet found its mark, she doubted she'd feel the pain.

When at last she cleared the overhang, she was too exhausted to feel any sense of triumph. She hauled herself over the top and rolled onto a narrow ledge. It was nothing more than a flat boulder, turned slick with rain and lichen, but no bed had ever felt so wonderful. If only she could lie here forever. If she could close her eyes and sleep! But there was no time to rest, no time to allow the agony to ease from her body; Susan was right behind her.

She staggered to her feet, her legs trembling with exhaustion, her body buffeted by the whistling wind. One of her shoes had dropped off during the climb and with every step, thorns bit into her bare foot. But here the ascent was easier and she had only a few yards to go until she reached the top of the ridge.

She never made it.

A final gunshot rang out. What she felt wasn't pain, but surprise. There was the dull punch of the bullet slamming into her shoulder. The sky spun above her. For a moment she swayed, as unsteady as a reed in the wind. Then she felt herself fall backward. She was rolling, over and over, tumbling toward oblivion.

It was a halekoa bush—one of those tough stubborn weeds that clamp their roots deep into Hawaiian soil—that saved her life. It snagged her by the legs, slowing her fall just enough to keep her from plunging over the edge of the boulder. As she lay there, fighting to make sense of where she was, she became aware of a strange shrieking in the distance; to her confused brain, it sounded like an infant's wail, and it grew steadily louder.

The hallucination dragged her into consciousness. Groggily she opened her eyes to the dull monochrome of a cloudy sky. The infant's cry suddenly turned into the rhythmic wail of police sirens. The sound of help. Of salvation.

Then, across her field of vision, a shadow moved. She struggled to make out the figure standing over her. Against the sky's fading light, Susan Santini's face was nothing more than a black cutout with wind-lashed hair.

Susan said nothing as she slowly pointed her gun at Kate's head. For a moment she stood there, her skirt flapping in the wind, the pistol clutched in both hands. A gust whipped the narrow ledge, making her sway uneasily on the slippery rock.

The siren's cry suddenly cut off; men's shouts rose up from the valley.

Kate struggled to sit up. The barrel was staring her in the face. She managed to say, quietly, "There's no reason to kill me now, Susan. Is there?"

"You know about William."

"So will they." Kate nodded feebly toward the distant voices, which were already moving closer.

"They won't. Not unless you tell them."

"How do you know I haven't?"

The gun wavered. "No!" Susan cried, her voice tinged with the first trace of panic. "You couldn't have told them! You weren't certain—"

"You need help, Susan. I'll see you get it. All the help you need."

The barrel still hovered at her head. It would take only a twitch of the finger, the clap of the pistol hammer, to make Kate's whole world disintegrate. She gazed up into that black circle, wondering if she would feel the bullet. How strange, that she could face her own death with such calmness. She had fought to stay alive and she had lost. Now all she could do was wait for the end.

Then, through the wind's scream, she heard a voice calling her name. *Another hallucination,* she thought. *It must be....*

But there it was again: David's voice, shouting her name, over and over.

Suddenly she wanted to live! She wanted to tell him all the things she'd been too proud to say. That life was too precious to waste on hurts of the past. That if he just gave her the chance, she could help him forget all the pain he'd ever suffered.

"Please, Susan," she whispered. "Put it down."

Susan shifted but her hands were still gripping the pistol. She seemed to be listening to the voices, moving closer along the old Pali road.

"Can't you see?" cried Kate. "If you kill me, you'll destroy your only chance of keeping your son!"

Her words seemed to drain all the strength from Susan's arms. Slowly, almost imperceptibly, she let the gun drop. For a moment she stood motionless, her head bent in a silent gesture of mourning. Then she turned and gazed over the ledge, at the road far below. "It's too late now," she said in a voice so soft it was almost drowned in the wind. "I've already lost him."

A chorus of shouts from below told them they'd been spotted.

Susan, her hair whipping like flames, stared down at the gathering of men. "It's better this way," she insisted. "He'll have only good memories of me. That's the way childhood should be, you know. Only good memories…"

Perhaps it was a sudden gust that threw Susan off balance; Kate could never be certain. All she knew was that one instant Susan was poised on the edge of the rock and then, in the next instant, she was gone.

She fell soundlessly, without uttering a cry.

It was Kate who sobbed. She collapsed back against the cold and unforgiving bed of stone. As the world spun around her she cried, silently, for the woman who had just died, and for the four others who had lost their lives. So many deaths, so much suffering. And all in the name of love.

16

David was the first to reach her.

He found her seventy-five feet up the mountainside, unconscious and shivering on a bloodstained boulder. What he did next had nothing to do with logic; it was pure panic. He ripped off his jacket and threw it over her body, only one thought in his mind. *You can't die. I won't let you. Do you hear me, Kate? You can't die!*

He cradled her in his arms and as the warmth of her blood seeped through his shirt, he said her name over and over, as though he could somehow keep her soul from drifting forever beyond his reach. He scarcely heard the shouts of the rescue workers or the ambulance sirens; his attention was focused on the rhythm of her breathing and the beating of her heart against his chest.

She was so cold, so still. If only he could give her his warmth. He had made just such a wish once before, when his only child had lain dying in his arms. *Not this time,* he prayed, pulling her tightly against him. *Don't take her from me, too....*

That plea rang over and over in his head as they carried her down the mountain. The descent ended in mass confusion as ambulance workers crowded in to help. David was shunted to the sidelines, a helpless observer of a battle he wasn't trained to fight.

He watched the ambulance scream off into the darkness. He imagined the emergency room, the lights, the people in white. He couldn't bear to think of Kate, lying helplessly in all that chaos. But that's where she would be soon. It was her only chance.

A hand clapped him gently on the shoulder. "You okay, Davy?" Pokie asked.

"Yeah." He sighed deeply. "Yeah."

"She'll be all right. I got a crystal ball on these things." He turned at the sound of a sneeze.

Sergeant Brophy approached, his face half-buried in a handkerchief. "They've brought the body up," said Brophy. "Got tangled up in all that—that—" he blew his nose "—shrubbery. Broken neck. Wanna take a look before it goes to the morgue?"

"Never mind," Pokie grunted. "I'll take your word for it." As they walked to the car, he asked, "How did Dr. Santini handle the news?"

"That's the weird thing," replied Brophy. "When I told him about his wife, he sort of acted like—well, he'd expected it."

Pokie frowned at the covered body of Susan Santini, now being loaded into the ambulance. He sighed. "Maybe he did. Maybe he knew all along what was happening. But he didn't want to admit it. Even to himself."

Brophy opened the car door. "Where to, Lieutenant?"

"The hospital. And move it." Pokie nodded toward David. "This man's got some serious waiting to do."

It was four hours before David was allowed to see her. Four hours of pacing the fourth-floor waiting room. Four hours of walking back and forth past the same *National Enquirer* headline on the coffee table: Woman's Head Joined To Baboon's Body.

There was only one other person in the room, a mule-faced man who slouched beneath a No Smoking sign, puffing desperately on a cigarette. He stubbed out the butt and reached for another. "Getting late," the man commented. That was the extent of their conversation. Two words, uttered in a monotone. The man never said who he was waiting for. He never spoke of fear. It was there, plain in his eyes.

At eleven o'clock, the mule-faced man was called into the recovery room and David was left alone. He stood at the window, listening to the wail of an approaching ambulance. For the hundredth time, he looked at his watch. She'd been in surgery three hours. How long did it take to remove a bullet? Had something gone wrong?

At midnight, a nurse at last poked her head into the room. "Are you Mr. Ransom?"

He spun around, his heart instantly racing. "Yes!"

"I thought you'd want to know. Dr. Chesne's out of surgery."

"Then... She's all right?"

"Everything went just fine."

He let out a breath so heavy its release left him floating. *Thank you,* he thought. *Thank you.*

"If you'd like to go home, we'll call you when she—"

"I have to see her."

"She's still unconscious."

"I have to see her."

"I'm sorry, but we only allow immediate family into..." Her voice trailed off as she saw the dangerous look in his eyes. She cleared her throat. "Five minutes, Mr. Ransom. That's all. You understand?"

Oh, he understood, all right. And he didn't give a damn. He pushed past her, through the recovery-room doors.

He found her lying on the last gurney, her small, pale form drowning in bright lights and plastic tubes. There was only a limp white curtain separating her from the next patient. David hovered at the foot of her stretcher, afraid to move close, afraid to touch her for fear he might break one of those fragile limbs. He was reminded of a princess in a glass bell, lying in some deep forest: untouchable, unreachable. A cardiac monitor chirped overhead, marking the rhythm of her heart. Beautiful music. Good and strong and steady. Kate's heart. He stood there, immobile, as the nurses fussed with tubes, adjusted IV fluids and oxygen. A doctor came to examine Kate's lungs. David felt useless. He was like a great big boulder in everyone's path. He knew he should leave and let them do their job, but something kept him rooted to his spot. One of the nurses pointed to her watch and said sternly, "We really can't work around you. You'll have to leave now."

But he didn't. He wouldn't. Not until he knew everything would be all right.

"She's waking up."

The light of a dozen suns seemed to burn through her closed eyelids. She heard voices, vaguely familiar, murmuring in the void above her. Slowly, painfully, she opened her eyes.

What she saw first was the light, brilliant and inescapable, glaring down at her. Bit by bit, she made out the smiling face of a woman, someone she knew from some dim and distant past, though she couldn't quite remember why. She focused on the name tag: Julie Sanders, RN. Julie. Now she remembered.

"Can you hear me, Dr. Chesne?" Julie asked.

Kate made a feeble attempt to nod.

"You're in the recovery room. Are you in pain?"

Kate didn't know. Her senses were returning one by one, and pain had yet to reawaken. It took her a moment to register all the signals her brain was receiving. She felt the hiss of oxygen in her nostrils and heard the soft beep of a cardiac monitor somewhere over the bed. But pain? No. She felt only a terrible sense of emptiness. And exhaustion. She wanted to sleep....

More faces had gathered around the bed. Another nurse, a stethoscope draped around her neck. Dr. Tam, dour as always. And then she heard a voice, calling softly to her.

"Kate?"

She turned. Framed against the glare of lights, David's face was blackly haggard. In wonder, she reached up to touch him but found that her wrist was hopelessly tangled in what seemed like a multitude of plastic tubes. Too weak to struggle, she let her hand drop back to the bed.

That's when he took it. Gently, as if he were afraid he might break her.

"You're all right," he whispered, pressing his lips to her palm. "Thank God you're all right...."

"I don't remember...."

"You've been in surgery." He gave her a small, tense smile. "Three hours. It seemed like forever. But the bullet's out."

She remembered, then. The wind. The ridge. And Susan, quietly slipping away like a phantom. "She's dead?"

He nodded. "There was nothing anyone could do."

"And Guy?"

"He won't be able to walk for a while. I don't know how he made it to that phone. But he did."

For a moment she lay in silence, thinking of Guy, whose life was now as shattered as his leg. "He saved my life. And now he's lost everything...."

"Not everything. He still has his son."

Yes, she thought. *William will always be Guy's son.* Not by blood, but by something much stronger: by love. Out of all this tragedy, at least one thing would remain intact and good.

"Mr. Ransom, you really will have to leave," insisted Dr. Tam.

David nodded. Then he bent over and dutifully gave Kate a gruff and awkward kiss. If he had told her he loved her, if he had said anything at all, she might have found some joy in that dry touch of lips. But too quickly his hand melted away from hers.

Things seemed to move in a blur. Dr. Tam began asking questions she was too dazed to answer. The nurses bustled around her bed, changing IV bottles, disconnecting wires, tucking in sheets. She was given a pain shot. Within minutes, she felt herself sliding irresistibly toward sleep.

As they moved her out of the recovery room, she fought
to stay awake. There was something important she had to say
to David, something that couldn't wait. But there were so
many people around and she lost track of his voice in the
confusing buzz of conversation. She felt a burst of panic that
this was her last chance to tell him she loved him. But even
to the very edge of consciousness, some last wretched scrap
of pride kept her silent. And so, in silence, she let herself be
dragged once again into darkness.

David stayed in her hospital room until almost dawn. He
sat by her bed, holding her hand, brushing the hair off her
face. Every so often he would say her name, half hoping she
would awaken. But whatever pain shot they'd given her was
industrial strength; she scarcely stirred all night. If only once
she'd called for him in her sleep, if she'd said even the first
syllable of his name, it would have been enough. He would
have known she needed him and then he would have told
her he needed her. It wasn't the sort of thing a man could
just come out and say to anyone. At least, *he* couldn't. In
truth, he was worse off than poor mute Charlie Decker. At
least Decker could express himself in a few lines of wretched
poetry.

It was a long drive home.

As soon as he walked in the door, he called the hospital
to check on her condition. ''Stable.'' That was all they'd say
but it was enough. He called a florist and ordered flowers
delivered to Kate's room. Roses. Since he couldn't think of
a message, he told the clerk to simply write ''David.'' He
fixed himself some coffee and toast and ate like a starved
man, which he was, since he'd missed supper the night before. Then, dirty, unshaven, exhausted, he went into the living room and threw himself on the couch.

He thought about all the reasons he couldn't be in love.
He'd carved out a nice, comfortable existence for himself.
He looked around at the polished floor, the curtains, the
books lined up in the glass cabinet. Then it struck him how

sterile it all was. This wasn't the home of a living, breathing man. It was a shell, the way he was a shell.

What the hell, he thought. She probably wouldn't want him anyway. Their affair had been rooted in need. She'd been terrified and he, conveniently, had been there. Soon she'd be back on her feet, her career on track. You couldn't keep a woman like Kate down for long.

He admired her and he wanted her. But did he love her? He hoped not.

Because he, better than anyone else, knew that love was nothing more than a setup for grief.

Dr. Clarence Avery stood awkwardly in the doorway of Kate's hospital room and asked if he could come in. He was carrying a half dozen hideously tinted green carnations, which he waved at her as though he had no idea what one did with flowers. Tinted green ones, anyway. The stems were still wrapped in supermarket cellophane, price tag and all.

"These are for you," he said, just in case she wasn't quite certain about that point. "I hope… I hope you're not allergic to carnations. Or anything."

"I'm not. Thank you, Dr. Avery."

"It's nothing, really. I just…" His gaze wandered to the dozen long-stemmed red roses set in a porcelain vase on the nightstand. "Oh. But I see you've already gotten flowers. Roses." Sadly, he looked down at his green carnations the way one might study a dead animal.

"I prefer carnations," she replied. "Could you put them in water for me? I think I saw a vase under the sink."

"Certainly." He took the flowers over to the sink and as he bent down, she saw that, as usual, his pants were wrinkled and his socks didn't match. The carnations looked somehow touching, flopping about in the huge, watery vase. What mattered most was that they'd been delivered in person, which was more than could be said about the roses.

They had arrived while she was still sleeping. The card said simply, "David." He hadn't called or visited. She thought maybe he'd decided this was the time to make the break. All morning she'd alternated between wanting to tear the flowers to bits and wanting to gather them up and hug them. Now that was an apt analogy—hugging thorns to one's breast.

"Here," she said. "Put the carnations right next to me. Where I can smell them." She brusquely shoved the roses aside, an act that made her wince. The surgical incision had left her with dozens of stitches and it had taken a hefty dose of narcotics just to dull the pain. Carefully she eased back against the pillows.

Pleased that his offering was given such a place of honor, Dr. Avery took a moment of silence to admire the limp blossoms. Then he cleared his throat. "Dr. Chesne," he began, "I should tell you this isn't just a—a social visit."

"It's not?"

"No. It has to do with your position here at Mid Pac."

"Then there's been a decision," she said quietly.

"With all the new evidence that's come out, well…" He gave a little shrug. "I suppose I should have taken your side earlier. I'm sorry I didn't. I suppose I was… I'm just sorry." Shuffling, he looked down at his ink-stained lab coat. "I don't know why I've held on to this blasted chairmanship. It's never given me anything but ulcers. Anyway, I'm here to tell you we're offering you your old job back. There'll be nothing on your record. Just a notation that a lawsuit was filed against you and later dropped. Which it will be. At least, that's what I'm told."

"My old job," she murmured. "I don't know." Sighing, she turned and looked out the window. "I'm not even sure I want it back. You know, Dr. Avery, I've been thinking. About other places."

"You mean another hospital?"

"Another town." She smiled at him. "It's not so surprising, is it? I've had a lot of time to think these last few days. I've been wondering if I don't belong somewhere else. Away from all this—this ocean." *Away from David.*

"Oh, dear."

"You'll find a replacement. There must be hundreds of doctors begging to come to paradise."

"No, it's not that. I'm just surprised. After all the work Mr. Ransom put into this, I thought certainly you'd—"

"Mr. Ransom? What do you mean?"

"All those calls he made. To every member of the hospital board."

A parting gesture, she thought. *At least I should be grateful for that.*

"It was quite a turnaround, I must say. A plaintiff's attorney asking—demanding—we reinstate a doctor! But this morning, when he presented the police evidence and we heard Dr. Santini's statement, well, it took the board a full five minutes to make a decision." He frowned. "Mr. Ransom gave us the idea you wanted your job back."

"Maybe I did once," she replied, staring at the roses and wondering why she felt no sense of triumph. "But things change. Don't they?"

"I suppose they do." Avery cleared his throat and shuffled a little more. "Your job is there if you want it. And we'll certainly be needing you on staff. Especially with my retirement coming up."

She looked up in surprise. "You're retiring?"

"I'm sixty-four, you know. That's getting along. I've never seen much of the country. Never had the time. My wife and I, we used to talk about traveling after my retirement. Barb would've wanted me to enjoy myself. Don't you think?"

Kate smiled. "I'm sure she would have."

"Anyway…" He shot another glance at the drooping carnations. "They are rather pretty, aren't they?" He walked out of the room, chuckling. "Yes. Yes, much better than roses, I think. Much better."

Kate turned once again to the flowers. Red roses. Green carnations. What an absurd combination. Just like her and David.

* * *

It was raining hard when David came to see her late that afternoon. She was sitting alone in the solarium, gazing through the watery window at the courtyard below. The nurse had just washed and brushed her hair and it was drying as usual into those frizzy, little-girl waves she'd always hated. She didn't hear him as he walked into the room. Only when he said her name did she turn and see him standing there, his hair damp and windblown, his suit beaded with rain. He looked tired. Almost as tired as she felt. She wanted him to pull her close, to take her in his arms, but he didn't. He simply bent over and gave her an automatic kiss on the forehead and then he straightened again.

"Out of bed, I see. You must be feeling better," he remarked.

She managed a wan smile. "I guess I never was one for lying around all day."

"Oh. I brought you these." Almost as an afterthought, he handed her a small foil-wrapped box of chocolates. "I wasn't sure they'd let you eat anything yet. Maybe later."

She looked down at the box resting in her lap. "Thank you," she murmured. "And thank you for the roses." Then she turned and stared out at the rain.

There was a long silence, as if both of them had run out of things to say. The rain slid down the solarium windows, casting a watery rainbow of light on her folded hands.

"I just spoke with Avery," he finally said. "I hear you're getting your old job back."

"Yes. He told me. I guess that's something else I have to thank you for."

"What's that?"

"My job. Avery said you made a lot of phone calls."

"Just a few. Nothing, really." He took a deep breath and continued with forced cheerfulness, "So. You should be back at work in the O.R. in no time. With a big raise in pay, I hope. It must feel pretty good."

"I'm not sure I'm taking it—the job."

"What? Why on earth wouldn't you?"

She shrugged. "You know, I've been thinking about other possibilities. Other places."

"You mean besides Mid Pac?"

"I mean…besides Hawaii." He didn't say a thing, so she added, "There's really nothing keeping me here."

There was another long silence. Softly he said, "Isn't there?"

She didn't answer. He watched her, sitting so quiet, so still in her chair. And he knew he could wait around till doomsday and there she'd still be. *A fine pair we are,* he thought in disgust. They were two so-called intelligent people, and they couldn't hunt up a single word between them.

"Dr. Chesne?" A nurse appeared in the doorway. "Are you ready to go back to your room?"

"Yes," Kate answered. "I think I'd like to sleep."

"You do look tired." The nurse glanced at David. "Maybe it's time you left, sir."

"No," said David, suddenly drawing himself to his full height.

"Excuse me?"

"I'm not going to leave. Not yet." He looked long and hard at Kate. "Not until I've finished making a fool of myself. So could you leave us alone?"

"But, sir—"

"Please."

The nurse hesitated. Then, sensing that something momentous was looming in the balance, she retreated from the solarium.

Kate was watching him, her green eyes filled with uncertainty. And maybe fear. He reached down and gently touched her face.

"Tell me again what you just said," he murmured. "That you have nothing to keep you here."

"I don't. What I mean is—"

"Now tell me the real reason you want to leave."

She was silent. But he saw the answer in her eyes, those soft and needy eyes. What he read there made him suddenly shake his head in wonder. "My God," he muttered. "You're a bigger coward than I am."

"A coward?"

"That's right. So am I." He turned away and with his hands in his pockets began to wander restlessly around the room. "I didn't plan to say this. Not yet, anyway. But here you're talking about leaving. And it seems I don't have much of a choice." He stopped and looked out the window. Outside, the world had gone silvery. "Okay." He sighed. "Since you're not going to say it, I guess I will. It's not easy for me. It's never been easy. After Noah died, I thought I'd taught myself not to feel. I've managed it up till now. Then I met you and..." He shook his head and laughed. "God, I wish I had one of Charlie Decker's poems handy. Maybe I could quote a few lines. Anything to sound halfway intelligible. Poor old Charlie had that much over me: his eloquence. For that I envy him." He looked at her and a half smile was on his lips. "I still haven't said it, have I? But you get the general idea."

"Coward," she whispered.

Laughing, he went to her and tilted her face up to his. "All right, then. I love you. I love your stubbornness and your pride. And your independence. I didn't want to. I thought I was going along just fine on my own. But now that it's happened, I can't imagine ever not loving you." He pulled away, offering her a chance to retreat.

She didn't. She remained perfectly still. Her throat seemed to have swollen shut. She was still clutching the little box of candy, trying to convince herself it was real. That he was real.

"It won't be easy, you know," he said.

"What won't?"

"Living with me. There'll be days you'll want to wring my neck or scream at me, anything to make me say 'I love you.' But just because I don't say it doesn't mean I don't feel it. Because I do." He let out a long sigh. "So. I guess that's about it. I hope you were listening. Because I'm not sure I could come up with a repeat performance. And damned if this time I forgot to bring my tape recorder.''

"I've been listening,'' she replied softly.

"And?'' he asked, not daring to let his gaze leave her face. "Do I hear the verdict? Or is the jury still out?''

"The jury,'' she whispered, "is in a state of shock. And badly in need of mouth-to-mouth—''

If resuscitation was what he'd intended, his kiss did quite the opposite. He lowered his face to hers and she felt the room spin. Every muscle of her neck seemed to go limp at once and her head sagged back against the chair.

"Now, fellow coward,'' he murmured, his lips hovering close to hers. "Your turn.''

"I love you,'' she said weakly.

"That's the verdict I was hoping for.''

She thought he would kiss her again but he suddenly pulled away and frowned. "You're looking awfully pale. I think I should call the nurse. Maybe a little oxygen—''

She reached up and wound her arms around his neck. "Who needs oxygen?'' she whispered, just before his mouth settled warmly on hers.

Epilogue

There was a brand-new baby visiting the house, a fact made apparent by the indignant squalls coming from the upstairs bedroom.

Jinx poked her head through the doorway. "What in heaven's name is the matter with Emma now?"

Gracie, her mouth clamped around a pale pink safety pin, looked up helplessly from the screaming infant. "It's all so new to me, Jinx. I'm afraid I've lost my touch."

"Your touch? When were you ever around babies?"

"Oh, you're right." Gracie sighed, tugging the pin out of her mouth. "I suppose I never did have the touch, did I? That explains why I'm doing such a shoddy job of it."

"Now, dear. Babies take practice, that's all. It's like the piano. All those scales, up and down, every day."

Gracie shook her head. "The piano's much easier." Resignedly, she stuffed the safety pin back between her lips. "And look at these impossible diapers! I just don't see how anyone could poke a pin through all that paper and plastic."

Jinx burst out in hoots of laughter, so loud that Gracie turned bright red with indignation. "And exactly what did I say that was so funny?" Gracie demanded.

"Darling, haven't you figured it out?" Jinx reached out and peeled open the adhesive flap. "You don't use pins. That's the whole *point* of disposable diapers." She looked down in astonishment as baby Emma suddenly let out a lusty howl.

"You see?" sniffed Gracie. "She didn't like your pun, either."

* * *

A leaf drifted down from the monkeypod tree and settled beside the fresh gathering of daisies. Chips of sunlight dappled the grass and danced on David's fair hair. How many times had he grieved alone in the shade of this tree? How many times had he stood in silent communion with his son? All the other visits seemed to blend together in a gray and dismal remembrance of mourning.

But today he was smiling. And in his mind, he could hear the smile in Noah's voice, as well.

Is that you, Daddy?

Yes, Noah. It's me. You have a sister.

I've always wanted a sister.

She sucks the same two fingers you did....

Does she?

And she always smiles when I walk in her room.

So did I. Remember?

Yes, I remember.

And you'll never forget, will you, Daddy? Promise me, you'll never forget.

No, I'll never forget. I swear to you, Noah, I will never, ever forget....

David turned and through his tears he saw Kate, standing a few feet away. No words were needed between them. Only a look. And an outstretched hand.

Together they walked away from that sad little patch of grass. As they emerged from the shade of the tree, David suddenly stopped and pulled her into his arms.

She touched his face. He felt the warmth of the sun in her fingertips. And he was healed.

He was healed.

TESS
GERRITSEN

WHISTLEBLOWER

First Published 1992
Third Australian Paperback Edition 2007
ISBN 978 1 741 16515 9

Published by
Mira Books
3 Gibbes Street
CHATSWOOD NSW 2067
AUSTRALIA

Printed and bound in Australia by
McPherson's Printing Group

PROLOGUE

Branches whipped his face, and his heart was pounding so hard he thought his chest would explode, but he couldn't stop running. Already, he could hear the man gaining on him, could almost imagine the bullet slicing through the night and slamming into his back. Maybe it already had. Maybe he was trailing a river of blood; he was too numb with terror to feel anything now, except the desperate hunger to live. The rain was pouring down his face, icy, blinding sheets of it, rattling on the dead leaves of winter. He stumbled through a pool of darkness and found himself sprawled flat on his belly in the mud. The sound of his fall was deafening. His pursuer, alerted by the sharp crack of branches, altered course and was now headed straight for him. The thud of a silencer, the zing of a bullet past his cheek, told him he'd been spotted. He forced himself to his feet and made a sharp right, zigzagging back toward the highway. Here in the woods, he was a dead man. But if he could flag down a car, if he could draw someone's attention, he might have a chance.

A crash of branches, a coarse oath, told him his pursuer had stumbled. He'd gained a few precious seconds. He kept running, moving only by an instinctive sense of direction. There was no light to guide his way, nothing except the dim glow of the clouds in the night sky. The road had to be just ahead. Any second now, his feet would hit pavement.

And then what? What if there's no car to flag down, no one to help me?

Then, through the trees ahead, he saw a faint flickering, two watery beams of light.

With a desperate burst of speed, he sprinted toward the car. His lungs were on fire, his eyes blinded by the lash of branches and rain. Another bullet whipped past him and thudded into a tree trunk, but the gunman behind him had suddenly lost all importance. All that mattered was those lights, beckoning him through the darkness, taunting him with the promise of salvation.

When his feet suddenly hit the pavement, he was shocked. The lights were still ahead, bobbing somewhere beyond the trees. Had he missed the car? Was it already moving away, around a curve? No, there it was, brighter now. It was coming this way. He ran to meet it, following the bend of the road and knowing all the time that here in the open, he was an easy target. The sound of his shoes slapping the wet road filled his ears. The lights twisted toward him. At that instant, he heard the gun fire a third time. The force of the impact made him stumble to his knees, and he was vaguely aware of the bullet tearing through his shoulder, of the warmth of his own blood dribbling down his arm, but he was oblivious to pain. He could focus only on staying alive. He struggled back to his feet, took a stumbling step forward...

And was blinded by the onrush of headlights. There was no time to throw himself out of the way, no time even to register panic. Tires screamed across the pavement, throwing up a spray of water.

He didn't feel the impact. All he knew was that he was suddenly lying on the ground and the rain was pouring into his mouth and he was very, very cold.

And that he had something to do, something important.

Feebly, he reached into the pocket of his windbreaker, and his fingers curled around the small plastic cylinder. He couldn't quite remember why it mattered so much, but it was still there and he was relieved. He clutched it tightly in his palm.

Someone was calling to him. A woman. He couldn't see her face through the rain, but he could hear her voice, hoarse with panic, floating through the buzz in his head. He tried to speak, tried to warn her that they had to get away, that death was waiting in the woods. But all that came out was a groan.

CHAPTER ONE

Three miles out of Redwood Valley, a tree had fallen across the road, and with the heavy rains and backed-up cars, it took Catherine Weaver nearly three hours to get past the town of Willits. By then it was already ten o'clock and she knew she wouldn't reach Garberville till midnight. She hoped Sarah wouldn't sit up all night waiting for her. But knowing Sarah, there'd be a supper still warm in the oven and a fire blazing in the hearth. She wondered how pregnancy suited her friend. Wonderfully, of course. Sarah had talked about this baby for years, had chosen its name—Sam or Emma—long before it was conceived. The fact she no longer had a husband was a minor point. "You can only wait around so long for the right father," Sarah had said. "Then you have to take matters into your own hands."

And she had. With her biological clock furiously ticking its last years away, Sarah had driven down to visit Cathy in San Francisco and had calmly selected a fertility clinic from the yellow pages. A liberal-minded one, of course. One that would understand the desperate longings of a thirty-nine-year-old single woman. The insemination itself had been a coolly clinical affair, she'd said later. Hop on the table, slip your feet into the stirrups, and five minutes later, you were pregnant. Well, almost. But it was a simple procedure, the donors were certifiably healthy, and best of all, a woman could fulfill her maternal instincts without all that foolishness about marriage.

Yes, the old marriage game. They'd both suffered through it. And after their divorces, they'd both carried on, albeit with battle scars.

Brave Sarah, thought Cathy. *At least she has the courage to go through with this on her own.*

The old anger washed through her, still potent enough to make her mouth tighten. She could forgive her ex-husband Jack for a lot of things. For his selfishness. His demands. His infidelity. But she could never forgive him for denying her the chance to have a child. Oh, she could have gone against his wishes and had a baby anyway, but she'd wanted him to want one as well. So she'd waited for the time to be right. But during their ten years of marriage, he'd never been "ready," never felt it was the "right time."

What he should have told her was the truth: that he was too self-centered to be bothered with a baby.

I'm thirty-seven years old, she thought. *I no longer have a husband. I don't even have a steady boyfriend. But I could be content, if only I could hold my own child in my arms.*

At least Sarah would soon be blessed.

Four months to go and then the baby was due. Sarah's baby. Cathy had to smile at that thought, despite the rain now pouring over her windshield. It was coming down harder now; even with the wipers thrashing at full speed, she could barely make out the road. She glanced at her watch and saw it was already eleven-thirty; there were no other cars in sight. If she had engine trouble out here, she'd probably have to spend the night huddled in the backseat, waiting for help to arrive.

Peering ahead, she tried to make out the road's dividing line and saw nothing but a solid wall of rain. This was ridiculous. She really should have stopped at that motel in Willits, but she hated the thought of being only fifty miles from her goal, especially when she'd already driven so far.

She spotted a sign ahead: Garberville, 10 Miles. So she was closer than she'd thought. Twenty-five miles more, then there'd be a turn-off and a five-mile drive through dense woods to Sarah's cedar house. The thought of being so close fueled her impatience. She fed the old Datsun some gas and sped up to forty-five miles an hour. It was a reckless thing to do, especially in these conditions, but the thought of a warm house and hot chocolate was just too tempting.

The road curved unexpectedly; startled, she jerked the wheel to the right and the car slid sideways, tobogganing wildly across the rain-slicked pavement. She knew enough not to slam on the brakes. Instead, she clutched the wheel, fighting to regain control. The tires skidded a few feet, a heart-stopping ride that took her to the very edge of the road. Just as she thought she'd clip the trees, the tires gripped the pavement. The car was still moving twenty miles an hour, but at least it was headed in a straight line. With clammy hands, she managed to negotiate the rest of the curve.

What happened next caught her completely by surprise. One instant she was congratulating herself for averting disaster, the next, she was staring ahead in disbelief.

The man had appeared out of nowhere. He was crouched in the road, captured like a wild animal in the glare of her headlights. Reflexes took over. She slammed on the brakes, but it was already too late. The screech of her tires was punctuated by the thud of the man's body against the hood of her car.

For what seemed like eternity, she sat frozen and unable to do anything but clutch the steering wheel and stare at the windshield wipers skating back and forth. Then, as the reality of what she'd just done sank in, she shoved the door open and dashed out into the rain.

At first she could see nothing through the downpour, only a glistening strip of blacktop lit by the dim glow of her taillights. *Where is he?* she thought frantically. With water streaming past her eyes, she traced the road backward, struggling to see in the darkness. Then, through the pounding rain, she heard a low moan. It came from somewhere off to the side, near the trees.

Shifting direction, she plunged into the shadows and sank ankle-deep in mud and pine needles. Again she heard the moan, closer now, almost within reach.

"Where are you?" she screamed. "Help me find you!"

"Here..." The answer was so weak she barely heard it, but it was all she needed. Turning, she took a few steps and practically stumbled over his crumpled body in the darkness. At first, he seemed to be only a confusing jumble of soaked clothes, then she managed to locate his hand and feel for his pulse. It was fast but steady, probably steadier than her own pulse, which was skipping wildly. His fingers suddenly closed over hers in a desperate grip. He rolled against her and struggled to sit up.

"Please! Don't move!" she said.

"Can't—can't stay here—"

"Where are you hurt?"

"No time. Help me. Hurry—"

"Not till you tell me where you're hurt!"

He reached out and grabbed her shoulder in a clumsy attempt to rise to his feet. To her amazement, he managed to pull himself halfway up. For an instant they wobbled against each other, then his strength seemed to collapse and they both slid to their knees in the mud. His breathing had turned harsh and irregular and she wondered about his injuries. If he was bleeding internally he could die within minutes. She had to get him to a hospital now, even if it meant dragging him back to the car.

"Okay. Let's try again," she said, grabbing his left arm and draping it around her neck. She was startled by his gasp of agony. Immediately she released him. His arm left a sticky trail of warmth around her neck. *Blood.*

"My other side's okay," he grunted. "Try again."

She shifted to his right side and pulled his arm over her neck. If she weren't so frantic, it would have struck her as a comical scene, the two of them struggling like drunkards to stand up. When at last he was on his feet and they stood swaying together in the mud, she wondered if he even had the strength to put one foot in front of the other. She certainly couldn't move them both. Though he was slender, he was also a great deal taller than she'd expected, and much more than her five-foot-five frame could support.

But something seemed to compel him forward, a kindling of some hidden reserves. Even through their soaked clothes, she could feel the heat of his body and could sense the urgency driving him onward. A dozen questions formed in her head, but she was breathing too hard to voice them. Her every effort had to be concentrated on getting him to the car, and then to a hospital.

Gripping him around the waist, she latched her fingers through his belt. Painfully they made their way to the road, struggling step by step. His arm felt taut as wire over her neck. It seemed everything about him was wound up tight. There was something desperate about the way his muscles strained to move forward. His urgency penetrated right through to her skin. It was a panic as palpable as the warmth of his body, and she was suddenly infected with his need to flee, a need made more desperate by the fact they could move no faster than they already were. Every few feet she had to stop and shove back her dripping hair just to see where she was going. And all around them, the rain and darkness closed off all view of whatever danger pursued.

The taillights of her car glowed ahead like ruby eyes winking in the night. With every step the man grew heavier and her legs felt so rubbery she thought they'd both topple in the road. If they did, she wouldn't have the strength to haul him back up again. Already, his head was sagging against her cheek and water trickled from his rain-matted hair down her neck. The simple act of putting one foot in front of the other was so automatic that she never even considered dropping him on the road and backing the car to him instead. And the taillights were already so close, just beyond the next veil of rain.

By the time she'd guided him to the passenger side, her arm felt ready to fall off. With the man on the verge of sliding from her grasp, she barely managed to wrench the door open. She had no strength left to be gentle; she simply shoved him inside.

He flopped onto the front seat with his legs still hanging out. She bent down, grabbed his ankles, and heaved them one by one into the car, noting with a sense of detachment that no man with feet this big could possibly be graceful.

As she slid into the driver's seat, he made a feeble attempt to raise his head, then let it sink back again. "Hurry," he whispered.

At the first turn of the key in the ignition, the engine sputtered and died. Dear God, she pleaded. Start. *Start!* She switched the key off, counted slowly to three, and tried again. This time the engine caught. Almost shouting with relief, she jammed it into gear and made a tire-screeching takeoff toward Garberville. Even a town that small must have a hospital or, at the very least, an emergency clinic. The question was: could she find it in this downpour? And what if she was wrong? What if the nearest medical help was in Willits, the other direction? She might be wasting precious minutes on the road while the man bled to death.

Suddenly panicked by that thought, she glanced at her passenger. By the glow of the dashboard, she saw that his head was still flopped back against the seat. He wasn't moving.

"Hey! Are you all right?" she cried.

The answer came back in a whisper. "I'm still here."

"Dear God. For a minute I thought..." She looked back at the road, her heart pounding. "There's got to be a clinic somewhere—"

"Near Garberville—there's a hospital—"

"Do you know how to find it?"

"I drove past it—fifteen miles..."

If he drove here, where's his car? she thought. "What happened?" she asked. "Did you have an accident?"

He started to speak but his answer was cut off by a sudden flicker of light. Struggling to sit up, he turned and stared at the headlights of another car far behind them. His whispered oath made her look sideways in alarm.

"What is it?"

"That car."

She glanced in the rearview mirror. "What about it?"

"How long's it been following us?"

"I don't know. A few miles. Why?"

The effort of keeping his head up suddenly seemed too much for him, and he let it sink back down with a groan. "Can't think," he whispered. "Christ, I can't think..."

He's lost too much blood, she thought. In a panic, she shoved hard on the gas pedal. The car seemed to leap through the rain, the steering wheel vibrating wildly as sheets of spray flew up from the tires. Darkness flew at dizzying speed against their windshield. *Slow down, slow down! Or I'll get us both killed.*

Easing back on the gas, she let the speedometer fall to a more manageable forty-five miles per hour. The man was struggling to sit up again.

"Please, keep your head down!" she pleaded.

"That car—"

"It's not there anymore."

"Are you sure?"

She looked at the rearview mirror. Through the rain, she saw only a faint twinkling of light, but nothing as definite as headlights. "I'm sure," she lied and was relieved to see him slowly settle back again. *How much farther?* she thought. *Five miles? Ten?* And then the next thought forced its way into her mind: *He might die before we get there.*

His silence terrified her. She needed to hear his voice, needed to be reassured that he hadn't slipped into oblivion. "Talk to me," she urged. "Please."

"I'm tired...."

"Don't stop. Keep talking. What—what's your name?"

The answer was a mere whisper: "Victor."

"Victor. That's a great name. I like that name. What do you do, Victor?"

His silence told her he was too weak to carry on any conversation. She couldn't let him lose consciousness! For some reason it suddenly seemed crucial to keep him awake, to keep him in touch with a living voice. If that fragile connection was broken, she feared he might slip away entirely.

"All right," she said, forcing her voice to remain low and steady. "Then *I'll* talk. You don't have to say a thing. Just listen. Keep listening. My name is Catherine. Cathy Weaver. I live in San Francisco, the Richmond district. Do you know the city?" There was no answer, but she sensed some movement in his head, a silent acknowledgement of her words. "Okay," she went on, mindlessly filling the silence. "Maybe you don't know the city. It really doesn't matter. I work with an independent film company. Actually, it's Jack's company. My ex-husband. We make horror films. Grade B, really, but they turn a profit. Our last one was *Reptilian*. I did the special-effects makeup. Really gruesome stuff. Lots of green scales and slime..." She laughed—it was a strange, panicked sound. It had an unmistakable note of hysteria.

She had to fight to regain control.

A wink of light made her glance up sharply at the rearview mirror. A pair of headlights was barely discernible through the rain. For a few seconds she watched them, debating whether to say anything to Victor. Then, like phantoms, the lights flickered off and vanished.

"Victor?" she called softly. He responded with an unintelligible grunt, but it was all she needed to be reassured that he was still alive. That he was listening. *I've got to keep him awake,* she thought, her mind scrambling for some new topic of conversation. She'd never been good at the glib sort of chitchat so highly valued at filmmakers' cocktail parties. What she needed was a joke, however stupid, as long as it was vaguely funny. *Laughter heals.* Hadn't she read it somewhere? That a steady barrage of comedy could shrink tumors? *Oh sure,* she chided herself. *Just make him laugh and the bleeding will miraculously stop....*

But she couldn't think of a joke, anyway, not a single damn one. So she returned to the topic that had first come to mind: her work.

"Our next project's slated for January. *Ghouls.* We'll be filming in Mexico, which I hate, because the damn heat always melts the makeup...."

She looked at Victor but saw no response, not even a flicker of movement. Terrified that she was losing him, she reached out to feel for his pulse and discovered that his hand was buried deep in the pocket of his windbreaker. She tried to tug it free, and to her amazement he reacted to her invasion with immediate and savage resistance. Lurching awake, he blindly lashed at her, trying to force her away.

"Victor, it's all right!" she cried, fighting to steer the car and protect herself at the same time. "It's all right! It's me, Cathy. I'm only trying to help!"

At the sound of her voice, his struggles weakened. As the tension eased from his body, she felt his head settle slowly against her shoulder. "Cathy," he whispered. It was a sound of wonder, of relief. "Cathy..."

"That's right. It's only me." Gently, she reached up and brushed back the tendrils of his wet hair. She wondered what color it was, a concern that struck her as totally irrelevant but nonetheless compelling. He reached for her hand. His fingers closed around hers in a grip that was surprisingly strong and steadying. *I'm still here,* it said. *I'm warm and alive and breathing.* He pressed her palm to his lips. So tender was the gesture, she was startled by the roughness of his unshaven jaw against her skin. It was a caress between strangers, and it left her shaken and trembling.

She returned her grip to the steering wheel and shifted her full attention back to the road. He had fallen silent again, but she couldn't ignore the weight of his head on her shoulder or the heat of his breath in her hair.

The torrent eased to a slow but steady rain, and she coaxed the car to fifty. The Sunnyside Up cafe whipped past, a drab little box beneath a single streetlight, and she caught a glimpse of Victor's face in the brief glow of light. She saw him only in profile: a high forehead, sharp nose, a jutting chin, and then the light was gone and he was only a shadow breathing softly against her. But she'd seen enough to know she'd never forget that face. Even as she peered through the darkness, his profile floated before her like an image burned into her memory.

"We have to be getting close," she said, as much to reassure herself as him. "Where a cafe appears, a town is sure to follow." There was no response. "Victor?" Still no response. Swallowing her panic, she sped up to fifty-five.

Though they'd passed the Sunnyside Up over a mile ago, she could still make out the streetlight winking on and off in her mirror. It took her a few seconds to realize it wasn't just one light she was watching but two, and that they were moving—a pair of headlights, winding along the highway. Was it the same car she'd spotted earlier?

Mesmerized, she watched the lights dance like twin wraiths among the trees, then, suddenly, they vanished and she saw only darkness. A ghost? she wondered irrationally. Any instant she expected the lights to rematerialize, to resume their phantom twinkling in the woods. She was watching the mirror so intently that she almost missed the road sign:

Garberville, Pop, 5,750
Gas—Food—Lodging

A half mile later streetlights appeared, glowing a hazy yellow in the drizzle; a flatbed truck splashed by, headed in the other direction. Though the speed limit had dropped to thirty-five, she kept her foot firmly on the gas pedal and for once in her life prayed for a police car to give chase.

The *Hospital* road sign seemed to leap out at her from nowhere. She braked and swerved onto the turnoff. A quarter mile away, a red *Emergency* sign directed her up a driveway to a side entrance. Leaving Victor in the front seat, she ran inside, through a deserted waiting room, and cried to a nurse sitting at her desk: "Please, help me! I've got a man in my car...."

The nurse responded instantly. She followed Cathy outside, took one look at the man slumped in the front seat, and yelled for assistance.

Even with the help of a burly ER physician, they had difficulty pulling Victor out of the car. He had slid sideways, and his arm was wedged under the emergency hand brake.

"Hey, Miss!" the doctor barked at Cathy. "Climb in the other side and free up his arm!"

Cathy scrambled to the driver's seat. There she hesitated. She would have to manipulate his injured arm. She took his elbow and tried to unhook it from around the brake, but discovered his wristwatch was snagged in the pocket of his windbreaker. After unsnapping the watchband, she took hold of his arm and lifted it over the brake. He responded with a groan of pure agony. The arm slid limply toward the floor.

"Okay!" said the doctor. "Arm's free! Now, just ease him toward me and we'll take it from there."

Gingerly, she guided Victor's head and shoulders safely past the emergency brake. Then she scrambled back outside to help load him onto the wheeled stretcher. Three straps were buckled into place. Everything became a blur of noise and motion as the stretcher was wheeled through the open double doors into the building.

"What happened?" the doctor barked over his shoulder at Cathy.

"I hit him—on the road—"

"When?"

"Fifteen—twenty minutes ago."

"How fast were you driving?"

"About thirty-five."

"Was he conscious when you found him?"

"For about ten minutes—then he sort of faded—"

A nurse said: "Shirt's soaked with blood. He's got broken glass in his shoulder."

In that mad dash beneath harsh fluorescent lights, Cathy had her first clear look at Victor, and she saw a lean, mud-streaked face, a jaw tightly squared in pain, a broad forehead matted damply with light brown hair. He reached out to her, grasping for her hand.

"Cathy—"

"I'm here, Victor."

He held on tightly, refusing to break contact. The pressure of his fingers in her flesh was almost painful. Squinting through the pain, he focused on her face. "I have to—have to tell you—"

"Later!" snapped the doctor.

"No, wait!" Victor was fighting to keep her in view, to hold her beside him. He struggled to speak, agony etching lines on his face.

Cathy bent close, drawn by the desperation of his gaze. "Yes, Victor," she whispered, stroking his hair, longing to ease his pain. This link between their hands, their gazes, felt forged in timeless steel. "Tell me."

"We can't delay!" barked the doctor. "Get him in the room."

All at once, Victor's hand was wrenched away from her as they whisked him into the trauma suite, a nightmarish room of stainless steel and blindingly bright lights. He was lifted onto the surgical table.

"Pulse 110," said a nurse. "Blood pressure eight-five over fifty!"

The doctor ordered, "Let's get two IVs in. Type and cross six units of blood. And get hold of a surgeon. We're going to need help...."

The machine-gun fire of voices, the metallic clang of cabinets and IV poles and instruments was deafening. No one seemed to notice Cathy standing in the doorway, watching in horrified fascination as a nurse pulled out a knife and began to tear off Victor's bloody clothing. With each rip, more and more flesh was exposed, until the shirt and windbreaker were shredded off, revealing a broad chest thickly matted with tawny hair. To the doctors and nurses, this was just another body to labor over, another patient to be saved. To Cathy, this was a living, breathing man, a man she cared about, if only because they had shared those last harrowing moments. The nurse shifted her attention to his belt, which she quickly unbuckled. With a few firm tugs, she peeled off his trousers and shorts and threw them into a pile with the other soiled clothing. Cathy scarcely noticed the man's nakedness, or the nurses and technicians shoving past her into the room. Her shocked gaze had focused on Victor's left shoulder, which was oozing fresh blood onto the table. She remembered how his whole body had resonated with pain when she'd grabbed that shoulder; only now did she understand how much he must have suffered.

A sour taste flooded her throat. She was going to be sick.

Struggling against the nausea, she somehow managed to stumble away and sink into a nearby chair. There she sat for a few minutes, oblivious to the chaos whirling around her. Looking down, she noted with instinctive horror the blood on her hands.

"There you are," someone said. A nurse had just emerged from the trauma room, carrying a bundle of the patient's belongings. She motioned Cathy over to a desk. "We'll need your name and address in case the doctors have any more questions. And the police will have to be notified. Have you called them?"

Cathy shook her head numbly. "I—I guess I should..."

"You can use this phone."

"Thank you."

It rang eight times before anyone answered. The voice that greeted her was raspy with sleep. Obviously, Garberville provided little late-night stimulation, even for the local police. The desk officer took down Cathy's report and told her he'd be in touch with her later, after they'd checked the accident scene.

The nurse had opened Victor's wallet and was flipping through the various ID cards for information. Cathy watched her fill in the blanks on a patient admission form: *Name: Victor Holland. Age: 41. Occupation: Biochemist. Next of kin: Unknown.*

So that was his full name. Victor Holland. Cathy stared down at the stack of ID cards and focused on what appeared to be a security pass for some company called Viratek. A color photograph showed Victor's quietly sober face, its green eyes gazing straight into the camera. Even if she had never seen his face, this was exactly how she would have pictured him, his expression unyielding, his gaze unflinchingly direct. She touched her palm, where he had kissed her. She could still recall how his beard had stung her flesh.

Softly, she asked, "Is he going to be all right?"

The nurse continued writing. "He's lost a lot of blood. But he looks like a pretty tough guy...."

Cathy nodded, remembering how, even in his agony, Victor had somehow dredged up the strength to keep moving through the rain. Yes, she knew just how tough a man he was.

The nurse handed her a pen and the information sheet. "If you could write your name and address at the bottom. In case the doctor has any more questions.''

Cathy fished out Sarah's address and phone number from her purse and copied them onto the form. ''My name's Cathy Weaver. You can get hold of me at this number.''

''You're staying in Garberville?''

''For three weeks. I'm just visiting.''

''Oh. Terrific way to start a vacation, huh?''

Cathy sighed as she rose to leave. ''Yeah. Terrific.''

She paused outside the trauma room, wondering what was happening inside, knowing that Victor was fighting for his life. She wondered if he was still conscious, if he would remember her. It seemed important that he *did* remember her.

Cathy turned to the nurse. ''You will call me, won't you? I mean, you'll let me know if he...''

The nurse nodded. ''We'll keep you informed.''

Outside, the rain had finally stopped and a belt of stars twinkled through a parting in the clouds. To Cathy's weary eyes, it was an exhilarating sight, that first glimpse of the storm's end. As she drove out of the hospital parking lot, she was shaking from fatigue. She never noticed the car parked across the street or the brief glow of the cigarette before it was snuffed out.

CHAPTER TWO

Barely a minute after Cathy left the hospital, a man walked into the emergency room, sweeping the smells of a stormy night in with him through the double doors. The nurse on duty was busy with the new patient's admission papers. At the sudden rush of cold air, she looked up to see a man approach her desk. He was about thirty-five, gaunt-faced, silent, his dark hair lightly feathered by gray. Droplets of water sparkled on his tan Burberry raincoat.

"Can I help you, sir?" she asked, focusing on his eyes, which were as black and polished as pebbles in a pond.

Nodding, he said quietly, "Was there a man brought in a short time ago? Victor Holland?"

The nurse glanced down at the papers on her desk. That was the name. Victor Holland. "Yes," she said. "Are you a relative?"

"I'm his brother. How is he?"

"He just arrived, sir. They're working on him now. If you'll wait, I can check on how he's doing—" She stopped to answer the ringing telephone. It was a technician calling with the new patient's laboratory results. As she jotted down the numbers, she noticed out of the corner of her eye that the man had turned and was gazing at the closed door to the trauma room. It suddenly swung open as an orderly emerged carrying a bulging plastic bag streaked with blood. The clamor of voices spilled from the room:

"Pressure up to 110 over 70!"

"OR says they're ready to go."

"Where's that surgeon?"

"On his way. He had car trouble."

"Ready for X rays! Everyone back!"

Slowly the door closed, muffling the voices. The nurse hung up just as the orderly deposited the plastic bag on her desk. "What's this?" she asked.

"Patient's clothes. They're a mess. Should I just toss 'em?"

"I'll take them home," the man in the raincoat cut in. "Is everything here?"

The orderly flashed the nurse an uncomfortable glance. "I'm not sure he'd want to...I mean, they're kind of...uh, dirty...."

The nurse said quickly, "Mr. Holland, why don't you let us dispose of the clothes for you? There's nothing worth keeping in there. I've already collected his valuables." She unlocked a drawer and pulled out a sealed manila envelope labeled: Holland, Victor. Contents: Wallet, Wristwatch. "You can take these home. Just sign this receipt."

The man nodded and signed his name: David Holland. "Tell me," he said, sliding the envelope in his pocket. "Is Victor awake? Has he said anything?"

"I'm afraid not. He was semiconscious when he arrived."

The man took this information in silence, a silence that the nurse found suddenly and profoundly disturbing. "Excuse me, Mr. Holland?" she asked. "How did you hear your brother was hurt? I didn't get a chance to contact any relatives...."

"The police called me. Victor was driving my car. They found it smashed up at the side of the road."

"Oh. What an awful way to be notified."

"Yes. The stuff of nightmares."

"At least someone was able to get in touch with you." She sifted through the sheaf of papers on her desk. "Can we get your address and phone number? In case we need to reach you?"

"Of course." The man took the ER papers, which he quickly scanned before scrawling his name and phone number on the blank marked Next of Kin. "Who's this Catherine Weaver?" he asked, pointing to the name and address at the bottom of the page.

"She's the woman who brought him in."

"I'll have to thank her." He handed back the papers.

"Nurse?"

She looked around and saw that the doctor was calling to her from the trauma room doorway. "Yes?"

"I want you to call the police. Tell them to get in here as soon as possible."

"They've been called, Doctor. They know about the accident—"

"Call them again. This is no accident."

"What?"

"We just got the X rays. The man's got a bullet in his shoulder."

"A *bullet?*" A chill went through the nurse's body, like a cold wind sweeping in from the night. Slowly, she turned toward the man in the raincoat, the man who'd claimed to be Victor Holland's brother. To her amazement, no one was there. She felt only a cold puff of night air, and then she saw the double doors quietly slide shut.

"Where the hell did he go?" the orderly whispered.

For a few seconds she could only stare at the closed doors. Then her gaze dropped and she focused on the empty spot on her desk. The bag containing Victor Holland's clothes had vanished.

"Why did the police call again?"

Cathy slowly replaced the telephone receiver. Even though she was bundled in a warm terry-cloth robe, she was shivering. She turned and stared across the kitchen at Sarah. "That man on the road—they found a bullet in his shoulder."

In the midst of pouring tea, Sarah glanced up in surprise. "You mean—someone *shot* him?"

Cathy sank down at the kitchen table and gazed numbly at the cup of cinnamon tea that Sarah had just slid in front of her. A hot bath and a soothing hour of sitting by the fireplace had made the night's events seem like nothing more than a bad dream. Here in Sarah's kitchen, with its chintz curtains and its cinnamon and spice smells, the violence of the real world seemed a million miles away.

Sarah leaned toward her. "Do they know what happened? Has he said anything?"

"He just got out of surgery." She turned and glanced at the telephone. "I should call the hospital again—"

"No. You shouldn't. You've done everything you possibly can." Sarah gently touched her arm. "And your tea's getting cold."

With a shaking hand, Cathy brushed back a strand of damp hair and settled uneasily in her chair. A bullet in his shoulder, she thought. Why? Had it been a random attack, a highway gunslinger blasting out the car window at a total stranger? She'd read about it in the newspapers, the stories of freeway arguments settled by the pulling of a trigger.

Or had it been a deliberate attack? Had Victor Holland been targeted for death?

Outside, something rattled and clanged against the house. Cathy sat up sharply. "What was that?"

"Believe me, it's not the bogeyman," said Sarah, laughing. She went to the kitchen door and reached for the bolt.

"Sarah!" Cathy called in panic as the bold slid open. "Wait!"

"Take a look for yourself." Sarah opened the door. The kitchen light swung across a cluster of trash cans sitting in the carport. A shadow slid to the ground and scurried away, trailing food wrappers across the driveway. "Raccoons," said Sarah. "If I don't tie the lids down, those pests'll scatter trash all over the yard." Another shadow popped its head out of a can and stared at her, its eyes glowing in the darkness. Sarah clapped her hands and yelled, "Go on, get lost!" The raccoon didn't budge. "Don't you have a home to go to?" At last, the raccoon dropped to the ground and ambled off into the trees. "They get bolder every year," Sarah sighed, closing the door. She turned and winked at Cathy. "So take it easy. This isn't the big city."

"Keep reminding me." Cathy took a slice of banana bread and began to spread it with sweet butter. "You know, Sarah, I think it'll be a lot nicer spending Christmas with you than it ever was with old Jack."

"Uh-oh. Since we're now speaking of ex-husbands—" Sarah shuffled over to a cabinet "—we might as well get in the right frame of mind. And tea just won't cut it." She grinned and waved a bottle of brandy.

"Sarah, you're not drinking alcohol, are you?"

"It's not for *me*." Sarah set the bottle and a single wine glass in front of Cathy. "But I think *you* could use a nip. After all, it's been a cold, traumatic night. And here we are, talking about turkeys of the male variety."

"Well, since you put it that way…" Cathy poured out a generous shot of brandy. "To the turkeys of the world," she declared and took a sip. It felt just right going down.

"So how *is* old Jack?" asked Sarah.

"Same as always."

"Blondes?"

"He's moved on to brunettes."

"It took him only a year to go through the world's supply of blondes?"

Cathy shrugged. "He might have missed a few."

They both laughed then, light and easy laughter that told them their wounds were well on the way to healing, that men were now creatures to be discussed without pain, without sorrow.

Cathy regarded her glass of brandy. "Do you suppose there *are* any good men left in the world? I mean, shouldn't there be *one* floating around somewhere? Maybe a mutation or something? One measly decent guy?"

"Sure. Somewhere in Siberia. But he's a hundred-and-twenty years old."

"I've always liked older men."

They laughed again, but this time the sound wasn't as light-hearted. So many years had passed since their college days together, the days when they had *known*, had never doubted, that Prince Charmings abounded in the world.

Cathy drained her glass of brandy and set it down. "What a lousy friend I am. Keeping a pregnant lady up all night! What time is it, anyway?"

"Only two-thirty in the morning."

"Oh, Sarah! Go to bed!" Cathy went to the sink and began wetting a handful of paper towels.

"And what are you going to do?" Sarah asked.

"I just want to clean up the car. I didn't get all the blood off the seat."

"I already did it."

"What? When?"

"While you were taking a bath."

"Sarah, you idiot."

"Hey, I didn't have a miscarriage or anything. Oh, I almost forgot." Sarah pointed to a tiny film canister on the counter. "I found that on the floor of your car."

Cathy shook her head and sighed. "It's Hickey's."

"Hickey! Now *there's* a waste of a man."

'He's also a good friend of mine.''

"That's all Hickey will ever be to a woman. A *friend*. So what's on the roll of film? Naked women, as usual?''

"I don't even want to know. When I dropped him off at the airport, he handed me a half-dozen rolls and told me he'd pick them up when he got back. Guess he didn't want to lug 'em all the way to Nairobi.''

"Is that where he went? Nairobi?''

"He's shooting 'gorgeous ladies of Africa' or something." Cathy slipped the film canister into her bathrobe pocket. "This must've dropped out of the glove compartment. Gee. I hope it's not pornographic.''

"Knowing Hickey, it probably is.''

They both laughed at the irony of it all. Hickman Von Trapp, whose only job it was to photograph naked females in erotic poses, had absolutely no interest in the opposite sex, with the possible exception of his mother.

"A guy like Hickey only goes to prove my point," Sarah said over her shoulder as she headed up the hall to bed.

"What point is that?''

"There really *are* no good men left in the world!''

It was the light that dragged Victor up from the depths of unconsciousness, a light brighter than a dozen suns, beating against his closed eyelids. He didn't want to wake up; he knew, in some dim, scarcely functioning part of his brain, that if he continued to struggle against this blessed oblivion he would feel pain and nausea and something else, something much, much worse: terror. Of what, he couldn't remember. Of death? No, no, this was death, or as close as one could come to it, and it was warm and black and comfortable. But he had something important to do, something that he couldn't allow himself to forget. He tried to think, but all he could remember was a hand, gentle but somehow strong, brushing his forehead, and a voice, reaching to him softly in the darkness.

My name is Catherine....

As her touch, her voice, flooded his memory, so too did the fear. Not for himself (he was dead, wasn't he?) but for her. Strong, gentle Catherine. He'd seen her face only briefly, could scarcely remember it, but somehow he knew she was beautiful, the way a blind man knows, without benefit of vision, that a rainbow or the sky or his own dear child's face is beautiful. And now he was afraid for her.

Where are you? he wanted to cry out.

"He's coming around," said a female voice (not Catherine's, it was too hard, too crisp) followed by a confusing rush of other voices.

"Watch that IV!"

"Mr. Holland, hold still. Everything's going to be all right—"

"I said, watch the IV!"

"Hand me that second unit of blood—"

"Don't move, Mr. Holland—"

Where are you, Catherine? The shout exploded in his head. Fighting the temptation to sink back into unconsciousness, he struggled to lift his eyelids. At first, there was only a blur of light and color, so harsh he felt it stab through his sockets straight to his brain. Gradually the blur took the shape of faces, strangers in blue, frowning down at him. He tried to focus but the effort made his stomach rebel.

"Mr. Holland, take it easy," said a quietly gruff voice. "You're in the hospital—the recovery room. They've just operated on your shoulder. You just rest and go back to sleep...."

No. No, I can't, he tried to say.

"Five milligrams of morphine going in," someone said, and Victor felt a warm flush creep up his arm and spread across his chest.

"That should help," he heard. "Now, sleep. Everything went just fine...."

You don't understand, he wanted to scream. *I have to warn her—* It was the last conscious thought he had before the lights once again were swallowed by the gentle darkness.

Alone in her husbandless bed, Sarah lay smiling. No, laughing! Her whole body seemed filled with laughter tonight. She wanted to sing, to dance. To stand at the open window and shout out her joy! It was all hormonal, she'd been told, this chemical pandemonium of pregnancy, dragging her body on a roller coaster of emotions. She knew she should rest, she should work toward serenity, but tonight she wasn't tired at all. Poor exhausted Cathy had dragged herself up the attic steps to bed. But here was Sarah, still wide awake.

She closed her eyes and focused her thoughts on the child resting in her belly. *How are you, my love? Are you asleep? Or are you listening, hearing my thoughts even now?*

The baby wiggled in her belly, then fell silent. It was a reply, secret words shared only between them. Sarah was almost glad there was no husband to distract her from this silent conversation, to lie here in jealousy, an outsider. There was only mother and child, the ancient bond, the mystical link.

Poor Cathy, she thought, riding those roller coaster emotions from joy to sadness for her friend. She knew Cathy yearned just as deeply for a child, but eventually time would snatch the chance away from her. Cathy was too much of a romantic to realize that the man, the circumstances, might never be right. Hadn't it taken Cathy ten long years to finally acknowledge that her marriage was a miserable failure? Not that Cathy hadn't tried to make it work. She had tried to the point of developing a monumental blind spot to Jack's faults, primarily his selfishness. It was surprising how a woman so bright, so intuitive, could have let things drag on as long as she did. But that was Cathy. Even at thirty-seven she was open and trusting and loyal to the point of idiocy.

The clatter of gravel outside on the driveway pricked Sarah's awareness. Lying perfectly still, she listened and for a moment heard only the familiar creak of the trees, the rustle of branches against the shake roof. Then—there it was again. Stones skittering across the road, and then the faint squeal of metal. Those raccoons again. If she didn't shoo them off now, they'd litter garbage all over the driveway.

Sighing, she sat up and hunted in the darkness for her slippers. Shuffling quietly out of her bedroom, she navigated instinctively down the hallway and into the kitchen. Her eyes found the night too comfortable; she didn't want to assault them with light. Instead of flipping on the carport switch, she grabbed the flashlight from its usual spot on the kitchen shelf and unlocked the door.

Outside, moonlight glowed dimly through the clouds. She pointed the flashlight at the trash cans, but her beam caught no raccoon eyes, no telltale scattering of garbage, only the dull reflection of stainless steel. Puzzled, she crossed the carport and paused next to the Datsun that Cathy had parked in the driveway.

That was when she noticed the light glowing faintly inside the car. Glancing through the window, she saw that the glove compartment was open. Her first thought was that it had somehow fallen open by itself or that she or Cathy had forgotten to close it. Then she spotted the road maps strewn haphazardly across the front seat.

With fear suddenly hissing in her ear, she backed away, but terror made her legs slow and stiff. Only then did she sense that someone was nearby, waiting in the darkness; she could feel his presence, like a chill wind in the night.

She wheeled around for the house. As she turned, the beam of her flashlight swung around in a wild arc, only to freeze on the face of a man. The eyes that stared down at her were as slick and as black as pebbles. She scarcely focused on the rest of his face: the hawk nose, the thin, bloodless lips. It was only the eyes she saw. They were the eyes of a man without a soul.

"Hello, Catherine," he whispered, and she heard, in his voice, the greeting of death.

Please, she wanted to cry out as she felt him wrench her hair backward, exposing her neck. *Let me live!*

But no sound escaped. The words, like his blade, were buried in her throat.

Cathy woke up to the quarreling of blue jays outside her window, a sound that brought a smile to her lips for it struck her as somehow whimsical, this flap and flutter of wings across the panes, this maniacal crackling of feathered enemies. So unlike the morning roar of buses and cars she was accustomed to. The blue jays' quarrel moved to the rooftop, and she heard their claws scratching across the shakes in a dance of combat. She trailed their progress across the ceiling, up one side of the roof and down the other. Then, tired of the battle, she focused on the window.

Morning sunlight cascaded in, bathing the attic room in a soft haze. Such a perfect room for a nursery! She could see all the changes Sarah had already made here—the Jack-and-Jill curtains, the watercolor animal portraits. The very prospect of a baby sleeping in this room filled her with such joy that she sat up, grinning, and hugged the covers to her knees. Then she glanced at her watch on the nightstand and saw it was already nine-thirty—half the morning gone!

Reluctantly, she left the warmth of her bed and poked around in her suitcase for a sweater and jeans. She dressed to the thrashing of blue jays in the branches, the battle having moved from the roof to the treetops. From the window, she watched them dart from twig to twig until one finally hoisted up the feathered version of a white flag and took off, defeated. The victor, his authority no longer in question, gave one last screech and settled back to preen his feathers.

Only then did Cathy notice the silence of the house, a stillness that magnified her every heartbeat, her every breath.

Leaving the room, she descended the attic steps and confronted the empty living room. Ashes from last night's fire mounded the grate. A silver garland drooped from the Christmas tree. A cardboard angel with glittery wings winked on the mantelpiece. She followed the hallway to Sarah's room and frowned at the rumpled bed, the coverlet flung aside. "Sarah?"

Her voice was swallowed up in the stillness. How could a cottage seem so immense? She wandered back through the living room and into the kitchen. Last night's teacups still sat in the sink. On the windowsill, an asparagus fern trembled, stirred by a breeze through the open door.

Cathy stepped out into the carport where Sarah's old Dodge was parked. "Sarah?" she called.

Something skittered across the roof. Startled, Cathy looked up and suddenly laughed as she heard the blue jay chattering in the tree above—a victory speech, no doubt. Even the animal kingdom had its conceits.

She started to head back into the house when her gaze swept past a stain on the gravel near the car's rear tire. For a few seconds she stared at the blot of rust-brown, unable to comprehend its meaning. Slowly, she moved alongside the car, her gaze tracing the stain backward along its meandering course.

As she rounded the rear of the car, the driveway came into full view. The dried rivulet of brown became a crimson lake in which a single swimmer lay open-eyed and still.

The blue jay's chatter abruptly ceased as another sound rose up and filled the trees. It was Cathy, screaming.

"Hey, mister. Hey, mister."

Victor tried to brush off the sound but it kept buzzing in his ear, like a fly that can't be shooed away.

"Hey, mister. You awake?"

Victor opened his eyes and focused painfully on a wry little face stubbled with gray whiskers. The apparition grinned, and darkness gaped where teeth should have been. Victor stared into that foul black hole of a mouth and thought: *I've died and gone to hell.*

"Hey, mister, you got a cigarette?"

Victor shook his head and barely managed to whisper: "I don't think so."

"Well, you got a dollar I could borrow?"

"Go away," groaned Victor, shutting his eyes against the day-light. He tried to think, tried to remember where he was, but his head ached and the little man's voice kept distracting him.

"Can't get no cigarettes in this place. Like a jail in here. Don't know why I don't just get up and walk out. But y'know, streets are cold this time of year. Been rainin' all night long. Least in here it's warm...."

Raining all night long... Suddenly Victor remembered. The rain. Running and running through the rain.

Victor's eyes shot open. "Where am I?"

"Three East. Land o' the bitches."

He struggled to sit up and almost gasped from the pain. Dizzily, he focused on the metal pole with its bag of fluid dripping slowly into the plastic intravenous tube, then stared at the bandages on his left shoulder. Through the window, he saw that the day was already drenched in sunshine. "What time is it?"

"Dunno. Nine o'clock, I guess. You missed breakfast."

"I've got to get out of here." Victor swung his legs out of bed and discovered that, except for a flimsy hospital gown, he was stark naked. "Where's my clothes? My wallet?"

The old man shrugged. "Nurse'd know. Ask her."

Victor found the call button buried among the bed sheets. He stabbed it a few times, then turned his attention to peeling off the tape affixing the IV tube to his arm.

The door hissed open and a woman's voice barked, *"Mr. Holland! What do you think you're doing?"*

"I'm getting out of here, that's what I'm doing," said Victor as he stripped off the last piece of tape. Before he could pull the IV out, the nurse rushed across the room as fast as her stout legs could carry her and slapped a piece of gauze over the catheter.

"Don't blame me, Miss Redfern!" screeched the little man.

"Lenny, go back to your own bed this instant! And as for you, Mr. Holland," she said, turning her steel-blue eyes on Victor, "you've lost too much blood." Trapping his arm against her massive biceps, she began to retape the catheter firmly in place.

"Just get me my clothes."

"Don't argue, Mr. Holland. You have to stay."

"Why?"

"Because you've got an IV, that's why!" she snapped, as if the plastic tube itself was some sort of irreversible condition.

"I want my clothes."

"I'd have to check with the ER. Nothing of yours came up to the floor."

"Then call the ER, damn you!" At Miss Redfern's disapproving scowl, he added with strained politeness, *"If* you don't mind."

It was another half hour before a woman showed up from the business office to explain what had happened to Victor's belongings.

"I'm afraid we—well, we seem to have...lost your clothes, Mr. Holland," she said, fidgeting under his astonished gaze.

"What do you mean, *lost?"*

"They were—" she cleared her throat "—er, stolen. From the emergency room. Believe me, this has never happened before. We're really very sorry about this, Mr. Holland, and I'm sure we'll be able to arrange a purchase of replacement clothing...."

She was too busy trying to make excuses to notice that Victor's face had frozen in alarm. That his mind was racing as he tried to remember, through the blur of last night's events, just what had happened to the film canister. He knew he'd had it in his pocket during the endless drive to the hospital. He remembered clutching it there, remembered flailing senselessly at the woman when she'd tried to pull his hand from his pocket. After that, nothing was clear, nothing was certain. *Have I lost it?* he thought. *Have I lost my only evidence?*

"…While the money's missing, your credit cards seem to be all there, so I guess that's something to be thankful for."

He looked at her blankly. "What?"

"Your valuables, Mr. Holland." She pointed to the wallet and watch she'd just placed on the bedside table. "The security guard found them in the trash bin outside the hospital. Looks like the thief only wanted your cash."

"And my clothes. Right."

The instant the woman left, Victor pressed the button for Miss Redfern. She walked in carrying a breakfast tray. "Eat, Mr. Holland," she said. "Maybe your behavior's all due to hypoglycemia."

"A woman brought me to the ER," he said. "Her first name was Catherine. I have to get hold of her."

"Oh, look! Eggs and Rice Krispies! Here's your fork—"

"Miss Redfern, will you forget the damned Rice Krispies!"

Miss Redfern slapped down the cereal box. "There is no need for profanity!"

"I have to find that woman!"

Without a word, Miss Redfern spun around and marched out of the room. A few minutes later she returned and brusquely handed him a slip of paper. On it was written the name Catherine Weaver followed by a local address.

"You'd better eat fast," she said. "There's a policeman coming over to talk to you."

"Fine," he grunted, stuffing a forkful of cold, rubbery egg in his mouth.

"And some man from the FBI called. He's on his way, too."

Victor's head jerked up in alarm. "The FBI? What was his name?"

"Oh, for heaven's sake, how should I know? Something Polish, I think."

Staring at her, Victor slowly put down his fork. "Polowski," he said softly.

"That sounds like it. Polowski." She turned and headed out of the room. "The FBI indeed," she muttered. "Wonder what he did to get *their* attention...."

Before the door had even swung shut behind her, Victor was out of bed and tearing at his IV. He scarcely felt the sting of the tape wrenching the hair off his arm; he had to concentrate on getting the hell out of this hospital before Polowski showed up. He was certain the FBI agent had set him up for that ambush last night, and he wasn't about to wait around for another attack.

He turned and snapped at his roommate, "Lenny, where are your clothes?"

Lenny's gaze traveled reluctantly to a cabinet near the sink. "Don't got no other clothes. Besides, they wouldn't fit you, mister..."

Victor yanked open the cabinet door and pulled out a frayed cotton shirt and a pair of baggy polyester pants. The pants were too short and about six inches of Victor's hairy legs stuck out below the cuffs, but he had no trouble fastening the belt. The real trouble was going to be finding a pair of size twelve shoes. To his relief, he discovered that the cabinet also contained a pair of Lenny's thongs. His heels hung at least an inch over the back edge, but at least he wouldn't be barefoot.

"Those are mine!" protested Lenny.

"Here. You can have this." Victor tossed his wristwatch to the old man. "You should be able to hock that for a whole new outfit."

Suspicious, Lenny put the watch up against his ear. "Piece of junk. It's not ticking."

"It's quartz."

"Oh. Yeah. I knew that."

Victor pocketed his wallet and went to the door. Opening it just a crack, he peered down the hall toward the nurses' station. The coast was clear. He glanced back at Lenny. "So long, buddy. Give my regards to Miss Redfern."

Slipping out of the room, Victor headed quietly down the hall, away from the nurses' station. The emergency stairwell door was at the far end, marked by the warning painted in red: Alarm Will Sound If Opened. He walked steadily towards it, willing himself not to run, not to attract attention. But just as he neared the door, a familiar voice echoed in the hall.

"Mr. Holland! You come back here this instant!"

Victor lunged for the door, slammed against the closing bar, and dashed into the stairwell.

His footsteps echoed against the concrete as he pounded down the stairs. By the time he heard Miss Redfern scramble after him into the stairwell, he'd already reached the first floor and was pushing through the last door to freedom.

"Mr. Holland!" yelled Miss Redfern.

Even as he dashed across the parking lot, he could still hear Miss Redfern's outraged voice echoing in his ears.

Eight blocks away he turned into a K Mart, and within ten minutes had bought a shirt, blue jeans, underwear, socks and a pair of size-twelve tennis shoes, all of which he paid for with his credit card. He tossed Lenny's old clothes into a trash can.

Before emerging back outside, he peered through the store window at the street. It seemed like a perfectly normal mid-December morning in a small town, shoppers strolling beneath a tacky garland of Christmas decorations, a half-dozen cars waiting patiently at a red light. He was just about to step out the door when he spotted the police car creeping down the road. Immediately he ducked behind an undressed mannequin and watched through the nude plastic limbs as the police car made its way slowly past the K Mart and continued in the direction of the hospital. They were obviously searching for someone. Was he the one they wanted?

He couldn't afford to risk a stroll down Main Street. There was no way of knowing who else besides Polowski was involved in the double cross.

It took him at least an hour on foot to reach the outskirts of town, and by then he was so weak and wobbly he could barely stand. The surge of adrenaline that had sent him dashing from the hospital was at last petering out. Too tired to take another step, he sank onto a boulder at the side of the highway and halfheartedly held out his thumb. To his immense relief, the next vehicle to come along—a pickup truck loaded with firewood—pulled over. Victor climbed in and collapsed gratefully on the seat.

The driver spat out the window, then squinted at Victor from beneath an Agway Seeds cap. "Goin' far?"

"Just a few miles. Oak Hill Road."

"Yep. I go right past it." The driver pulled back onto the road. The truck spewed black exhaust as they roared down the highway, country music blaring from the radio.

Through the plucked strains of guitar music, Victor heard a sound that made him sit up sharply. A siren. Whipping his head around, he saw a patrol car zooming up fast behind them. *That's it,* thought Victor. *They've found me. They're going to stop this truck and arrest me....*

But for what? For walking away from the hospital? For insulting Miss Redfern? Or had Polowski fabricated some charge against him?

With a sense of impending doom, he waited for the patrol car to overtake them and start flashing its signal to pull over. In fact, he was so certain they *would* be pulled over that when the police car sped right past them and roared off down the highway, he could only stare ahead in amazement.

"Must be some kinda trouble," his companion said blandly, nodding at the rapidly vanishing police car.

Victor managed to clear his throat. "Trouble?"

"Yep. Don't get much of a chance to use that siren of theirs but when they do, boy oh boy, do they go to town with it."

With his heart hammering against his ribs, Victor sat back and forced himself to calm down. He had nothing to worry about. The police weren't after him, they were busy with some other concern. He wondered what sort of small-town catastrophe could warrant blaring sirens. Probably nothing more exciting than a few kids out on a joyride.

By the time they reached the turnoff to Oak Hill Road, Victor's pulse had settled back to normal. He thanked the driver, climbed out, and began the trek to Catherine Weaver's house. It was a long walk, and the road wound through a forest of pines. Every so often he'd pass a mailbox along the road and, peering through the trees, would spot a house. Catherine's address was coming up fast.

What on earth should he say to her? Up till now he'd concentrated only on reaching her house. Now that he was almost there, he had to come up with some reasonable explanation for why he'd dragged himself out of a hospital bed and trudged all this way to see her. A simple *thanks for saving my life* just wouldn't do it. He had to find out if she had the film canister. But she, of course, would want to know why the damn thing was so important.

You could tell her the truth.

No, forget that. He could imagine her reaction if he were to launch into his wild tale about viruses and dead scientists and double-crossing FBI agents. *The FBI is out to get you? I see. And who else is after you, Mr. Holland?* It was so absurdly paranoid he almost felt like laughing. No, he couldn't tell her any of it or he'd end up right back in a hospital, and this time in a ward that would make Miss Redfern's Three East look like paradise.

She didn't need to know any of it. In fact, she was better off ignorant. The woman had saved his life, and the last thing he wanted to do was put her in any danger. The film was all he wanted from her. After today, she'd never see him again.

He was so busy debating what to tell her that he didn't notice the police cars until well after he'd rounded the road's bend. Suddenly he froze, confronted by three squad cars—probably the entire police fleet of Garberville—parked in front of a rustic cedar house. A half-dozen neighbors lingered in the gravel driveway, shaking their heads in disbelief. Good God, had something happened to Catherine?

Swallowing the urge to turn and flee, Victor propelled himself forward, past the squad cars and through the loose gathering of onlookers, only to be stopped by a uniformed officer.

"I'm sorry, sir. No one's allowed past this point."

Dazed, Victor stared down and saw that the police had strung out a perimeter of red tape. Slowly, his gaze moved beyond the tape, to the old Datsun parked near the carport. Was that Catherine's car? He tried desperately to remember if she'd driven a Datsun, but last night it had been so dark and he'd been in so much pain that he hadn't bothered to pay attention. All he could remember was that it was a compact model, with scarcely enough room for his legs. Then he noticed the faded parking sticker on the rear bumper: Parking Permit, Studio Lot A.

I work for an independent film company, she'd told him last night.

It was Catherine's car.

Unwillingly, he focused on the stained gravel just beside the Datsun, and even though the rational part of him knew that that peculiar brick red could only be dried blood, he wanted to deny it. He wanted to believe there was some other explanation for that stain, for this ominous gathering of police.

He tried to speak, but his voice sounded like something dragged up through gravel.

"What did you say, sir?" the police officer asked.

"What—what happened?"

The officer shook his head sadly. "Woman was killed here last night. Our first murder in ten years."

"Murder?" Victor's gaze was still fixed in horror on the blood-stained gravel. "But—*why?*"

The officer shrugged. "Don't know yet. Maybe robbery, though I don't think he got much." He nodded at the Datsun. "Car was the only thing broken into."

If Victor said anything at that point, he never remembered what it was. He was vaguely aware of his legs carrying him back through the onlookers, past the three police cars, toward the road. The sunshine was so brilliant it hurt his eyes and he could barely see where he was going.

I killed her, he thought. *She saved my life and I killed her....*

Guilt slashed its way to his throat and he could scarcely breathe, could barely take another step for the pain. For a long time he stood there at the side of the road, his head bent in the sunshine, his ears filled with the sound of blue jays, and mourned a woman he'd never known.

When at last he was able to raise his head again, rage fueled the rest of his walk back to the highway, rage against Catherine's murderer. Rage at himself for having put her in such danger. It was the film the killer had been searching for, and he'd probably found it in the Datsun. If he hadn't, the house would have been ransacked, as well.

Now what? thought Victor. He dismissed the possibility that his briefcase—with most of the evidence—might still be in his wrecked car. That was the first place the killer would have searched. Without the film, Victor was left with no evidence at all. It would all come down to his word against Viratek's. The newspapers would dismiss him as nothing more than a disgruntled ex-employee. And after Polowski's double cross, he couldn't trust the FBI.

At that last thought, he quickened his pace. The sooner he got out of Garberville, the better. When he got back to the highway, he'd hitch another ride. Once safely out of town, he could take the time to plan his next move.

He decided to head south, to San Francisco.

CHAPTER THREE

From the window of his office at Viratek, Archibald Black watched the limousine glide up the tree-lined driveway and pull to a stop at the front entrance. Black snorted derisively. The cowboy was back in town, damn him. And after all the man's fussing about the importance of secrecy, about keeping his little visit discreet, the idiot had the gall to show up in a limousine—with a uniformed driver, no less.

Black turned from the window and paced over to his desk. Despite his contempt for the visitor, he had to acknowledge the man made him uneasy, the way all so-called men of action made him uneasy. Not enough brains behind all that muscle. Too much power in the hands of imbeciles, he thought. Is this an example of who we have running the country?

The intercom buzzed. "Mr. Black?" said his secretary. "A Mr. Tyrone is here to see you."

"Send him in, please," said Black, smoothing the scorn from his expression. He was wearing a look of polite deference when the door opened and Matthew Tyrone walked into the office.

They shook hands. Tyrone's grip was unreasonably firm, as though he was trying to remind Black of their relative positions of power. His bearing had all the spit and polish of an ex-marine, which Tyrone was. Only the thickening waist betrayed the fact that Tyrone's marine days had been left far behind.

"How was the flight from Washington?" inquired Black as they sat down.

"Terrible service. I tell you, commercial flights aren't what they used to be. To think the average American pays good money for the privilege."

"I imagine it can't compare with Air Force One."

Tyrone smiled. "Let's get down to business. Tell me where things stand with this little crisis of yours."

Black noted Tyrone's use of the word *yours. So now it's my problem,* he thought. Naturally. That's what they meant by deniability: When things go wrong, the other guy gets the blame. If any of this leaked out, Black's head would be the one to fall. But then, that's why this contract was so lucrative—because he—meaning Viratek—was willing to take that risk.

"We've recovered the documents," said Black. "And the film canisters. The negatives are being developed now."

"And your two employees?"

Black cleared his throat. "There's no need to take this any further."

"They're a risk to national security."

"You can't just kill them off!"

"Can't we?" Tyrone's eyes were a cold, gun-metal gray. An appropriate color for someone who called himself "the Cowboy." You didn't argue with anyone who had eyes like that. Not if you had an instinct for self-preservation.

Black dipped his head deferentially. "I'm not accustomed to this sort of…business. And I don't like dealing with your man Savitch."

"Mr. Savitch has performed well for us before."

"He killed one of my senior scientists!"

"I assume it was necessary."

Black looked down unhappily at his desk. Just the thought of that monster Savitch made him shudder.

"Why, exactly, did Martinique go bad?"

Because he had a conscience, thought Black. He looked at Tyrone. "There was no way to predict it. He'd worked in commercial R and D for ten years. He'd never presented a security problem before. We only found out last week that he'd taken classified documents. And then Victor Holland got involved…."

"How much does Holland know?"

"Holland wasn't involved with the project. But he's clever. If he looked over those papers, he might have pieced it together."

Now Tyrone was agitated, his fingers drumming the desktop. "Tell me about Holland. What do you know about him?"

"I've gone over his personnel file. He's forty-one years old, born and raised in San Diego. Entered the seminary but dropped out after a year. Went on to Stanford, then MIT. Doctorate in biochemistry. He was with Viratek for four years. One of our most promising researchers.''

''What about his personal life?''

''His wife died three years ago of leukemia. Keeps pretty much to himself these days. Quiet kind of guy, likes classical jazz. Plays the saxophone in some amateur group.''

Tyrone laughed. ''Your typical nerd scientist.'' It was just the sort of moronic comment an ex-marine like Tyrone would make. It was an insult that grated on Black. Years ago, before he created Viratek Industries, Black too had been a research biochemist.

''He should be a simple matter to dispose of,'' said Tyrone. ''Inexperienced. And probably scared.'' He reached for his briefcase. ''Mr. Savitch is an expert on these matters. I suggest you let him take care of the problem.''

''Of course.'' In truth, Black didn't think he had any choice. Nicholas Savitch was like some evil, frightening force that, once unleashed, could not be controlled.

The intercom buzzed. ''Mr. Gregorian's here from the photo lab,'' said the secretary.

''Send him in.'' Black glanced at Tyrone. ''The film's been developed. Let's see just what Martinique managed to photograph.''

Gregorian walked in carrying a bulky envelope. ''Here are those contact prints you requested,'' he said, handing the bundle across the desk to Black. Then he cupped his hand over his mouth, muffling a sound suspiciously like laughter.

''Yes, Mr. Gregorian?'' inquired Black.

''Nothing, sir.''

Tyrone cut in, ''Well, let's see them!''

Black removed the five contact sheets and lay them out on the desk for everyone to see. The men stared.

For a long time, no one spoke. Then Tyrone said, ''Is this some sort of joke?''

Gregorian burst out laughing.

Black said, ''What the hell is this?''

''Those are the negatives you gave me, sir,'' Gregorian insisted. ''I processed them myself.''

"These are the photos you got back from Victor Holland?" Tyrone's voice started soft and rose slowly to a roar. "Five rolls of *naked women?*"

"There's been a mistake," said Black. "It's the wrong film—"

Gregorian laughed harder.

"Shut up!" yelled Black. He looked at Tyrone. "I don't know how this happened."

"Then the roll we want is still out there?"

Black nodded wearily.

Tyrone reached for the phone. "We need to clean things up. Fast."

"Who are you calling?" asked Black.

"The man who can do the job," said Tyrone as he punched in the numbers. "Savitch."

In his motel room on Lombard Street, Victor paced the avocado-green carpet, wracking his brain for a plan. Any plan. His well-organized scientist's mind had already distilled the situation into the elements of a research project. Identify the problem: someone is out to kill me. State your hypothesis: Jerry Martinique uncovered something dangerous and he was killed for it. Now they think I have the information—and the evidence. Which I don't. Goal: Stay alive. Method: *Any damn way I can!*

For the last two days, his only strategy had consisted of holing up in various cheap motel rooms and pacing the carpets. He couldn't hide out forever. If the feds were involved, and he had reason to believe they were, they'd soon have his credit card charges traced, would know exactly where to find him.

I need a plan of attack.

Going to the FBI was definitely out. Sam Polowski was the agent Victor had contacted, the one who'd arranged to meet him in Garberville. No one else should have known about that meeting. Sam Polowski had never shown up.

But someone else had. Victor's aching shoulder was a constant reminder of that near-disastrous rendezvous.

I could go to the newspapers. But how would he convince some skeptical reporter? Who would believe his stories of a project so dangerous it could kill millions? They would think his tale was some fabrication of a paranoid mind.

And I am not paranoid.

He paced over to the TV and switched it on to the five o'clock news. A perfectly coiffed anchorwoman smiled from the screen as she read a piece of fluff about the last day of school, happy children, Christmas vacation. Then her expression sobered. Transition. Victor found himself staring at the TV as the next story came on.

"And in Garberville, California, there have been no new leads in the murder investigation of a woman found slain Wednesday morning. A houseguest found Sarah Boylan, 39, lying in the driveway, dead of stab wounds to the neck. The victim was five months pregnant. Police say they are puzzled by the lack of motive in this terrible tragedy, and at the present time there are no suspects. Moving on to national news…"

No, no, no! Victor thought. She wasn't pregnant. Her name wasn't Sarah. It's a mistake….

Or was it?

My name is Catherine, she had told him.

Catherine Weaver. Yes, he was sure of the name. He'd remember it till the day he died.

He sat on the bed, the facts spinning around in his brain. Sarah. Cathy. A murder in Garberville.

When at last he rose to his feet, it was with a swelling sense of urgency, even panic. He grabbed the hotel room phone book and flipped to the *W*s. He understood now. The killer had made a mistake. If Cathy Weaver was still alive, she might have that roll of film—or know where to find it. Victor had to reach her.

Before someone else did.

Nothing could have prepared Cathy for the indescribable sense of gloom she felt upon returning to her flat in San Francisco. She had thought she'd cried out all her tears that night in the Garberville motel, the night after Sarah's death. But here she was, still bursting into tears, then sinking into deep, dark meditations. The drive to the city had been temporarily numbing. But as soon as she'd climbed the steps to her door and confronted the deathly silence of her second-story flat, she felt overwhelmed once again by grief. And be-wilderment. Of all the people in the world to die, why Sarah?

She made a feeble attempt at unpacking. Then, forcing herself to stay busy, she surveyed the refrigerator and saw that her shelves were practically empty. It was all the excuse she needed to flee her apartment. She pulled a sweater over her jeans and, with a sense of escape, walked the four blocks to the neighborhood grocery store. She bought only the essentials, bread and eggs and fruit. Enough to tide her over for a few days, until she was back on her feet and could think clearly about any sort of menu.

Carrying a sack of groceries in each arm, she walked through the gathering darkness back to her apartment building. The night was chilly, and she regretted not wearing a coat. Through an open win-dow, a woman called, "Time for dinner!" and two children playing kickball in the street turned and scampered for home.

By the time Cathy reached her building, she was shivering and her arms were aching from the weight of the groceries. She trudged up the steps and, balancing one sack on her hip, managed to pull out her keys and unlock the security door. Just as she swung through, she heard footsteps, then glimpsed a blur of movement rushing toward her from the side. She was swept through the door-way, into the building. A grocery bag tumbled from her arms, spill-ing apples across the floor. She stumbled forward, catching herself on the wood banister. The door slammed shut behind her.

She spun around, ready to fight off her attacker.

It was Victor Holland.

"You!" she whispered in amazement.

He didn't seem so sure of *her* identity. He was frantically search-ing her face, as though trying to confirm he had the right woman. "Cathy Weaver?"

"What do you think you're—"

"Where's your apartment?" he cut in.

"What?"

"We can't stand around out here."

"It's—it's upstairs—"

"Let's go." He reached for her arm but she pulled away.

"My groceries," she said, glancing down at the scattered apples.

He quickly scooped up the fruit, tossed it in one of the bags, and nudged her toward the stairs. "We don't have a lot of time."

Cathy allowed herself to be herded up the stairs and halfway down the hall before she stopped dead in her tracks. "Wait a minute. You tell me what this is all about, Mr. Holland, and you tell me right now or I don't move another step!"

"Give me your keys."

"You can't just—"

"Give me your keys!"

She stared at him, shocked by the command. Suddenly she realized that what she saw in his eyes was panic. They were the eyes of a hunted man.

Automatically she handed him her keys.

"Wait here," he said. "Let me check the apartment first."

She watched in bewilderment as he unlocked her door and cautiously eased his way inside. For a few moments she heard nothing. She pictured him moving through the flat, tried to estimate how many seconds each room would require for inspection. It was a small flat, so why was he taking so long?

Slowly she moved toward the doorway. Just as she reached it, his head popped out. She let out a little squeak of surprise. He barely caught the bag of groceries as it slipped from her grasp.

"It's okay," he said. "Come on inside."

The instant she stepped over the threshold, he had the door locked and bolted behind her. Then he quickly circled the living room, closing the drapes, locking windows.

"Are you going to tell me what's going on?" she asked, following him around the room.

"We're in trouble."

"You mean *you're* in trouble."

"No. I mean *we*. Both of us." He turned to her, his gaze clear and steady. "Do you have the film?"

"What are you talking about?" she asked, utterly confused by the sudden shift of conversation.

"A roll of film. Thirty-five millimeter. In a black plastic container. Do you have it?"

She didn't answer. But an image from that last night with Sarah had already taken shape in her mind: a roll of film on the kitchen counter. Film she'd thought belonged to her friend Hickey. Film she'd slipped into her bathrobe pocket and later into her purse. But she wasn't about to reveal any of this, not until she found out why he wanted it. The gaze she returned to him was purposefully blank and unrevealing.

Frustrated, he forced himself to take a deep breath, and started over. "That night you found me—on the highway—I had it in my pocket. It wasn't with me when I woke up in the hospital. I might have dropped it in your car."

"Why do you want this roll of film?"

"I need it. As evidence—"

"For what?"

"It would take too long to explain."

She shrugged. "I've got nothing better to do at the moment—"

"*Damn it!*" He stalked over to her. Taking her by the shoulders, he forced her to look at him. "Don't you understand? That's why your friend was killed! The night they broke into your car, they were looking for that film!"

She stared at him, a look of sudden comprehension and horror. "Sarah..."

"Was in the wrong place at the wrong time. The killer must have thought she was *you*."

Cathy felt trapped by his unrelenting gaze. And by the inescapable threat of his revelation. Her knees wobbled, gave way. She sank into the nearest chair and sat there in numb silence.

"You have to get out of here," he said. "Before they find you. Before they figure out you're the Cathy Weaver they're looking for."

She didn't move. She couldn't move.

"Come on, Cathy. There isn't much time!"

"What was on that roll of film?" she asked softly.

"I told you. Evidence. Against a company called Viratek."

She frowned. "Isn't—isn't that the company you work for?"

"Used to work for."

"What did they do?"

"They're involved in some sort of illegal research project. I can't tell you the particulars."

"Why not?"

"Because I don't know them. I'm not the one who gathered the evidence. A colleague—a friend—passed it to me, just before he was killed."

"What do you mean by killed?"

"The police called it an accident. I think otherwise."

"You're saying he was murdered over a research project?" She shook her head. "Must have been dangerous stuff he was working on."

"I know this much. It involves biological weapons. Which makes the research illegal. And incredibly dangerous."

"Weapons? For what government?"

"Ours."

"I don't understand. If this is a federal project, that makes it all legal, right?"

"Not by a long shot. People in high places have been known to break the rules."

"How high are we talking about?"

"I don't know. I can't be sure of anyone. Not the police, not the Justice Department. Not the FBI."

Her eyes narrowed. The words she was hearing sounded like paranoid ravings. But the voice—and the eyes—were perfectly sane. They were sea-green, those eyes. They held an honesty, a steadiness that should have been all the assurance she needed.

It wasn't. Not by a long shot.

Quietly she said, "So you're telling me the FBI is after you. Is that correct?"

Sudden anger flared in his eyes, then just as quickly, it was gone. Groaning, he sank onto the couch and ran his hands through his hair. "I don't blame you for thinking I'm nuts. Sometimes I wonder if I'm all there. I thought if I could trust anyone, it'd be you...."

"Why me?"

He looked at her. "Because you're the one who saved my life. You're the one they'll try to kill next."

She froze. No, no, this was insane. Now he was pulling her into his delusion, making her believe in his nightmare world of murder and conspiracy. She wouldn't let him! She stood up and started to walk away, but his voice made her stop again.

"Cathy, think about it. Why was your friend Sarah killed? Because they thought she was *you*. By now they've figured out they killed the wrong woman. They'll have to come back and do the job right. Just in case you know something. In case you have evidence—''

"This is crazy!" she cried, clapping her hands over her ears. "No one's going to—''

"They already have!" He whipped out a scrap of newspaper from his shirt pocket. "On my way over here, I happened to pass a newsstand. This was on the front page." He handed her the piece of paper.

She stared in bewilderment at the photograph of a middle-aged woman, a total stranger. "San Francisco woman shot to death on front doorstep," read the accompanying headline.

"This has nothing to do with me," she said.

"Look at her name."

Cathy's gaze slid to the third paragraph, which identified the victim.

Her name was Catherine Weaver.

The scrap of newsprint slipped from her grasp and fluttered to the floor.

"There are three Catherine Weavers in the San Francisco phone book," he said. "That one was shot to death at nine o'clock this morning. I don't know what's happened to the second. She might already be dead. Which makes you next on the list. They've had enough time to locate you."

"I've been out of town—I only got back an hour ago—''

"Which explains why you're still alive. Maybe they came here earlier. Maybe they decided to check out the other two women first."

She shot to her feet, suddenly frantic with the need to flee. "I have to pack my things—''

"No. Let's just get the hell out of here."

Yes, do what he says! an inner voice screamed at her.

She nodded. Turning, she headed blindly for the door. Halfway there, she halted. "My purse—''

"Where is it?"

She headed back, past a curtained window. "I think I left it by the—''

Her next words were cut off by an explosion of shattering glass. Only the closed curtains kept the shards from piercing her flesh. Pure reflex sent Cathy diving to the floor just as the second gun blast went off. An instant later she found Victor Holland sprawled on top of her, covering her body with his as the third bullet slammed into the far wall, splintering wood and plaster.

The curtains shuddered, then hung still.

For a few seconds Cathy was paralyzed by terror, by the weight of Victor's body on hers. Then panic took hold. She squirmed free, intent on fleeing the apartment.

"Stay down!" Victor snapped.

"They're trying to kill us!"

"Don't make it easy for them!" He dragged her back to the floor. "We're getting out. But not through the front door."

"How—"

"Where's your fire escape?"

"My bedroom window."

"Does it go to the roof?"

"I'm not sure—I think so—"

"Then let's move it."

On hands and knees they crawled down the hall, into Cathy's unlit bedroom. Beneath the window they paused, listening. Outside, in the darkness, there was no sound. Then, from downstairs in the lobby, came the tinkle of breaking glass.

"He's already in the building!" hissed Victor. He yanked open the window. "Out, out!"

Cathy didn't need to be prodded. Hands shaking, she scrambled out and lowered herself onto the fire escape. Victor was right behind her.

"Up," he whispered. "To the roof."

And then what? she wondered, climbing the ladder to the third floor, past Mrs. Chang's flat. Mrs. Chang was out of town this week, visiting her son in New Jersey. The apartment was dark, the windows locked tight. No way in there.

"Keep going," said Victor, nudging her forward.

Only a few more rungs to go.

At last, she pulled herself up and over the edge and onto the asphalt roof. A second later, Victor dropped down beside her. Potted plants shuddered in the darkness. It was Mrs. Chang's rooftop garden, a fragrant mélange of Chinese herbs and vegetables.

Together, Victor and Cathy weaved their way through the plants and crossed to the opposite edge of the roof, where the next building abutted theirs.

"All the way?" said Cathy.

"All the way."

They hopped onto the adjoining roof and ran across to the other side, where three feet of emptiness separated them from the next building. She didn't pause to think of the perils of that leap, she simply flung herself across the gap and kept running, aware that every step took her farther and farther from danger.

On the roof of the fourth building, Cathy finally halted and stared over the edge at the street below. End of the line. It suddenly occurred to her that it was a very long drop to the ground below. The fire escape looked as sturdy as a Tinkertoy.

She swallowed. "This probably isn't a good time to tell you this, but—"

"Tell me what?"

"I'm afraid of heights."

He clambered over the edge. "Then don't look down."

Right, she thought, slithering onto the fire escape. *Don't look down.* Her palms were so slick with sweat she could barely grip the rungs. Suddenly seized by an attack of vertigo, she froze there, clinging desperately to that flimsy steel skeleton.

"Don't stop now!" Victor whispered up to her. "Just keep moving!"

Still she didn't move. She pressed her face against the rung, so hard she felt the rough edge bite into her flesh.

"You're okay, Cathy!" he said. "Come on."

The pain became all-encompassing, blocking out the dizziness, even the fear. When she opened her eyes again, the world had steadied. On rubbery legs, she descended the ladder, pausing on the third floor landing to wipe her sweaty palms on her jeans. She continued downward, to the second-floor landing. It was still a good fifteen-foot drop to the ground. She unlatched the extension ladder and started to slide it down, but it let out such a screech that Victor immediately stopped her.

"Too noisy. We have to jump!"

"But—"

To her astonishment, he scrambled over the railing and dropped to the ground. "Come on!" he hissed from below. "It's not that far. I'll catch you."

Murmuring a prayer, she lowered herself over the side and let go.

To her surprise he did catch her—but held on only for a second. The bullet wound had left his injured shoulder too weak to hold on. They both tumbled to the ground. She landed smack on top of him, her legs astride his hips, their faces inches apart. They stared at each other, so stunned they could scarcely breathe.

Upstairs, a window slid open and someone yelled, "Hey, you bums! If you don't clear out this instant, I'm calling the cops!"

Instantly Cathy rolled off Victor, only to stagger into a trash can. The lid fell off and slammed like a cymbal against the sidewalk.

"That's it for rest stops," Victor grunted and scrambled to his feet. *"Move it."*

They took off at a wild dash down the street, turned up an alley, and kept running. It was a good five blocks before they finally stopped to catch their breath. They glanced back.

The street was deserted.

They were safe!

Nicholas Savitch stood beside the neatly made bed and surveyed the room. It was every inch a woman's room, from the closet hung with a half-dozen simple but elegant dresses, to the sweetly scented powders and lotions lined up on the vanity table. It took only a single circuit around the room to tell him about the woman whose bedroom this was. She was slim, a size seven dress, size six-and-a-half shoe. The hairs on the brush were brown and shoulder-length. She owned only a few pieces of jewelry, and she favored natural scents, rosewater and lavender. Her favorite color was green.

Back in the living room, he continued to gather information. The woman subscribed to the Hollywood trade journals. Her taste in music, like her taste in books, was eclectic. He noticed a scrap of newspaper lying on the floor. He picked it up and glanced at the article. Now this was interesting. The death of Catherine Weaver I had not gone unnoticed by Catherine Weaver III.

He pocketed the article. Then he saw the purse, lying on the floor near the shattered window.

Bingo.

He emptied the contents on the coffee table. Out tumbled a wallet, checkbook, pens, loose change, and...an address book. He opened it to the *B*s. There he found the name he was looking for: Sarah Boylan.

He now knew this was the Catherine Weaver he'd been seeking. What a shame he'd wasted his time hunting down the other two.

He flipped through the address book and spotted a half dozen or so San Francisco listings. The woman may have been clever enough to slip away from him this time. But staying out of sight was a more difficult matter. And this little book, with its names of friends and relatives and colleagues, could lead him straight to her.

Somewhere in the distance, a police siren was wailing.

It was time to leave.

Savitch took the address book and the woman's wallet and headed out the door. Outside, his breath misted in the cold air as he walked at a leisurely pace down the street,

He could afford to take his time.

But for Catherine Weaver and Victor Holland, time was running out.

CHAPTER FOUR

There was no time to rest. They jogged for the next six blocks, miles and miles, it seemed to Cathy. Victor moved tirelessly, leading her down side streets, avoiding busy intersections. She let him do the thinking and navigating. Her terror slowly gave way to numbness and a disorienting sense of unreality. The city itself seemed little more than a dreamscape, asphalt and streetlights and endless twists and turns of concrete. The only reality was the man striding close beside her, his gaze alert, his movements swift and sure. She knew he too must be afraid, but she couldn't see his fear.

He took her hand; the warmth of that grasp, the strength of those fingers, seemed to flow into her cold, exhausted limbs.

She quickened her pace. "I think there's a police substation down that street," she said. "If we go a block or two further—"

"We're not going to the police."

"What?" She stopped dead, staring at him.

"Not yet. Not until I've had a chance to think this through."

"Victor," she said slowly. "Someone is trying to kill us. Trying to kill *me*. What do you mean, you need time to *think this through?*"

"Look, we can't stand around talking about it. We have to get off the streets." He grabbed her hand again. "Come on."

"Where?"

"I have a room. It's only a few blocks away."

She let him drag her only a few yards before she mustered the will to pull free. "Wait a minute. Just *wait.*"

He turned, his face a mask of frustration, and confronted her. "Wait for what? For that maniac to catch up? For the bullets to start flying again?"

"For an explanation!"

"I'll explain it all. When we're safe."

She backed away. "Why are you afraid of the police?"

"I can't be sure of them."

"Do you have a reason to be afraid? What have you done?"

With two steps he closed the gap between them and grabbed her hard by the shoulders. "I just pulled you out of a death trap, remember? The bullets were going through your window, not mine!"

"Maybe they were aimed at you!"

"Okay!" He let her go, let her back away from him. "You want to try it on your own? Do it. Maybe the police'll be a help. Maybe not. But I can't risk it. Not until I know all the players behind this."

"You—you're letting me go?"

"You were never my prisoner."

"No." She took a breath—it misted in the cold air. She glanced down the street, toward the police substation. "It's...the reasonable thing to do," she muttered, almost to reassure herself. "That's what they're there for."

"Right."

She frowned, anticipating what lay ahead. "They'll ask a lot of questions."

"What are you going to tell them?"

She looked at him, her gaze unflinchingly meeting his. "The truth."

"Which'll be at best, incomplete. And at worst, unbelievable."

"I have broken glass all over my apartment to prove it."

"A drive-by shooting. Purely random."

"It's their job to protect me."

"What if they don't think you need protection?"

"I'll tell them about you! About Sarah."

"They may or may not take you seriously."

"They have to take me seriously! Someone's trying to kill me!" Her voice, shrill with desperation, seemed to echo endlessly through the maze of streets.

Quietly he said, "I know."

She glanced back toward the substation. "I'm going."

He said nothing.

"Where will you be?" she asked.

"On my own. For now."

She took two steps away, then stopped. "Victor?"

"I'm still here."

"You did save my life. Thank you."

He didn't respond. She heard his footsteps slowly walk away. She stood there thinking, wondering if she was doing the right thing. Of course she was. A man afraid of the police—with a story as paranoid as his was—had to be dangerous.

But he saved my life.

And once, on a rainy night in Garberville, she had saved his.

She replayed all the events of the last week. Sarah's murder, never explained. The other Catherine Weaver, shot to death on her front doorstep. The film canister that Sarah had retrieved from the car, the one Cathy had slipped into her bathrobe pocket...

Victor's footsteps had faded.

In that instant she realized she'd lost the only man who could help her find the answers to all those questions, the one man who'd stood by her in her darkest moment of terror. The one man she knew, by some strange intuition, she could trust. Facing that deserted street, she felt abandoned and utterly friendless. In sudden panic, she whirled around and called out: "Victor!"

At the far end of the block, a silhouette stopped and turned. He seemed an island of refuge in that crazy, dangerous world. She started toward him, her legs moving her faster and faster, until she was running, yearning for the safety of his arms, the arms of a man she scarcely knew. Yet it didn't feel like a stranger's arms gathering her to his chest, welcoming her into his protective embrace. She felt the pounding of his heart, the grip of his fingers against her back, and something told her that this was a man she could depend upon, a man who wouldn't fold when she needed him most.

"I'm right here," he murmured. "Right here." He stroked through her windblown hair, his fingers burying deep in the tangled strands. She felt the heat of his breath against her face, felt her own quick and shuddering response. And then, all at once, his mouth hungrily sought hers and he was kissing her. She responded with a kiss just as desperate, just as needy. Stranger though he was, he had been there for her and he was still here, his arms sheltering her from the terrors of the night.

She burrowed her face against his chest, longing to press ever deeper, ever closer. "I don't know what to do! I'm so afraid, Victor, and I don't know what to do...."

"We'll work this out together. Okay?" He cupped her face in his hands and tilted it up to his. "You and I, we'll beat this thing."

She nodded. Searching his eyes, connecting with that rock-solid gaze, she found all the assurance she needed.

A wind gusted down the street. She shivered in its wake. "What do we do first?" she whispered.

"First," he said, pulling off his windbreaker and draping it over her shoulders, "We get you warmed up. And inside." He took her hand. "Come on. A hot bath, a good supper, and you'll be operating on all cylinders again."

It was another five blocks to the Kon-Tiki Motel. Though not exactly a five-star establishment, the Kon-Tiki was comfortingly drab and anonymous, one of a dozen on motel row. They climbed the steps to Room 214, overlooking the half-empty parking lot. He unlocked the door and motioned her inside.

The rush of warmth against her cheeks was delicious. She stood in the center of that utterly charmless space and marveled at how good it felt to be safely surrounded by four walls. The furnishings were spare: a double bed, a dresser, two nightstands with lamps, and a single chair. On the wall was a framed print of some nameless South Pacific island. The only luggage she saw was a cheap nylon bag on the floor. The bedcovers were rumpled, recently napped in, the pillows punched up against the headboard.

"Not much," he said. "But it's warm. And it's paid for." He turned on the TV. "We'd better keep an eye on the news. Maybe they'll have something on the Weaver woman."

The Weaver woman, she thought. *It could have been me.* She was shivering again, but now it wasn't from the cold. Settling onto the bed she stared numbly at the TV, not really seeing what was on the screen. She was more aware of *him.* He was circling the room, checking the windows, fiddling with the lock on the door. He moved quietly, efficiently, his silence a testimony to the dangers of their situation. Most men she knew began to babble nonsense when they were scared; Victor Holland simply turned quiet. His mere presence was overwhelming. He seemed to fill the room.

He moved to her side. She flinched as he took her hands and

gently inspected them, palm side up. Looking down, she saw the bloodied scratches, the flakes of rust from the fire escape embedded in her skin.

"I guess I'm a mess," she murmured.

He smiled and stroked her face. "You could use some washing up. Go ahead. I'll get us something to eat."

She retreated into the bathroom. Through the door she could hear the drone of the TV, the sound of Victor's voice ordering a pizza over the phone. She ran hot water over her cold, numb hands. In the mirror over the sink she caught an unflattering glimpse of herself, her hair a tangled mess, her chin smudged with dirt. She washed her face, rubbing new life, new circulation into those frigid cheeks. Glancing down, she noticed Victor's razor on the counter. The sight of that blade cast her situation into a new focus—a frightening one. She picked up the razor, thinking how lethal that blade looked, how vulnerable she would be tonight. Victor was a large man, at least six foot two, with powerful arms. She was scarcely five foot five, a comparative weakling. There was only one bed in the next room. She had come here voluntarily. What would he assume about her? That she was a willing victim? She thought of all the ways a man could hurt her, kill her. It wouldn't take a razor to finish the job. Victor could use his bare hands. *What am I doing here?* she wondered. *Spending the night with a man I scarcely know?*

This was not the time to have doubts. She'd made the decision. She had to go by her instincts, and her instincts told her Victor Holland would never hurt her.

Deliberately she set down the razor. She would have to trust him. She was afraid not to.

In the other room, a door slammed shut. Had he left?

Opening the door a crack, she peered out. The TV was still on. There was no sign of Victor. Slowly she emerged, to find she was alone. She began to circle the room, searching for clues, anything that would tell her more about the man. The bureau drawers were empty, and so was the closet. Obviously he had not moved into this room for a long stay. He'd planned only one night, maybe two. She went to the nylon bag and glanced inside. She saw a clean pair of socks, an unopened package of underwear, and a day-old edition of the *San Francisco Chronicle.* All it told her was that the man kept himself informed and he traveled light.

Like a man on the run.

She dug deeper and came up with a receipt from an automatic teller machine. Yesterday he'd tried to withdraw cash. The machine had printed out the message: *Transaction cannot be completed. Please contact your bank.* Why had it refused him the cash? she wondered. Was he overdrawn? Had the machine been out of order?

The sound of a key grating in the lock caught her by surprise. She glanced up as the door swung open.

The look he gave her made her cheeks flush with guilt. Slowly she rose to her feet, unable to answer that look of accusation in his eyes.

The door swung shut behind him.

"I suppose it's a reasonable thing for you to do," he said. "Search my things."

"I'm sorry. I was just…" She swallowed. "I had to know more about you."

"And what terrible things have you dug up?"

"Nothing!"

"No deep dark secrets? Don't be afraid. Tell me, Cathy."

"Only…only that you had trouble getting cash out of your account."

He nodded. "A frustrating state of affairs. Since by my estimate I have a balance of six thousand dollars. And now I can't seem to touch it." He sat down in the chair, his gaze still on her face. "What else did you learn?"

"You—you read the newspaper."

"So do a lot of people. What else?"

She shrugged. "You wear boxer shorts."

Amusement flickered in his eyes. "Now we're getting personal."

"You…" She took a deep breath. "You're on the run."

He looked at her a long time without saying a word.

"That's why you won't go to the police," she said. "Isn't it?"

He turned away, gazing not at her but at the far wall. "There are reasons."

"Give me one, Victor. One good reason is all I need and then I'll shut up."

He sighed. "I doubt it."

"Try me. I have every reason to believe you."

"You have every reason to think I'm paranoid." Leaning forward, he ran his hands over his face. "Lord, sometimes *I* think I must be."

Quietly she went to him and knelt down beside his chair. "Victor, these people who are trying to kill me—who are they?"

"I don't know."

"You said it might involve people in high places."

"It's just a guess. It's a case of federal money going to illegal research. Deadly research."

"And federal money has to be doled out by someone in authority."

He nodded. "This is someone who's bent the rules. Someone who could be hurt by a political scandal. He just might try to protect himself by manipulating the Bureau. Or even your local police. That's why I won't go to them. That's why I left the room to make my call."

"When?"

"While you were in the bathroom. I went to a pay phone and called the police. I didn't want it traced."

"You just said you don't want them involved."

"This call I had to make. There's a third Catherine Weaver in that phone book. Remember?"

A third victim on the list. Suddenly weak, she sat down on the bed. "What did you say?" she asked softly.

"That I had reason to think she might be in danger. That she wasn't answering her phone."

"You tried it?"

"Twice."

"Did they listen to you?"

"Not only did they listen, they demanded to know my name. That's when I picked up the cue that something must already have happened to her. At that point I hung up and hightailed it out of the booth. A call can be traced in seconds. They could've had me surrounded."

"That makes three," she whispered. "Those two other women. And me."

"They have no way of finding you. Not as long as you stay away from your apartment. Stay out of—"

They both froze in panic.

Someone was knocking on the door.

They stared at each other, fear mirrored in their eyes. Then, after a moment's hesitation, Victor said: "Who is it?"

"Domino's," called a thin voice.

Cautiously, Victor eased open the door. A teenage boy stood outside, wielding a bag and a flat cardboard box.

"Hi!" chirped the boy. "A large combo with the works, two Cokes and extra napkins. Right?"

"Right." Victor handed the boy a few bills. "Keep the change," he said and closed the door. Turning, he gave Cathy a sheepish look. "Well," he admitted. "Just goes to show you. Sometimes a knock at the door really is just the pizza man."

They both laughed, a sound not of humor but of frayed nerves. The release of tension seemed to transform his face, melted his wariness to warmth. Erase those haggard lines, she thought, and he could almost be called a handsome man.

"I tell you what," he said. "Let's not think about this mess right now. Why don't we just get right down to the really important issue of the day. Food."

Nodding, she reached out for the box. "Better hand it over. Before I eat the damn bedspread."

While the ten o'clock news droned from the television set, they tore into the pizza like two ravenous animals. It was a greasy and utterly satisfying banquet on a motel bed. They scarcely bothered with conversation—their mouths were too busy devouring cheese and pepperoni. On the TV, a dapper anchorman announced a shakeup in the mayor's office, the resignation of the city manager, news that, given their current situation, seemed ridiculously trivial. Scarcely thirty seconds were devoted to that morning's killing of Catherine Weaver I; as yet, no suspects were in custody. No mention was made of any second victim by the same name.

Victor frowned. "Looks like the other woman didn't make it to the news."

"Or nothing's happened to her." She glanced at him questioningly. "What if the second Cathy Weaver is all right? When you called the police, they might've been asking you routine questions. When you're on edge, it's easy to—''

"Imagine things?" The look he gave her almost made her bite her tongue.

"No," she said quietly. "Misinterpret. The police can't respond to every anonymous call. It's natural they'd ask for your name."

"It was more than a request, Cathy. They were champing at the bit to interrogate me."

"I'm not doubting your word. I'm just playing devil's advocate. Trying to keep things level and sane in a crazy situation."

He looked at her long and hard. At last he nodded. "The voice of a rational woman," he sighed. "Exactly what I need right now. To keep me from jumping at my own shadow."

"And remind you to eat." She held out another slice of pizza. "You ordered this giant thing. You'd better help me finish it."

The tension between them instantly evaporated. He settled onto the bed and accepted the proferred slice. "That maternal look becomes you," he noted wryly. "So does the pizza sauce."

"What?" She swiped at her chin.

"You look like a two-year-old who's decided to fingerpaint her face."

"Good grief, can you hand me the napkins?"

"Let me do it." Leaning forward, he gently dabbed away the sauce. As he did, she studied his face, saw the laugh lines creasing the corners of his eyes, the strands of silver intertwined with the brown hair. She remembered the photo of that very face, pasted on a Viratek badge. How somber he'd looked, the unsmiling portrait of a scientist. Now he appeared young and alive and almost happy.

Suddenly aware that she was watching him, he looked up and met her gaze. Slowly his smile faded. They both went very still, as though seeing, in each other's eyes, something they had not noticed before. The voices on the television seemed to fade into a far-off dimension. She felt his fingers trace lightly down her cheek. It was only a touch, but it left her shivering.

She asked, softly, "What happens now, Victor? Where do we go from here?"

"We have several choices."

"Such as?"

"I have friends in Palo Alto. We could turn to them."

"Or?"

"Or we could stay right where we are. For a while."

Right where we are. In this room, on this bed. She wouldn't mind that. Not at all.

She felt herself leaning toward him, drawn by a force against which she could offer no resistance. Both his hands came up to cradle her face, such large hands, but so infinitely gentle. She closed her eyes, knowing that this kiss, too, would be a gentle one.

And it was. This wasn't a kiss driven by fear or desperation. This was a quiet melting together of warmth, of souls. She swayed against him, felt his arms circle behind her to pull her inescapably close. It was a dangerous moment. She could feel herself tottering on the edge of total surrender to this man she scarcely knew. Already, her arms had found their way around his neck and her hands were roaming through the silver-streaked thickness of his hair.

His kisses dropped to her neck, exploring all the tender rises and hollows of her throat. All the needs that had lain dormant these past few years, all the hungers and desires, seemed to stir inside her, awakening at his touch.

And then, in an instant, the magic slipped away. At first she didn't understand why he suddenly pulled back. He sat bolt upright. The expression on his face was one of frozen astonishment. Bewildered, she followed his gaze and saw that he was focused on the television set behind her. She turned to see what had captured his attention.

A disturbingly familiar face stared back from the screen. She recognized the Viratek logo at the top, the straight-ahead gaze of the man in the photo. Why on earth would they be broadcasting Victor Holland's ID badge?

"...Sought on charges of industrial espionage. Evidence now links Dr. Holland to the death of a fellow Viratek researcher, Dr. Gerald Martinique. Investigators fear the suspect has already sold extensive research data to a European competitor...."

Neither one of them seemed able to move from the bed. They could only stare in disbelief at the newscaster with the Ken doll haircut. The station switched to a commercial break, raisins dancing crazily on a field, proclaiming the wonders of California sunshine. The lilting music was unbearable.

Victor rose to his feet and flicked off the television.

Slowly he turned to look at her. The silence between them grew agonizing.

"It's not true," he said quietly. "None of it."

She tried to read those unfathomable green eyes, wanting desperately to believe him. The taste of his kisses were still warm on her lips. The kisses of a con artist? *Is this just another lie? Has everything you've told me been nothing but lies? Who and what are you, Victor Holland?*

She glanced sideways, at the telephone on the bedside stand. It was so close. One call to the police, that's all it would take to end this nightmare.

"It's a frame-up," he said. "Viratek's releasing false information."

"Why?"

"To corner me. What easier way to find me than to have the police help them?"

She edged toward the phone.

"Don't, Cathy."

She froze, startled by the threat in his voice.

He saw the instant fear in her eyes. Gently he said, "Please. Don't call. I won't hurt you. I promise you can walk right out that door if you want. But first listen to me. Let me tell you what happened. Give me a chance."

His gaze was steady and absolutely believable. And he was right beside her, ready to stop her from making a move. Or to break her arm, if need be. She had no other choice. Nodding, she settled back down on the bed.

He began to pace, his feet tracing a path in the dull green carpet.

"It's all some—some incredible lie," he said. "It's crazy to think I'd kill him. Jerry Martinique and I were the best of friends. We both worked at Viratek. I was in vaccine development, he was a microbiologist. His specialty was viral studies. Genome research."

"You mean—like chromosomes?"

"The viral equivalent. Anyway, Jerry and I, we helped each other through some bad times. He'd gone through a painful divorce and I…" He paused, his voice dropping. "I lost my wife three years ago. To leukemia."

So he'd been married. Somehow it surprised her. He seemed like the sort of man who was far too independent to have ever said, "I do."

"About two months ago," he continued, "Jerry was transferred to a new research department. Viratek had been awarded a grant for some defense project. It was top security—Jerry couldn't talk about it. But I could see he was bothered by something that was going on in that lab. All he'd say to me was, 'They don't understand the danger. They don't know what they're getting into.' Jerry's field was the alteration of viral genes. So I assume the project had something to do with viruses as weapons. Jerry was fully aware that those weapons are outlawed by international agreement."

"If he knew it was illegal, why did he take part in it?"

"Maybe he didn't realize at first what the project was aiming for. Maybe they sold it to him as purely defensive research. In any event, he got upset enough to resign from the project. He went right to the top—the founder of Viratek. Walked into Archibald Black's office and threatened to go public if the project wasn't terminated. Four days later he had an accident." Anger flashed in Victor's eyes. It wasn't directed at her, but the fury in that gaze was frightening all the same.

"What happened to him?" she asked.

"His wrecked car was found at the side of the road. Jerry was still inside. Dead, of course." Suddenly, the anger was gone, replaced by overwhelming weariness. He sank onto the bed. "I thought the accident investigation would blow everything into the open. It was a farce. The local cops did their best, but then some federal transportation "expert" showed up on the scene and took over. He said Jerry must've fallen asleep at the wheel. Case closed. That's when I realized just how deep this went. I didn't know who to go to, so I called the FBI in San Francisco. Told them I had evidence."

"You mean the film?" asked Cathy.

Victor nodded. "Just before he was killed, Jerry told me about some duplicate papers he'd stashed away in his garden shed. After the…accident, I went over to his house. Found the place ransacked. But they never bothered to search the shed. That's how I got hold of the evidence, a single file and a roll of film. I arranged a meeting with one of the San Francisco agents, a guy named Sam Polowski. I'd already talked to him a few times on the phone. He offered to meet me in Garberville. We wanted to keep it private, so we agreed to a spot just outside of town. I drove down, fully expecting him to show. Well, someone showed up, all right. Someone who ran me off the road." He paused and looked straight at her. "That's the night you found me."

The night my whole life changed, she thought.

"You have to believe me," he said.

She studied him, her instincts battling against logic. The story was just barely plausible, halfway between truth and fantasy. But the man looked solid as stone.

Wearily she nodded. "I do believe you, Victor. Maybe I'm crazy. Or just gullible. But I do."

The bed shifted as he sat down beside her. They didn't touch, yet she could almost feel the warmth radiating between them.

"That's all that matters to me right now," he said. "That you know, in your heart, I'm telling the truth."

"In my heart?" She shook her head and laughed. "My heart's always been a lousy judge of character. No, I'm guessing. I'm going by the fact you kept me alive. By the fact there's another Cathy Weaver who's now dead…"

Remembering the face of that other woman, the face in the newspaper, she suddenly began to shake. It all added up to the terrible truth. The gun blasts into her apartment, the other dead Cathy. And Sarah, poor Sarah.

She was gulping in shaky breaths, hovering on the verge of tears.

She let him take her in his arms, let him pull her down on the bed beside him. He murmured into her hair, gentle words of comfort and reassurance. He turned off the lamp. In darkness they held each other, two frightened souls joined against a terrifying world. She felt safe there, tucked away against his chest. This was a place where no one could hurt her. It was a stranger's arms, but from the smell of his shirt to the beat of his heart, it all seemed somehow familiar. She never wanted to leave that spot, ever.

She trembled as his lips brushed her forehead. He was stroking her face now, her neck, warming her with his touch. When his hand slipped beneath her blouse, she didn't protest. Somehow it seemed

so natural, that that hand would come to lie at her breast. It wasn't
the touch of a marauder, it was simply a gentle reminder that she
was in safekeeping.

And yet, she found herself responding....

Her nipple tingled and grew taut beneath his cupping hand. The
tingling spread, a warmth that crept to her face and flushed her
cheeks. She reached for his shirt and began to unbutton it. In the
darkness she was slow and clumsy. By the time she finally slid her
hand under the fabric, they were both breathing hard and fast with
anticipation.

She brushed through the coarse mat of hair, stroking her way
across that broad chest. He took in a sharp breath as her fingers
skimmed a delicate circle around his nipple.

If playing with fire had been her intention, then she had just
struck the match.

His mouth was suddenly on hers, seeking, devouring. The force
of his kiss pressed her onto her back, trapping her head against the
pillows. For a dizzy eternity she was swimming in sensations, the
scent of male heat, the unyielding grip of his hands imprisoning her
face. Only when he at last drew away did they both come up for
air.

He stared down at her, as though hovering on the edge of temptation.

"This is crazy," he whispered.

"Yes. Yes, it is—"

"I never meant to do this—"

"Neither did I."

"It's just that you're scared. We're both scared. And we don't
know what the hell we're doing."

"No." She closed her eyes, felt the unexpected bite of tears. "We
don't. But I *am* scared. And I just want to be held. Please, Victor.
Hold me, that's all. Just hold me."

He pulled her close, murmuring her name. This time the embrace
was gentle, without the fever of desire. His shirt was still unbut-
toned, his chest bared. And that's where she lay her head, against
that curling nest of hair. Yes, he was right, so wise. They were
crazy to be making love when they both knew it was fear, nothing
else, that had driven their desire. And now the fever had broken.

A sense of peace fell over her. She curled up against him. Exhaustion robbed them both of speech. Her muscles gradually fell limp as sleep tugged her into its shadow. Even if she tried to, she could not move her arms or legs. Instead she was drifting free, like a wraith in the darkness, floating somewhere in a warm and inky sea.

Vaguely she was aware of light sliding past her eyelids.

The warmth encircling her body seemed to melt away. No, she wanted it back, wanted *him* back! An instant later she felt him shaking her.

"Cathy. Come on, wake up!"

Through drowsy eyes she peered at him. "Victor?"

"Something's going on outside."

She tumbled out of bed and followed him to the window. Through a slit in the curtains she spotted what had alarmed him: a patrol car, its radio crackling faintly, parked by the motel registration door. At once she snapped wide awake, her mind going over the exits from their room. There was only one.

"Out, now!" he ordered. "Before we're trapped."

He eased open the door. They scrambled out onto the walkway. The frigid night air was like a slap in the face. She was already shivering, more from fear than from the cold. Running at a crouch, they moved along the walkway, away from the stairs, and ducked past the ice machine.

Below, they heard the lobby door open and the voice of the motel manager: "Yeah, that'll be right upstairs. Gee, he sure seemed like a nice-enough guy...."

Tires screeched as another patrol car pulled up, lights flashing.

Victor gave her a push. *"Go!"*

They slipped into a breezeway and scurried through, to the other side of the building. No stairways there! They climbed over the walkway railing and dropped into the parking lot.

Faintly they heard a banging, then the command: "Open up! This is the police."

At once they were sprinting instinctively for the shadows. No one spotted them, no one gave chase. Still they kept running, until they'd left the Kon-Tiki Motel blocks and blocks behind them, until they were so tired they were stumbling.

At last Cathy slowed to a halt and leaned back against a doorway, her breath coming out in clouds of cold mist. "How did they find you?" she said between gasps.

"It couldn't have been the call...." Suddenly he groaned. "My credit card! I had to use it to pay the bill."

"Where now? Should we try another motel?"

He shook his head. "I'm down to my last forty bucks. I can't risk a credit card again."

"And I left my purse at the apartment. I—I'm not sure I want to—"

"We're not going back for it. They'll be watching the place."

They. Meaning the killers.

"So we're broke," she said weakly.

He didn't answer. He stood with his hands in his pockets, his whole body a study in frustration. "You have friends you can go to?"

"I think so. Uh, no. She's out of town till Friday. And what would I tell her? How would I explain you?"

"You can't. And we can't handle any questions right now."

That leaves out most of my friends, she thought. Nowhere to go, no one to turn to. Unless...

No, she'd promised herself never to sink that low, never to beg for *that* particular source of help.

Victor glanced up the street. "There's a bus stop over there." He reached in his pocket and took out a handful of money. "Here," he said. "Take it and get out of the city. Go visit some friends on your own."

"What about you?"

"I'll be okay."

"Broke? With everyone after you?" She shook her head.

"I'll only make things more dangerous for you." He pressed the money into her hand.

She stared down at the wad of bills, thinking: *This is all he has. And he's giving it to me.* "I can't," she said.

"You have to."

"But—"

"Don't argue with me." The look in his eyes left no alternative. Reluctantly she closed her fingers around the money.

"I'll wait till you get on the bus. It should take you right past the station."

"Victor?"

He silenced her with a single look. Placing both hands on her shoulders, he stood her before him. "You'll be fine," he said. Then he pressed a kiss to her forehead. For a moment his lips lingered, and the warmth of his breath in her hair left her trembling. "I wouldn't leave you if I thought otherwise."

The roar of a bus down the block made them both turn.

"There's your limousine," he whispered. "Go." He gave her a nudge. "Take care of yourself, Cathy."

She started toward the bus stop. Three steps, four. She slowed and came to a halt. Turning, she saw that he had already edged away into the shadows.

"Get on it!" he called.

She looked at the bus. *I won't do it,* she thought.

She turned back to Victor. "I know a place! A place we can both stay!"

"What?"

"I didn't want to use it but—"

Her words were drowned out as the bus wheezed to the stop, then roared away.

"It's a bit of a walk," she said. "But we'd have beds and a meal. And I can guarantee no one would call the police."

He came out of the shadows. "Why didn't you think of this earlier?"

"I did think of it. But up till now, things weren't, well…desperate enough."

"Not desperate enough," he repeated slowly. He moved toward her, his face taut with incredulity. "Not *desperate* enough? Hell, lady. I'd like to know exactly what kind of crisis would qualify!"

"You have to understand, this is a last resort. It's not an easy place for me to turn to."

His eyes narrowed in suspicion. "This place is beginning to sound worse and worse. What are we talking about? A flophouse?"

"No, it's in Pacific Heights. You could even call the place a mansion."

"Who lives there? A friend?"

"Quite the opposite."

His eyebrow shot up. "An enemy?"

"Close." She let out a sigh of resignation. "My ex-husband."

CHAPTER FIVE

"Jack, open up! Jack!" Cathy banged again and again on the door of the formidable Pacific Heights home. There was no answer. Through the windows they saw only darkness.

"Damn you, Jack!" She gave the door a slap of frustration. "Why aren't you *ever* home when I need you?"

Victor glanced around at the neighborhood of elegant homes and neatly trimmed shrubbery. "We can't stand around out here all night."

"We're not going to," she muttered. Crouching on her knees, she began to dig around in a red-brick planter.

"What are you doing?"

"Something I swore I'd never do." Her fingers raked the loamy soil, searching for the key Jack kept buried under the geraniums. Sure enough, there it was, right where it had always been. She rose to her feet, clapping the dirt off her hands. "But there are limits to my pride. Threat of death being one of them." She inserted the key and felt a momentary dart of panic when it didn't turn. But with a little jiggling, the lock at last gave way. The door swung open to the faint gleam of a polished wood floor, a massive bannister.

She motioned Victor inside. The solid thunk of the door closing behind them seemed to shut out all the dangers of the night. Cloaked in the darkness, they both let out a sigh of relief.

"Just what kind of terms are you on with your ex-husband?" Victor asked, following her blindly through the unlit foyer.

"Speaking. Barely."

"He doesn't mind you wandering around his house?"

"Why not?" She snorted. "Jack lets half the human race wander through his bedroom. The only prerequisite being XX chromosomes."

She felt her way into the pitch-dark living room and flipped on the light switch. There she froze in astonishment and stared at the two naked bodies intertwined on the polar bear rug.

"Jack!" she blurted out.

The larger of the two bodies extricated himself and sat up. "Hello, Cathy!" He raked his hand through his dark hair and grinned. "Seems like old times."

The woman lying next to him spat out a shocking obscenity, scrambled to her feet, and stormed off in a blur of wild red hair and bare bottom toward the bedroom.

"That's Lulu," yawned Jack, by way of introduction.

Cathy sighed. "I see your taste in women hasn't improved."

"No, sweetheart, my taste in women hit a high point when I married you." Unmindful of his state of nudity, Jack rose to his feet and regarded Victor. The contrast between the two men was instantly apparent. Though both were tall and lean, it was Jack who possessed the striking good looks, and he knew it. He'd always known it. Vanity wasn't a label one could ever pin on Victor Holland.

"I see you brought a fourth," said Jack, giving Victor the once-over. "So, what'll it be, folks? Bridge or poker?"

"Neither," said Cathy.

"That opens up all *sorts* of possibilities."

"Jack, I need your help."

He turned and looked at her with mock incredulity. *"No!"*

"You know damn well I wouldn't be here if I could avoid it!"

He winked at Victor. "Don't believe her. She's still madly in love with me."

"Can we get serious?"

"Darling, you never did have a sense of humor."

"Damn you, Jack!" Everyone had a breaking point and Cathy had reached hers. She couldn't help it; without warning she burst into tears. "For once in your life will you *listen* to me?"

That's when Victor's patience finally snapped. He didn't need a degree in psychology to know this Jack character was a first-class jerk. Couldn't he see that Cathy was exhausted and terrified? Up till this moment, Victor had admired her for her strength. Now he ached at the sight of her vulnerability.

It was only natural to pull her into his arms, to ease her tear-streaked face against his chest. Over her shoulder, he growled out an oath that impugned not only Jack's name but that of Jack's mother as well.

The other man didn't seem to take offense, probably because he'd been called far worse names, and on a regular basis. He simply crossed his arms and regarded Victor with a raised eyebrow. "Being protective, are we?"

"She needs protection."

"From what, pray tell?"

"Maybe you haven't heard. Three days ago, someone murdered her friend Sarah."

"Sarah…Boylan?"

Victor nodded. "Tonight, someone tried to kill Cathy."

Jack stared at him. He looked at his ex-wife. "Is this true? What he's saying?"

Cathy, wiping away tears, nodded.

"Why didn't you tell me this to begin with?"

"Because you were acting like an ass to begin with!" she shot back.

Down the hall came the *click-click* of high-heeled shoes. "She's absolutely right!" yelled a female voice from the foyer. "You *are* an ass, Jack Zuckerman!" The front door opened and slammed shut again. The thud seemed to echo endlessly through the mansion.

There was a long silence.

Suddenly, through her tears, Cathy laughed. "You know what, Jack? I *like* that woman."

Jack crossed his arms and gave his ex-wife the critical once-over. "Either I'm going senile or you forgot to tell me something. Why haven't you gone to the police? Why bother old Jack about this?"

Cathy and Victor glanced at each other.

"We can't go to the police," Cathy said.

"I assume this has to do with *him?*" He cocked a thumb at Victor. Cathy let out a breath. "It's a complicated story…."

"It must be. If you're afraid to go to the police."

"I can explain it," said Victor.

"Mm-hm. Well." Jack reached for the bathrobe lying in a heap by the polar bear rug. "Well," he said again, calmly tying the sash. "I've always enjoyed watching creativity at work. So let's have it."

He sat down on the leather couch and smiled at Victor. "I'm waiting. It's showtime."

Special Agent Sam Polowski lay shivering in his bed, watching the eleven o'clock news. Every muscle in his body ached, his head pounded, and the thermometer at his bedside read an irrefutable 101 degrees. So much for changing flat tires in the pouring rain. He wished he could get his hands on the joker who'd punched that nail in his tire while he was grabbing a quick bite at that roadside cafe. Not only had the culprit managed to keep Sam from his appointment in Garberville, thereby shredding the Viratek case into confetti, Sam had also lost track of his only contact in the affair: Victor Holland. And now, the flu.

Sam reached over for the bottle of aspirin. To hell with the ulcer. His head hurt. And when it came to headaches, there was nothing like Mom's time-tested remedy.

He was in the midst of gulping down three tablets when the news about Victor Holland flashed on the screen.

"...New evidence links the suspect to the murder of fellow Viratek researcher, Dr. Gerald Martinique...."

Sam sat up straight in bed. "What the hell?" he growled at the TV.

Then he grabbed the telephone.

It took six rings for his supervisor to answer. "Dafoe?" Sam said. "This is Polowski."

"Do you know what time it is?"

"Have you seen the late-night news?"

"I happen to be in bed."

"There's a story on Viratek."

A pause. "Yeah, I know. I cleared it."

"What's with this crap about industrial espionage? They're making Holland out to be a—"

"Polowski, drop it."

"Since when did he become a murder suspect?"

"Look, just consider it a cover story. I want him brought in. For his own good."

"So you sic him with a bunch of trigger-happy cops?"

"I said drop it."

"But—"

"You're off the case." Dafoe hung up.

Sam stared in disbelief at the receiver, then at the television, then back at the receiver.

Pull me off the case? He slammed the receiver down so hard the bottle of aspirin tumbled off the nightstand.

That's what you think.

"I think I've heard about enough," said Jack, rising to his feet. "I want this man out of my house. And I want him out now."

"Jack, please!" said Cathy. "Give him a chance—"

"You're buying this ridiculous tale?"

"I believe him."

"Why?"

She looked at Victor and saw the clear fire of honesty burning in his eyes. "Because he saved my life."

"You're a fool, babycakes." Jack reached for the phone. "You yourself saw the TV. He's wanted for murder. If you don't call the police, I will."

But as Jack picked up the receiver, Victor grabbed his arm. "No," he said. Though his voice was quiet, it held the unmistakable note of authority.

The two men stared at each other, neither willing to back down.

"This is more than just a case of murder," said Victor. "This is deadly research. The manufacture of illegal weapons. This could reach all the way to Washington."

"Who in Washington?"

"Someone in control. Someone with the federal funds to authorize that research."

"I see. Some lofty public servant is out knocking off scientists. With the help of the FBI."

"Jerry wasn't just any scientist. He had a conscience. He was a whistleblower who would've taken this to the press to stop that research. The political fallout would've been disastrous, for the whole administration."

"Wait. Are we talking Pennsylvania Avenue?"

"Maybe."

Jack snorted. "Holland, I *make* Grade B horror films. I don't live them."

"This isn't a film. This is real. Real bullets, real bodies."

"Then that's all the more reason I want nothing to do with it." Jack turned to Cathy. "Sorry, sweetcakes. It's nothing personal, but I detest the company you keep."

"Jack," she said. "You have to help us!"

"You, I'll help. Him—no way. I draw the line at lunatics and felons."

"You heard what he said! It's a frame-up!"

"You are so gullible."

"Only about you."

"Cathy, it's all right," said Victor. He was standing very still, very calm. "I'll leave."

"No, you won't." Cathy shot to her feet and stalked over to her ex-husband. She stared him straight in the eye, a gaze so direct, so accusing, he seemed to wilt right down into a chair. "You owe it to me, Jack. You owe me for all the years we were married. All the years I put into *your* career, *your* company, *your* idiotic flicks. I haven't asked for anything. You have the house. The Jaguar. The bank account. I never asked because I didn't want to take a damn thing from this marriage except my own soul. But now I'm asking. This man saved my life tonight. If you ever cared about me, if you ever loved me, even a little, then you'll do me this favor."

"Harbor a criminal?"

"Only until we figure out what to do next."

"And how long might that take? Weeks? Months?"

"I don't know."

"Just the kind of definite answer I like."

Victor said, "I need time to find out what Jerry was trying to prove. What it is Viratek's working on—"

"You had one of his files," said Jack. "Why didn't you read the blasted thing?"

"I'm not a virologist. I couldn't interpret the data. It was some sort of RNA sequence, probably a viral genome. A lot of the data was coded. All I can be sure of is the name: Project Cerberus."

"Where is all this vital evidence now?"

"I lost the file. It was in my car the night I was shot. I'm sure they have it back."

"And the film?"

Victor sank into a chair, his face suddenly lined by weariness. "I don't have it. I was hoping that Cathy…" Sighing, he ran his hands through his hair. "I've lost that, too."

"Well," said Jack. "Give or take a few miracles, I'd say this puts your chances at just about zero. And I'm known as an optimist."

"I know where the film is," said Cathy.

There was a long silence. Victor raised his head and stared at her. "What?"

"I wasn't sure about you—not at first. I didn't want to tell you until I could be certain—"

Victor shot to his feet. *"Where is it?"*

She flinched at the sharpness of his voice. He must have noticed how startled she was—his next words were quiet but urgent. "I need that film, Cathy. Before they find it. Where is it?"

"Sarah found it in my car. I didn't know it was yours! I thought it was Hickey's."

"Who's Hickey?"

"A photographer—a friend of mine—"

Jack snorted. "Hickey. Now *there's* a ladies' man."

"He was in a rush to get to the airport," she continued. "At the last minute he left me with some rolls of film. Asked me to take care of them till he got back from Nairobi. But all his film was stolen from my car."

"And my roll?" asked Victor.

"It was in my bathrobe pocket the night Sarah—the night she—" She paused, swallowing at the mention of her friend. "When I got back here, to the city, I mailed it to Hickey's studio."

"Where's the studio?"

"Over on Union Street. I mailed it this afternoon—"

"So it should be there sometime tomorrow." He began to pace the room. "All we have to do is wait for the mail to arrive."

"I don't have a key."

"We'll find a way in."

"Terrific," sighed Jack. "Now he's turning my ex-wife into a burglar."

"We're only after the film!" said Cathy.

"It's still breaking and entering, sweetie."

"You don't have to get involved."

"But you're asking me to harbor the breakers and enterers."

"Just one night, Jack. That's all I'm asking."

"That sounds like one of *my* lines."

"And your lines always work, don't they?"

"Not this time."

"Then here's another line to chew on: 1988. Your federal tax return. Or lack of one."

Jack froze. He glowered at Victor, then at Cathy. "That's below the belt."

"Your most vulnerable spot."

"I'll get around to filing—"

"More words to chew on. Audit. IRS. Jail."

"Okay, okay!" Jack threw his arms up in surrender. "God, I *hate* that word."

"What, *jail?*"

"Don't laugh, babycakes. The word could soon apply to all of us." He turned and headed for the stairs.

"Where are you going?" Cathy demanded.

"To make up the spare beds. Seems I have houseguests for the night...."

"Can we trust him?" Victor asked after Jack had vanished upstairs.

Cathy sank back on the couch, all the energy suddenly drained from her body, and closed her eyes. "We have to. I can't think of anywhere else to go...."

She was suddenly aware of his approach, and then he was sitting beside her, so close she could feel the overwhelming strength of his presence. He didn't say a word, yet she knew he was watching her.

She opened her eyes and met his gaze. So steady, so intense, it seemed to infuse her with new strength.

"I know it wasn't easy for you," he said. "Asking Jack for favors."

She smiled. "I've always wanted to talk tough with Jack." Ruefully she added, "Until tonight, I've never quite been able to pull it off."

"My guess is, talking tough isn't in your repertoire."

"No, it isn't. When it comes to confrontation, I'm a gutless wonder."

"For a gutless wonder, you did pretty well. In fact, you were magnificent."

"That's because I wasn't fighting for me. I was fighting for you."

"You don't consider yourself worth fighting for?"

She shrugged. "It's the way I was raised. I was always told that sticking up for yourself was unladylike. Whereas sticking up for other people was okay."

He nodded gravely. "Self-sacrifice. A fine feminine tradition."

That made her laugh. "Spoken like a man who knows women well."

"Only two women. My mother and my wife."

At the mention of his dead wife, she fell silent. She wondered what the woman's name was, what she'd looked like, how much he'd loved her. He must have loved her a great deal—she'd heard the pain in his voice earlier that evening when he'd mentioned her death. She felt an unexpected stab of envy that this unnamed wife had been so loved. What Cathy would give to be as dearly loved by a man! Just as quickly she suppressed the thought, appalled that she could be jealous of a dead woman.

She turned away, her face tinged with guilt. "I think Jack will go along," she said. "Tonight, at least."

"That was blackmail, wasn't it? That stuff about the tax return?"

"He's a careless man. I just reminded him of his oversight."

Victor shook his head. "You are amazing. Jumping along rooftops one minute, blackmailing ex-husbands the next."

"You're so right," said Jack, who'd reappeared at the bottom of the stairs. "She is an amazing woman. I can't wait to see what she'll do next."

Cathy rose wearily to her feet. "At this point I'll do anything." She slipped past Jack and headed up the stairs. "Anything I have to to stay alive."

The two men listened to her footsteps recede along the hall. Then they regarded each other in silence.

"Well," said Jack with forced cheerfulness. "What's next on the agenda? Scrabble?"

"Try solitaire," said Victor, hauling himself off the couch. He was in no mood to share pleasantries with Jack Zuckerman. The man was slick and self-centered and he obviously went through women the way most men went through socks. Victor had a hard time imagining what Cathy had ever seen in the man. That is, aside from Jack's good looks and obvious wealth. There was no denying the fact he was a classic hunk, with the added attraction of money thrown in. Maybe it was that combination that had dazzled her.

A combination I'll certainly never possess, he thought.

He crossed the room, then stopped and turned. "Zuckerman?" he asked. "Do you still love your wife?"

Jack looked faintly startled by the question. "Do I still love her? Well, let me see. No, not exactly. But I suppose I have a sentimental attachment, based on ten years of marriage. And I respect her."

"Respect her? You?"

"Yes. Her talents. Her technical skill. After all, she's my number-one makeup artist."

That's what she meant to him. An asset he could use. *Thinking of himself, the jerk.* If there was anyone else Victor could turn to, he would. But the one man he would've trusted—Jerry—was dead. His other friends might already be under observation. Plus, they weren't in the sort of tax brackets that allowed private little hideaways in the woods. Jack, on the other hand, had the resources to spirit Cathy away to a safe place. Victor could only hope the man's sentimental attachment was strong enough to make him watch out for her.

"I have a proposition," said Victor.

Jack instantly looked suspicious. "What might that be?"

"I'm the one they're really after. Not Cathy. I don't want to make things any more dangerous for her than I already have."

"Big of you."

"It's better if I go off on my own. If I leave her with you, will you keep her safe?"

Jack shifted, looked down at his feet. "Well, sure. I guess so."

"Don't guess. Can you?"

"Look, we start shooting a film in Mexico next month. Jungle scenes, black lagoons, that sort of stuff. Should be a safe-enough place."

"That's next month. What about now?"

"I'll think of something. But first you get yourself out of the picture. Since you're the reason she's in danger in the first place."

Victor couldn't disagree with that last point. *Since the night I met her I've caused her nothing but trouble.*

He nodded. "I'm out of here tomorrow."

"Good."

"Take care of Cathy. Get her out of the city. Out of the country. Don't wait."

"Yeah. Sure."

Something about the way Jack said it, his hasty, whatever-you-say tone, made Victor wonder if the man gave a damn about anyone but himself. But at this point Victor had no choice. He had to trust Jack Zuckerman.

As he climbed the stairs to the guest rooms, it occurred to him that, come morning, it would be goodbye. A quiet little bond had formed between them. He owed his life to her and she to him. That was the sort of link one could never break.

Even if we never see each other again.

In the upstairs hall, he paused outside her closed door. He could hear her moving around the room, opening and closing drawers, squeaking bedsprings.

He knocked on the door. "Cathy?"

There was a pause. Then, "Come in."

One dim lamp lit the room. She was sitting on the bed, dressed in a ridiculously huge man's shirt. Her hair hung in damp waves to her shoulders. The scent of soap and shampoo permeated the shadows. It reminded him of his wife, of the shower smells and feminine sweetness. He stood there, pierced by a sense of longing he hadn't felt in over a year, longing for the warmth, the love, of a woman. Not just any woman. He wasn't like Jack, to whom a soft body with the right equipment would be sufficient. What Victor wanted was the heart and soul; the package they came wrapped in was only of minor importance.

His own wife Lily hadn't been beautiful; neither had she been unattractive. Even at the end, when the ravages of illness had left her shrunken and bruised, there had been a light in her eyes, a gentle spirit's glow.

The same glow he'd seen in Catherine Weaver's eyes the night she'd saved his life. The same glow he saw now.

She sat with her back propped up on pillows. Her gaze was silently expectant, maybe a little fearful. She was clutching a handful of tissues. *Why were you crying?* he wondered.

He didn't approach; he stood just inside the doorway. Their gazes locked together in the gloom. "I've just talked with Jack," he said.

She nodded but said nothing.

"We both agree. It's better that I leave as soon as possible. So I'll be taking off in the morning."

"What about the film?"

"I'll get it. All I need is Hickey's address."

"Yes. Of course." She looked down at the tissues in her fist.

He could tell she wanted to say something. He went to the bed and sat down. Those sweet woman smells grew intoxicating. The neckline of her oversized shirt sagged low enough to reveal a tempting glimpse of shadow. He forced himself to focus on her face.

"Cathy, you'll be fine. Jack said he'd watch out for you. Get you out of the city."

"Jack?" What sounded like a laugh escaped her throat.

"You'll be safer with him. I don't even know where I'll be going. I don't want to drag you into this—"

"But you already have. You've dragged me in over my head, Victor. What am I supposed to do now? I can't just—just sit around and wait for you to fix things. I owe it to Sarah—"

"And I owe it to you not to let you get hurt."

"You think you can hand me over to Jack and make everything be fine again? Well, it won't be fine. Sarah's dead. Her baby's dead. And somehow it's not just your fault. It's mine as well."

"No, it's not. Cathy—"

"It is my fault! Did you know she was lying there in the driveway all night? In the rain. In the cold. There she was, dying, and I slept through the whole damn thing...." She dropped her face in her hands. The guilt that had been tormenting her since Sarah's death at last burst through. She began to cry, silently, ashamedly, unable to hold back the tears any longer.

Victor's response was automatic and instinctively male. He pulled her against him and gave her a warm, safe place to cry. As soon as he felt her settle into his arms, he knew it was a mistake. It was too perfect a fit. She felt as if she belonged there, against his heart, felt that if she ever pulled away there would be left a hole so gaping it could never be filled. He pressed his lips to her damp hair and inhaled her heady scent of soap and warm skin. That gentle fragrance was enough to drown a man with need. So was the softness of her face, the silken luster of that shoulder peeking out from beneath the shirt. And all the time he was stroking her hair, murmuring inane words of comfort, he was thinking: *I have to leave her. For her sake I have to abandon this woman. Or I'll get us both killed.*

"Cathy," he said. It took all the willpower he could muster to pull away. He placed his hands on her shoulders, made her look at him. Her gaze was confused and brimming with tears. "We have to talk about tomorrow."

She nodded and swiped at the tears on her cheeks.

"I want you out of the city, first thing in the morning. Go to Mexico with Jack. Anywhere. Just keep out of sight."

"What will you do?"

"I'm going to take a look at that roll of film, see what kind of evidence it has."

"And then?"

"I don't know yet. Maybe I'll take it to the newspapers. The FBI is definitely out."

"How will I know you're all right? How do I reach you?"

He thought hard, fighting the distraction of her scent, her hair. He found himself stroking the bare skin of her shoulder, marveling at how smooth it felt beneath his fingers.

He focused on her face, on the look of worry in her eyes. "Every other Sunday I'll put an ad in the Personals. *Los Angeles Times.* It'll be addressed to, let's say, Cora. Anything I need to tell you will be there."

"Cora." She nodded. "I'll remember."

They looked at each other, a silent acknowledgment that this parting had to be. He cupped her face and pressed a kiss to her mouth. She barely responded; already, it seemed, she had said her goodbyes.

He rose from the bed and started for the door. There he couldn't resist asking, one more time: "You'll be all right?"

She nodded, but it was too automatic. The sort of nod one gave to dismiss an unimportant question. "I'll be fine. After all, I'll have Jack to watch over me."

He didn't miss the faint note of irony in her reply. Jack, it seemed, didn't inspire confidence in either of them. *What's my alternative? Drag her along with me as a moving target?*

He gripped the doorknob. No, it was better this way. He'd already ripped her life apart; he wasn't going to scatter the pieces as well.

As he was leaving, he took one last backward glance. She was still huddled on the bed, her knees drawn up to her chest. The over-sized shirt had slid off one bare shoulder. For a moment he thought she was crying. Then she raised her head and met his gaze. What he saw in her eyes wasn't tears. It was something far more moving, something pure and bright and beautiful.

Courage.

In the pale light of dawn, Savitch stood outside Jack Zuckerman's house. Through the fingers of morning mist, Savitch studied the curtained windows, trying to picture the inhabitants within. He wondered who they were, in which room they slept, and whether Catherine Weaver was among them.

He'd find out soon.

He pocketed the black address book he'd taken from the woman's apartment. The name C. Zuckerman and this Pacific Heights address had been written on the inside front cover. Then the Zuckerman had been crossed out and replaced with Weaver. She was a divorcée, he concluded. Under Z, he'd found a prominent listing for a man named Jack, with various phone numbers and addresses, both foreign and domestic. Her ex-husband, he'd confirmed, after a brief chat with another name listed in the book. Pumping strangers for information was a simple matter. All it took was an air of authority and a cop's ID. The same ID he was planning to use now.

He gave the house one final perusal, taking in the manicured lawns and shrubbery, the trellis with its vines of winter-dormant wisteria. A successful man, this Jack Zuckerman. Savitch had always admired men of wealth. He gave his jacket a final tug to assure himself that the shoulder holster was concealed. Then he crossed the street to the front porch and rang the doorbell.

CHAPTER SIX

At first light, Cathy awakened. It wasn't a gentle return but a startling jerk back to consciousness. She was instantly aware that she was not in her own bed and that something was terribly wrong. It took her a few seconds to remember exactly what it was. And when she did remember, the sense of urgency was so compelling she rose at once from bed and began to dress in the semidarkness. *Have to be ready to run...*

The creak of floorboards in the next room told her that Victor was awake as well, probably planning his moves for the day. She rummaged through the closet, searching for things he might need in his flight. All she came up with was a zippered nylon bag and a raincoat. She searched the dresser next and found a few men's socks. She also found a collection of women's underwear. *Damn Jack and all his women,* she thought with sudden irritation and slammed the drawer shut. The thud was still resonating in the room when another sound echoed through the house.

The doorbell was ringing.

It was only seven o'clock, too early for visitors or deliverymen. Suddenly her door swung open. She turned to see Victor, his face etched with tension.

"What should we do?" she asked.

"Get ready to leave. Fast."

"There's a back door—"

"Let's go."

They hurried along the hall and had almost reached the top of the stairs when they heard Jack's sleepy voice below, grumbling: "I'm coming, dammit! Stop that racket, I'm coming!"

The doorbell rang again.

"Don't answer it!" hissed Cathy. "Not yet—"

Jack had already opened the door. Instantly Victor snatched Cathy back up the hall, out of sight. They froze with their backs against the wall, listening to the voices below.

"Yeah," they heard Jack say. "I'm Jack Zuckerman. And who are you?"

The visitor's voice was soft. They could tell only that it was a man.

"Is that so?" said Jack, his voice suddenly edged with panic. "You're with the *FBI,* you say? And what on earth would the *FBI* want with my *ex-wife?*"

Cathy's gaze flew to Victor. She read the frantic message in his eyes: *Which way out?*

She pointed toward the bedroom at the end of the hall. He nodded. Together they tiptoed along the carpet, all the time aware that one misstep, one loud creak, might be enough to alert the agent downstairs.

"Where's your warrant?" they heard Jack demand of the visitor. "Hey, wait a minute! You can't just barge in here without a court order or something!"

No time left! thought Cathy in panic as she slipped into the last room. They closed the door behind them.

"The window!" she whispered.

"You mean jump?"

"No." She hurried across the room and gingerly eased the window open. "There's a trellis!"

He glanced down dubiously at the tangled vines of wisteria. "Are you sure it'll hold us?"

"I know it will," she said, swinging her leg over the sill. "I caught one of Jack's blondes hanging off it one night. And believe me, she was a *big* girl." She glanced down at the ground far below and felt a sudden wave of nausea as the old fear of heights washed through her. "God," she muttered. "Why do we always seem to be hanging out of windows?"

From somewhere in the house came Jack's outraged shout: "You can't go up there! You haven't shown me your warrant!"

"Move!" snapped Victor.

Cathy lowered herself onto the trellis. Branches clawed her face as she scrambled down the vine. An instant after she landed on the dew-soaked grass, Victor dropped beside her.

At once they were on their feet and sprinting for the cover of shrubbery. Just as they rolled behind the azalea bushes, they heard a second-floor window slide open, and then Jack's voice complaining loudly: "I know my rights! This is an illegal search! I'm going to call my lawyer!"

Don't let him see us! prayed Cathy, burrowing frantically into the bush. She felt Victor's body curl around her back, his arms pulling her tightly to him, his breath hot and ragged against her neck. For an eternity they lay shivering in the grass as mist swirled around them.

"You see?" they heard Jack say. "There's no one here but me. Or would you like to check the garage?"

The window slid shut.

Victor gave Cathy a little push. "Go," he whispered. "The end of the hedge. We'll run from there."

On hands and knees she crawled along the row of azalea bushes. Her soaked jeans were icy and her palms scratched and bleeding, but she was too numbed by terror to feel any pain. All her attention was focused on moving forward. Victor was crawling close behind her. When she felt him bump up against her hip, it occurred to her what a ridiculous view he had, her rump swaying practically under his nose.

She reached the last bush and stopped to shove a handful of tangled hair off her face. "That house next?" she asked.

"Go for it!"

They both took off like scared rabbits, dashing across the twenty yards of lawn between houses. Once they reached the cover of the next house, they didn't stop. They kept running, past parked cars and early-morning pedestrians. Five blocks later, they ducked into a coffee shop. Through the front window, they glanced out at the street, watching for signs of pursuit. All they saw was the typical Monday morning bustle: the stop-and-go traffic, the passersby bundled up in scarves and overcoats.

From the grill behind them came the hiss and sizzle of bacon. The smell of freshly brewed coffee wafted from the counter burner. The aromas were almost painful; they reminded Cathy that she and Victor probably had a total of forty dollars between them. Damn it, why hadn't she begged, borrowed or stolen some cash from Jack?

"What now?" she asked, half hoping he'd suggest blowing the rest of their cash on breakfast.

He scanned the street. "Let's go on."

"Where?"

"Hickey's studio."

"Oh." She sighed. Another long walk, and all on an empty stomach.

Outside, a car passed by bearing the bumper sticker: Today is the First Day of the Rest of Your Life.

Lord, I hope it gets better than this, she thought. Then she followed Victor out the door and into the morning chill.

Field Supervisor Larry Dafoe was sitting at his desk, pumping away at his executive power chair. Upper body strength, he always said, was the key to success as a man. Bulk out those muscles *pull!*, fill out that size forty-four jacket *pull!*, and what you got was a pair of shoulders that'd impress any woman, intimidate any rival. And with this snazzy 700-buck model, you didn't even have to get out of your chair.

Sam Polowski watched his superior strain at the system of wires and pulleys and thought the device looked more like an exotic instrument of torture.

"What you gotta understand," gasped Dafoe, "is that there are other *pull!* issues at work here. Things you know nothing about."

"Like what?" asked Polowski.

Dafoe released the handles and looked up, his face sheened with a healthy sweat. "If I was at liberty to tell you, don't you think I already would've?"

Polowski looked at the gleaming black exercise handles, wondering whether he'd benefit from an executive power chair. Maybe a souped-up set of biceps was what he needed to get a little respect around this office.

"I still don't see what the point is," he said. "Putting Victor Holland in the hot seat."

"The point," said Dafoe, "is that you don't call the shots."

"I gave Holland my word he'd be left out of this mess."

"He's *part* of the mess! First he claims he has evidence, then he pulls a vanishing act."

Jack scowled at him. He drummed his fingers against the door frame. He debated. At last he stepped aside. "As a law-abiding citizen, I suppose it is my duty." Grudgingly, he waved the man in. "Oh, just come in, Polowski. I'll tell you what I know."

The window shattered, raining slivers into the gloomy space beyond.

Cathy winced at the sound. "Sorry, Hickey," she said under her breath.

"We'll make it up to him," said Victor, knocking off the remaining shards. "We'll send him a nice fat check. You see anyone?"

She glanced up and down the alley. Except for a crumpled newspaper tumbling past the trash cans, nothing moved. A few blocks away, car horns blared, the sounds of another Union Street traffic jam.

"All clear," she whispered.

"Okay." Victor draped his windbreaker over the sill. "Up you go."

He gave her a lift to the window. She clambered through and landed among the glass shards. Seconds later, Victor dropped down beside her.

They were standing in the studio dressing room. Against one wall hung a rack of women's lingerie; against the other were makeup tables and a long mirror.

Victor frowned at a cloud of peach silk flung over one of the chairs. "What kind of photos does your friend take, anyway?"

"Hickey specializes in what's politely known as 'boudoir portraits.'"

Victor's startled gaze turned to a black lace negligee hanging from a wall hook. "Does that mean what I think it means?"

"What do you think it means?"

"You know."

She headed into the next room. "Hickey insists it's not pornography. It's tasteful erotic art...." She stopped in her tracks as she came face-to-face with a photo blowup on the wall. Naked limbs—eight, maybe more—were entwined in a sort of human octopus. Nothing was left to the imagination. Nothing at all.

"Tasteful," Victor said dryly.

"That must be one of his, uh, commercial assignments."

"I wonder what product they were selling."

She turned and found herself staring at another photograph. This time it was two women, drop-dead gorgeous and wearing not a stitch.

"Another commercial assignment?" Victor inquired politely over her shoulder.

She shook her head. "Don't ask."

In the front room they found a week's worth of mail piled up beneath the door slot, darkroom catalogues and advertising flyers. The roll of film Cathy had mailed the day before was not yet in the mound.

"I guess we just sit around and wait for the postman," she said.

He nodded. "Seems like a safe-enough place. Any chance your friend keeps food around?"

"I seem to remember a refrigerator in the other room."

She led Victor into what Hickey had dubbed his "shooting gallery." Cathy flipped the wall switch and the vast room was instantly illuminated by a dazzling array of spotlights.

"So this is where he does it," said Victor, blinking in the sudden glare. He stepped over a jumble of electrical cords and slowly circled the room, regarding with humorous disbelief the various props. It was a strange collection of objects: a genuine English phone booth, a street bench, an exercise bicycle. In a place of honor sat a four-poster bed. The ruffled coverlet was Victorian; the handcuffs dangling from the bedposts were not.

Victor picked up one of the cuffs and let it fall again. "Just how good a friend *is* this Hickey guy, anyway?"

"None of this stuff was here when he shot me a month ago."

"He photographed *you?*" Victor turned and stared at her.

She flushed, imagining the images that must be flashing through his mind. She could feel his gaze undressing her, posing her in a sprawl across that ridiculous four-poster bed. With the handcuffs, no less.

"It wasn't like—like these other photos," she protested. "I mean, I just did it as a favor...."

"A favor?"

"It was a purely *commercial* shot!"

"Oh."

"I was fully dressed. In overalls, as a matter of fact. I was supposed to be a plumber."

"A lady plumber?"

"I was an emergency stand-in. One of his models didn't show up that day, and he needed someone with an ordinary face. I guess that's me. Ordinary. And it really was just my face."

"And your overalls."

"Right."

They looked at each other and burst out laughing.

"I can guess what you were thinking," she said.

"I don't even want to *tell* you what I was thinking." He turned and glanced around the room. "Didn't you say there was some food around here?"

She crossed the room to the refrigerator. Inside she found a shelf of film plus a jar of sweet pickles, some rubbery carrots and half a salami. In the freezer they discovered real treasures: ground Sumatran coffee and a loaf of sourdough bread.

Grinning, she turned to him. "A feast!"

They sat together on the four-poster bed and gnawed on salami and half-frozen sourdough, all washed down with cups of coffee. It was a bizarre little picnic, paper plates with pickles and carrots resting in their laps, the spotlights glaring down like a dozen hot suns from the ceiling.

"Why did you say that about yourself?" he asked, watching her munch a carrot.

"Say what?"

"That you're ordinary. So ordinary that you get cast as the lady plumber?"

"Because I am ordinary."

"I don't think so. And I happen to be a pretty good judge of character."

She looked up at a wall poster featuring one of Hickey's super models. The woman stared back with a look of glossy confidence. "Well, I certainly don't measure up to *that*."

"*That*," he said, "is pure fantasy. *That* isn't a real woman, but an amalgam of makeup, hairspray and fake eyelashes."

"Oh, I know that. That's my job, turning actors into some movie-goer's fantasy. Or nightmare, as the case may be." She reached into the jar and fished out the last pickle. "No, I really meant *underneath* it all. Deep inside, I *feel* ordinary."

"I think you're quite extraordinary. And after last night, I should know."

She gazed down, at the limp carrot stretched out like a little corpse across the paper plate. "There was a time—I suppose there's always that time, for everyone, when we're still young, when we feel special. When we feel the world's meant just for us. The last time I felt that way was when I married Jack." She sighed. "It didn't last long."

"Why did you marry him?"

"I don't know. Dazzle? I was only twenty-three, a mere appren-tice on the set. He was the director." She paused. "He was *God.*"

"He impressed you, did he?"

"Jack can be very impressive. He can turn on the power, the charisma, and just overwhelm a gal. Then there was the champagne, the suppers, the flowers. I think what attracted him to me was that I didn't immediately fall for him. That I wasn't swooning at his every look. He thought of me as a challenge, the one he finally conquered." She gave him a rueful look. "That accomplished, he moved onto bigger and better things. That's when I realized that I wasn't particularly special. That I'm really just a perfectly ordinary woman. It's not a bad feeling. It's not as if I go through life longing to be someone different, someone special."

"Then who do you consider special?"

"Well, my grandmother. But she's dead."

"Venerable grandmothers always make the list."

"Okay, then. Mother Teresa."

"She's on everyone's list."

"Kate Hepburn. Gloria Steinem. My friend Sarah..." Her voice faded. Looking down, she added softly: "But she's dead, too."

Gently he took her hand. With a strange sense of wonder she watched his long fingers close over hers and thought about how the strength she felt in that grasp reflected the strength of the man him-self. Jack, for all his dazzle and polish, had never inspired a fraction of the confidence she now felt in Victor. No man ever had.

He was watching her with quiet sympathy. "Tell me about Sarah," he said.

Cathy swallowed, trying to stem the tears. "She was absolutely lovely. I don't mean in *that* way." She nodded at the photo of Hickey's picture-perfect model. "I mean, in an inner sort of way. It was this look in her eyes. A perfect calmness. As though she'd found exactly what she wanted while all the rest of us were still grubbing around for lost treasure. I don't think she was born like that. She came to it, all by herself. In college, we were both pretty unsure of ourselves. Marriage certainly didn't help either of us. My divorce—it was nothing short of devastating. But Sarah's divorce only seemed to make her stronger. Better able to take care of herself. When she finally got pregnant, it was exactly as she planned it. There wasn't a father, you see, just a test tube. An anonymous donor. Sarah used to say that the primeval family unit wasn't man, woman and child. It was just woman and child. I thought she was brave, to take that step. She was a lot braver than I could ever be...." She cleared her throat. "Anyway, Sarah *was* special. Some people simply are."

"Yes," he said. "Some people are."

She looked up at him. He was staring off at the far wall, his gaze infinitely sad. What had etched those lines of pain in his face? She wondered if lines so deep could ever be erased. There were some losses one never got over, never accepted.

Softly she asked, "What was your wife like?"

He didn't answer at first. She thought: *Why did I ask that? Why did I have to bring up such terrible memories?*

He said, "She was a kind woman. That's what I'll always remember about her. Her kindness." He looked at Cathy and she sensed it wasn't sadness she saw in those eyes, but acceptance.

"What was her name?"

"Lily. Lillian Dorinda Cassidy. A mouthful for such a tiny woman." He smiled. "She was about five foot one, maybe ninety pounds sopping wet. It used to scare me, how small she always seemed. Almost breakable. Especially toward the end, when she'd lost all that weight. It seemed as if she'd shrunk down to nothing but a pair of big brown eyes."

"She must have been young when she died."

"Only thirty-eight. It seemed so unfair. All her life, she'd done everything right. Never smoked, hardly ever touched a glass of wine. She even refused to eat meat. After she was diagnosed, we kept trying to figure out how it could've happened. Then it occurred to us what might have caused it. She grew up in a small town in Massachusetts. Directly downwind from a nuclear power plant."

"You think that was it?"

"One can never be sure. But we asked around. And we learned that, just in her neighborhood, at least twenty families had someone with leukemia. It took four years and a class-action suit to force an investigation. What they found was a history of safety violations going back all the way to the plant's opening."

Cathy shook her head in disbelief. "And all those years they allowed it to operate?"

"No one knew about it. The violations were hushed up so well even the federal regulators were kept in the dark."

"They shut it down, didn't they?"

He nodded. "I can't say I got much satisfaction, seeing the plant finally close. By that time Lily was gone. And all the families, well, we were exhausted by the fight. Even though it sometimes felt as though we were banging our heads against a wall, we knew it was something we had to do. *Somebody* had to do it, for all the Lilys of the world." He looked up, at the spotlights shining above. "And here I am again, still banging my head against walls. Only this time, it feels like the Great Wall of China. And the lives at stake are yours and mine."

Their gazes met. She sat absolutely still as he lightly stroked down the curve of her cheek. She took his hand, pressed it to her lips. His fingers closed over hers, refusing to release her hand. Gently he tugged her close. Their lips met, a tentative kiss that left her longing for more.

"I'm sorry you were pulled into this," he murmured. "You and Sarah and those other Cathy Weavers. None of you asked to be part of it. And somehow I've managed to hurt you all."

"Not you, Victor. You're not the one to blame. It's this windmill you're tilting at. This giant, dangerous windmill. Anyone else would have dropped his lance and fled. You're still going at it."

"I didn't have much of a choice."

"But you did. You could have walked away from your friend's death. Turned a blind eye to whatever's going on at Viratek. That's what Jack would have done."

"But I'm not Jack. There are things I can't walk away from. I'd always be thinking of the Lilys. All the thousands of people who might get hurt."

At the mention once again of his dead wife, Cathy felt some unbreachable barrier form between them—the shadow of Lily, the wife she'd never met. Cathy drew back, at once aching from the loss of his touch.

"You think that many people could die?" she asked.

"Jerry must have thought so. There's no way to predict the outcome. The world's never seen the effects of all-out biological warfare. I like to think it's because we're too smart to play with our own self-destruction. Then I think of all the crazy things people have done over the years and it scares me...."

"Are viral weapons that dangerous?"

"If you alter a few genes, make it just a little more contagious, raise the kill ratio, you'd end up with a devastating strain. The research alone is hazardous. A single slip-up in lab security and you could have millions of people accidentally infected. And no means of treatment. It's the kind of worldwide disaster a scientist doesn't want to think about."

"Armageddon."

He nodded, his gaze frighteningly sane. "If you believe in such a thing. That's exactly what it'd be."

She shook her head. "I don't understand why these things are allowed."

"They aren't. By international agreement, they're outlawed. But there's always some madman lurking in the shadows who wants that extra bit of leverage, that weapon no one else has."

A madman. That's what one would have to be, to even think of unleashing such a weapon on the world. She thought of a novel she'd read, about just such a plague, how the cities had lain dead and decaying, how the very air had turned poisonous. But those were only the nightmares of science fiction. This was real.

From somewhere in the building came the sound of whistling.

Cathy and Victor both sat up straight. The melody traveled along the hall, closer and closer, until it stopped right outside Hickey's door. They heard a rustling, then the slap of magazines hitting the floor.

"It's here!" said Cathy, leaping to her feet.

Victor was right behind her as she hurried into the front room. She spotted it immediately, sitting atop the pile: a padded envelope, addressed in her handwriting. She scooped it up and ripped the envelope open. Out slid the roll of film. The note she'd scribbled to Hickey fluttered to the floor. Grinning in triumph, she held up the canister. "Here's your evidence!"

"We hope. Let's see what we've got on the roll. Where's the darkroom?"

"Next to the dressing room." She handed him the film. "Do you know how to process it?"

"I've done some amateur photography. As long as I've got the chemicals I can—" He stopped and glanced over at the desk.

The phone was ringing.

Victor shook his head. "Ignore it," he said and turned for the darkroom.

As they left the reception room, they heard the answering machine click on. Hickey's voice, smooth as silk, spoke on the recording. "This is the studio of Hickman Von Trapp, specializing in tasteful and artistic images of the female form...."

Victor laughed. "Tasteful?"

"It depends on your taste," said Cathy as she followed him up the hall.

They had just reached the darkroom when the recording ended and was followed by the message beep. An agitated voice rattled from the speaker. "Hello? Hello, Cathy? If you're there, answer me, will you? There's an FBI agent looking for you—some guy named Polowski—"

Cathy stopped dead. "It's Jack!" she said, turning to retrace her steps toward the front room.

The voice on the speaker had taken on a note of panic. "I couldn't help it—he made me tell him about Hickey. Get out of there now!"

The message clicked off just as Cathy grabbed the receiver. "Hello? *Jack?*"

She heard only the dial tone. He'd already hung up. Hands shaking, she began to punch in Jack's phone number.

"There's no time!" said Victor.

"I have to talk to him—"

He grabbed the receiver and slammed it down. "Later! We have to get out of here!"

She nodded numbly and started for the door. There she halted. "Wait. We need money!" She turned back to the reception desk and searched the drawers until she found the petty cash box. Twenty-two dollars was all it contained. "Always keep just enough for decent coffee beans," Hickey used to say. She pocketed the money. Then she reached up and yanked one of Hickey's old raincoats from the door hook. He wouldn't miss it. And she might need it for concealment. "Okay," she said, slipping on the coat. "Let's go."

They paused only a second to check the corridor. From another suite came the faint echo of laughter. Somewhere above, high heels clicked across a wooden floor. With Victor in the lead, they darted down the hall and out the front door.

The midday sun seemed to glare down on them like an accusing eye. Quickly they fell into step with the rest of the lunch crowd, the businessmen and artists, the Union Street chic. No one glanced their way. But even with people all around her, Cathy felt conspicuous. As though, in this bright cityscape of crowds and concrete, she was the focus of the painter's eye.

She huddled deeper into the raincoat, wishing it were a mantle of invisibility. Victor had quickened his pace, and she had to run to keep up.

"Where do we go now?" she whispered.

"We've got the film. Now I say we head for the bus station."

"And then?"

"Anywhere." He kept his gaze straight ahead. "As long as it's out of this city."

CHAPTER SEVEN

That pesky FBI agent was ringing his doorbell again.

Sighing, Jack opened the front door. "Back already?"

"Damn right I'm back." Polowski stamped in and shoved the door closed behind him. "I want to know where to find 'em next."

"I told you, Mr. Polowski. Over on Union Street there's a studio owned by Mr. Hickman—"

"I've been to Von Whats-his-name's studio."

Jack swallowed. "You didn't find them?"

"You knew I wouldn't. You warned 'em, didn't you?"

"Really, I don't know why you're harrassing me. I've tried to be—"

"They left in a hurry. The door was wide open. Food was still lying around. They left the empty cash box just sitting on the desk."

Jack drew himself up in outrage. "Are you calling my ex-wife a petty thief?"

"I'm calling her a desperate woman. And I'm calling you an imbecile for screwing things up. Now where is she?"

"I don't know."

"Who would she turn to?"

"No one I know."

"Think harder."

Jack stared down at Polowski's turgid face and marveled that any human being could be so unattractive. Surely the process of natural selection would have dictated against such unacceptable genes?

Jack shook his head. "I honestly don't know."

It was the truth, and Polowski must have sensed it. After a moment of silent confrontation, he backed off. "Then maybe you can tell me this. Why did you warn them?"

"It—it was—" Jack shrugged helplessly. "Oh, I don't know!

After you left, I wasn't sure I'd done the right thing. I wasn't sure whether to trust you. *He* doesn't trust you.''

''Who?''

''Victor Holland. He thinks you're in on some conspiracy. Frankly, the man struck me as just the slightest bit paranoid.''

''He has a right to be. Considering what's happened to him so far.'' Polowski turned for the door.

''Now what happens?''

''I keep looking for them.''

''Where?''

''You think I'd tell *you?*'' He stalked out. ''Don't leave town, Zuckerman,'' he snapped over his shoulder. ''I'll be back to see you later.''

''I don't think so,'' Jack muttered softly as he watched the other man lumber back to his car. He looked up and saw there wasn't a cloud in the sky. Smiling to himself, he shut the door.

It would be sunny in Mexico, as well.

Someone had left in a hurry.

Savitch strolled through the rooms of the photo studio, which had been left unlocked. He noted the scraps of a meal on the four-poster bed: crumbs of sourdough bread, part of a salami, an empty pickle jar. He also took note of the coffee cups: there were two of them. Interesting, since Savitch had spotted only one person leaving the studio, a squat little man in a polyester suit. The man hadn't been there long. Savitch had observed him climb into a dark green Ford parked at a fifteen-minute meter. The meter still had three minutes remaining.

Savitch continued his tour of the studio, eyeing the tawdry photos, wondering if this wasn't another waste of his time. After all, every other address he'd pulled from the woman's black book had turned up no sign of her. Why should Hickman Von Trapp's address be any different?

Still, he couldn't shake the instinct that he was getting close. Clues were everywhere. He read them, put them together. Today, this studio had been visited by two hungry people. They'd entered through a broken window in the dressing room. They'd eaten scraps taken from the refrigerator. They (or the man in the polyester suit) had emptied the petty cash box.

Savitch completed his tour and returned to the front room. That's when he noticed the telephone message machine blinking on and off.

He pressed the play button. The string of messages seemed endless. The calls were for someone named Hickey—no doubt the Hickman Von Trapp of the address book. Savitch lazily circled the room, half listening to the succession of voices. Business calls for the most part, inquiring about appointments, asking when proofs would be ready and would he like to do the shoot for *Snoop* magazine? Near the door, Savitch halted and stooped down to sift through the pile of mail. It was boring stuff, all addressed to Von Trapp. Then he noticed, off to the side, a loose slip of paper. It was a note, addressed to Hickey.

"Feel awful about this, but someone stole all those rolls of film from my car. This was the only one left. Thought I'd get it to you before it's lost, as well. Hope it's enough to save your shoot from being a complete waste—"

It was signed "Cathy."

He stood up straight. Catherine Weaver? It had to be! The roll of film—where the hell was the roll of film?

He rifled through the mail, searching, searching. He turned up only a torn envelope with Cathy Weaver's return address. The film was gone. In frustration, he began to fling magazines across the room. Then, in mid-toss, he froze.

A new message was playing on the recorder.

"Hello? Hello, Cathy? If you're there, answer me, will you? There's an FBI agent looking for you—some guy named Polowski. I couldn't help it—he made me tell him about Hickey. Get out of there now!"

Savitch stalked over to the answering machine and stared down as the mechanism automatically whirred back to the beginning. He replayed it.

Get out of there now!

There was now no doubt. Catherine Weaver had been here, and Victor Holland was with her. But who was this agent Polowski and why was he searching for Holland? Savitch had been assured that the Bureau was off the case. He would have to check into the matter.

He crossed over to the window and stared out at the bright sunshine, the crowded sidewalks. So many faces, so many strangers. Where, in this city, would two terrified fugitives hide? Finding them would be difficult, but not impossible.

He left the suite and went outside to a pay phone. There he dialed a Washington, D.C., number. He wasn't fond of asking the Cowboy for help, but now he had no choice. Victor Holland had his hands on the evidence, and the stakes had shot sky-high.

It was time to step up the pursuit.

The clerk yelled, "Next window, please!" and closed the grate.

"Wait!" cried Cathy, tapping at the pane. "My bus is leaving right now!"

"Which one?"

"Number 23 to Palo Alto—"

"There's another at seven o'clock."

"But—"

"I'm on my dinner break."

Cathy stared helplessly as the clerk walked away. Over the PA system came the last call for the Palo Alto express. Cathy glanced around just in time to see the Number 23 roar away from the curb.

"Service just ain't what it used to be," an old man muttered behind her. "Get there faster usin' yer damn thumb."

Sighing, Cathy shifted to the next line, which was eight-deep and slow as molasses. The woman at the front was trying to convince the clerk that her social security card was an acceptable ID for a check.

Okay, Cathy thought. *So we leave at seven o'clock. That puts us in Palo Alto at eight. Then what? Camp in a park? Beg a few scraps from a restaurant? What does Victor have in mind…?*

She glanced around and spotted his broad back hunched inside one of the phone booths. Whom could he possibly be calling? She saw him hang up and run his hand wearily through his hair. Then he picked up the receiver and dialed another number.

"Next!" Someone tapped Cathy on the shoulder. "Go ahead, Miss."

Cathy turned and saw that the ticket clerk was waiting. She stepped to the window.

"Where to?" asked the clerk.

"I need two tickets to…" Cathy's voice suddenly faded.

"Where?"

Cathy didn't speak. Her gaze had frozen on a poster tacked right beside the ticket window. The words Have You seen This Man? appeared above an unsmiling photo of Victor Holland. And at the bottom were listed the charges: Industrial espionage and murder. If you have any information about this man, please contact your local police or the FBI.

"Lady, you wanna go somewhere or not?"

"What?" Cathy's gaze jerked back to the clerk, who was watching her with obvious annoyance. "Oh. Yes, I'm—I'd like two tickets. To Palo Alto." Numbly she handed over a fistful of cash. "One way."

"Two to Palo Alto. That bus will depart at 7:00, Gate 11."

"Yes. Thank you…" Cathy took the tickets and turned to leave the line. That's when she spotted the two policemen, standing just inside the front entrance. They seemed to be scanning the terminal, searching—for what?

In a panic, her gaze shot to the phone booth. It was empty. She stared at it with a sense of abandonment. *You left me! You left me with two tickets to Palo Alto and five bucks in my pocket! Where are you, Victor?*

She couldn't stand here like an idiot. She had to do something, had to move. She pulled the raincoat tightly around her shoulders and forced herself to stroll across the terminal. *Don't let them notice me,* she prayed. *Please. I'm nobody. Nothing.* She paused at a chair and picked up a discarded *San Francisco Chronicle.* Then, thumbing through the Want Ads, she sauntered right past the two policemen. They didn't even glance at her as she went out the front entrance.

Now what? she wondered, pausing amidst the confusion of a busy sidewalk. Automatically she started to walk and had taken only half a dozen steps down the street when she was wrenched sideways, into an alley.

She reeled back against the trash cans and almost sobbed with relief. "Victor!"

"Did they see you?"

"No. I mean, yes, but they didn't seem to care—"

"Are you sure?" She nodded. He turned and slapped the wall in frustration. "What the hell do we do now?"

"I have the tickets."

"We can't use them."

"How are we going to get out of town? Hitchhike? Victor, we're down to our last five dollars!"

"They'll be watching every bus that leaves. And they've got my face plastered all over the damn terminal!" He slumped back against the wall and groaned. "*Have you seen this man?* God, I looked like some two-bit gangster."

"It wasn't the most flattering photo."

He managed to laugh. "Have you *ever* seen a flattering wanted poster?"

She leaned back beside him, against the wall. "We've got to get out of this city, Victor."

"Amend that. *You've* got to get out."

"What's that supposed to mean?"

"The police aren't looking for you. So *you* take that bus to Palo Alto. I'll put you in touch with some old friends. They'll see you make it somewhere safe."

"No."

"Cathy, they've probably got my mug posted in every airport and car rental agency in town! We've spent almost all our money for those bus tickets. I say you use them!"

"I'm not leaving you."

"You don't have a choice."

"Yes I do. I choose to stick to you like glue. Because you're the only one I feel safe with. The only one I can count on!"

"I can move faster on my own. Without you slowing me down." He looked off, toward the street. "Hell, I don't even *want* you around."

"I don't believe that."

"Why should I care what you believe?"

"Look at me! Look at me and say that!" She grabbed his arm, willing him to face her. "Say you don't want me around!"

He started to speak, to repeat the lie. She knew then that it *was* a lie; she could see it in his eyes. And she saw something else in that gaze, something that took her breath away.

He said, "I don't—I won't have you—"

She just stood there, looking up at him, waiting for the truth to come.

What she didn't expect was the kiss. She never remembered how it happened. She only knew that all at once his arms were around her and she was being swept up into some warm and safe and wonderful place. It started as an embrace more of desperation than passion, a coming together of two terrified people. But the instant their lips met, it became something much more. This went beyond fear, beyond need. This was a souls' joining, one that wouldn't be broken, even after this embrace was over, even if they never touched again.

When at last they drew apart and stared at each other, the taste of him was still fresh on her lips.

"You see?" she whispered. "I was right. You do want me around. You do."

He smiled and touched her cheek. "I'm not a very good liar."

"And I'm not leaving you. You need me. You can't show your face, but I can! I can buy bus tickets, run errands—"

"What I really need," he sighed, "is a new face." He glanced out at the street. "Since there's no plastic surgeon handy, I suggest we hoof it over to the BART station. It'll be crowded at this hour. We might make it to the East Bay—"

"God, I'm such an *idiot!*" she groaned. "A new face is exactly what you need!" She turned toward the street. "Come on. There isn't much time...."

"Cathy?" He followed her up the alley. They both paused, scanning the street for policemen. There were none in sight. "Where are we going?" he whispered.

"To find a phone booth."

"Oh. And who are we calling?"

She turned and the look she gave him was distinctly pained. "Someone we both know and love."

* * *

Jack was packing his suitcase when the phone rang. He considered not answering it, but something about the sound, an urgency that could only have been imagined, made him pick up the receiver. He was instantly sorry he had.

"Jack?"

He sighed. "Tell me I'm hearing things."

"Jack, I'm going to talk fast because your phone might be tapped—"

"You don't say."

"I need my kit. The whole shebang. And some cash. I swear I'll pay it all back. Get it for me right now. Then drop it off where we shot the last scene of *Cretinoid*. You know the spot."

"Cathy, you wait a minute! I'm in trouble enough as it is!"

"One hour. That's all I can wait."

"It's rush hour! I can't—"

"It's the last favor I'll ask of you." There was a pause. Then, softly, she added, "Please."

He let out a breath. "This is the absolute last time, right?"

"One hour, Jack. I'll be waiting."

Jack hung up and stared at his suitcase. It was only half packed, but it would have to do. He sure as hell wasn't coming back *here* tonight.

He closed the suitcase and carried it out to the Jaguar. As he drove away it suddenly occurred to him that he'd forgotten to cancel his date with Lulu tonight.

No time now, he thought. I've got more important things on my mind—like getting out of town.

Lulu would be mad as a hornet, but he'd make it up to her. Maybe a pair of diamond ear studs. Yeah, that would do the trick.

Good old Lulu, so easy to please. Now there was a woman he could understand.

The corner of Fifth and Mission was a hunker-down, chew-the-fat sort of gathering place for the street folk. At five forty-five it was even busier than usual. Rumor had it the soup kitchen down the block was fixing to serve beef Bourguignonne, which, as those who remembered better days and better meals could tell you, was made with red wine. No one passed up the chance for a taste of the grape, even if every drop of alcohol was simmered clean out of it. And so they stood around on the corner, talking of other meals they'd had, of the weather, of the long lines at the unemployment office.

No one noticed the two wretched souls huddled in the doorway of the pawnshop.

Lucky for us, thought Cathy, burying herself in the folds of the raincoat. The sad truth was, they were both beginning to fit right into this crowd. Just a moment earlier she'd caught sight of her own reflection in the pawnshop window and had almost failed to recognize the disheveled image staring back. *Has it been that long since I've combed my hair? That long since I've had a meal or a decent night's sleep?*

Victor looked no better. A torn shirt and two days' worth of stubble on his jaw only emphasized that unmistakable look of exhaustion. He could walk into that soup kitchen down the block and no one would look twice.

He's going to look a hell of a lot worse when I get through with him, she thought with a grim sense of humor.

If Jack ever showed up with the kit.

"It's 6:05," Victor muttered. "He's had an hour."

"Give him time."

"We're running out of time."

"We can still make the bus." She peered up the street, as though by force of will she could conjure up her ex-husband. But only a city bus barreled into view. *Come on, Jack, come on! Don't let me down this time....*

"Will ya lookit that!" came a low growl, followed by general murmurs of admiration from the crowd.

"Hey, pretty boy!" someone called as the group gathered on the corner to stare. "What'd you have to push to get yerself wheels like that?"

Through the gathering of men, Cathy spied the bright gleam of chrome and burgundy. "Get away from my car!" demanded a querulous voice. "I just had her waxed!"

"Looks like Pretty Boy got hisself lost. Turned down the wrong damn street, did ya?"

Cathy leaped to her feet. "He's here!"

She and Victor pushed through the crowd to find Jack standing guard over the Jaguar's gleaming finish.

"Don't—don't touch her!" he snapped as one man ran a grimy finger across the hood. "Why can't you people go find yourselves a job or something?"

"A job?" someone yelled. "What's that?"

"Jack!" called Cathy.

Jack let out a sigh of relief when he spotted her. "This is the last favor. The absolute *last* favor—"

"Where is it?" she asked.

Jack walked around to the trunk, where he slapped away another hand as it stroked the Jaguar's burgundy flank. "It's right here. The whole kit and kaboodle." He swung out the makeup case and handed it over. "Delivered as promised. Now I gotta run."

"Where are you going?" she called.

"I don't know." He climbed back into the car. "Somewhere. Anywhere!"

"Sounds like we're headed in the same direction."

"God, I hope not." He started the engine and revved it up a few times.

Someone yelled: "So long, Pretty Boy!"

Jack gazed out dryly at Cathy. "You know, you really should do something about the company you keep. Ciao, sweetcakes."

The Jaguar lurched away. With a screech of tires, it spun around the corner and vanished into traffic.

Cathy turned and saw that every eye was watching her. Automatically, Victor moved close beside her, one tired and hungry man facing a tired and hungry crowd.

Someone called out: "So who's the jerk in the Jag?"

"My ex-husband," said Cathy.

"Doin' a lot better than you are, honey."

"No kidding." She held up the makeup case and managed a careless laugh. "I ask the creep for my clothes, he throws me a change of underwear."

"Babe, now ain't that just the way it works?"

Already, the men were wandering away, regrouping in doorways,

or over by the corner newsstands. The Jaguar was gone, and so was
their interest.

Only one man stood before Cathy and Victor, and the look he
gave them was distinctly sympathetic. "That's all he left you, huh?
Him with that nice, fancy car?" He turned to leave, then glanced
back at them. "Say, you two need a place to stay or somethin'? I
got a lot of friends. And I hate to see a lady out in the cold."

"Thanks for the offer," said Victor, taking Cathy's hand. "But
we've got a bus to catch."

The man nodded and shuffled away, a kind but unfortunate soul
whom the streets had not robbed of decency.

"We have a half hour to get on that bus," said Victor, hurrying
Cathy along. "Better get to work."

They were headed up the street, toward the cover of an alley,
when Cathy suddenly halted. "Victor—"

"What's the matter?"

"Look." She pointed at the newsstand, her hand shaking.

Beneath the plastic cover was the afternoon edition of the *San
Francisco Examiner.* The headline read: "Two Victims, Same
Name. Police Probe Coincidence." Beside it was a photo of a young
blond woman. The caption was hidden by the fold, but Cathy didn't
need to read it. She could already guess the woman's name.

"Two of them," she whispered. "Victor, you were right...."

"All the more reason for us to get out of town." He pulled on
her arm. "Hurry."

She let him lead her away. But even as they headed down the
street, even as they left the newsstand behind them, she carried that
image in her mind: the photograph of a blond woman, the second
victim.

The second Catherine Weaver.

Patrolman O'Hanley was a helpful soul. Unlike too many of his
colleagues, O'Hanley had joined the force out of a true desire to
serve and protect. The "Boy Scout" was what the other men called
him behind his back. The epithet both annoyed and pleased him. It
told him he didn't fit in with the rough-and-tumble gang on the
force. It also told him he was above it all, above the petty bribe-
taking and backbiting and maneuverings for promotion. He wasn't

out to glorify the badge on his chest. What he wanted was the chance to pat a kid on the head, rescue an old granny from a mugging.

That's why he found this particular assignment so frustrating. All this standing around in the bus depot, watching for a man some witness *might* have spotted a few hours ago. O'Hanley hadn't noticed any such character. He'd eyeballed every person who'd walked in the door. A sorry lot, most of them. Not surprising since, these days, anyone with the cash to spare took a plane. By the looks of these folks, none of 'em could spare much more than pennies. Take that pair over there, huddled together in the waiting area. A father and daughter, he figured, and both of 'em down on their luck. The daughter was bundled up in an old raincoat, the collar pulled up to reveal only a mop of windblown hair. The father was an even sorrier sight, gaunt-faced, white-whiskered, about as old as Methuselah. Still, there was a remnant of pride in the old codger— O'Hanley could see it in the way the man held himself, stiff and straight. Must've been an impressive fellow in his younger years since he was still well over six feet tall.

The public speaker announced final boarding for number fourteen to Palo Alto.

The old man and his daughter rose to their feet.

O'Hanley watched with concern as the pair shuffled across the terminal toward the departure gate. The woman was carrying only one small case, but it appeared to be a heavy one. And she already had her hands full, trying to guide the old man in the right direction. But they were making progress, and O'Hanley figured they'd make it to the bus okay.

That is, until the kid ran into them.

He was about six, the kind of kid no mother wants to admit she produced, the kind of kid who gives all six-year-olds a bad name. For the last half hour the boy had been tearing around the terminal, scattering ashtray sand, tipping over suitcases, banging locker doors. Now he was running. Only this kid was doing it *backward*.

O'Hanley saw it coming. The old man and his daughter were crossing slowly toward the departure gate. The kid was scuttling toward them. Intersecting paths, inevitable collision. The kid slammed into the woman's knees; the case flew out of her grasp.

She stumbled against her companion. O'Hanley, paralyzed, expected the codger to keel over. To his surprise, the old man simply caught the woman in his arms and handily set her back on her feet.

By now O'Hanley was hurrying to their aid. He got to the woman just as she'd regained her footing. "You folks okay?" he asked.

The woman reacted as though he'd slapped her. She stared up at him with the eyes of a terrified animal. "What?" she said.

"Are you okay? Looked to me like he hit you pretty hard."

She nodded.

"How 'bout you, Gramps?"

The woman glanced at her companion. It seemed to O'Hanley that there was a lot being said in that glance, a lot he wasn't privy to.

"We're both fine," the woman said quickly. "Come on, Pop. We'll miss our bus."

"Can I give you a hand with him?"

"That's mighty kind of you, officer, but we'll do fine." The woman smiled at O'Hanley. Something about that smile wasn't right. As he watched the pair shuffle off toward bus number fourteen, O'Hanley kept trying to figure it out. Kept trying to put his finger on what was wrong with that pair of travelers.

He turned away and almost tripped over the fallen case. The woman had forgotten it. He snatched it up and started to run for the bus. Too late; the number fourteen to Palo Alto was already pulling away. O'Hanley stood helplessly on the curb, watching the taillights vanish around the corner.

Oh, well.

He turned in the makeup case at Lost and Found. Then he stationed himself once again at the entrance. Seven o'clock already and still no sighting of the suspect Victor Holland.

O'Hanley sighed. What a waste of a policeman's time.

Five minutes out of San Francisco, aboard the number fourteen bus, the old man turned to the woman in the raincoat and said, "This beard is killing me."

Laughing, Cathy reached up and gave the fake whiskers a tug. "It did the trick, didn't it?"

"No kidding. We practically got a police escort to the getaway bus.'' He scratched furiously at his chin. ''Geez, how do those actors stand this stuff, anyway? The itch is driving me up a wall.''

''Want me to take it off?''

''Better not. Not till we get to Palo Alto.''

Another hour, she thought. She sat back and gazed out at the highway gliding past the bus window. ''Then what?'' she asked softly.

''I'll knock on a few doors. See if I can dig up an old friend or two. It's been a long time, but I think there are still a few in town.''

''You used to live there?''

''Years ago. Back when I was in college.''

''Oh.'' She sat up straight. ''A *Stanford* man.''

''Why do you make it sound just a tad disreputable?''

''I rooted for the Bears, myself.''

''I'm consorting with the arch enemy?''

Giggling, she burrowed against his chest and inhaled the warm, familiar scent of his body. ''It seems like another lifetime. Berkeley and blue jeans.''

''Football. Wild parties.''

''Wild parties?'' she asked. ''You?''

''Well, *rumors* of wild parties.''

''Frisbee. Classes on the lawn...''

''Innocence,'' he said softly.

They both fell silent.

''Victor?'' she asked. ''What if your friends aren't there any longer? Or what if they won't take us in?''

''One step at a time. That's how we have to take it. Otherwise it'll all seem too overwhelming.''

''It already does.''

He squeezed her tightly against him. ''Hey, we're doing okay. We made it out of the city. In fact, we waltzed out right under the nose of a cop. I'd call that pretty damn impressive.''

Cathy couldn't help grinning at the memory of the earnest young Patrolman O'Hanley. ''All policemen should be so helpful.''

''Or blind,'' Victor snorted. ''I can't believe he called me *Gramps*.''

''When I set out to change a face, I do it right.''

''Apparently.''

She looped her arm through his and pressed a kiss to one scowling, bewhiskered cheek. "Can I tell you a secret?"

"What's that?"

"I'm crazy about older men."

The scowl melted away, slowly reformed into a dubious smile. "How much older are we talking about?"

She kissed him again, this time full on the lips. "Much older."

"Hm. Maybe these whiskers aren't so bad, after all." He took her face in his hands. This time he was the one kissing her, long and deeply, with no thought of where they were or where they were going. Cathy felt herself sliding back against the seat, into a space that was inescapable and infinitely safe.

Someone behind them hooted: "Way to go, Gramps!"

Reluctantly, they pulled apart. Through the flickering shadows of the bus, Cathy could see the twinkle in Victor's eyes, the gleam of a wry smile.

She smiled back and whispered, "Way to go, Gramps."

The posters with Victor Holland's face were plastered all over the bus station.

Polowski couldn't help a snort of irritation as he gazed at that unflattering visage of what he knew in his gut was an innocent man. A damn witchhunt, that's what this'd turned into. If Holland wasn't already scared enough, this public stalking would surely send him diving for cover, beyond the reach of those who could help him. Polowski only hoped it'd also be beyond the reach of those with less benign intentions.

With all these posters staring him in the face, Holland would've been a fool to stroll through this bus depot. Still, Polowski had an instinct about these things, a sense of how people behaved when they were desperate. If he were in Holland's shoes, a killer on his trail and a woman companion to worry about, he knew what *he'd* do—get the hell out of San Francisco. A plane was unlikely. According to Jack Zuckerman, Holland was operating on a thin wallet. A credit card would've been out of the question. That also knocked out a rental car. What was left? It was either hitchhike or take the bus.

Polowski was betting on the bus.

His last piece of info supported that hunch. The tap on Zuckerman's phone had picked up a call from Cathy Weaver. She'd arranged some sort of drop-off at a site Polowski couldn't identify at first. He'd spent a frustrating hour asking around the office, trying to locate someone who'd not only seen Zuckerman's forgettable film, *Cretinoid,* but could also pinpoint where the last scene was filmed. The Mission District, some movie nut file clerk had finally told him. Yeah, she was sure of it. The monster came up through the manhole cover right at the corner of Fifth and Mission and slurped down a derelict or two just before the hero smashed him with a crated piano. Polowski hadn't stayed to hear the rest; he'd made a run for his car.

By that time, it was too late. Holland and the woman were gone, and Zuckerman had vanished. Polowski found himself cruising down Mission, his doors locked, his windows rolled up, wondering when the local police were going to clean up the damn streets.

That's when he remembered the bus depot was only a few blocks away.

Now, standing among the tired and slack-jawed travelers at the bus station, he was beginning to think he'd wasted his time. All those wanted posters staring him in the face. And there was a cop standing over by the coffee machine, taking furtive sips from a foam cup.

Polowski strolled over to the cop. "FBI," he said, flashing his badge.

The cop—he was scarcely more than a boy—instantly straightened. "Patrolman O'Hanley, sir."

"Seeing much action?"

"Uh—you mean today?"

"Yeah. Here."

"No, sir." O'Hanley sighed. "Pretty much a bust. I mean, I could be out on patrol. Instead they got me hanging around here eyeballing faces."

"Surveillance?"

"Yes, sir." He nodded at the poster of Holland. "That guy. Everyone's hot to find him. They say he's a spy."

"Do they, now?" Polowski took a lazy glance around the room. "Seen anyone around here who looks like him?"

"Not a one. I been watching every minute."

Polowski didn't doubt it. O'Hanley was the kind of kid who, if you asked him to, would scrub the Captain's boots with a toothbrush. He'd do a good job of it, too.

Obviously Holland hadn't come through here. Polowski turned to leave. Then another thought came to mind, and he turned back to O'Hanley. "The suspect may be traveling with a woman," he said. He pulled out a photo of Cathy Weaver, one Jack Zuckerman had been persuaded to donate to the FBI. "Have you seen her come through here?"

O'Hanley frowned. "Gee. She sure does look like... Naw. That can't be her."

"Who?"

"Well, there was this woman in here 'bout an hour ago. Kind of a down and outer. Some little brat ran smack into her. I sort've brushed her off and sent her on her way. She looked a lot like this gal, only in a lot worse shape."

"Was she traveling alone?"

"She had an old guy with her. Her pop, I think."

Suddenly Polowski was all ears. That instinct again—it was telling him something. "What did this old man look like?"

"Real old. Maybe seventy. Had this bushy beard, lot of white hair."

"How tall?"

"Pretty tall. Over six feet..." O'Hanley's voice trailed off as his gaze focused on the wanted poster. Victor Holland was six foot three. O'Hanley's face went white. "Oh, God..."

"Was it him?"

"I—I can't be sure—"

"Come on, come on!"

"I just don't know... Wait. The woman, she dropped a makeup case! I turned it in at that window there—"

It took only a flash of an FBI badge for the clerk in Lost and Found to hand over the case. The instant Polowski opened the thing, he knew he'd hit pay dirt. It was filled with theatrical makeup supplies. Stenciled inside the lid was: Property of Jack Zuckerman Productions.

He slammed the lid shut. "Where did they go?" he snapped at O'Hanley.

"They—uh, they boarded a bus right over there. That gate. Around seven o'clock."

Polowski glanced up at the departure schedule. At seven o'clock, the number fourteen had departed for Palo Alto.

It took him ten minutes to get hold of the Palo Alto depot manager, another five minutes to convince the man this wasn't just another Prince-Albert-in-the-can phone call.

"The number fourteen from San Francisco?" came the answer. "Arrived twenty minutes ago."

"What about the passengers?" pressed Polowski. "You see any of 'em still around?"

The manager only laughed. "Hey, man. If you had a choice, would *you* hang around a stinking bus station?"

Muttering an oath, Polowski hung up.

"Sir?" It was O'Hanley. He looked sick. "I messed up, didn't I? I let him walk right past me. I can't believe—"

"Forget it."

"But—"

Polowski headed for the exit. "You're just a rookie," he called over his shoulder. "Chalk it up to experience."

"Should I call this in?"

"I'll take care of it. I'm headed there, anyway."

"Where?"

Polowski shoved open the station door. "Palo Alto."

CHAPTER EIGHT

The front door was answered by an elderly oriental woman whose command of English was limited.

"Mrs. Lum? Remember me? Victor Holland. I used to know your son."

"Yes, yes!"

"Is he here?"

"Yes." Her gaze shifted to Cathy now, as though the woman didn't want her second visitor to feel left out of the conversation.

"I need to see him," said Victor. "Is Milo here?"

"Milo?" At last here was a word she seemed to know. She turned and called out loudly in Chinese.

Somewhere a door squealed open and footsteps stamped up the stairs. A fortyish oriental man in blue jeans and chambray shirt came to the front door. He was a dumpling of a fellow, and he brought with him the vague odor of chemicals, something sharp and acidic. He was wiping his hands on a rag.

"What can I do for you?" he asked.

Victor grinned. "Milo Lum! Are you still skulking around in your mother's basement?"

"Excuse me?" Milo inquired politely. "Am I supposed to know you, sir?"

"Don't recognize an old horn player from the Out of Tuners?"

Milo stared in disbelief. "Gershwin? That can't be *you?*"

"Yeah, I know," Victor said with a laugh. "The years haven't been kind."

"I didn't want to say anything, but..."

"I won't take it personally. Since—" Victor peeled off his false beard "—the face isn't all mine."

Milo gazed down at the lump of fake whispers, hanging like a dead animal in Victor's grasp. Then he stared up at Victor's jaw, still blotchy with spirit gum. "This is some kind of joke on old Milo, right?" He stuck his head out the door, glancing past Victor at the sidewalk. "And the other guys are hiding out there somewhere, waiting to yell *surprise!* Aren't they? Some big practical joke."

"I wish it were a joke," said Victor.

Milo instantly caught the undertone of urgency in Victor's voice. He looked at Cathy, then back at Victor. Nodding, he stepped aside. "Come in, Gersh. Sounds like I have some catching up to do."

Over a late supper of duck noodle soup and jasmine tea, Milo heard the story. He said little; he seemed more intent on slurping down the last of his noodles. Only when the ever-smiling Mrs. Lum had bowed good-night and creaked off to bed did Milo offer his comment.

"When you get in trouble, man, you sure as hell do it right."

"Astute as always, Milo," sighed Victor.

"Too bad we can't say the same for the cops," Milo snorted. "If they'd just bothered to ask around, they would've learned you're harmless. Far as I know, you're guilty of only one serious crime."

Cathy looked up, startled. "What crime?"

"Assaulting the ears of victims unlucky enough to hear his saxophone."

"This from a piccolo player who practises with earplugs," observed Victor.

"That's to drown out extraneous noise."

"Yeah. Mainly your own."

Cathy grinned. "I'm beginning to understand why you called yourselves the Out of Tuners."

"Just some healthy self-deprecating humor," said Milo. "Something we needed after we failed to make the Stanford band." Milo rose, shoving away from the kitchen table. "Well, come on. Let's see what's on that mysterious roll of film."

He led them along the hall and down a rickety set of steps to the basement. The chemical tang of the air, the row of trays lined up on a stainless-steel countertop and the slow drip, drip of water from the faucet told Cathy she was standing in an enormous darkroom. Tacked on the walls was a jumble of photos. Faces, mostly, apparently snapped around the world. Here and there she spotted a newsworthy shot: soldiers storming an airport, protestors unfurling a banner.

"Is this your job, Milo?" she asked.

"I wish," said Milo, agitating the developing canister. "No, I just work in the ol' family business."

"Which is?"

"Shoes. Italian, Brazilian, leather, alligator, you name it, we import it." He cocked his head at the photos. "That's how I get my exotic faces. Shoe-buying trips. I'm an expert on the female arch."

"For that," said Victor, "he spent four years at Stanford."

"Why not? Good a place as any to study the fine feet of the fair sex." A timer rang. Milo poured out the developer, removed the roll of film, and hung it up to dry. "Actually," he said, squinting at the negatives, "it was my dad's dying request. He wanted a son with a Stanford degree. I wanted four years of nonstop partying. We both got our wishes." He paused and gazed off wistfully at his photos. "Too bad I can't say the same of the years since then."

"What do you mean?" asked Cathy.

"I mean the partying's long since over. Gotta earn those profits, keep up those sales. Never thought life'd come down to the bottom line. Whatever happened to all that rabble-rousing potential, hey, Gersh? We sort of lost it along the way. All of us, Bach and Ollie and Roger. The Out of Tuners finally stepped into line. Now we're all marching to the beat of the same boring drummer." He sighed and glanced at Victor. "You make out anything on those negatives?"

Victor shook his head. "We need prints."

Milo flipped off the lights, leaving only the red glow of the darkroom lamp. "Coming up."

As Milo laid out the photographic paper, Victor asked, "What happened to the other guys? They still around?"

Milo flipped the exposure switch. "Roger's VP at some multinational bank in Tokyo. Into silk suits and ties, the whole nine yards. Bach's got an electronics firm in San José."

"And Ollie?"

"What can I say about Ollie?" Milo slipped the first print into the bath. "He's still lurking around in that lab over at Stanford Med. I doubt he ever sees the light of day. I figure he's got some secret chamber in the basement where he keeps his assistant Igor chained to the wall.''

"This guy I have to meet," said Cathy.

"Oh, he'd love you." Victor laughed and gave her arm a squeeze. "Seeing as he's probably forgotten what the female of the species looks like."

Milo slid the print into the next tray. "Yeah, Ollie's the one who never changed. Still the night owl. Still plays a mean clarinet." He glanced at Victor. "How's the sax, Gersh? You keeping it up?"

"Haven't played in months."

"Lucky neighbors."

"How did you ever get that name?" asked Cathy. "Gersh?"

"Because," said Milo, wielding tongs as he transferred another batch of prints between trays, "he's a firm believer in the power of George Gershwin to win a lady's heart. 'Someone to Watch Over Me,' wasn't that the tune that made Lily say…'' Milo's voice suddenly faded. He looked at his friend with regret.

"You're right," said Victor quietly. "That was the tune. And Lily said yes."

Milo shook his head. "Sorry. Guess I still have a hard time remembering she's gone."

"Well, she is," said Victor, his voice matter-of-fact. Cathy knew there was pain buried in the undertones. But he hid it well. "And right now," Victor said, "we've got other things to think about."

"Yeah." Milo, chastened, turned his attention back to the prints he'd just developed. He fished them out and clipped the first few sheets on the line to dry. "Okay, Gersh. Tell us what's on this roll that's worth killing for."

Milo switched on the lights.

Victor stood in silence for a moment, frowning at the first five dripping prints. To Cathy, the data was meaningless, only a set of numbers and codes, recorded in an almost illegible hand.

"Well," grunted Milo. "That sure tells me a lot."

Victor's gaze shifted quickly from one page to the next. He paused at the fifth photo, where a column ran down the length of the page. It contained a series of twenty-seven entries, each one a date followed by the same three letters: EXP.

"Victor?" asked Cathy. "What does it mean?"

He turned to them. It was the look in his eyes that worried her. The stillness. Quietly he said, "We need to call Ollie."

"You mean tonight?" asked Milo. "Why?"

"This isn't just some experiment in test tubes and petri dishes. They've gone beyond that, to clinical trials." Victor pointed to the last page. "These are monkeys. Each one was infected with a new virus. A manmade virus. And in every case the results were the same."

"You mean this?" Milo pointed to the last column. "EXP?"

"It stands for expired," said Victor. "They all died."

Sam Polowski sat on a bench in the Palo Alto bus terminal and wondered: If I wanted to disappear, where would I go next? He watched a dozen or so passengers straggle off to board the 210 from San José, noting they were by and large the Birkenstock and backpack set. Probably Stanford students heading off for Christmas break. He wondered why it was that students who could afford such a pricey university couldn't seem to scrape up enough to buy a decent pair of jeans. Or even a decent haircut, for that matter.

At last Polowski rose and automatically dusted off his coat, a habit he'd picked up from his early years of hanging around the seamier side of town. Even if the grime wasn't actually visible, he'd always *felt* it was there, coating any surface he happened to brush against, ready to cling to him like wet paint.

He made one phone call—to Dafoe's answering machine, to tell him Victor Holland had moved on to Palo Alto. It was, after all, his responsibility to keep his supervisor informed. He was glad he only had to talk to a recording and not to the man himself.

He left the bus station and strolled down the street, heading Lord knew where, in search of a spark, a hunch. It was a nice-enough neighborhood, a nice-enough town. Palo Alto had its old professors' houses, its bookshops and coffee houses where university types, the ones with the beards and wire-rim glasses, liked to sit and argue the meaning of Proust and Brecht and Goethe. Polowski remembered his own university days, when, after being subjected to an hour of such crap from the students at the next table, he had finally stormed over to them and yelled, "Maybe Brecht meant it that way, maybe not. But can you guys answer this? *What the hell difference does it make?*"

This did not, needless to say, enhance his reputation as a serious scholar.

Now, as he paced along the street, no doubt in the footsteps of more serious philosophers, Polowski turned over in his head the question of Victor Holland. More specifically the question of where such a man, in his desperation, would hide. He stalked past the lit windows, the glow of TVs, the cars spilling from garages. Where in this warren of suburbia was the man hiding?

Holland was a scientist, a musician, a man of few but lasting friendships. He had a Ph.D. from MIT, a B.S. from Stanford. The university was right up the road. The man must know his way around here. Maybe he still had friends in the neighborhood, people who'd take him in, keep his secrets.

Polowski decided to take another look at Holland's file. Somewhere in the Viratek records, there had to be some employment reference, some recommendation from a Stanford contact. A friend Holland might turn to.

Sooner or later, he would have to turn to *someone.*

It was after midnight when Dafoe and his wife returned home. He was in an excellent mood, his head pleasantly abuzz with champagne, his ears still ringing with the heart-wrenching aria from *Samson and Delilah.* Opera was a passion for him, a brilliant staging of courage and conflict and *amore,* a vision of life so much grander than the petty little world in which he found himself. It launched him to a plane of such thrilling intensity that even his own wife took on exciting new aspects. He watched her peel off her coat and kick off her shoes. Forty pounds overweight, hair streaked with silver, yet she had her attractions. *It's been three weeks. Surely she'll let me tonight....*

But his wife ignored his amorous looks and wandered off to the kitchen. A moment later, the rumble of the automatic dishwasher announced another of her fits of housecleaning.

In frustration, Dafoe turned and stabbed the blinking button on his answering machine. The message from Polowski completely destroyed any amorous intentions he had left.

"…Reason to believe Holland is in, or has just left, the Palo Alto area. Following leads. Will keep you informed.…"

Polowski, you half-wit. Is following orders so damn difficult?

It was 3:00 a.m. Washington time. An ungodly hour, but he made the phone call.

The voice that answered was raspy with sleep. "Tyrone here."

"Cowboy, this is Dafoe. Sorry to wake you."

The voice became instantly alert, all sleep shaken from it. "What's up?"

"New lead on Holland. I don't know the particulars, but he's headed south, to Palo Alto. May still be there."

"The university?"

"It is the Stanford area."

"That may be a very big help."

"Anything for an old buddy. I'll keep you posted."

"One thing, Dafoe."

"Yeah?"

"I can't have any interference. Pull all your people out. We'll take it from here."

Dafoe paused. "I might…have a problem."

"A problem?" The voice, though quiet, took on a razor's edge.

"It's, uh, one of my men. Sort of a wild card. Sam Polowski. He's got this Holland case under his skin, wants to go after him."

"There's such a thing as a direct order."

"At the moment, Polowski's unreachable. He's in Palo Alto, digging around in God knows what."

"Loose cannons. I don't like them."

"I'll pull him back as soon as I can."

"Do that. And keep it quiet. It's a matter of utmost security."

After Dafoe hung up, his gaze shifted automatically to the photo on the mantelpiece. It was a '68 snapshot of him and the Cowboy: two young marines, both of them grinning, their rifles slung over their shoulders as they stood ankle-deep in a rice paddy. It was a crazy time, when one's very life depended on the loyalty of buddies. When Semper Fi applied not only to the corps in general but to each other in particular. Matt Tyrone was a hero then, and he was a hero now. Dafoe stared at that smiling face in the photo, disturbed by the threads of envy that had woven into his admiration for the man. Though Dafoe had much to be proud of—a solid eighteen years in the FBI, maybe even a shot at assistant director somewhere in his stars, he couldn't match the heady climb of Matt Tyrone in the NSA. Though Dafoe wasn't clear as to exactly what position the Cowboy held in the NSA, he had heard that Tyrone regularly attended cabinet meetings, that he held the trust of the president, that he dealt in secrets and shadows and security. He was the sort of man the country needed, a man for whom patriotism was more than mere flag-waving and rhetoric; it was a way of life. Matt Tyrone would do more than die for his country; he'd live for it.

Dafoe couldn't let such a man, such a friend, down.

He dialed Sam Polowski's home phone and left a message on the recorder.

This is a direct order. You are to withdraw from the Holland case immediately. Until further notice you are on suspension.

He was tempted to add, *by special request from my friends in Washington,* but thought better of it. No room for vanity here. The Cowboy had said national security was at stake.

Dafoe had no doubt it truly was. He'd gotten the word from Matt Tyrone. And Matt Tyrone's authority came direct from the President himself.

"This does not look good. This does not look good at all."

Ollie Wozniak squinted through his wire-rim glasses at the twenty-four photographs strewn across Milo's dining table. He held one up for a closer look. Through the bottle-glass lens, one pale blue eye stared out, enormous. One only saw Ollie's eyes; everything else, hollow cheeks, pencil lips and baby-fine hair, seemed to recede into the background pallor. He shook his head and picked up another photo.

"You're right, of course," he said. "Some of these I can't interpret. I'd like to study 'em later. But these here are definitely raw mortality data. Rhesus monkeys, I suspect." He paused and added quietly, "I hope."

"Surely they wouldn't use people for this sort of thing," said Cathy.

"Not officially." Ollie put down the photo and looked at her. "But it's been done."

"Maybe in Nazi Germany."

"Here, too," said Victor.

"What?" Cathy looked at him in disbelief.

"Army studies in germ warfare. They released colonies of Serratia Marcescens over San Francisco and waited to see how far the organism spread. Infections popped up in a number of Bay Area hospitals. Some of the cases were fatal."

"I can't believe it," murmured Cathy.

"The damage was unintentional, of course. But people died just the same."

"Don't forget Tuskegee," said Ollie. "People died in those experiments, too. And then there was that case in New York. Mentally retarded kids in a state hospital who were deliberately exposed to hepatitis. No one died there, but the ethics were just as shaky. So it's been done. Sometimes in the name of humanity."

"Sometimes not," said Victor.

Ollie nodded. "As in this particular case."

"What exactly are we talking about here?" asked Cathy, nodding at the photos. "Is this medical research? Or weapons development?"

"Both." Ollie pointed to one of the photos on the table. "By all appearances, Viratek's engaged in biological weapons research. They've dubbed it Project Cerberus. From what I can tell, the organism they're working on is an RNA virus, extremely virulent, highly contagious, producing over eighty-percent mortality in its lab animal hosts. This photo here—" he tapped one of the pages "—shows the organism produces vesicular skin lesions on the infected subjects."

"Vesicular?"

"Blisterlike. That could be one route of transmission, the fluid in those lesions." He sifted through the pile and pulled out another page. "This shows the time course of the illness. The viral counts, periods of infectiousness. In almost every case the course is the same. The subject's exposed here." He pointed to Day One on the time graph. "Minor signs of illness here at Day Seven. Full-blown pox on Day Twelve. And here—" he tapped the graph at Day Fourteen "—the deaths begin. The time varies, but the result's the same. They all die."

"You used the word *pox*," said Cathy.

Ollie turned to her, his eyes like blue glass. "Because that's what it is."

"You mean like chickenpox?"

"I wish it was. Then it wouldn't be so deadly. Almost everyone gets exposed to chickenpox as a kid, so most of us are immune. But this one's a different story."

"Is it a new virus?" asked Milo.

"Yes and no." He reached for an electron micrograph. "When I saw this I thought there was something weirdly familiar about all this. The appearance of the organism, the skin lesions, the course of illness. The whole damn picture. It reminded me of something I haven't read about in decades. Something I never dreamed I'd see again."

"You're saying it's an old virus?" said Milo.

"Ancient. But they've made some modifications. Made it more infectious. And deadlier. Which turns this into a real humdinger of a weapon, considering the millions of folks it's already killed."

"Millions?" Cathy stared at him. "What are we talking about?"

"A killer we've known for centuries. Smallpox."

"That's impossible!" said Cathy. "From what I've read, we conquered smallpox. It's supposed to be extinct."

"It was," said Victor. "For all practical purposes. Worldwide vaccination wiped it out. Smallpox hasn't been reported in decades. I'm not even sure they still make the vaccine. Ollie?"

"Not available. No need for it since the virus has vanished."

"So where did *this* virus come from?" asked Cathy.

Ollie shrugged. "Probably someone's closet."

"Come on."

"I'm serious. After smallpox was eradicated, a few samples of virus were kept alive in government labs, just in case someone needed it for future research. It's the scientific skeleton in the closet, so to speak. I'd assume those labs are top security. Because if any of the virus got out, there could be a major epidemic." He looked at the stack of photos. "Looks like security's already been breached. Someone obviously got hold of the virus."

"Or had it handed to them," said Victor. "Courtesy of the U.S. government."

"I find that incredible, Gersh," said Ollie. "This is a powderkeg experiment you're talking about. No committee would approve this sort of project."

"Right. That's why I think this is a maverick operation. It's easy to come up with a scenario. Bunch of hardliners cooking this up over at NSA. Or joint chiefs of staff. Or even the Oval Office. Someone says: 'World politics have changed. We can't get away with nuking the enemy. We need a new weapons option, one that'll work well against a Third World army. Let's find one.' And some guy in that room, some red, white and blue robot, will take that as the go-ahead. International law be damned."

"And since it's unofficial," said Cathy, "it'd be completely deniable."

"Right. The administration could claim it knew nothing."

"Sounds like Iran-Contra all over again."

"With one big difference," said Ollie. "When Iran-Contra fell apart, all you had were a few ruined political careers. If Project Cerberus goes awry, what you'll have is a few million dead people."

"But Ollie," said Milo. "I got vaccinated for smallpox when I was a kid. Doesn't that mean I'm safe?"

"Probably. Assuming the virus hasn't been altered too much. In fact, everyone over 35 is probably okay. But remember, there's a whole generation after us that never got the vaccine. Young adults and kids. By the time you could manufacture enough vaccine for them all, we'd have a raging epidemic."

"I'm beginning to see the logic of this weapon," said Victor. "In any war, who makes up the bulk of combat soldiers? Young adults."

Ollie nodded. "They'd be hit bad. As would the kids."

"A whole generation," Cathy murmured. "And only the old would be spared." She glanced at Victor and saw, mirrored in his eyes, the horror she felt.

"They chose an appropriate name," said Milo.

Ollie frowned. "What?"

"Cerberus. The three-headed dog of Hades." Milo looked up, visibly shaken. "Guardian of the dead."

* * *

It wasn't until Cathy was fast asleep and Milo had retired upstairs that Victor finally broached the subject to Ollie. It had troubled him all evening, had shadowed his every moment since they'd arrived at Milo's house. He couldn't look at Cathy, couldn't listen to the sound of her voice or inhale the scent of her hair without thinking of the terrible possibilities. And in the deepest hours of night, when it seemed all the world was asleep except for him and Ollie, he made the decision.

"I need to ask you a favor," he said.

Ollie gazed at him across the dining table, steam wafting up from his fourth cup of coffee. "What sort of favor?"

"It has to do with Cathy."

Ollie's gaze shifted to the woman lying asleep on the living room floor. She looked very small, very defenseless, curled up beneath the comforter. Ollie said, "She's a nice woman, Gersh."

"I know."

"There hasn't really been anyone since Lily. Has there?"

Victor shook his head. "I guess I haven't felt ready for it. There were always other things to think about...."

Ollie smiled. "There are always excuses. I should know. People keep telling me there's a glut of unattached female baby boomers. I haven't noticed."

"And I never bothered to notice." Victor looked at Cathy. "Until now."

"What're you gonna do with her, Gersh?"

"That's what I need you for. I'm not the safest guy to hang around with these days. A woman could get hurt."

Ollie laughed. "Hell, a *guy* could get hurt."

"I feel responsible for her. And if something happened to her, I'm not sure I could ever..." He let out a long sigh and rubbed his bloodshot eyes. "Anyway, I think it's best if she leaves."

"For where?"

"She has an ex-husband. He'll be working down in Mexico for a few months. I think she'd be pretty safe."

"You're sending her to her ex-husband?"

"I've met him. He's a jerk, but at least she won't be alone down there."

"Does Cathy agree to this?"

"I didn't ask her."

"Maybe you should."

"I'm not giving her a choice."

"What if she wants the choice?"

"I'm not in the mood to take any crap, Okay? I'm doing this for her own good."

Ollie took off his glasses and cleaned them on the tablecloth. "Excuse me for saying this, Gersh, but if it was me, I'd want her nearby, where I could sort of keep an eye on her."

"You mean where I can watch her get killed?" Victor shook his head. "Lily was enough. I won't go through it with Cathy."

Ollie thought it over for a moment, then he nodded. "What do you want me to do?"

"Tomorrow I want you to take her to the airport. Buy her a ticket to Mexico. Let her use your name. Mrs. Wozniak. Make sure she gets safely off the ground. I'll pay you back when I can."

"What if she won't get on the plane? Do I just shove her aboard?"

"Do whatever it takes, Ollie. I'm counting on you."

Ollie sighed. "I guess I can do it. I'll call in sick tomorrow. That'll free up my day." He looked at Victor. "I just hope you know what you're doing."

So do I, thought Victor.

Ollie rose to his feet and tucked the envelope with the photos under his arm. "I'll get back to you in the morning. After I show these last two photos to Bach. Maybe he can identify what those grids are."

"If it's anything electronic, Bach'll figure it out."

Together they walked to the door. There they paused and regarded each other, two old friends who'd grown a little grayer and, Victor hoped, a little wiser.

"Somehow it'll all work out," said Ollie. "Remember. The system's there to be beaten."

"Sounds like the old Stanford radical again."

"It's been a long time." Grinning, Ollie gave Victor a clap on the back. "But we're still not too old to raise a little hell, hey, Gersh? See you in the morning."

Victor waved as Ollie walked away into the darkness. Then he closed the door and turned off all the lights.

In the living room he sat beside Cathy and watched her sleep. The glow of a streetlight spilled in through the window onto her tumbled hair. *Ordinary,* she had called herself. Perhaps, if she'd been a stranger he'd merely passed on the street, he might have thought so, too. A chance meeting on a rainy highway in Garberville had made it impossible for him to ever consider this woman ordinary. In her gentleness, her kindness, she was very much like Lily.

In other ways, she was very different.

Though he'd cared about his wife, though they'd never stopped being good friends, he'd found Lily strangely passionless, a pristine, spiritual being trapped by human flesh. Lily had never been comfortable with her own body. She'd undress in the dark, make love— the rare times they did—in the dark. And then, the illness had robbed her of what little desire she had left.

Gazing at Cathy, he couldn't help wondering what passions might lie harbored in her still form.

He cut short the speculation. What did it matter now? Tomorrow, he'd send her away. *Get rid of her,* he thought brutally. It was necessary. He couldn't think straight while she was around. He couldn't stay focused on the business at hand: exposing Viratek. Jerry Martinique had counted on him. Thousands of potential victims counted on him. He was a scientist, a man who prided himself on logic. His attraction to this particular woman was, in the grand scheme of things, clearly unimportant.

That was what the scientist in him said.

That problem finally settled, he decided to get some rest while he could. He kicked off his shoes and stretched out beside her to sleep. The comforter was large enough—they could share it. He climbed beneath it and lay for a moment, not touching her, almost afraid to share her warmth.

She whimpered in her sleep and turned toward him, her silky hair tumbling against his face.

This was more than he could resist. Sighing, he wrapped his arms around her and felt her curl up against his chest. It was their last night together. They might as well spend it keeping each other warm.

That was how he fell asleep, with Cathy in his arms.

Only once during the night did he awaken. He had been dreaming of Lily. They were walking together, in a garden of pure white flowers. She said absolutely nothing. She simply looked at him with profound sadness, as if to say, *Here I am, Victor. I've come back to you. Why doesn't that make you happy?* He couldn't answer her. So he simply took her in his arms and held her.

He'd awakened to find he was holding Cathy, instead.

Joy instantly flooded his heart, warmed the darkest corners of his soul. It took him by surprise, that burst of happiness; it also made him feel guilty. But there it was. And the joy was all too short-lived. He remembered that today she'd be going away.

Cathy, Cathy. What a complication you've become.

He turned on his side, away from her, mentally building a wall between them.

He concentrated on the dream, trying to remember what had happened. He and Lily had been walking. He tried to picture Lily's face, her brown eyes, her curly black hair. It was the face of the woman he'd been married to for ten years, a face he should know well.

But the only face he saw when he closed his eyes was that of Catherine Weaver.

It took Nicholas Savitch only two hours to pack his bags and drive down to Palo Alto. The word from Matt Tyrone was that Holland had slipped south to the Stanford area, perhaps to seek out old friends. Holland was, after all, a Stanford man. Maybe not the red-and-white rah-rah Cardinals type, but a Stanford man nonetheless. These old school ties could run deep. It was only a guess on Savitch's part; he'd never gone beyond high school. His education consisted of what a hungry and ambitious boy could pick up on Chicago's south side. Mainly a keen, almost uncanny knack for crawling into another man's head, for sensing what a particular man would think and do in a given situation. Call it advanced street psychology. Without spending a day in college, Savitch had earned his degree.

Now he was putting it to use.

The *finder,* they called him. He liked that name. He grinned as he drove, his leather-gloved hands expertly handling the wheel. Nicholas Savitch, diviner of human souls, the hunter who could ferret a man out of deepest hiding.

In most cases it was a simple matter of logic. Even while on the run, most people conformed to old patterns. It was the fear that did it. It made them seek out their old comforts, cling to their usual habits. In a strange town, the familiar was precious, even if it was only the sight of those ubiquitous golden arches.

Like every other fugitive, Victor Holland would seek the familiar.

Savitch turned his car onto Palm Drive and pulled up in front of the Stanford Arch. The campus was silent; it was 2:00 a.m. Savitch sat for a moment, regarding the silent buildings, Holland's alma mater. Here, in his former stomping grounds, Holland would turn to old friends, revisit old haunts. Savitch had already done his homework. He carried, in his briefcase, a list of names he'd culled from the man's file. In the morning he'd start in on those names, knock on neighbors' doors, flash his government ID, ask about new faces in the neighborhood.

The only possible complication was Sam Polowski. By last report, the FBI agent was also in town, also on Holland's trail. Polowski was a dogged operator. It'd be messy business, taking out a Bureau man. But then, Polowski was only a cog, the way the Weaver woman was only a cog, in a much bigger wheel.

Neither of them would be missed.

CHAPTER NINE

In the cold, clear hours before dawn, Cathy woke up shaking, still trapped in the threads of a nightmare. She had been walking in a world of concrete and shadow, where doorways gaped and silhouettes huddled on street corners. She drifted among them, one among the faceless, taking refuge in obscurity, instinctively avoiding the light. No one pursued her; no attacker lunged from the alleys. The real terror lay in the unending maze of concrete, the hard echoes of the streets, the frantic search for a safe place.

And the certainty that she would never find it.

For a moment she lay in the darkness, curled up beneath a down comforter on Milo's living room floor. She barely remembered having crawled under the covers; it must have been sometime after three when she'd fallen asleep. The last she remembered, Ollie and Victor were still huddled in the dining room, discussing the photographs. Now there was only silence. The dining room, like the rest of the house, lay in shadow.

She turned on her back, and her shoulder thumped against something warm and solid. Victor. He stirred, murmuring something she couldn't understand.

"Are you awake?" she whispered.

He turned toward her and in his drowsiness enfolded her in his arms. She knew it was only instinct that drew him to her, the yearning of one warm body for another. Or perhaps it was the memory of his wife sleeping beside him, in his mind always there, always waiting to be held. For the moment, she let him cling to the dream. *While he's still half asleep, let him believe I'm Lily,* she thought. *What harm can there be? He needs the memory. And I need the comfort.*

She burrowed into his arms, into the safe spot that once had belonged to another. She took it without regard for the consequences, willing to be swept up into the fantasy of being, for this moment, the one woman in the world he loved. How good it felt, how protected and cared for. From the soap-and-sweat smell of his chest to the coarse fabric of his shirt, it was sanctuary. He was breathing warmly into her hair now, whispering words she knew were for another, pressing kisses to the top of her head. Then he trapped her face in his hands and pressed his lips to hers in a kiss so undeniably needy it ignited within her a hunger of her own. Her response was instinctive and filled with all the yearning of a woman too long a stranger to love.

She met his kiss with one just as deep, just as needy.

At once she was lost, whirled away into some grand and glorious vortex. He stroked down her face, her neck. His hands moved to the buttons of her blouse. She arched against him, her breasts suddenly aching to be touched. It had been so long, so long.

She didn't know how the blouse fell open. She knew only that one moment his fingers were skimming the fabric, and the next moment, they were cupping her flesh. It was that unexpected contact of skin on forbidden skin, the magic torment of his fingers caressing her nipple, that made any last resistance fall away. How many chances were left to them? How many nights together? She longed for so many more, an eternity, but this might be all they had. She welcomed it, welcomed him, with all the passion of a woman granted one last taste of love.

With a knowing touch, she slid her hands down his shirt, undoing buttons, stroking her way through the dense hair of his chest, to the top of his trousers. There she paused, feeling his startled intake of breath, knowing that he too was past retreat.

Together they fumbled at buttons and zippers, both of them suddenly feverish to be free. It all fell away in a tumult of cotton and lace. And when the last scrap of clothing was shed, when nothing came between them but the velvet darkness, she reached up and pulled him to her, on her.

It was a joyful filling, as if, in that first deep thrust within her, he also reached some long-empty hollow in her soul.

"Please," she murmured, her voice breaking into a whimper.

He fell instantly still. "Cathy?" he asked, his hands anxiously cupping her face. "What—"

"Please. Don't stop...."

His soft laughter was all the reassurance she needed. "I have no intention of stopping," he whispered. "None whatsoever..."

And he didn't stop. Not until he had taken her with him all the way, higher and further than any man ever could, to a place beyond thought or reason. Only when release came, wave flooding upon wave, did she know how very high and far they had climbed.

A sweet exhaustion claimed them.

Outside, in the grayness of dawn, a bird sang. Inside, the silence was broken only by the sound of their breathing.

She sighed into the warmth of his shoulder. "Thank you."

He touched her face. "For what?"

"For making me feel...wanted again."

"Oh, Cathy."

"It's been such a long time. Jack and I, we—we stopped making love way before the divorce. It was me, actually. I couldn't bear having him..." She swallowed. "When you don't love someone anymore, when they don't love you, it's hard to let yourself be... touched."

He brushed his fingers down her cheek. "Is it still hard? Being touched?"

"Not by you. Being touched by you is like...being touched the very first time."

By the window's pale light she saw him smile. "I hope your very first time wasn't too awful."

Now she smiled. "I don't remember it very well. It was such a frantic, ridiculous thing on the floor of a college dorm room."

He reached out and patted the carpet. "I see you've come a long way."

"Haven't I?" she laughed. "But floors can be terribly romantic places."

"Goodness. A carpet connoisseur. How do dorm room and living room floors compare?"

"I couldn't tell you. It's been such a long time since I was eighteen." She paused, hovering on the edge of baring the truth. "In fact," she admitted, "it's been a long time since I've been with anyone."

Softly he said, "It's been a long time for both of us."

She let that revelation hang for a moment in the semi-darkness. "Not—not since Lily?" she finally asked.

"No." A single word, yet it revealed so much. The three years of loyalty to a dead woman. The grief, the loneliness. How she wanted to fill that womanless chasm for him! To be his savior, and he, hers. Could she make him forget? No, not forget; she couldn't expect him ever to forget Lily. But she wanted a space in his heart for herself, a very large space designed for a lifetime. A space to which no other woman, dead or alive, could ever lay claim.

"She must have been a very special woman," she said.

He ran a strand of her hair through his fingers. "She was very wise, very aware. And she was kind. That's something I don't always find in a person."

She's still part of you, isn't she? She's still the one you love.

"It's the same sort of kindness I find in you," he said.

His fingers had slid to her face and were now stroking her cheek. She closed her eyes, savoring his touch, his warmth. "You hardly know me," she whispered.

"But I do. That night, after the accident, I survived purely on the sound of your voice. And the touch of your hand. I'd know them both, anywhere."

She opened her eyes and gazed at him. "Would you really?"

He pressed his lips to her forehead. "Even in my sleep."

"But I'm not Lily. I could never be Lily."

"That's true. You can't be. No one can."

"I can't replace what you lost."

"What makes you think that's what I want? Some sort of replacement? She was my wife. And yes, I loved her." By the way he said it, his answer invited no exploration.

She didn't try.

From somewhere in the house came the jingle of a telephone. After two rings it stopped. Faintly they heard Milo's voice murmuring upstairs.

Cathy sat up and reached automatically for her clothes. She dressed in silence, her back turned to Victor. A new modesty had sprung up between them, the shyness of strangers.

"Cathy," he said. "People do move on."

"I know."

"You've gotten over Jack."

She laughed, a small, tired sound. "No woman ever really gets over Jack Zuckerman. Yes, I'm over the worst of it. But every time a woman falls in love, really falls in love, it takes something out of her. Something that can never be put back."

"It also gives her something."

"That depends on who you fall in love with, doesn't it?"

Footsteps thumped down the stairs, creaked across the dining room. A wide-awake Milo stood in the doorway, his uncombed hair standing out like a brush. "Hey, you two!" he hissed. "Get up! Hurry."

Cathy rose to her feet in alarm. "What is it?"

"That was Ollie on the phone. He called to say some guy's in the area, asking questions about you. He's already been down to Bach's neighborhood."

"What?" Now Victor was on his feet and hurriedly stuffing his legs into his trousers.

"Ollie figures the guy'll be knocking around here next. Guess they know who your friends are."

"Who was asking the questions?"

"Claimed he was FBI."

"Polowski," muttered Victor, pulling his shirt on. "Has to be."

"You know him?"

"The same guy who set me up. The guy who's been tailing us ever since."

"How did he know we're here?" said Cathy. "No one could've followed us—"

"No one had to. They have my profile. They know I have friends here." Victor glanced at Milo. "Sorry, buddy. Hope this doesn't get you into trouble."

Milo's laugh was distinctly tense. "Hey, I didn't do nothin' wrong. Just harbored a felon." The bravado suddenly melted away. He asked, "Exactly what kind of trouble should I expect?"

"Questions," said Victor, quickly buttoning his shirt. "Lots of 'em. Maybe they'll even take a look around. Just keep cool, tell 'em you haven't heard from me. Think you can do it?"

"Sure. But I don't know about Ma—"

"Your Ma's no problem. Just tell her to stick to Chinese." Victor grabbed the envelope of photos and glanced at Cathy. "Ready?"

"Let's get out of here. Please."

"Back door," Milo suggested.

They followed him through the kitchen. A glance told them the way was clear. As he opened the door, Milo added, "I almost forgot. Ollie wants to see you this afternoon. Something about those photos."

"Where?"

"The lake. Behind the boathouse. You know the place."

They stepped out into the chill dampness of morning. Fog-borne silence hung in the air. *Will we ever stop running?* thought Cathy. *Will we never stop listening for footsteps?*

Victor clapped his friend on the shoulder. "Thanks, Milo. I owe you a big one."

"And one of these days I plan to collect!" Milo hissed as they slipped away.

Victor held up his hand in farewell. "See you around."

"Yeah," Milo muttered into the mist. "Let's hope not in jail."

The Chinese man was lying. Though the man betrayed nothing in his voice, no hesitation, no guilty waver, still Savitch knew this Mr. Milo Lum was hiding something. His eyes betrayed him.

He was seated on the living room couch, across from Savitch. Off to the side sat Mrs. Lum in an easy chair, smiling uncomprehendingly. Savitch might be able to use the old biddy; for now, it was the son who held his interest.

"I can't see why you'd be after him," said Milo. "Victor's as clean as they come. At least, he was when I knew him. But that was a long time ago."

"How far back?" asked Savitch politely.

"Oh, years. Yeah. Haven't seen him since. No, sir."

Savitch raised an eyebrow. Milo shifted on the couch, shuffled his feet, glanced pointlessly around the room.

"You and your mother live here alone?" Savitch asked.

"Since my dad died."

"No tenants? No one else lives here?"

"No. Why?"

"There were reports of a man fitting Holland's description in the neighborhood."

"Believe me, if Victor was wanted by the police, he wouldn't hang around here. You think I'd let a murder suspect in the house? With just me and my old Ma?"

Savitch glanced at Mrs. Lum, who merely smiled. The old woman had sharp, all-seeing eyes. A survivor's eyes.

It was time for Savitch to confirm his hunch. "Excuse me," he said, rising to his feet. "I had a long drive from the city. May I use your restroom?"

"Uh, sure. Down that hall."

Savitch headed into the bathroom and closed the door. Within seconds he'd spotted the evidence he was looking for. It was lying on the tiled floor: a long strand of brown hair. Very silky, very fine.

Catherine Weaver's shade.

It was all the proof he needed to proceed. He reached under his jacket for the shoulder holster and pulled out the semiautomatic. Then he gave his crisp white shirt a regretful pat. Messy business, interrogation. He would have to watch the bloodstains.

He stepped out into the hall, casually holding his pistol at his side. He'd go for the old woman first. Hold the barrel to her head, threaten to pull the trigger. There was an uncommonly strong bond between this mother and son. They would protect each other at all costs.

Savitch was halfway down the hall when the doorbell rang. He halted. The front door was opened and a new voice said, "Mr. Milo Lum?"

"And who the hell are you?" came Milo's weary reply.

"The name's Sam Polowski. FBI."

Every muscle in Savitch's body snapped taut. No choice now; he had to take the man out.

He raised his pistol. Soundlessly, he made his way down the hall toward the living room.

"*Another* one?" came Milo's peevish voice. "Look, one of your guys is already here—"

"What?"

"Yeah, he's back in the—"

Savitch stepped out and was swinging his pistol toward the front doorway when Mrs. Lum shrieked.

Milo froze. Polowski didn't. He rolled sideways just as the bullet thudded into the door frame, splintering wood.

By the time Savitch got off a second shot, Polowski was crawling somewhere behind the couch and the bullet slammed uselessly into the stuffing. That was it for chances—Polowski was armed.

Savitch decided it was time to vanish.

He turned and darted back up the hall, into a far bedroom. It was the mother's room; it smelled of incense and old-lady perfume. The window slid open easily. Savitch kicked out the screen, scrambled over the sill and sank heel-deep into the muddy flower bed. Cursing, he slogged away, trailing clumps of mud across the lawn.

He heard, faintly, "Halt! FBI!" but continued running.

He nursed his rage all the way back to the car.

Milo stared in bewilderment at the trampled pansies. "What the hell was that all about?" he demanded. "Is this some sort of FBI practical joke?"

Sam Polowski didn't answer; he was too busy tracking the footprints across the grass. They led to the sidewalk, then faded into the road's pebbly asphalt.

"Hey!" yelled Milo. "What's going on?"

Polowski turned. "I didn't really see him. What did he look like?"

Milo shrugged. "I dunno. Efrem Zimbalist-type."

"Meaning?"

"Tall, clean-cut, great build. Typical FBI."

There was a silence as Milo regarded Polowski's sagging belly.

"Well," amended Milo, "maybe not *typical*..."

"What about his face?"

"Lemme think. Brown hair? Maybe brown eyes?"

"You're not sure."

"You know how it is. All you white guys look alike to me."

An eruption of rapid Chinese made them both turn. Mrs. Lum had followed them out onto the lawn and was jabbering and gesticulating.

"What's she saying?" asked Polowski.

"She says the man was about six foot one, had straight dark brown hair parted on the left, brown eyes, almost black, a high forehead, a narrow nose and thin lips, and a small tattoo on his inside left wrist."

"Uh—is that all?"

"The tattoo read PJX."

Polowski shook his head in amazement. "Is she always this observant?"

"She can't exactly converse in English. So she does a lot of watching."

"Obviously." Polowski took out a pen and began to jot the information in a notebook.

"So who was this guy?" prodded Milo.

"Not FBI."

"How do I know *you're* FBI."

"Do I look like it?"

"No."

"Only proves my point."

"What?"

"If I wanted to pretend I was an agent, wouldn't I at least try to *look* like one? Whereas, if I *am* one, I wouldn't bother to try and look like one."

"Oh."

"Now." Polowski slid the notebook in his pocket. "You're still going to insist you haven't seen, or heard from, Victor Holland?"

Milo straightened. "That's right."

"And you don't know how to get in touch with him?"

"I have no idea."

"That's too bad. Because I could be the one to save his life. I've already saved yours."

Milo said nothing.

"Just why the hell do you think that guy was here? To pay a social visit? No, he was after information." Polowski paused and added, ominously, "And believe me, he would've gotten it."

Milo shook his head. "I'm confused."

"So am I. That's why I need Holland. He has the answers. But I need him alive. That means I need to find him before the other guy does. Tell me where he is."

Polowski and Milo looked at each other long and hard.

"I don't know," said Milo. "I don't know what to do."

Mrs. Lum was chattering again. She pointed to Polowski and nodded.

"Now what's she saying?" asked Polowski.

"She says you have big ears."

"For that, I can look in the mirror."

"What she means is, the size of your ears indicates sagacity."

"Come again?"

"You're a smart dude. She thinks I should listen to you."

Polowski turned and grinned at Mrs. Lum. "Your mother is a great judge of character." He looked back at Milo. "I wouldn't want anything to happen to her. Or you. You both have to get out of town."

Milo nodded. "On that particular point, we both agree." He turned toward the house.

"What about Holland?" called Polowski. "Will you help me find him?"

Milo took his mother by the arm and guided her across the lawn. Without even a backward look he said, "I'm thinking about it."

"It was those two photos. I just couldn't figure them out," said Ollie.

They were standing on the boathouse pier, overlooking the bed of Lake Lagunita. The lake was dry now, as it was every winter, drained to a reedy marsh until spring. They were alone, the three of them, sharing the lake with only an occasional duck. In the spring, this would be an idyllic spot, the water lapping the banks, lovers drifting in rowboats, here and there a poet lolling under the trees. But today, under black clouds, with a cold mist rising from the reeds, it was a place of utter desolation.

"I knew they weren't biological data," said Ollie. "I kept thinking they looked like some sort of electrical grid. So this morning, right after I left Milo's, I took 'em over to Bach's, down in San José. Caught him at breakfast."

"Bach?" asked Cathy.

"Another member of the Out of Tuners. Great bassoon player. Started an electronics firm a few years back and now he's working with the big boys. Anyway, the first thing he says as I walk in the door is, 'Hey, did the FBI get to you yet?' And I said, 'What?' and he says, 'They just called. For some reason they're looking for Gershwin. They'll probably get around to you next.' And that's when I knew I had to get you two out of Milo's house, stat.''

"So what did he say about those photos?''

"Oh, yeah.'' Ollie reached into his briefcase and pulled out the photos. "Okay. This one here, it's a circuit diagram. An electronic alarm system. Very sophisticated, very secure. Designed to be breached by use of a keypad code, punched in at this point here. Probably at an entryway. You seen anything like it at Viratek?''

Victor nodded. "Building C-2. Where Jerry worked. The keypad's in the hall, right by the Special Projects door.''

"Ever been inside that door?''

"No. Only those with top clearance can get through. Like Jerry.''

"Then we'll have to visualize what comes next. Going by the diagram, there's another security point here, probably another keypad. Right inside the first door, they've stationed a camera system.''

"You mean like a bank camera?'' asked Cathy.

"Similar. Only I'd guess this one's being monitored twenty-four hours a day.''

"They went first class, didn't they?'' said Victor. "Two secured doors, plus inspection by a guard. Not to mention the guard at the outside gate.''

"Don't forget the laser lattice.''

"What?''

"This inner room here.'' Ollie pointed to the diagram's core. "Laser beams, directed at various angles. They'll detect movement of just about anything bigger than a rat.''

"How do the lasers get switched off?''

"Has to be done by the security guard. The controls are on his panel.''

"You can tell all this from the diagram?'' asked Cathy. "I'm impressed.''

"No problem.'' Ollie grinned. "Bach's firm designs security systems.''

Victor shook his head. "This looks impossible. We can't get through all that.''

Cathy frowned at him. "Wait a minute. What are you talking about? You aren't considering going into that building, are you?"

"We discussed it last night," said Victor. "It may be the only way—"

"Are you crazy? Viratek's out to kill us and you want to break *in?*"

"It's the proof we need," said Ollie. "You try going to the newspapers or the Justice Department and they'll demand evidence. You can bet Viratek's going to deny everything. Even if someone does launch an investigation, all Viratek has to do is toss the virus and, *poof!* your evidence is gone. No one can prove a thing."

"You have photos—"

"Sure. A few pages of animal data. The virus is never identified. And all that evidence could've been fabricated by, say, some disgruntled ex-employee."

"So what *is* proof? What do you need, another dead body? Victor's, for instance?"

"What we need is the virus—a virus that's supposed to be extinct. Just a single vial and the case against them is nailed shut."

"Just a single vial. Right." Cathy shook her head. "I don't know what I'm worried about. No one can get through those doors. Not without the keypad codes."

"Ah, but those we have!" Ollie flipped to the second photo. "The mysterious numbers. See, they finally make sense. Two sets of seven digits. Not phone numbers at all! Jerry was pointing the way through Viratek's top security."

"What about the lasers?" she pointed out, her agitation growing. They couldn't be serious! Surely they could see the futility of this mission. She didn't care if her fear showed; she had to be their voice of reason. "And then there's the guards," she said. "Two of them. Do you have a way past them? Or did Jerry also leave you the formula for invisibility?"

Ollie glanced uneasily at Victor. "Uh, maybe I should let you two discuss this first. Before we make any other plans."

"I thought I was part of all this," said Cathy. "Part of every decision. I guess I was wrong."

Neither man said a thing. Their silence only fueled Cathy's anger.

She thought: *So you left me out of this. You didn't respect my opinion enough to ask me what I think, what I want.*

Without a word she turned and walked away.

Moments later, Victor caught up with her. She was standing on the dirt path, hugging herself against the cold. She heard his approach, sensed his uncertainty, his struggle to find the right words. For a moment he simply stood beside her, not speaking.

"I think we should run," she said. She gazed over the dry lake bed and shivered. The wind that swept across the reeds was raw and biting; it sliced right through her sweater. "I want to get away," she said. "I want to go somewhere warm. Some place where the sun's shining, where I can lie on a beach and not worry about who's watching me from the bushes...." Suddenly reminded of the terrible possibilities, she turned and glanced at the oaks hulking behind them. She saw only the fluttering of dead leaves.

"I agree with you," said Victor quietly.

"You do?" She turned to him, relieved. "Let's go, Victor! Let's leave now. Forget this crazy idea. We can catch the next bus south—"

"This very afternoon. You'll be on your way."

"*I* will?" She stared at him, at first not willing to accept what she'd heard. Then the meaning of his words sank in. "You're not coming."

Slowly he shook his head. "I can't."

"You mean you won't."

"Don't you see?" He took her by the shoulders, as though to shake some sense into her. "We're backed into a corner. Unless we do something—I do something—we'll always be running."

"Then let's *run!*" She reached for him, her fingers clutching at his windbreaker. She wanted to scream at him, to tear away his cool mask of reason and get to the raw emotions beneath. They had to be there, buried deep in that logical brain of his. "We could go to Mexico," she said. "I know a place on the coast—in Baja. A little hotel near the beach. We could stay there a few months, wait until things are safer—"

"It'll never be safer."

"Yes, it will! They'll forget about us—"

"You're not thinking straight."

"I am. I'm thinking I want to stay alive."

"And that's exactly why I have to do this." He took her face in his hands, trapping it so she could look nowhere but at him. No longer was he the lover, the friend—his voice now held the cold, steady note of authority and she hated the sound of it. "I'm trying to keep you alive," he said. "With a future ahead of you. And the only way I can do that is to blow this thing wide open so the world knows about it. I owe it to you. And I owe it to Jerry."

She wanted to argue with him, to plead with him to go with her, but she knew it was useless. What he said was true. Running would only be a temporary solution, one that would give them a few sweet months of safety, but a temporary one just the same.

"I'm sorry, Cathy," he said softly. "I can't think of any other way—"

"—But to get rid of me," she finished for him.

He released her. She stepped back, and the sudden gulf between them left her aching. She couldn't bear to look at him, knowing that the pain she felt wouldn't be reflected in his eyes. "So how does it work?" she said dully. "Do I leave tonight? Will it be plane, train or automobile?"

"Ollie will drive you to the airport. I've asked him to buy you the ticket under his name—Mrs. Wozniak. He'll have to be the one to see you off. We thought it'd be safer if I didn't come along to the airport."

"Of course."

"That'll get you to Mexico. Ollie'll give you enough cash to keep you going for a while. Enough to get you anywhere you want to go from there. Baja. Acapulco. Or just hang around with Jack if you think that's best."

"Jack." She turned away, unwilling to show her tears. "Right."

"Cathy." She felt his hand on her shoulder, as though he wanted to turn her toward him, to pull her back one last time into his arms. She refused to move.

Footsteps approached. They both glanced around to see Ollie, standing a few feet away. "Ready to go?" he asked.

There was a long silence. Then Victor nodded. "She's ready."

"Uh, look," Ollie mumbled, suddenly aware that he'd stepped

in at a bad time. "My car's over by the boathouse. If you want, I can, uh, wait for you there...."

Cathy furiously dashed away her tears. "No," she said with sudden determination. "I'm coming."

Victor stood watching her, his gaze veiled by some cool, impenetrable mist.

"Goodbye, Victor," she said.

He didn't answer. He just kept looking at her through that terrible mist.

"If I—if I don't see you again..." She stopped, struggling to be just as brave, just as invulnerable. "Take care of yourself," she finished. Then she turned and followed Ollie down the path.

Through the car window, she glimpsed Victor, still standing on the lake path, his hands jammed in his pockets, his shoulders hunched against the wind. He didn't wave goodbye; he merely watched them drive away.

It was an image she'd carry with her forever, that last, fading view of the man she loved. The man who'd sent her away.

As Ollie turned the car onto the road, she sat stiff and silent, her fists balled in her lap, the pain in her throat so terrible she could scarcely breathe. Now he was behind them. She couldn't see him, but she knew he was still standing there, as unmoving as the oaks that surrounded him. *I love you,* she thought. *And I will never see you again.*

She turned to look out. He was a distant figure now, almost lost among the trees. In a gesture of farewell, she reached up and gently touched the window.

The glass was cold.

"I have to stop off at the lab," said Ollie, turning into the hospital parking lot. "I just remembered I left the checkbook in my desk. Can't get you a plane ticket without it."

Cathy nodded dully. She was still in a state of shock, still trying to accept the fact that she was now on her own. That Victor had sent her away.

Ollie pulled into a stall marked Reserved, Wozniak. "This'll only take a sec."

"Shall I come in with you?"

"You'd better wait in the car. I work with a very nosy bunch. They see me with a woman and they want to know everything. Not that there's ever anything to know." He climbed out and shut the door. "Be right back."

Cathy watched him stride away and vanish into a side entrance. She had to smile at the thought of Ollie Wozniak squiring around a woman—any woman. Unless it was someone with a Ph.D. who could sit through his scientific monologues.

A minute passed.

Outside, a bird screeched. Cathy glanced out at the trees lining the hospital driveway and spotted the jay, perched among the lower branches. Nothing else moved, not even the leaves.

She leaned back and closed her eyes.

Too little sleep, too much running, had taken its toll. Exhaustion settled over her, so profound she thought she would never again be able to move her limbs. *A beach,* she thought. *Warm sand. Waves washing at my feet...*

The jay's cry cut off in mid-screech. Only vaguely did Cathy register the sudden silence. Then, even through her half sleep, she sensed the shadowing of the window, like a cloud passing before the sun.

She opened her eyes. A face was staring at her through the glass.

Panic sent her lunging for the lock button. Before she could jam it down, the door was wrenched open. A badge was thrust up to her face.

"FBI!" the man barked. "Out of the car, please."

Slowly Cathy emerged, to stand weak-kneed against the door. *Ollie,* she thought, her gaze darting toward the hospital entrance. *Where are you?* If he appeared, she had to be ready to bolt, to flee across the parking lot and into the woods. She doubted the man with the badge would be able to keep up; his stubby legs and thick waist didn't go along with a star athlete.

But he must have a gun. If I bolt, would he shoot me in the back?

"Don't even think about it, Miss Weaver," the man said. He took her arm and gave her a nudge toward the hospital entrance. "Go on. Inside."

"But—"

"Dr. Wozniak's waiting for us in the lab."

Waiting didn't exactly describe Ollie's predicament. Bound and trussed would have been a better description. She found Ollie bent over double in his office, handcuffed to the foot of his desk, while three of his lab colleagues stood by gaping in amazement.

"Back to work, folks," said the agent as he herded the onlookers out of the office. "Just a routine matter." He shut the door and locked it. Then he turned to Cathy and Ollie. "I have to find Victor Holland," he said. "And I have to find him fast."

"Man," Ollie muttered into his chest. "This guy sounds like a broken record."

"Who are you?" demanded Cathy.

"The name's Sam Polowski. I work out of the San Francisco office." He pulled out his badge and slapped it on the desk. "Take a closer look if you want. It's official."

"Uh, excuse me?" called Ollie. "Could I maybe, possibly, get into a more comfortable position?"

Polowski ignored him. His attention was focused on Cathy. "I don't think I need to spell it out for you, Miss Weaver. Holland's in trouble."

"And you're one of his biggest problems," she retorted.

"That's where you're wrong." Polowski moved closer, his gaze unflinching, his voice absolutely steady. "I'm one of his hopes. Maybe his only hope."

"You're trying to kill him."

"Not me. Someone else, someone who's going to succeed. Unless I can stop it."

She shook her head. "I'm not stupid! I know about you. What you've been trying to—"

"Not me. The other guy." He reached for the telephone on the desk. "Here," he said, holding the receiver out to her. "Call Milo Lum. Ask him what happened at his house this morning. Maybe he'll convince you I'm on your side."

Cathy stared at the man, wondering what sort of game he was playing. Wondering why she was falling for it. *Because I want so much to believe him.*

"He's alone out there," said Polowski. "One man trying to buck the U.S. government. He's new to the game. Sooner or later he's going to slip, do something stupid. And that'll be it." He dialed the phone for her and again held out the receiver. "Go on. Talk to Lum."

She heard the phone ring three times, followed by Milo's answer "Hello? Hello?"

Slowly she took the receiver. "Milo?"

"Is that you? Cathy? God, I was hoping you'd call—"

"Listen, Milo. I need to ask you something. It's about a man named Polowski."

"I've met him."

"You *have?*" She looked up and saw Polowski nodding.

"Lucky for me," said Milo. "The guy's got the charm of an old shoe but he saved my life. I don't know what Gersh was talking about. Is Gersh around? I have to—"

"Thanks, Milo," she murmured. "Thanks a lot." She hung up.

Polowski was still looking at her.

"Okay," she said. "I want your side of it. From the beginning."

"You gonna help me out?"

"I haven't decided." She crossed her arms. "Convince me."

Polowski nodded. "That's just what I plan to do."

CHAPTER TEN

For Victor it was a long and miserable afternoon. After leaving the lake, he wandered around the campus for a while, ending up at last in the main quad. There in the courtyard, standing among the buildings of sandstone and red tile, Victor struggled to keep his mind on the business at hand: exposing Viratek. But his thoughts kept shifting back to Cathy, to that look she'd given him, full of hurt abandonment.

As if I'd betrayed her.

If she could just see the good sense in his actions. He was a scientist, a man whose life and work was ruled by logic. Sending her away was the logical thing to do. The authorities were closing in, the noose was growing ever tighter. He could accept the danger to himself. After all, he'd chosen to take on Jerry's battle, to see this through to the end.

What he hadn't chosen was to put Cathy in danger. *Now she's out of the mess and on her way to a safe place. One less thing to worry about. Time to put her out of my mind.*

As if I could.

He stared up at one of the courtyard's Romanesque arches and reminded himself, once again, of the wisdom of his actions. Still, the uneasiness remained. Where was she? Was she safe? She'd been gone only an hour and he missed her already.

He gave a shrug, as though by that gesture, he could somehow cast off the fears. Still they remained, constant and gnawing. He found a place under the eaves and huddled on the steps to wait for Ollie's return.

At dusk he was still waiting. By the last feeble light of day, he paced the stone courtyard. He counted and recounted the number of hours it should've taken Ollie to drive to San José Airport and return. He added in traffic time, red lights, ticket-counter delays.

Surely three hours was enough. Cathy had to be on a plane by now, jetting for warmer climes.

Where was Ollie?

At the sound of the first footstep, he spun around. For a moment he couldn't believe what he was seeing, couldn't understand how she could be standing there, silhouetted beneath the sandstone archway. "Cathy?" he said in amazement.

She stepped out, into the courtyard. "Victor," she said softly. She started toward him, slowly at first, and then, in a jubilant burst of flight, ran toward his waiting arms. He swept her up, swung her around, kissed her hair, her face. He didn't understand why she was here but he rejoiced that she was.

"I don't know if I've done the right thing," she murmured. "I hope to God I have."

"Why did you come back?"

"I wasn't sure—I'm still not sure—"

"Cathy, what are you doing here?"

"You can't fight this alone! And he can help you—"

"Who can?"

From out of the twilight came another voice, gruff and startling. "*I* can."

At once Victor stiffened. His gaze shifted back to the arch behind Cathy. A man emerged and walked slowly toward him. Not a tall man, he had the sort of body that, in a weight-loss ad, would've been labeled Before. He came up to Victor and planted himself squarely on the courtyard stones.

"Hello, Holland," he said. "I'm glad we've finally met. The name is Sam Polowski."

Victor turned and looked in disbelief at Cathy. "Why?" he asked in quiet fury. "Just tell me that. *Why?*"

She reacted as though he'd delivered a physical blow. Tentatively she reached for his arm; he pulled away from her at once.

"He wants to help," she said, her voice wretched with pain. "*Listen* to him!"

"I'm not sure there's any point to listening. Not now." He felt his whole body go slack in defeat. He didn't understand it, would never understand it. It was over, the running, the scraping along on fear and hope. All because Cathy had betrayed him. He turned matter-of-factly to Polowski. "I take it I'm under arrest," he said.

"Hardly," said Polowski, nodding toward the archway. "Seeing as he's got my gun."

"What?"

"Hey, Gersh! Over here!" Ollie yelled. "See, I got him covered!"

Polowski winced. "Geez, do ya have to wave the damn thing?"

"Sorry," said Ollie.

"Now, does that convince you, Holland?" asked Polowski. "You think I'd hand my piece over to an idiot like him if I didn't want to talk to you?"

"He's telling the truth," insisted Cathy. "He gave the gun to Ollie. He was willing to take the risk, just to meet you face-to-face."

"Bad move, Polowski," said Victor bitterly. "I'm wanted for murder, remember? Industrial espionage? How do you know I won't just blow you away?"

"'Cause I know you're innocent."

"That makes a difference, does it?"

"It does to me."

"Why?"

"You're caught up in something big, Holland. Something that's going to eat you up alive. Something that's got my supervisor doing backflips to keep me off the case. I don't like being pulled off a case. It hurts my delicate ego."

The two men gazed at each other through the gathering darkness, each sizing up the other.

At last Victor nodded. He looked at Cathy, a quiet plea for forgiveness, for not believing in her. When at last she came into his arms, he felt the world had suddenly gone right again.

He heard a deliberate clearing of a throat. Turning, he saw Polowski hold out his hand. Victor took it in a handshake that could very well be his doom—or his salvation.

"You've led me on a long, hard chase," said Polowski. "I think it's time we worked together."

* * *

"Basically," said Ollie, "What we have here is just your simple, everyday mission impossible."

They were assembled in Polowski's hotel room, a five-member team that Milo had just dubbed the "Older, Crazier Out of Tuners," or Old COOTS for short. On the table in the center of the room lay potato chips, beer and the photos detailing Viratek's security system. There was also a map of the Viratek compound, forty acres of buildings and wooded grounds, all of it surrounded by an electrified fence. They had been studying the photos for an hour now, and the job that lay before them looked hopeless.

"No easy way in," said Ollie, shaking his head. "Even if those keypad codes are still valid, you're faced with the human element of recognition. Two guards, two positions. No way they're gonna let you pass."

"There has to be a way," said Polowski. "Come on, Holland. You're the egghead. Use that creative brain of yours."

Cathy looked at Victor. While the others had tossed ideas back and forth, he had said very little. *And he's the one with the most at stake—his life,* she thought. It took incredible courage—or foolhardiness—even to consider such a desperate move. Yet here he was, calmly scanning the map as though he were planning nothing more dangerous than a Sunday drive.

He must have felt her gaze, for he slung his arm around her and tugged her close. Now that they were reunited, she savored every moment they shared, committed to memory every look, every caress. Soon he could be wrenched away from her. Even now he was making plans to enter what looked like a death trap.

He pressed a kiss to the top of her head. Then, reluctantly, he turned his attention back to the map.

"The electronics I'm not worried about," he said. "It's the human element. The guards."

Milo cocked his head toward Polowski. "I still say ol' J. Edgar here should get a warrant and raid the place."

"Right," snorted Polowski. "By the time that order gets through the judge and Dafoe and your Aunt Minnie's cousin, Viratek'll have that lab turned into a baby-milk factory. No, we need to get in on our own. Without anyone getting word of it." He looked at Ollie. "And you're sure this is the only evidence we'll need?"

Ollie nodded. "One vial should do it. Then we take it to a reputable lab, have them confirm it's smallpox, and your case is airtight."

"They'll have no way around it?"

"None. The virus is officially extinct. Any company caught playing with a live sample is, ipso facto, dead meat."

"I like that," said Polowski. "That ipso facto stuff. No fancy Viratek attorney can argue that one away."

"But first you gotta get hold of a vial," said Ollie. "And from where I'm standing, it looks impossible. Unless we're willing to try armed robbery."

For one frightening moment, Polowski actually seemed to give that thought serious consideration. "Naw," he conceded. "Wouldn't go over well in court."

"Besides which," said Ollie, "I refuse to shoot another human being. It's against my principles."

"Mine, too," said Milo.

"But theft," said Ollie, "that's acceptable."

Polowski looked at Victor. "A group with high moral standards."

Victor grinned. "Holdovers from the sixties."

"Sounds like we're back to the first option," said Cathy. "We have to steal the virus." She focused on the map of the compound, noting the electrified fence that circled the entire complex. The main road led straight to the front gate. Except for an unpaved fire road, labeled *not maintained,* no other approaches were apparent.

"All right," she said. "Assume you do get through the front gate. You still have to get past two locked doors, two separate guards and a laser grid. Come on."

"The doors are no problem," said Victor. "It's the two guards."

"Maybe a diversion?" suggested Milo. "How about we set a fire?"

"And bring in the town fire department?" said Victor. "Not a good idea. Besides, I've dealt with this night guard at the front gate. I know him. And he goes strictly by the book. Never leaves the booth. At the first hint of anything suspicious, he'll hit the alarm button."

"Maybe Milo could whip up a fake security pass," said Ollie.

"You know, the way he used to fix us up with those fake drivers' licenses."

"He falsified IDs?" said Polowski.

"Hey, I just changed the age to twenty-one!" protested Milo.

"Made great passports, too," said Ollie. "I had one from the kingdom of Booga Booga. It got me right past the customs official in Athens."

"Yeah?" Polowski looked impressed. "So what about it, Holland? Would it work?"

"Not a chance. The guard has a master list of top-security employees. If he doesn't know the face, he'll do a double check."

"But he does let some people through automatically?"

"Sure. The bigwigs. The ones he recognizes on—" Victor suddenly paused and turned to stare at Cathy "—on sight. Lord. It just might work."

Cathy took one look at his face and immediately read his mind. "No," she said. "It's not that easy! I need to see the subject! I need molds of his face. Detailed photos from every angle—"

"But you *could* do it. You do it all the time."

"On film it works! But this is face-to-face!"

"It's at night, through a car window. Or through a video camera. If you could just make me pass for one of the exec's—"

"What are you talking about?" demanded Polowski.

"Cathy's a makeup artist. You know, horror films, special effects."

"This is different!" Cathy said. The difference being it was Victor's life on the line. No, he couldn't ask her to do this. If anything went wrong, she would be responsible. Having his death on her conscience would be more than she could live with.

She shook her head, praying he'd read the deadly earnestness in her gaze. "There's too much at stake," she insisted. "It's not as simple as—as filming *Slimelords*!"

"You did *Slimelords*?" asked Milo. "Terrific flick!"

"Besides," said Cathy, "it's not that easy, copying a face. I have to cast a mold, to get the features just right. For that I need a model."

"You mean the real guy?" asked Polowski.

"Right. The real guy. And I hardly think you're going to get some Viratek executive to sit down and let me slap plaster all over his face.''

There was a long silence.

''That does present a problem,'' said Milo.

''Not necessarily.''

They all turned and looked at Ollie.

''What are you thinking?'' asked Victor.

''About this guy who works with me once in a while. Down in the lab...'' Ollie looked up, and the grin on his face was distinctly smug. ''He's a veterinarian.''

The events of the past few weeks had weighed heavily on Archibald Black, so heavily, in fact, that he found it difficult to carry on with those everyday tasks of life. Just driving to and from his office at Viratek was an ordeal. And then, to sit down at his desk and face his secretary and pretend that nothing, absolutely nothing, was wrong—that was almost more than he could manage. He was a scientist, not an actor.

Not a criminal.

But that's what they would call him, if the experiments in C wing ever came to light. His instinct was to shut the lab down, to destroy the contents of those incubators. But Matthew Tyrone insisted the work continue. They were so close to completion. After all, Defense had underwritten the project, and Defense expected a product. This matter of Victor Holland was only a minor glitch, soon to be solved. The thing to do was carry on.

Easy for Tyrone to say, thought Black. *Tyrone had no conscience to bother him.*

These thoughts had plagued him all day. Now, as Black packed up his briefcase, he felt desperate to flee forever this teak-and-leather office, to take refuge in some safe and anonymous job. It was with a sigh of relief that he walked out the door.

It was dark when he pulled into his gravel driveway. The house, a saltbox of cedar and glass tucked among the trees, looked cold and empty and in need of a woman. Perhaps he should call his neighbor Muriel. She always seemed to appreciate an impromptu dinner together. Her snappy wit and green Jell-O salad almost made up for the fact she was 75. What a shame his generation didn't produce many Muriels.

He stepped out of his car and started up the path to the front door. Halfway there, he heard a soft *whht!* and almost simultaneously, a sharp pain stung his neck. Reflexively he slapped at it; something came away in his hands. In wonderment, he stared down at the dart, trying to understand where it had come from and how such a thing had managed to lodge in his neck. But he found he couldn't think straight. And then he found he was having trouble seeing, that the night had suddenly darkened to a dense blackness, that his legs were being sucked into some sort of quagmire. His briefcase slipped from his grasp and thudded to the ground.

I'm dying, he thought. And then, *Will anyone find me here?*

It was his last conscious thought before he collapsed onto the leaf-strewn path.

"Is he dead?"

Ollie bent forward and listened for Archibald Black's breathing. "He's definitely alive. But out cold." He looked up at Polowski and Victor. "Okay, let's move it. He'll be out for only an hour or so."

Victor grabbed the legs, Ollie and Polowski, the arms. Together they carried the unconscious man a few dozen yards through the woods, toward the clearing where the van was parked.

"You—you sure we got an hour?" gasped Polowski.

"Plus or minus," said Ollie. "The tranquilizer's designed for large animals, so the dose was only an estimate. And this guy's heavier than I expected." Ollie was panting now. "Hey, Polowski, he's slipping. Pull your weight, will ya?"

"I am! I think his right arm's heavier than his left."

The van's side door was already open for them. They rolled Black inside and slid the door closed. A bright light suddenly glared, but the unconscious man didn't even twitch.

Cathy knelt down at his side and critically examined the man's face.

"Can you do it?" asked Victor.

"Oh, I can do it," she said. "The question is, will you pass for him?" She glanced up and down the man's length, then back at

Victor. "Looks about your size and build. We'll have to darken your hair, give you a widow's peak. I think you'll pass." She turned and glanced at Milo, who was already poised with his camera. "Take your photos. A few shots from every angle. I need lots of hair detail."

As Milo's strobe flashed again and again, Cathy donned gloves and an apron. She pointed to a sheet. "Drape him for me," she directed. "Everything but his face. I don't want him to wake up with plaster all over his clothes."

"Assuming he wakes up at all," said Milo, frowning down at Black's inert form.

"Oh, he'll wake up," said Ollie. "Right where we found him. And if we do the job right, Mr. Archibald Black will never know what hit him."

It was the rain that awakened him. The cold droplets pelted his face and dribbled into his open mouth. Groaning, Black turned over and felt gravel bite into his shoulder. Even in his groggy state it occurred to him that this did not make sense. Slowly he took stock of all the things that were not as they should be: the rain falling from the ceiling, the gravel in his bed, the fact he was still wearing his shoes...

At last he managed to shake himself fully awake. He found to his puzzlement that he was sitting in his driveway, and that his briefcase was lying right beside him. By now the rain had swelled to a downpour—he had to get out of the storm. Half crawling, half walking, Black managed to make it up the porch steps and into the house.

An hour later, huddled in his kitchen, a cup of coffee in hand, he tried to piece together what had happened. He remembered parking his car. He'd taken out his briefcase and apparently had managed to make it halfway up the path. And then...what?

A vague ache worried its way into his awareness. He rubbed his neck. That's when he remembered something strange had happened, just before he blacked out. Something associated with that ache in his neck.

He went to a mirror and looked. There it was, a small puncture in the skin. An absurd thought popped into his head: *Vampires.*

Right. *Damn it, Archibald. You are a scientist. Come up with a rational explanation.*

He went to the laundry hamper and fished out his damp shirt. To his alarm he spotted a droplet of blood on the lapel. Then he saw what had caused it: a common, everyday tailor's pin. It was still lodged in the collar, no doubt left there by the dry cleaners. There was his rational explanation. He'd been pricked by a collar pin and the pain had sent him into a faint.

In disgust, he threw the shirt down. First thing in the morning, he was going to complain to the Tidy Girl cleaners and demand they do his suit for free.

Vampires, indeed.

"Even with bad lighting, you'll be lucky if you pass," said Cathy.

She stood back and gave Victor a long, critical look. Slowly she walked around him, eyeing the newly darkened hair, the resculpted face, the new eye color. It was as close as she could make it, but it wasn't good enough. It would never be good enough, not when Victor's life was at stake.

"I think he's the spitting image," said Polowski. "What's the problem now?"

"The problem is, I suddenly realize it's a crazy idea. I say we call it off."

"You've been working on him all afternoon. You got it right down to the damn freckles on his nose. What else can you improve on?"

"I don't know. I just don't feel *good* about this!"

There was a silence as she confronted the four men.

Ollie shook his head. "Women's intuition. That's a dangerous thing to disregard."

"Well, here's *my* intuition," said Polowski. "I think it'll work. And I think it's our best option. Our chance to nail the case."

Cathy turned to Victor. "You're the one who'll get hurt. It's your decision." What she really wanted to say was, *Please. Don't do it. Stay with me. Stay alive and safe and mine.* But she knew, looking into his eyes, that he'd already made his decision, and no matter how much she might wish for it, he would never really be hers.

"Cathy," he said. "It'll work. You have to believe that."

"The only thing I believe," she said, "is that you're going to get killed. And I don't want to be around to watch it."

Without another word, she turned and walked out the door.

Outside, in the parking lot of the Rockabye Motel, she stood in the darkness and hugged herself. She heard the door shut, and then his footsteps moved toward her across the blacktop.

"You don't have to stay," he said. "There's still that beach in Mexico. You could fly there tonight, be out of this mess."

"Do you want me to go?"

A pause, then, "Yes."

She shrugged, a poor attempt at nonchalance. "All right. I suppose it all makes perfect sense. I've done my part."

"You saved my life. At the very least, I owe you a measure of safety."

She turned to him. "Is that what weighs most on your mind, Victor? The fact that you *owe* me?"

"What weighs most on my mind is that you might get caught in the crossfire. I'm prepared to walk through those doors at Viratek. I'm prepared to do a lot of stupid things. But I'm not prepared to watch you get hurt. Does that make any sense?" He pulled her against him, into a place that felt infinitely warm and safe. "Cathy, Cathy. I'm not crazy. I don't want to die. But I don't see any way around this...."

She pressed her face against his chest, felt his heartbeat, so steady, so regular. She was afraid to think of that heart not beating, of those arms no longer alive to hold her. He was brave enough to go through with this crazy scheme; couldn't she somehow dredge up the same courage? She thought, *I've come this far with you. How could I dream of walking away? Now that I know I love you?*

The motel door opened, and light arced across the parking lot. "Gersh?" said Ollie. "It's getting late. If we want to go ahead, we'll have to leave now."

Victor was still looking at her. "Well?" he said. "Do you want Ollie to take you to the airport?"

"No." She squared her shoulders. "I'm coming with you."

"Are you sure that's what you want to do?"

"I'm never sure of anything these days. But on this I've decided.

I'll stick it out." She managed a smile. "Besides, you might need me on the set. In case your face falls off."

"I need you for a hell of a lot more than that."

"Gersh?"

Victor reached out for Cathy's hand. She let him take it. "We're coming," he said. "Both of us."

"I'm approaching the front gate. One guard in the booth. No one else around. Copy?"

"Loud and clear," said Polowski.

"Okay. Here I go. Wish me luck."

"We'll be tuned in. Break a leg." Polowski clicked off the microphone and glanced at the others. "Well, folks, he's on his way."

To what? Cathy wondered. She glanced around at the other faces. There were four of them huddled in the van. They'd parked a half mile from Viratek's front gate. Close enough to hear Victor's transmissions, but too far away to do him much good. With the microphone link, they could mark his progress.

They could also mark his death.

In silence, they waited for the first hurdle.

"Evening," said Victor, pulling up at the gate.

The guard peered out through the booth window. He was in his twenties, cap on straight, collar button fastened. This was Pete Zahn, Mr. By-the-book Extraordinaire. If anyone was to cut the operation short, it would be this man. Victor made a brave attempt at a smile and prayed his mask wouldn't crack. It seemed an eternity, that exchange of looks. Then, to Victor's relief, the man smiled back.

"Working late, Dr. Black?"

"Forgot something at the lab."

"Must be important, huh? To make a special trip at midnight."

"These government contracts. Gotta be done on time."

"Yeah." The guard waved him through. "Have a nice night."

Heart pounding, Victor pulled through the gate. Only when he'd rounded the curve into the empty parking lot did he manage a sigh of relief. "First base," he said into the microphone. "Come on, guys. Talk to me."

"We're here," came the response. It was Polowski.

"I'm heading into the building—can't be sure the signal will get through those walls. So if you don't hear from me—"

"We'll be listening."

"I've got a message for Cathy. Put her on."

There was a pause, then he heard, "I'm here, Victor."

"I just wanted to tell you this. I'm coming back. I promise. Copy?"

He wasn't sure if it was just the signal's waiver, but he thought he heard the beginning of tears in her reply. "I copy."

"I'm going in now. Don't leave without me."

It took Pete Zahn only a minute to look up Archibald Black's license plate number. He kept a Rolodex in the booth, though he seldom referred to it as he had a good memory for numbers. He knew every executive's license by heart. It was his own little mind game, a test of his cleverness. And the plate on Dr. Black's car just didn't seem right.

He found the file card. The auto matched up okay: a gray 1991 Lincoln sedan. And he was fairly certain that *was* Dr. Black sitting in the driver's seat. But the license number was all wrong.

He sat back and thought about it for a while, trying to come up with all the possible explanations. That Black was simply driving a different auto. That Black was playing a joke on him, testing him.

That it hadn't been Archibald Black, at all.

Pete reached for the telephone. The way to find out was to call Black's home. It was after midnight, but it had to be done. If Black didn't answer the phone, then that must be him in the Lincoln. And if he *did* answer, then something was terribly wrong and Black would want to know about it.

Two rings. That's all it took before a groggy voice answered, "Hello?"

"This is Pete Zahn, night man at Viratek. Is this—is this Dr. Black?"

"Yes."

"Dr. *Archibald* Black?"

"Look, it's late! What is it?"

"I don't know how to tell you this, Dr. Black, but..." Pete cleared his throat. "Your double just drove through the gate...."

* * *

"I'm through the front door. Heading up the hall to the security wing. In case anyone's listening." Victor didn't expect a reply, and he heard none. The building was a concrete monstrosity, designed to last forever. He doubted a radio signal would make it through these walls. Though he'd been on his own from the moment he'd entered the front gate, at least he'd had the comfort of knowing his friends were listening in on the progress. Now he was truly alone.

He moved at a casual pace to the locked door marked Authorized Personnel Only. A camera hung from the ceiling, its lens pointed straight at him. He pointedly ignored it and turned his attention to the security keypad mounted on the wall. The numbers Jerry had given him had gotten him through the front door; would the second combination get him through this one? His hands were sweating as he punched in the seven digits. He felt a dart of panic as a beep sounded and a message flashed on the screen: *Incorrect security code. Access denied.*

He could feel the sweat building up beneath the mask. Were the numbers wrong? Had he simply transposed two digits? He knew someone was watching him through the camera, wondering why he was taking so long. He took a deep breath and tried again. This time, he entered the digits slowly, deliberately. He braced himself for the warning beep. To his relief, it didn't go off.

Instead, a new message appeared. *Security code accepted. Please enter.*

He stepped through, into the next room.

Third hurdle, he thought in relief as the door closed behind him. Now for the home run.

Another camera, mounted in a corner, was pointed at him. Acutely conscious of that lens, he made his way across the room to the inner lab door. He turned the knob and a warning bell sounded.

Now what? he thought. Only then did he notice the red light glowing over the door, and the warning *Laser grid activated.* He needed a key to shut it off. He saw no other way to deactivate it, no way to get past it, into the room beyond.

It was time for desperate measures, time for a little chutzpah. He patted his pockets, then turned and faced the camera. "Hello?" He waved.

A voice answered over an intercom. "Is there a problem, Dr. Black?"

"Yes. I can't seem to find my keys. I must have left them at home...."

"I can cut the lasers from here."

"Thanks. Gee, I don't know how this happened."

"No problem."

At once the red warning light shut off. Cautiously Victor tried the door; it swung open. He gave the camera a goodbye wave and entered the last room.

Inside, to his relief, there were no cameras anywhere—at least, none that he could spot. A bit of breathing space, he thought. He moved into the lab and took a quick survey of his surroundings. What he saw was a mind-numbing display of space-age equipment—not just the expected centrifuges and microscopes, but instruments he'd never seen before, all of them brand-new and gleaming. He headed through the decontamination chamber, past the laminar flow unit, and went straight to the incubators. He opened the door.

Glass vials tinkled in their compartments. He took one out. Pink fluid glistened within. The label read Lot #341. Active.

This must be it, he thought. This was what Ollie had told him to look for. Here was the stuff of nightmares, the grim reaper distilled to sub-microscopic elements.

He removed two vials, fitted them into a specially padded cigarette case, and slipped it into his pocket. *Mission accomplished,* he thought in triumph as he headed back through the lab. All that lay before him was a casual stroll back to his car. Then the champagne...

He was halfway across the room when the alarm bell went off.

He froze, the harsh ring echoing in his ears.

"Dr. Black?" said the guard's voice over some hidden intercom. "Please don't leave. Stay right where you are."

Victor spun around wildly, trying to locate the speaker. "What's going on?"

"I've just been asked to detain you. If you'll hold on, I'll find out what—"

Victor didn't wait to hear the reason—he bolted for the door. Even as he reached it, he heard the whine of the lasers powering on, felt something slash his arm. He shoved through the first door, dashed across the anteroom and out the security door, into the hallway.

Everywhere, alarms were going off. The whole damn building had turned into an echo chamber of ringing bells. His gaze shot right, to the front entrance. No, not that way—the guard was stationed there.

He sprinted left, toward what he hoped was a fire exit. Somewhere behind him a voice yelled, "Halt!" He ignored it and kept running. At the end of the hall he slammed against the opening bar and found himself in a stairwell. No exit, only steps leading up and down. He wasn't about to be trapped like a rat in the basement. He headed up the stairs.

One flight into his climb, he heard the stairwell door slam open on the first floor. Again a voice commanded, "Halt or I'll shoot!"

A bluff, he thought.

A pistol shot exploded, echoing up the concrete stairwell.

Not a bluff. With new desperation, he pushed through the landing door, into the second-floor hallway. A line of closed doors stretched before him. Which one, which one? There was no time to think. He ducked into the third room and softly shut the door behind him.

In the semidarkness, he spotted the gleam of stainless steel and glass beakers. Another lab. Only this one had a large window, now shimmering with moonlight, looming over the far countertop.

From down the hall came the slam of a door being kicked open and the guard's shouted command: "Freeze!"

He was down to one last escape route. Victor grabbed a chair, raised it over his head, and flung it at the window. The glass shattered, raining moonlight-silvered shards into the darkness below. He scarcely bothered to look before he leapt. Bracing himself for the impact, he jumped from the window and landed in a tangle of shrubbery.

"Halt!" came a shout from above.

That was enough to jar Victor back to his feet. He sprinted off across a lawn, into the cover of trees. Glancing back, he saw no pursuing shadow. The guard wasn't about to risk his neck leaping out any window.

Got to make it out the gate...

Victor circled around the building, burrowing his way through bushes and trees to a stand of oaks. From there he could view the front gate, way off in the distance. What he saw made his heart sink.

Floodlights illuminated the entrance, glaring down on the four security cars blocking the driveway. Now a panel truck pulled up. The driver went around to the back and opened the doors. At his command two German shepherds leaped out and danced around, barking at his feet.

Victor backed away, stumbling deeper into the grove of oaks. *No way out,* he thought, glancing behind him at the fence, topped with coils of barbed wire. Already, the dogs' barking was moving closer. *Unless I can sprout wings and fly, I'm a dead man....*

CHAPTER ELEVEN

"Something's wrong!" Cathy cried as the first security car drove past.

Polowski touched her arm. "Easy. It could be just a routine patrol."

"No. Look!" Through the trees, they spotted three more cars, all roaring down the road at top speed toward Viratek.

Ollie muttered a surprisingly coarse oath and reached for the microphone.

"Wait!" Polowski grabbed his hand. "We can't risk a transmission. Let him contact us first."

"If he's in trouble—"

"Then he already knows it. Give him a chance to make it out on his own."

"What if he's trapped?" said Cathy. "Are we just going to sit here?"

"We don't have a choice. Not if they've blockaded the front gate—"

"We *do* have a choice!" said Cathy, scrambling forward into the driver's seat.

"What the hell are you doing?" demanded Polowski.

"Giving him a fighting chance. If we don't—"

They all fell instantly silent as a transmission suddenly hissed over the receiver. "Looks like I got myself in a bind, guys. Don't see a way out. You copy?"

Ollie snatched up the microphone. "Copy, Gersh. What's your situation?"

"Bad."

"Specify."

"Front gate's blocked and lit up like a football field. Big time alarms going off. They just brought in the dogs—"

"Can you get over the fence?"

"Negative. It's electrified. Low voltage, but more than I can handle. You guys better hit the road without me."

Polowski grabbed the microphone and barked, "Did you get the stuff?"

Cathy turned and snapped: "Forget that! Ask him where he is. *Ask him!*"

"Holland?" said Polowski. "Where are you?"

"At the northeast perimeter. Fence goes all the way around. Look, get moving. I'll manage—"

"Tell him to head for the east fence!" Cathy said. "Near the midpoint!"

"What?"

"Just tell him!"

"Go to the east fence," Polowski said into the microphone. "Midpoint."

"I copy."

Polowski looked up at Cathy in puzzlement. "What the hell are you thinking of?"

"This is a getaway car, right?" she muttered as she turned on the engine. "I say we put it to its intended use!" She threw the van into gear and spun it around, onto the road.

"Hey, you're going the wrong way!" yelled Milo.

"No, I'm not. There's a fire road, just off to the left somewhere. There it is." She made a sharp turn, onto what was little more than a dirt track. They bounced along, crashing through tree branches and shrubs, a ride so violently spine-shaking it was all they could do to hang on.

"How did you find this *wonderful* road?" Polowski managed to ask.

"It was on the map. I saw it when we were studying the plans for Viratek."

"Is this a scenic route? Or does it go somewhere?"

"The east fence. Used to be the construction entrance for the compound. I'm hoping it's still clear enough to get through...."

"And then what happens?"

Ollie sighed. "Don't ask."

Cathy steered around a bush that had sprung up in her path and

ran head-on into a sapling. Her passengers tumbled to the floor.
"Sorry," she muttered. Reversing gear, she spun them back on the
road. "It should be just ahead...."

A barrier of chain link suddenly loomed before them. Instantly
she cut the lights. Through the darkness, they could hear dogs barking, moving in. Where was he?

Then they saw him, flitting through the moonlight. He was running. Somewhere off to the side, a man shouted and gunfire spat
the ground.

"Brace yourselves!" yelled Cathy. She snapped on her seatbelt
and gripped the steering wheel. Then she stepped on the gas.

The van jerked forward like a bronco, barreled through the un-
derbrush, and slammed into the fence. The chain link sagged; electrical sparks hissed in the night. Cathy threw the gears into reverse,
backed up, and hit the gas again.

The fence toppled; barbed wire scraped across the windshield.

"We're through!" said Ollie. He yanked open the sliding door
and yelled: "Come on, Gersh! Come on!"

The running figure zigzagged across the grass. All around him,
gunfire exploded. He made a last flying leap across the coil of
barbed wire and stumbled.

"Come on, Gersh!"

Gunfire spattered the van.

Victor struggled back to his feet. They heard the rip of clothing,
then he was reaching up to them, being dragged inside, to safety.

The door slammed shut. Cathy backed up, wheeled the van
around and slammed on the gas pedal.

They leaped forward, bouncing through the bushes and across
ruts. Another round of bullets pinged the van. Cathy was oblivious
to it. She focused only on getting them back to the main road. The
sound of gunfire receded. At last the trees gave way to a familiar
band of blacktop. She turned left and gunned the engine, anxious
to put as many miles as possible between them and Viratek.

Off in the distance, a siren wailed.

"We got company!" said Polowski.

"Which way now?" Cathy cried. Viratek lay behind them; the
sirens were approaching from ahead.

"I don't know! Just get the hell out of here!"

As yet her view of the police cars was blocked by trees, but she could hear the sirens moving rapidly closer. *Will they let us pass? Or will they pull us over?*

Almost too late she spotted a clearing, off to the side. On sudden impulse she veered off the pavement, and the van bounced onto a stubbly field.

"Don't tell me," groaned Polowski. "Another fire road?"

"Shut up!" she snapped and steered straight for a clump of bushes. With a quick turn of the wheel, she circled behind the shrubbery and cut her lights.

It was just in time. Seconds later, two patrol cars, lights flashing, sped right past the concealing bushes. She sat frozen, listening as the sirens faded in the distance. Then, in the darkness, she heard Milo say softly, "Her name is Bond. Jane Bond."

Half laughing, half crying, Cathy turned as Victor scrambled beside her, onto the front seat. At once she was in his arms, her tears wetting his shirt, her sobs muffled in the depths of his embrace. He kissed her damp cheeks, her mouth. The touch of his lips stilled her tremors.

From the back came the sound of a throat being cleared. "Uh, Gersh?" inquired Ollie politely. "Don't you think we ought to get moving?"

Victor's mouth was still pressed against Cathy's. Reluctantly he broke contact but his gaze never left her face. "Sure," he murmured, just before he pulled her back for another kiss. "But would somebody else mind driving...?"

"Here's where things get dangerous," said Polowski. He was at the wheel now, as they headed south toward San Francisco. Cathy and Victor sat in front with Polowski; in the back of the van, Milo and Ollie lay curled up asleep like two exhausted puppies. From the radio came the soft strains of a country western song. The dials glowed a vivid green in the darkness.

"We've finally got the evidence," said Polowski. "All we need to hang 'em. They'll be desperate. Ready to try anything. From here on out, folks, it's going to be a game of cat and mouse."

As if it wasn't already, thought Cathy as she huddled closer to Victor. She longed for a chance to be alone with him. There had been no time for tearful reunions, no time for any confessions of love. They'd spent the last two hours on a harrowing journey down backroads, always avoiding the police. By now the break-in at Viratek would have been reported to the authorities. The state police would be on the lookout for a van with frontal damage.

Polowski was right. Things were only getting more dangerous.

"Soon as we hit the city," said Polowski, "we'll get those vials off to separate labs. Independent confirmation. That should wipe any doubts away. You know names we can trust, Holland?"

"Fellow alum back in New Haven. Runs the hospital lab. I can trust him."

"Yale? Great. That'll have clout."

"Ollie has a pal at UCSF. They'll take care of the second vial."

"And when those reports get back, I know a certain journalist who loves to have a little birdie chirp in his ear." Polowski gave the steering wheel a satisfied slap. "Viratek, you are dead meat."

"You enjoy this, don't you?" said Cathy.

"Workin' the right side of the law? I say it's good for the soul. It keeps your mind sharp and your feet on their toes. It helps you stay young."

"Or die young," said Cathy.

Polowski laughed. "Women. They just never understand the game."

"I don't understand it, at all."

"I bet Holland here does. He just had the adrenaline high of his life. Didn't you?"

Victor didn't answer. He was gazing ahead at the blacktop stretching before their headlights.

"Well, wasn't it a high?" asked Polowski. "To claw your way to hell and back again? To know you made it through on nothing much more than your wits?"

"No," said Victor quietly. "Because it's not over yet."

Polowski's grin faded. He turned his attention back to the road. "Almost," he said. "It's almost over."

They passed a sign: San Francisco: 12 Miles.

Four in the morning. The stars were mere pinpricks in a sky washed out by streetlights. In a North Beach doughnut shop, five weary souls had gathered around steaming coffee and cheese Danish. Only one other table was occupied, by a man with bloodshot eyes and shaking hands. The girl behind the counter sat with her nose buried in a paperback. Behind her, the coffee machine hissed out a fresh brew.

"To the Old Coots," said Milo, raising his cup. "Still the best ensemble around."

They all raised their cups. "To the Old Coots!"

"And to our newest and fairest member," said Milo. "The beautiful—the intrepid—"

"Oh, *please*," said Cathy.

Victor wrapped his arm around her shoulder. "Relax and be honored. Not everyone gets into this highly selective group."

"The only requirement," said Ollie, "is that you have to play a musical instrument badly."

"But I don't play anything."

"No problem." Ollie fished out a piece of waxed paper from the pile of Danishes and wrapped it around his pocket comb. "Kazoo."

"Fitting," said Milo. "Since that was Lily's instrument."

"Oh." She took the comb. Lily's instrument. It always came back to *her*, the ghost who would forever be there. Suddenly the air of celebration was gone, as though swept away by the cold wind of dawn. She glanced at Victor. He was looking out the window, at the garishly lit streets. *What are you thinking? Are you wishing she was here? That it wasn't me being presented this silly kazoo, but her?*

She put the comb to her lips and hummed an appropriately out-of-tune version of "Yankee Doodle." Everyone laughed and clapped, even Victor. But when the applause was over, she saw the sad and weary look in his eyes. Quietly she set the kazoo down on the table.

Outside, a delivery truck roared past. It was 5:00 a.m.; the city was stirring.

"Well, folks," said Polowski, slapping down a dollar tip. "We got a hotshot reporter to roust outta bed. And then you and I—" he looked at Victor "—have a few deliveries to make. When's United leave for New Haven?"

"At ten-fifteen," said Victor.

"Okay. I'll buy you the plane tickets. In the meantime, you see if you can't grow yourself a new mustache or something." Polowski glanced at Cathy. "You're going with him, right?"

"No," she said, looking at Victor.

She was hoping for a reaction, any reaction. What she saw was a look of relief. And, strangely, resignation.

He didn't try to change her mind. He simply asked, "Where will you be going?"

She shrugged. "Maybe I should stick to our original plan. You know, head south. Hang out with Jack for a while. What do you think?"

It was his chance to stop her. His chance to say, *No, I want you around. I won't let you leave, not now, not ever.* If he really loved her, that's exactly what he would say.

Her heart sank when he simply nodded and said, "I think it's a good idea."

She blinked back the tears before anyone could see them. With an indifferent smile she looked at Ollie. "So I guess I'll need a ride. When are you and Milo heading home?"

"Right now, I guess," said Ollie, looking bewildered. "Seeing as our job's pretty much done."

"Can I hitch along? I'll catch the bus at Palo Alto."

"No problem. In fact, you can sit in the honored front seat."

"Long as you don't let her behind the wheel," grumbled Milo. "I want a nice, quiet drive home if you don't mind."

Polowski rose to his feet. "Then we're all set. Everyone's got a place to go. Let's do it."

Outside, on a street rumbling with early-morning traffic, with their friends standing only a few yards away, Cathy and Victor said their goodbyes. It wasn't the place for sentimental farewells. Perhaps that was all for the best. At least she could leave with some trace of dignity. At least she could avoid hearing, from his lips, the brutal truth. She would simply walk away and hold on to the fantasy that he loved her. That in their brief time together she'd managed to work her way, just a little, into his heart.

"You'll be all right?" he asked.

"I'll be fine. And you?"

"I'll manage." He thrust his hands in his pockets and looked off at a bus idling near the corner. "I'll miss you," he said. "But I know it doesn't make sense for us to be together. Not under the circumstances."

I would stay with you, she thought. *Under any circumstances. If I only knew you wanted me.*

"Anyway," he said with a sigh, "I'll let you know when things are safe again. When you can come home."

"And then?"

"And then we'll take it from there," he said softly.

They kissed, a clumsy, polite kiss, all the more hurried because they knew their friends were watching. There was no passion here, only the cool, dry lips of a man saying goodbye. As they pulled apart, she saw his face blur away through the tears.

"Take care of yourself, Victor," she said. Then, shoulders squared, she turned and walked toward Ollie and Milo.

"Is that it?" asked Ollie.

"That's it." Brusquely she rubbed her hand across her eyes. "I'm ready to go."

"Tell me about Lily," she said.

The first light of dawn was already streaking the sky as they drove past the boxy row homes of Pacifica, past the cliffs where sea waves crashed and gulls swooped and dove.

Ollie, his gaze on the road, asked: "What do you want to know?"

"What kind of woman was she?"

"She was a nice person," said Ollie. "And brainy. Though she never went out of her way to impress people, she was probably the smartest one of all of us. Definitely brighter than Milo."

"And a lot better-looking than Ollie," piped a voice from the backseat.

"A real kind, real decent woman. When she and Gersh got married, I remember thinking, 'he's got himself a saint.'" He glanced at Cathy, suddenly noticing her silence. "Of course," he added quickly, "not every man *wants* a saint. I know I'd be happier with a lady who can be a little goofy." He flashed Cathy a grin. "Someone who might, say, crash a van through an electrified fence, just for kicks."

It was a sweet thing to say, a comment designed to lift her spirits. It couldn't take the edge off her pain.

She settled back and watched dawn lighten the sky. How she needed to get away! She thought about Mexico, about warm water and hot sand and the tang of fresh fish and lime. She would throw herself into working on that new film. Of course, Jack would be on the set, Jack with his latest sweetie pie in tow, but she could handle that now. Jack would never be able to hurt her again. She was beyond that now, beyond being hurt by any man.

The drive to Milo's house seemed endless.

When at last they pulled up in the driveway, the dawn had already blossomed into a bright, cold morning. Milo climbed out and stood blinking in the sunshine.

"So, guys," he said through the car window. "Guess here's where we go our separate ways." He looked at Cathy. "Mexico, right?"

She nodded. "Puerto Vallarta. What about you?"

"I'm gonna catch up with Ma in Florida. Maybe get a load of Disney World. Wanna come, Ollie?"

"Some other time. I'm going to go get some sleep."

"Don't know what you're missing. Well, it's been some adventure. I'm almost sorry it's over." Milo turned and headed up the walk to his house. On the front porch he waved and yelled, "See you around!" Then he vanished through the front door.

Ollie laughed. "Milo and his ma, together? Disney World'll never be the same." He reached for the ignition. "Next stop, the bus station. I've got just enough gas to get us there and—"

He didn't get a chance to turn the key.

A gun barrel was thrust in the open car window. It came to rest squarely against Ollie's temple.

"Get out, Dr. Wozniak," said a voice.

Ollie's reply came out in a bare croak. "What—what do you want?"

"Do it now." The click of the hammer being cocked was all the coaxing Ollie needed.

"Okay, okay! I'm getting out!" Ollie scrambled out and backed away, his hands raised in surrender.

Cathy, too, started to climb out, but the gunman snapped, "Not you! You stay inside."

"Look," said Ollie, "You can have the damn car! You don't need her—"

"But I do. Tell Mr. Holland I'll be in contact. Regarding Ms. Weaver's future." He went around and opened the passenger door. "You, into the driver's seat!" he commanded her.

"No. Please—"

The gun barrel dug into her neck. "Need I ask again?"

Trembling, she moved behind the wheel. Her knee brushed the car keys, still dangling from the ignition. The man slid in beside her. Though the gun barrel was still thrust against her neck, it was the man's eyes she focused on. They were black, fathomless. If any spark of humanity lurked in those depths, she couldn't see it.

"Start the engine," he said.

"Where—where are we going?"

"For a drive. Somewhere scenic."

Her thoughts were racing, seeking some means of escape, but she came up with nothing. That gun was insurmountable.

She turned on the ignition.

"Hey!" yelled Ollie, grabbing at the door. "You can't do this!"

Cathy screamed, "Ollie, no!"

The gunman had already shifted his aim out the window.

"Let her go!" yelled Ollie. "Let her—"

The gun went off.

Ollie staggered backward, his face a mask of astonishment.

Cathy lunged at the gunman. Pure animal rage, fueled by the instinct to survive, sent her clawing first for his eyes. At the last split second he flinched away. Her nails scraped down his cheek, drawing blood. Before he could shift his aim, she grabbed his wrist, wrenching desperately for control of the gun. He held fast. Not with all her strength could she keep the gun at bay, keep the barrel from turning toward her.

It was the last image she registered: that black hole, slowly turning until it was pointed straight at her face.

Something lashed at her from the side. Pain exploded in her head, shattering the world into a thousand slivers of light.

They faded, one by one, into darkness.

CHAPTER TWELVE

"Victor's here," said Milo.

It seemed to take Ollie forever to register their presence. Victor fought the urge to shake him to consciousness, to drag the words out of his friend's throat. He was forced to wait, the silence broken only by the hiss of oxygen, the gurgle of the suction tube. At last Ollie stirred and squinted through pain-glazed eyes at the three men standing beside his bed. "Gersh. I didn't—couldn't—" He stopped, exhausted by the effort just to talk.

"Easy, Ollie," said Milo. "Take it slow."

"Tried to stop him. Had a gun..." Ollie paused, gathering the strength to continue.

Victor listened fearfully for the next terrible words to come out. He was still in a state of disbelief, still hoping that what Milo had told him was one giant mistake, that Cathy was, at this very moment, on a bus somewhere to safety. Only two hours ago he'd been ready to board a plane for New Haven. Then he'd been handed a message at the United gate. It was addressed to passenger Sam Polowski, the name on his ticket. It had consisted of only three words: *Call Milo immediately.*

Passenger "Sam Polowski" never did board the plane.

Two hours, he thought in anguish. *What have they done to her in those two long hours?*

"This man—what did he look like?" asked Polowski.

"Didn't see him very well. Dark hair. Face sort of...thin."

"Tall? Short?"

"Tall."

"He drove off in your car?"

Ollie nodded.

"What about Cathy?" Victor blurted out, his control shattered. "He—didn't hurt her? She's all right?"

There was a pause that, to Victor, seemed like an eternity in hell. Ollie's gaze settled mournfully on Victor. "I don't know."

It was the best Victor could hope for. *I don't know.* It left open the possibility that she was still alive.

Suddenly agitated, he began to pace the floor. "I know what he wants," he said. "I know what I have to give him—"

"You can't be serious," said Polowski. "That's our evidence! You can't just hand it over—"

"That's exactly what I'm going to do."

"You don't even know how to contact him!"

"He'll contact *me*." He spun around and looked at Milo. "He must've been watching your house all this time. Waiting for one of us to turn up. That's where he'll call."

"If he calls," said Polowski.

"He will." Victor touched his jacket pocket, where the two vials from Viratek still rested. "I have what he wants. He has what I want. I think we're both ready to make a trade."

The sun, glaring and relentless, was shining in her eyes. She tried to escape it, tried to close her lids tighter, to stop those rays from piercing through to her brain, but the light followed her.

"Wake up. *Wake up!*"

Icy water slapped her face. Cathy gasped awake, coughing, rivulets of water trickling from her hair. She struggled to make out the face hovering above her. At first all she saw was a dark oval against the blinding circle of light. Then the man moved away and she saw eyes like black agate, a slash of a mouth. A scream formed in her throat, to be instantly frozen by the cold barrel of a gun against her cheek.

"Not a sound," he said. "Got that?"

In silent terror she nodded.

"Good." The gun slid away from her cheek and was tucked under his jacket. "Sit up."

She obeyed. Instantly the room began to spin. She sat clutching her aching head, the fear temporarily overshadowed by waves of pain and nausea. The spell lasted for only a few moments. Then, as the nausea faded, she became aware of a second man in the room, a large, broad-shouldered man she'd never before seen. He sat off in a corner, saying nothing, but watching her every move. The room itself was small and windowless. She couldn't tell if it was day or night. The only furniture was a chair, a card table and the cot she was sitting on. The floor was a bare slab of concrete. *We're in a basement,* she thought. She heard no other sounds, either outside or in the building. Were they still in Palo Alto? Or were they a hundred miles away?

The man in the chair crossed his arms and smiled. Under different circumstances, she might have considered that smile a charming one. Now it struck her as frighteningly inhuman. "She seems awake enough," he said. "Why don't you proceed, Mr. Savitch?"

The man called Savitch loomed over her. "Where is he?"

"Who?" she said.

Her answer was met by a ringing slap to her cheek. She sprawled backwards on the cot.

"Try again," he said, dragging her back up to a sitting position. "Where is Victor Holland?"

"I don't know."

"You were with him."

"We—we split up."

"Why?"

She touched her mouth. The sight of blood on her fingers shocked her temporarily into silence.

"Why?"

"He—" She bowed her head. Softly she said, "He didn't want me around."

Savitch let out a snort. "Got tired of you pretty quick, did he?"

"Yes," she whispered. "I guess he did."

"I don't know why."

She shuddered as the man ran his finger down her cheek, her throat. He stopped at the top button of her blouse. *No,* she thought. *Not that.*

To her relief, the man in the chair suddenly cut in. "This is getting us nowhere."

Savitch turned to the other man. "You have another sug-gestion, Mr. Tyrone?"

"Yes. Let's try using her in a different way." Fearfully Cathy watched as Tyrone moved to the card table and opened a satchel.

"Since we can't go to him," he said, "we'll have Holland come to us." He turned and smiled at her. "With your help, of course."

She stared at the cellular telephone he was holding. "I told you. I don't know where he is."

"I'm sure one of his friends will track him down."

"He's not stupid. He wouldn't come for me—"

"You're right. He's not stupid." Tyrone began to punch in a phone number. "But he's a man of conscience. And that's a flaw that's every bit as fatal." He paused, then said into the telephone, "Hello? Mr. Milo Lum? I want you to pass this message to Victor Holland for me. Tell him I have something of his. Something that won't be around much longer..."

"It's him!" hissed Milo. "He wants to make a deal."

Victor shot to his feet. "Let me talk to him—"

"Wait!" Polowski grabbed his arm. "We have to take this slow. Think about what we're—"

Victor pulled his arm free and snatched the receiver from Milo. "This is Holland," he barked into the phone. "Where is she?"

The voice on the other end paused, a silence designed to emphasize just who held the upper hand. "She's with me. She's alive."

"How do I know that?"

"You'll have to take my word for it."

"Word, hell! I want proof!"

Again there was a silence. Then, through the crackle of the line, came another voice, so tremulous, so afraid, it almost broke his heart. "Victor, it's me."

"Cathy?" He almost shouted with relief. "Cathy, are you all right?"

"I'm...fine."

"Where are you?"

"I don't know—I think—" She stopped. The silence was agonizing. "I can't be sure."

"He hasn't hurt you?"

A pause. "No."

She's not telling me the truth, he thought. *He's done something to her...*

"Cathy, I promise. You'll be all right. I swear to you I'll—"

"Let's talk business." The man was back on the line.

Victor gripped the receiver in fury. "If you hurt her, if you just touch her, I swear I'll—"

"You're hardly in a position to bargain."

Victor felt a hand grasp his arm. He turned and met Polowski's gaze. *Keep your head* was the message he saw. *Go along with him. Make a bargain. It's the only way to buy time.*

Nodding, Victor fought to regain control. When he spoke again, his voice was calm. "Okay. You want the vials, they're yours."

"Not good enough."

"Then I'll throw myself into the bargain. A trade. Is that acceptable?"

"Acceptable. You and the vials in exchange for her life."

An anguished cry of *"No!"* pierced the dialogue. It was Cathy, somewhere in the background, shouting, "Don't, Victor! They're going to—"

Through the receiver, Victor heard the thud of a blow, followed by soft moans of pain. All his control shattered. He was screaming now, cursing, begging, anything to make the man stop hurting her. The words ran together, making no sense. He couldn't see straight, couldn't think straight.

Again, Polowski took his arm, gave it a shake. Victor, breathing hard, stared at him through a gaze blurred by tears. Polowski's eyes advised: *Make the deal. Go on.*

Victor swallowed and closed his eyes. *Give me strength,* he thought. He managed to ask, "When do we make the exchange?"

"Tonight. At 2:00 a.m."

"Where?"

"East Palo Alto. The old Saracen Theater."

"But it's closed. It's been closed for—"

"It'll be open. Just you, Holland. I spot anyone else and the first bullet has her name on it. Clear?"

"I want a guarantee! I want to know she'll be—"

He was answered by silence. And then, seconds later, he heard a dial tone.

Slowly he hung up.

"Well? What's the deal?" demanded Polowski.

"At 2:00 a.m. Saracen Theater."

"Half an hour. That barely gives us time to set up a—"

"I'm going alone."

Milo and Polowski stared at him. "Like hell," said Polowski.

Victor grabbed his jacket from out of the closet. He gave the pocket a quick pat; the cigarette case was right where he'd left it. He turned and reached for the door.

"But Gersh!" said Milo. "He's gonna kill you!"

Victor paused in the doorway. "Probably," he said softly. "But it's Cathy's only chance. And it's a chance I have to take."

"He won't come," said Cathy.

"Shut up," Matt Tyrone snapped and shoved her forward.

As they moved down the glass-strewn alley behind the Saracen Theater, Cathy frantically searched her mind for some way to sabotage this fatal meeting. It *would* be fatal, not just for Victor, but for her, as well. The two men now escorting her through the darkness had no intention of letting her live. The best she could hope for was that Victor would survive. She had to do what she could to better his chances.

"He's already got his evidence," she said. "You think he'd give that up just for me?"

Tyrone glanced at Savitch. "What if she's right?"

"Holland's coming," said Savitch. "I know how he thinks. He's not going to leave the little woman behind." Savitch gave Cathy's cheek a deceptively gentle caress. "Not when he knows exactly what we'll do to her."

Cathy flinched away, repelled by his touch. *What if he really doesn't come?* she thought. *What if he does the sensible thing and leaves me to die?*

She wouldn't blame him.

Tyrone gave her a push up the steps and into the building. "Inside. Move."

"I can't see," she protested, feeling her way along a pitch-black passage. She stumbled over boxes, brushed past what felt like heavy drapes. "It's too dark—"

"Then let there be light," said a new voice.

The lights suddenly sprang on, so bright she was temporarily blinded. She raised her hand to shield her eyes. Through the glare she could make out a third man, looming before her. Beyond him, the floor seemed to drop away into a vast blackness.

They were standing on a theater stage. It was obvious no performer had trod these boards in years. Ragged curtains hung like cobwebs from the rafters. Panels of an old set, the ivy-hung battlements of a medieval castle, still leaned at a crazy tilt against the back wall, framed by a pair of mops.

Tyrone said, "Any problems, Dafoe?"

"None," said the new man. "I've reconned the building. One door at the front, one backstage. The emergency side doors are padlocked. If we block both exits, he's trapped."

"I see the FBI deserves its fine reputation."

Dafoe grinned and dipped his head. "I knew the Cowboy would want the very best."

"Okay, Ms. Weaver." Tyrone shoved Cathy forward, toward a chair placed directly under the spotlight. "Let's put you right where he can see you. Center stage."

It was Savitch who tied her to the chair. He knew exactly what he was doing. She had no hope of working her hands free from such tight, professional knots.

He stepped back, satisfied with his job. "She's not going anywhere," he said. Then, as an afterthought, he ripped off a strip of cloth tape and slapped it over her mouth. "So we don't have any surprises," he said.

Tyrone glanced at his watch. "Zero minus fifteen. Positions, gentlemen."

The three men slipped away into the shadows, leaving Cathy alone on the empty stage. The spotlight beating down on her face was hot as the midday sun. Already she could feel beads of sweat forming on her forehead. Though she couldn't see them, by their voices she could guess the positions of the three men. Tyrone was close by. Savitch was at the back of the theater, near the building's front entrance. And the man named Dafoe had stationed himself somewhere above, in one of the box seats. Three different lines of fire. No route of escape.

Victor, don't be a fool, she thought. *Stay away...*

And if he doesn't come? She couldn't bear to consider that possibility, either, for it meant he was abandoning her. It meant he didn't care enough even to make the effort to save her.

She closed her eyes against the spotlight, against the tears. *I love you. I could take anything, even this, if I only knew you loved me.*

Her hands were numb from the ropes. She tried to wriggle the bonds looser, but only succeeded in rubbing her wrists raw. She fought to remain calm, but with every minute that passed, her heart seemed to pound harder. A drop of sweat trickled down her temple.

Somewhere in the shadows ahead, a door squealed open and closed. Footsteps approached, their pace slow and deliberate. She strained to see against the spotlight's glare, but could make out only the hint of shadow moving through shadow.

The stage floorboards creaked behind her as Tyrone strolled out from the wings. "Stop right where you are, Mr. Holland," he said.

CHAPTER THIRTEEN

Another spotlight suddenly sprang on, catching Victor in its glare. He stood halfway up the aisle, a lone figure trapped in a circle of brilliance.

You came for me! she thought. *I knew, somehow I knew, that you would....*

If only she could shout to him, warn him about the other two men. But the tape had been applied so tightly that the only sound she could produce was a whimper.

"Let her go," said Victor.

"You have something we want first."

"I said, *let her go!*"

"You're hardly in a position to bargain." Tyrone strolled out of the wings, onto the stage. Cathy flinched as the icy barrel of a gun pressed against her temple. "Let's see it, Holland," said Tyrone.

"Untie her first."

"I could shoot you both and be done with it."

"Is this what it's come to?" yelled Victor. "Federal dollars for the murder of civilians?"

"It's all a matter of cost and benefit. A few civilians may have to die now. But if this country goes to war, think of all the millions of Americans who'll be saved!"

"I'm thinking of the Americans you've already killed."

"Necessary deaths. But you don't understand that. You've never seen a fellow soldier die, have you, Holland? You don't know what a helpless feeling it is, to watch good boys from good American towns get cut to pieces. With this weapon, they won't have to. It'll be the enemy dying, not us."

"Who gave you the authority?"

"I gave myself the authority."

"And who the hell are *you?*"

"A patriot, Mr. Holland! I do the jobs no one else in the Administration'll touch. Someone says, 'Too bad our weapons don't have a higher kill ratio.' That's my cue to get one developed. They don't even have to ask me. They can claim total ignorance."

"So you're the fall guy."

Tyrone shrugged. "It's part of being a good soldier. The willingness to fall on one's sword. But I'm not ready to do that yet."

Cathy tensed as Tyrone clicked back the gun hammer. The barrel was still poised against her skull.

"As you can see," said Tyrone, "the cards aren't exactly stacked in her favor."

"On the other hand," Victor said calmly, "how do you know I've brought the vials? What if they're stashed somewhere, a publicity time bomb ticking away? Kill her now and you'll never find out."

Deadlock. Tyrone lowered the pistol. He and Victor faced each other for a moment. Then Tyrone reached into his pocket, and Cathy heard the click of a switchblade. "This round goes to you, Holland," he said as he cut the bindings. The sudden rush of circulation back into Cathy's hands was almost painful. Tyrone ripped the tape off her mouth and yanked her out of the chair. "She's all yours!"

Cathy scrambled off the stage. On unsteady legs, she moved up the aisle, toward the circle of the spotlight, toward Victor. He pulled her into his arms. Only by the thud of his racing heart did she know how close he was to panic.

"Your turn, Holland," called Tyrone.

"Go," Victor whispered to her. "Get out of here."

"Victor, he has two other men—"

"Let's have it!" yelled Tyrone.

Victor hesitated. Then he reached into his jacket and pulled out a cigarette case. "They'll be watching me," he whispered. "You move for the door. Go on. *Do it.*"

She stood paralyzed by indecision. She couldn't leave him to die. And she knew the other two gunmen were somewhere in the darkness, watching their every move.

"She stays where she is!" said Tyrone. "Come on, Holland. The vials!"

Victor took a step further, then another.

"No further!" commanded Tyrone.

Victor halted. "You want it, don't you?"

"Put it down on the floor."

Slowly Victor set the cigarette case down by his feet.

"Now slide it to me."

Victor gave the case a shove. It skimmed down the aisle and came to a rest in the orchestra pit.

Tyrone dropped from the stage.

Victor began to back away. Taking Cathy's hand, he edged her slowly up the aisle, toward the exit.

As if on cue, the click of pistol hammers being snapped back echoed through the theater. Reflexively, Victor spun around, trying to sight the other gunmen. It was impossible to see anything clearly against the glare of the spotlight.

"You're not leaving yet," said Tyrone, reaching down for the case. Gingerly he removed the lid. In silence he stared at the contents.

This is it, thought Cathy. *He has no reason to keep us alive, now that he has what he wants....*

Tyrone's head shot up. "Double cross," he said. Then, in a roar, *"Double cross! Kill them!"*

His voice was still reverberating through the far reaches of the theater when, all at once, the lights went out. Blackness fell, so impenetrable that Cathy had to reach out to get her bearings.

That's when Victor pulled her sideways, down a row of theater seats.

"Stop them!" screamed Tyrone in the darkness.

Gunfire seemed to erupt from everywhere at once. As Cathy and Victor scurried on hands and knees along the floor, they could hear bullets thudding into the velvet-backed seats. The gunfire quickly became random, a blind spraying of the theater.

"Hold your fire!" yelled Tyrone. "Listen for them!"

The gunfire stopped. Cathy and Victor froze in the darkness, afraid to give away their position. Except for the pounding of her own pulse, Cathy heard absolute silence. *We're trapped. We make a single move and they'll know where we are.*

Scarcely daring to breathe, she reached back and pulled off her shoe. With a mighty heave, she threw it blindly across the theater.

The clatter of the shoe's landing instantly drew a new round of gunfire. In the din of ricocheting bullets, Victor and Cathy scurried along the remainder of the row and emerged in the side aisle.

Again, the gunfire stopped.

"No way out, Holland!" yelled Tyrone. "Both doors are covered! It's just a matter of time...."

Somewhere above, in a theater balcony, a light suddenly flickered on. It was Dafoe, holding aloft a cigarette lighter. As the flame leapt brightly, casting its terrible light against the shadows, Victor shoved Cathy to the floor behind a seat.

"I know they're here!" shouted Tyrone. "See 'em, Dafoe?"

As Dafoe moved the flame, the shadows shifted, revealing new forms, new secrets. "I'll spot 'em any second. Wait. I think I see—"

Dafoe suddenly jerked sideways as a shot rang out. The flame's light danced crazily on his face as he wobbled for a moment on the edge of the balcony. He reached out for the railing, but the rotten wood gave way under his weight. He pitched forward, his body tumbling into a row of seats.

"Dafoe!" screamed Tyrone. "Who the hell—"

A tongue of flame suddenly slithered up from the floor. Dafoe's lighter had set fire to the drapes! The flames spread quickly, dancing their way along the heavy velvet fabric, toward the rafters. As the first flames touched wood, the fire whooshed into a roar.

By the light of the inferno, all was revealed: Victor and Cathy, cowering in the aisle. Savitch, standing near the entrance, semi-automatic at the ready. And onstage, Tyrone, his expression demonic in the fire's glow.

"They're yours, Savitch!" ordered Tyrone.

Savitch aimed. This time there was no place for them to hide, no shadows to scurry off to. Cathy felt Victor's arm encircle her in a last protective embrace.

The gun's explosion made them both flinch. Another shot; still she felt no pain. She glanced at Victor. He was staring at her, as though unable to believe they were both alive.

They looked up to see Savitch, his shirt stained in a spreading abstract of blood, drop to his knees.

"Now's your chance!" yelled a voice. *"Move, Holland!"*

They whirled around to see a familiar figure silhouetted against the flames. Somehow, Sam Polowski had magically appeared from behind the drapes. Now he pivoted, pistol clutched in both hands, and aimed at Tyrone.

He never got a chance to squeeze off the shot.

Tyrone fired first. The bullet knocked Polowski backward and sent him sprawling against the smoldering velvet seats.

"Get out of here!" barked Victor, giving Cathy a push toward the exit. "I'm going back for him—"

"Victor, you can't!"

But he was on his way. Through the swirling smoke she could see him moving at a half crouch between rows of seats. *He needs help. And time's running out....*

Already the air was so hot it seemed to sear its way into her throat. Coughing, she dropped to the floor and took in a few breaths of relatively smoke-free air. She still had time to escape. All she had to do was crawl up the aisle and out the theater door. Every instinct told her to flee now, while she had the chance.

Instead, she turned from the exit and followed Victor into the maelstrom.

She could just make out his figure, scrambling before a solid wall of fire. She raised her arm to shield her face against the heat. Squinting into the smoke, she crawled forward, moving ever closer to the flames. "Victor!" she screamed.

She was answered only by the fire's roar, and by a sound even more ominous: the creak of wood. She glanced up. To her horror she saw that the rafters were sagging and on the verge of collapse.

Panicked, she scurried blindly forward, toward where she'd last spotted Victor. He was no longer visible. In his place was a whirlwind of smoke and flame. Had he already escaped? Was she alone, trapped in this blazing tinderbox?

Something slapped against her cheek. She stared, at first uncomprehending, at the human hand dangling before her face. Slowly she followed it up, along the bloodied arm, to the lifeless eyes of Dafoe. Her cry of terror seemed to funnel into the fiery cyclone.

"Cathy?"

She turned at the sound of Victor's shout. That's when she saw him, crouching in the aisle just a few feet away. He had Polowski under the arms and was struggling to drag him toward the exit. But the heat and smoke had taken its toll; he was on the verge of collapse.

"The roof's about to fall!" she screamed.

"Get out!"

"Not without you!" She scrambled forward and grabbed Polowski's feet. Together they hauled their burden up the aisle, across carpet that was already alight with sparks. Step by step they neared the top of the aisle. Only a few yards to go!

"I've got him," gasped Victor. "Go—open the door—"

She rose to a half crouch and turned.

Matt Tyrone stood before her.

"Victor!" she sobbed.

Victor, his face a mask of soot and sweat, turned to meet Tyrone's gaze. Neither man said a word. They both knew the game had been played out. Now the time had come to finish it.

Tyrone raised his gun.

Just as he did, they heard the loud crack of splintering wood. Tyrone glanced up as one of the rafters sagged, spilling a shower of burning tinder.

That brief distraction was all the time Cathy needed. In an act of sheer desperation she lunged at Tyrone's legs, knocking him backward. The gun flew from his grasp and slid off beneath a row of seats.

At once Tyrone was back on his feet. He aimed a savage kick at her. The blow hit her in the ribs, an impact so agonizing she hadn't the breath to cry out. She simply sprawled in the aisle, stunned and utterly helpless to ward off any other blows.

Through the darkness gathering before her eyes, she saw two figures struggling. Victor and Tyrone. Framed against a sea of fire, they grappled for each other's throats. Tyrone threw a punch; Victor staggered back a few paces. Tyrone charged him like a bull. At the last instant Victor sidestepped him and Tyrone met only empty air. He stumbled and sprawled forward, onto the smoldering carpet. Enraged, he rose to his knees, ready to charge again.

The crack of collapsing timber made him glance skyward.

He was still staring up in astonishment as the beam crashed down on his head.

Cathy tried to cry out Victor's name but no sound escaped. The smoke had left her throat too parched and swollen. She struggled to her knees. Polowski was lying beside her, groaning. Flames were everywhere, shooting up from the floor, clambering up the last untouched drapes.

Then she saw him, stumbling toward her through that vision of hellfire. He grabbed her arm and shoved her toward the exit.

Somehow, they managed to tumble out the door, dragging Polowski behind them. Coughing, choking, they pulled him across the street to the far sidewalk. There they collapsed.

The night sky suddenly lit up as an explosion ripped through the theater. The roof collapsed, sending up a whoosh of flames so brilliant they seemed to reach to the very heavens. Victor threw his body over Cathy's as the windows in the building above shattered, raining splinters onto the sidewalk.

For a moment there was only the sound of the flames, crackling across the street. Then, somewhere in the distance, a siren wailed.

Polowski stirred and groaned.

"Sam!" Victor turned his attention to the wounded man. "How you doing, buddy?"

"Got...got one helluva stitch in my side...."

"You'll be fine." Victor flashed him a tense grin. "Listen! Hear those sirens? Help's on the way."

"Yeah." Polowski, eyes narrowed in pain, stared up at the flame-washed sky.

"Thanks, Sam," said Victor softly.

"Had to. You...too damn stupid to listen..."

"We got her back, didn't we?"

Polowski's gaze shifted to Cathy. "We—we did okay."

Victor rubbed a hand across his smudged and weary face. "But we're back to square one. I've lost the evidence—"

"Milo..."

"It's all in there." Victor stared across at the flames now engulfing the old theater.

"Milo has it," whispered Sam.

"What?"

"You weren't looking. Gave it to Milo."

Victor sat back in bewilderment. "You mean you *took* them? You took the vials?"

Polowski nodded.

"You—you stupid son of a—"

"Victor!" said Cathy.

"He stole my bargaining chip!"

"He saved our lives!"

Victor stared down at Polowski.

Polowski returned a pained grin. "Dame's got a head on her shoulders," he murmured. "Listen to her."

The sirens, which had risen to a scream, suddenly cut off. Men's shouts at once sliced through the hiss and roar of the flames. A burly fireman loped over from the truck and knelt beside Polowski.

"What've we got here?"

"Gunshot wound," said Victor. "And a wise-ass patient."

The fireman nodded. "No problem, sir. We can handle both."

By the time they'd loaded Polowski into an ambulance, the Saracen Theater had been reduced to little more than a dying bonfire. Victor and Cathy watched the taillights of the ambulance vanish, heard the fading wail of the siren, the hiss of water on the flames.

He turned to her. Without a word he pulled her into his arms and held her long and hard, two silent figures framed against a sea of smoldering flames and chaos. They were both so weary neither knew which was holding the other up. Yet even through her exhaustion, Cathy felt the magic of that moment. It was eerily beautiful, that last sputtering glow, the reflections dancing off the nearby buildings. Beautiful and frightening and final.

"You came for me," she murmured. "Oh, Victor, I was so afraid you wouldn't...."

"Cathy, you knew I would!"

"I *didn't* know. You had your evidence. You could have left me—"

"No, I couldn't." He buried a kiss in her singed hair. "Thank God I wasn't already on that plane. They'd have had you, and I'd have been two thousand miles away."

Footsteps crunched toward them across the glass-littered pavement. "Excuse me," a voice said. "Are you Victor Holland?"

They turned to see a man in a rumpled parka, a camera slung over his shoulder, watching them.

"Who are you?" asked Victor.

The man held out his hand. "Jay Wallace. *San Francisco Chronicle.* Sam Polowski called me, said there'd be some fireworks in case I wanted to check it out." He gazed at the last remains of the Saracen Theater and shook his head. "Looks like I got here a little too late."

"Wait. *Sam* called you? When?"

"Maybe two hours ago. If he wasn't my ex-brother-in-law, I'd a hung up on him. For days he's been dropping hints he had a story to spill. Never followed through, not once. I almost didn't come tonight. You know, it's a helluva long drive down here from the city."

"He told you about me?"

"He said you had a story to tell."

"Don't we all?"

"Some stories are better than others." The reporter glanced around, searching. "So where is Sam, anyway? Or didn't the Bozo show up?"

"That Bozo," said Victor, his voice tight with anger, "is a goddamn hero. Stick *that* in your article."

More footsteps approached. This time it was two police officers. Cathy felt Victor's muscles go taut as he turned to face them.

The senior officer spoke. "We've just been informed that a gunshot victim was taken to the ER. And that you were found on the scene."

Victor nodded. His look of tension suddenly gave way to one of overwhelming exhaustion. And resignation. He said, quietly, "I was present. And if you search that building, you'll find three more bodies."

"Three?" The two cops glanced at each other.

"Musta been some fireworks," muttered the reporter.

The senior officer said, "Maybe you'd better give us your name, sir."

"My name..." Victor looked at Cathy. She read the message in those weary eyes: *We've reached the end. I have to tell them. Now they'll take me away from you, and God knows when we'll see each other again....*

She felt his hand tighten around hers. She held on, knowing with every second that passed that he would soon be wrenched from her grasp.

His gaze still focused on her face, he said, "My name is Victor Holland."

"Holland... Victor Holland?" said the officer. "Isn't that..."

And still Victor was looking at her. Until they'd clapped on the handcuffs, until he'd been pulled away, toward a waiting squad car, his gaze was locked on her.

She was left anchorless, shivering among the dying embers.

"Ma'am, you'll have to come with us."

She looked up, dazed, at the policeman. "What?"

"Hey, she doesn't have to!" cut in Jay Wallace. "You haven't charged her with anything!"

"Shut up, Wallace."

"I've had the court beat. I know her rights!"

Quietly Cathy said, "It doesn't matter. I'll come with you, officer."

"Wait!" said Wallace. "I wanna talk to you first! I got just a few questions—"

"She can talk to you later," snapped the policeman, taking Cathy by the arm. "*After* she talks to us."

The policemen were polite, even kind. Perhaps it was her docile acceptance of the situation, perhaps they could sense she was operating on her last meager reserves of strength. She answered all their questions. She let them examine the rope burns on her wrists. She told them about Ollie and Sarah and the other Catherine Weavers. And the whole time, as she sat in that room in the Palo Alto police station, she kept hoping she'd catch a glimpse of Victor. She knew he had to be close by. Were they, at that very moment, asking him these same questions?

At dawn, they released her.

Jay Wallace was waiting outside near the front steps. "I have to talk to you," he said as she walked out.

"Please. Not now. I'm tired...."

"Just a few questions."

"I can't. I need to—to—" She stopped. And there, standing on that cold and empty street, she burst into tears. "I don't know what to do," she sobbed. "I don't know how to help him. How to reach him."

"You mean Holland? They've already taken him to San Francisco."

"What?" She raised her startled gaze to Wallace.

"An hour ago. The big boys from the Justice Department came down as an escort. I hear tell they're flying him straight to Washington. First-class treatment all the way."

She shook her head in bewilderment. "Then he's all right—he's not under arrest—"

"Hell, lady," said Wallace, laughing. "The man is now a genuine hero."

A hero. But she didn't care what they called him, as long as he was safe.

She took a deep breath of bitingly chill air. "Do you have a car, Mr. Wallace?" she asked.

"It's parked right around the corner."

"Then you can give me a ride."

"Where to?"

"To…" She paused, wondering where to go, where Victor would look for her. Of course. Milo's. "To a friend's house," she said. "I want to be there when Victor calls."

Wallace pointed the way to the car. "I hope it's a long drive," he said. "I got a lot of gaps to fill in before this story goes to press."

Victor didn't call.

For four days she sat waiting near the phone, expecting to hear his voice. For four days, Milo and his mother brought her tea and cookies, smiles and sympathy. On the fifth day, when she still hadn't heard from him, those terrible doubts began to haunt her. She remembered that day by the lake bed, when he'd tried to send her away with Ollie. She thought of all the words he could have said, but never had. True, he'd come back for her. He'd knowingly walked straight into a trap at the Saracen Theater. But wouldn't he have done that for any of his friends? That was the kind of man he was. She'd saved his life once. He remembered his debts, and he paid them back. It had to do with honor.

It might have nothing to do with love.

She stopped waiting by the phone. She returned to her flat in San Francisco, cleaned up the glass, had the windows replaced, the walls replastered. She took long walks and paid frequent visits to Ollie and Polowski in the hospital. Anything to stay away from that silent telephone.

She got a call from Jack. "We're shooting next week," he whined. "And the monster's in terrible shape. All this humidity! Its face keeps melting into green goo. Get down here and do something about it, will you?"

She told him she'd think about it.

A week later she decided. Work was what she needed. Green goo and cranky actors—it was better than waiting for a call that would never come.

She reserved a one-way flight from San José to Puerto Vallarta. Then she packed, throwing in her entire wardrobe. A long stay, that's what she planned, a long vacation.

But before she left, she would drive down to Palo Alto. She had promised to pay Sam Polowski one last visit.

CHPATER FOURTEEN

(AP) Washington.

Administration spokesman Richard Jungkuntz repeated today that neither the President nor any of his staff had any knowledge of biological weapons research being conducted at Viratek Industries in California. Viratek's Project Cerberus, which involved development of genetically altered viruses, was clearly in violation of international law. Recent evidence, gathered by reporter Jay Wallace of the *San Francisco Chronicle,* has revealed that the project received funds directly authorized by the late Matthew Tyrone, a senior aide to the Secretary of Defense.

In today's Justice Department hearings, delayed four hours because of heavy snowstorms, Viratek president Archibald Black testified for the first time, promising to reveal, to the best of his knowledge, the direct links between the Administration and Project Cerberus. Yesterday's testimony, by former Viratek employee Dr. Victor Holland, has already outlined a disturbing tale of deception, cover-ups and possibly murder.

The Attorney General's office continues to resist demands by Congressman Leo D. Fanelli that a special prosecutor be appointed...

Cathy put down the newspaper and smiled across the hospital solarium at her three friends. "Well, guys. Aren't you lucky to be here in sunny California and not freezing your you-know-what's off in Washington."

"Are you kidding?" groused Polowski. "I'd give anything to be in on those hearings right now. Instead of hooked up to all these—

these *doohickeys.*'' He gave his intravenous line a tug, clanging a bottle against the pole.

"Patience, Sam," said Milo. "You'll get to Washington."

"Ha! Holland's already told 'em the good stuff. By the time they get around to hearing my testimony, it'll be back-page news."

"I don't think so," said Cathy. "I think it'll be front-page news for a long time to come." She turned and looked out the window at the sunshine glistening on the grass. *A long time to come.* That's how long it would be before she'd see Victor again. If ever. Three weeks had already passed since she'd last laid eyes on him. Via Jay Wallace in Washington, she'd heard that it was like a shark-feeding whenever Victor appeared in public, mobs of reporters and federal attorneys and Justice Department officials. No one could get near him.

Not even me, she thought.

It had been a comfort, having these three new friends to talk to. Ollie had bounced back quickly and was discharged—or kicked out, as Milo put it—a mere eight days after being shot. Polowski had had a rougher time of it. Post-operative infections, plus a bad case of smoke inhalation, had prolonged his stay to the point that every day was another trial of frustration for him. He wanted out. He wanted back on the beat.

He wanted a real, honest-to-God cheeseburger and a cigarette.

One more week, the doctors said.

At least there's an end to his waiting in sight, Cathy thought. *I don't know when I'll see or hear from Victor again.*

The silence was to be expected, Polowski had told her. Sequestration of witnesses. Protective custody. The Justice Department wanted an airtight case, and for that it would keep its star witness incommunicado. For the rest of them, depositions had been sufficient. Cathy had given her testimony two weeks before. Afterward, they'd told her she was free to leave town any time she wished.

Now she had a plane ticket to Mexico in her purse.

She was through with waiting for telephone calls, through with wondering whether he loved her or missed her. She'd been through this before with Jack, the doubts, the fears, the slow but inevitable realization that something was wrong. She knew enough not to be hurt again, not this way.

At least, out of all this pain, I've discovered three new friends.
Ollie and Polowski and Milo, the most unlikely trio on the face of
the earth.

"Look, Sam," said Milo, reaching into his backpack. "We
brought ya something."

"No more hula-girl boxer shorts, okay? Caught hell from the
nurses for that one."

"Naw. It's something for your lungs. To remind you to breathe
deep."

"Cigarettes?" Polowski asked hopefully.

Milo grinned and held up his gift. "A kazoo!"

"I really needed one."

"You really do need it," said Ollie, opening up his clarinet case.
"Seeing as we brought our instruments today and we weren't about
to leave you out of this particular gig."

"You're not serious."

"What better place to perform?" said Milo, giving his piccolo a
quick and loving rubdown. "All these sick, depressed patients lying
around, in need of a bit of cheering up. Some good music."

"Some peace and quiet!" Polowski turned pleading eyes to Cathy. "They're not serious."

She looked him in the eye and took out her kazoo. "Dead serious."

"Okay, guys," said Ollie. "Hit it!"

Never before had the world heard such a rendering of "California, Here I Come!" And, if the world was lucky, never again. By
the time they'd played the last note, nurses and patients had spilled
into the solarium to check on the source of that terrible screeching.

"Mr. Polowski!" said the head nurse. "If your visitors can't
behave—"

"You'll throw 'em out?" asked Polowski hopefully.

"No need," said Ollie. "We're packing up the pipes. By the
way, folks, we're available for private parties, birthdays, cocktail
hours. Just get in touch with our business manager—" at this, Milo
smiled and waved "—to set up your own special performance."

Polowski groaned, "I want to go back to bed."

"Not yet," said the nurse. "You need the extra stimulation."

Then, with a sly wink at Ollie, she turned and whisked out of the room.

"Well," said Cathy. "I think I've done my part to cheer you up. Now it's time I hit the road."

Polowski looked at her in astonishment. "You're leaving me with these lunatics?"

"Have to. I have a plane to catch."

"Where you going?"

"Mexico. Jack called to say they're shooting already. So I thought I'd get on down there and whip up a few monsters."

"What about Victor?"

"What about him?"

"I thought—that is—" Polowski looked at Ollie and Milo. Both men merely shrugged. "He's going to miss you."

"I don't think so." She turned once again to gaze out the window. Below, in the walkway, an old woman sat in a wheelchair, her wan face turned gratefully to the sun. Soon Cathy would be enjoying that very sunshine, somewhere on a Mexican beach.

By their silence, she knew the three men didn't know what to say. After all, Victor was their friend, as well. They couldn't defend or condemn him. Neither could she. She simply loved him, in ways that made her decision to leave all the more right. She'd been in love before, she knew that the very worst thing a woman can sense in a man is indifference.

She didn't want to be around to see it in Victor's eyes.

Gathering up her purse, she said, "Guys, I guess this is it."

Ollie shook his head. "I really wish you'd hang around. He'll be back any day. Besides, you can't break up our great little quartet."

"Sam can take my place on the kazoo."

"No way," said Polowski.

She planted a kiss on his balding head. "Get better. The country needs you."

Polowski sighed. "I'm glad somebody does."

"I'll write you from Mexico!" She slung her purse over her shoulder and turned. One step was all she managed before she halted in astonishment.

Victor was standing in the doorway, a suitcase in hand. He cocked his head. "What's this about Mexico?"

She couldn't answer. She just kept staring at him, thinking how unfair it was that the man she was trying so hard to escape should look so heartbreakingly wonderful.

"You got back just in time," said Ollie. "She's leaving."

"What?" Victor dropped his suitcase and stared at her in dismay. Only then did she notice his wrinkled clothes, the day-old growth of beard shadowing his face. The toe of a sock poked out from a corner of the closed suitcase.

"You can't be leaving," he said.

She cleared her throat. "It was unexpected. Jack needs me."

"Did something happen? Is there some emergency?"

"No, it's just that they're filming and, oh, things are a royal mess on the set...." She glanced at her watch, a gesture designed to speed her escape. "Look, I'll miss my plane. I promise I'll give you a call when I get to—"

"You're not his only makeup artist."

"No, but—"

"He can do the movie without you."

"Yes, but—"

"Do you *want* to leave? Is that it?"

She didn't answer. She could only look at him mutely, the anguish showing plainly in her eyes.

Gently, firmly, he took her hand. "Excuse us, guys," he said to the others. "The lady and I are going for a walk."

Outside, leaves blew across the brown winter lawn. They walked beneath a row of oak trees, through patches of sun and shadow. Suddenly he stopped and pulled her around to face him.

"Tell me now," he said. "What gave you this crazy idea of leaving?"

She looked down. "I didn't think it made much difference to you."

"Wouldn't make a *difference?* Cathy, I was climbing the walls! Thinking of ways to get out of that hotel room and back to you! You have no idea how I worried. I wondered if you were safe—if this whole crazy mess was really over. The lawyers wouldn't let me call out, not until the hearings were finished. I did manage to sneak out and call Milo's house. No one answered."

"We were probably here, visiting Sam."

"And I was going crazy. They had me answering the same damn questions over and over again. And all I could think of was how much I missed you." He shook his head. "First chance I got, I flew the coop. And got snowed in for hours in Chicago. But I made it. I'm here. Just in time, it seems." Gently he took her by the shoulders. "Now. Tell me. Are you still flying off to Jack?"

"I'm not leaving for Jack. I'm leaving for *myself.* Because I know this won't work."

"Cathy, after what we've been through together, we can make *anything* work."

"Not—not this."

Slowly he let his hands drop, but his gaze remained on her face. "That night we made love," he said softly. "That didn't tell you something?"

"But it wasn't *me* you were making love to! You were thinking of Lily—"

"*Lily?*" He shook his head in bewilderment. "Where does she come in?"

"You loved her so much—"

"And you loved Jack once. Remember?"

"I fell out of love. You never did. No matter how much I try, I'll never measure up to her. I won't be smart enough or kind enough—"

"Cathy, stop."

"I won't be *her.*"

"I don't want you to be her! I want the woman who'll hang off fire escapes with me and—and drag me off the side of the road. I want the woman who saved my life. The woman who calls herself average. The woman who doesn't know just how extraordinary she really is." He took her face in his hands and tilted it up to his. "Yes, Lily was a wonderful woman. She was wise and kind and caring. But she wasn't you. And she and I—we weren't the perfect couple. I used to think it was my fault, that if I were just a better lover—"

"You're a wonderful lover, Victor."

"No. Don't you see, it's *you.* You bring it out in me. All the want and need." He pulled her face close to his and his voice dropped to a whisper. "When you and I made love that night, it was like the very first time for me. No, it was even better. Because I loved you.''

"And I loved you,'' she whispered.

He pulled her into his arms and kissed her, his fingers burrowing deep into her hair. "Cathy, Cathy,'' he murmured. "We've been so busy trying to stay alive we haven't had time to say all the things we should have....''

His arms suddenly stiffened as a startling round of applause erupted above them. They looked up. Three grinning faces peered down at them from a hospital balcony.

"Hit it, boys!'' yelled Ollie.

A clarinet, piccolo and kazoo screeched into concert. The melody was doubtful. Still, Cathy thought she recognized the familiar strains of George Gershwin. "Someone to Watch Over Me.''

Victor groaned. "I say we try this again, but with a different band. And no audience.''

She laughed. "Mexico?''

"Definitely.'' He grabbed her hand and pulled her toward a taxi idling at the curb.

"But, Victor!'' she protested. "What about our luggage? All my clothes—''

He cut her off with another kiss, one that left her dizzy and breathless and starved for more.

"Forget the luggage,'' she whispered. "Forget everything. "Let's just go....''

They climbed into the taxi. That's when the band on the hospital balcony abruptly switched to a new melody, one Cathy didn't at first recognize. Then, out of the muddy strains, the kazoo screeched out a solo that, for a few notes, was perfectly in tune. They were playing *Tannhäuser*. Wedding music!

"What the hell's that terrible noise?'' asked the taxi driver.

"Music,'' said Victor, grinning down at Cathy. "The most beautiful music in the world.''

She fell into his arms, and he held her there.

The taxi pulled away from the curb. But even as they drove away, even as they left the hospital far behind them, they thought they could hear it in the distance: the sound of Sam Polowski's kazoo, playing one last fading note of farewell.